THE VIEW FROM THE TOP

RACHEL LACEY

The View from the Top

COPYRIGHT

To my grandma, Mary Eva, for showing me the power of unconditional love.

ONE

Diana Devlin didn't often trade her heels for hiking boots, but as she got her first glimpse of the valley through the trees ahead, she knew today's hike would be worth the effort. The breeze kissed her cheeks, cool and refreshing on this June afternoon, lightly scented with pine and earth. She couldn't hear anything but the occasional chirp of a bird and the whisper of the wind through the trees, and it was oddly exhilarating.

A world away from her twenty-second-floor office in Boston. There were perks to scouting acquisitions in scenic locales, allowing Diana a rare chance to leave the city behind and indulge in a few hours of nature. She was currently thirty minutes into a three-mile hike to the summit of Crescent Peak to see the famous waterfall that the town of Crescent Falls, Vermont, was named after. There were several easier hikes to the base of the falls, but Diana wanted to see the view from the top.

Right now, her view consisted mostly of trees, although they were a nice change from the high-rise buildings she usually looked out at. She twisted the cap off her water bottle and took a sip. So far, the hike hadn't been as challenging as the concierge at her hotel had led her to expect. The man had been so concerned when she told him which trail she'd picked, all but insisting she choose an easier hike, but Diana wouldn't be deterred.

Although she'd recently celebrated her fortieth birthday, she was in excellent shape. She ran most evenings after work and visited the gym several times a week. She'd done a lot of hiking as a girl when she visited her family's vacation home in Western Massachusetts, enough to know she enjoyed pushing herself on more difficult trails, especially if they promised a stunning vista as a reward. The challenge exhilarated her.

And she'd come prepared. Her backpack contained plenty of water and snacks, Band-Aids for potential blisters or scrapes, and her phone so she could snap photos of the scenery. The trail offered a quick peek at the valley before beginning a steeper climb. It crisscrossed up the side of a hill in a series of switchbacks to make the incline more manageable.

Diana began the climb enthusiastically, pleased that the boots she'd purchased this morning were holding up well and not causing any pain. By the time she'd completed the first two switchbacks, her thighs were burning. At the third, she had to pause to catch her breath. *Phew.* Okay, the elevation on this climb was no joke.

She had broken out in a sweat by the time the trail leveled off on a narrow ridge overlooking the valley she'd glimpsed earlier. She lifted a hand to swat at the bugs circling her head. They didn't seem to bite, but they were extremely annoying. A wooden sign marker indicated that the Crescent Peak Summit Trail branched off to the left, the Blossom Trail continuing on the right. Diana veered left, following the red diamond trail markers that had been her guide since she left the parking lot.

A rock beside the trail had been painted so that its surface looked like a bright pink flower. Diana would have thought she'd dislike the idea of someone painting a flower on a rock, but this was surprisingly pretty and added a welcome splash of color along the trail. She pulled out her phone and snapped a photo.

She paused at the flower rock for another drink of water and to catch her breath, but the gnats became unbearable every time she stopped, buzzing around her head. The concierge at the hotel hadn't warned her to bring bug spray. Sucking in a deep breath, she forged on. The trail was steeper in this section, rising steadily up the side of the mountain. She crossed a stream by balancing on a series of stepping stones before heading up another steep incline.

"For fuck's sake," Diana huffed as she grabbed a nearby tree to keep her balance. At the top of the hill, the trail crossed a rocky outcrop that was equal parts beautiful and intimidating. Thank goodness she had on new boots designed for this.

Diana pressed a palm against the nearest rock and stuck her left boot into a crevice to gain purchase. She scrambled over several rocks, straining and sweating and swearing, before she reached the top, and... "Oh, wow."

The view here was even more magnificent, and she was probably only halfway to the summit. She sat, dangling her feet over the side of a rock as she ate a protein bar and had another drink of water, doing her best to ignore the gnats. This trail was intense. She understood now why the concierge had tried to discourage her from attempting it, but he had underestimated her. Most people did.

She'd take a selfie in front of the distinctive tower at the top so she could show him when she got back to the hotel. According to the pamphlet she'd read this morning, a woman named Elizabeth Abington had commissioned the tower to be built in the early 1800s to remind her of the castles of her native England. Now, a crumbling stone tower stood at the summit of one of the tallest peaks in central Vermont, delighting tourists.

Diana couldn't wait to see it. She held in a groan as she stood. Her legs were going to be sore tomorrow, but it would be worth the pain. This was a much more exhilarating workout than the machines at the gym.

Today, she'd conquer the mountain, and tomorrow, she'd lay the groundwork for her next corporate purchase. The inn she hoped to acquire would be a valuable addition to the Devlin Hotels portfolio, one more stepping stone on her path to CEO.

Diana carefully made her way along the edge of the rock before plunging back into the trees. She'd encountered a few other hikers near the base of the trail, but hadn't passed another person in at least thirty minutes. It was oddly peaceful. Living and working in the city, she so rarely found herself alone, except when she was at home.

The path continued to run along the ridgeline, and Diana followed, pausing periodically to sip her water. She finished her first bottle faster than she'd anticipated. Now she was halfway through her water, but not yet halfway through her hike. She'd have to be more sparing with her water consumption from here on out.

She kept walking, annoyed to realize she was still out of breath from that last incline. Her thighs and calves burned, and she had a stitch in her side. This climb was taking more out of her than she'd expected.

"The view from the top will be worth it," she murmured to herself.

There was an odd cry from overhead. An eagle, perhaps? It sounded like something she'd heard on TV. She looked up, shielding her eyes from the sun with her hand as she watched a large bird glide by, far above the treetops. Well, that was cool.

Still looking up at the eagle, she tripped over an uneven spot on the trail and pitched forward, catching herself against a tree trunk. The water bottle slipped from her fingers and dropped to the ground, rolling away from her.

"Shit." She lunged, dropping to her hands and knees, but the bottle was picking up speed now. It rolled down the steep side of the ridgeline she'd been walking along before dropping off into the valley below. Just like that, it was gone, leaving Diana with no water.

Her shoulders slumped. Stubbornly, she turned her gaze toward the way forward. Diana never gave up. When the going got tough, she outmaneuvered her opponent and kept going. But continuing a strenuous hike without water? Well, she might be stubborn, but she wasn't stupid.

With a sigh, she looked around for a trail marker to orient herself, but all she saw was trees. Trees in every direction. She'd been walking along this ridgeline, but as she looked behind herself, she saw several others like it. Which one had she come from? When was the last time she'd seen a trail marker? Because now that she was really paying attention, the area around her didn't contain a visible trail.

For the first time since she'd set out, she felt a frisson of fear. These woods were vast...and desolate. A person could *really* get lost out here. Squaring her shoulders, she turned around and began to backtrack in her best guess of where she'd come from.

It didn't take long to realize she'd gotten it wrong. She'd traversed the ridgeline, but it seemed like she was on the wrong side of the hill she'd been climbing. Nothing looked familiar. She unzipped her backpack and pulled out her cell phone, but there was no service. Of course not. She was miles from civilization, so far out she hadn't seen another human in at least an hour.

Diana had officially fucked up, and that wasn't something she admitted easily. She was tired and thirsty, surrounded by a cloud of obnoxious bugs, and she had no freaking idea where she was. That pang of fear swept through her again, causing her heart rate to tick up. Automatically, she reached for the sensory key chain dangling from the side of her backpack, rubbing her thumb over the textured strip she kept there to help calm her anxiety.

She recalled that she'd watched a survival show once where the advice was given that if you were ever lost in the woods to stay put and wait for rescue, but no one knew she was out here. Okay, the hotel concierge knew, but he might have gone home for the day already. It wasn't his job to make sure she made it back to the hotel safely. It could be days before the hotel realized she was missing.

No, staying put wasn't an option. Surely if she walked around this general area, she'd find the trail, or at least *a* trail. Any trail would do at this point, as long as it led her back to civilization. Diana started walking, slow and steady, searching every tree for a marker and every stretch of the forest for anything man-made.

Thirty minutes later, she was truly beginning to panic. Her throat was parched, and her skin felt flushed. She was so thirsty she was considering a drink from the next mountain stream she stumbled across. Surely it would be better to risk whatever was in the water than to become too dehydrated to hike out of here.

She'd decided to keep moving downhill, hoping that once she reached the bottom of the hill, she'd encounter a path or road. Plus, walking down was easier and gave her some reassurance that she wasn't going in circles.

A flash of color through the trees caught her eye, something bright orange that didn't seem to belong out here in the middle of the forest. Diana shielded her eyes. It was a person! A woman wearing an orange top, just on the other side of the hill.

Her knees shook with relief, before she looked down and saw the perilously steep and rocky hillside she'd have to traverse to get to her. Could she make it down without breaking her neck? Only one way to find out. As adrenaline surged through her system, Diana began her descent.

PURPLE ASTERS HAD ALWAYS BEEN her favorite. Emily dabbed her brush against the canvas, capturing the vivid hue of the flowers before her with their thin, delicate petals. It was unusual to see an aster in full bloom this early in the year—usually, they didn't peak until August or even September—but this one had flowered early, and she couldn't resist painting it.

Emily had already completed the mountains that made up the backdrop for today's painting. Now she just had to finish a few final details on the purple asters that were the star of this canvas. She smiled. Flowers made her happy. Painting made her happy. And painting flowers made her happiest of all.

She was fortunate to earn a steady income from her

artwork. It wasn't enough to live on—not yet—but hopefully she'd reach that milestone soon. In the meantime, she didn't mind working part-time behind the front desk at her grandmothers' inn to help pay the bills.

Emily swapped her brush for a painter's knife, sharpening the edge of each purple petal while she added texture to the canvas. Her hand was as steady as a surgeon's as she slid the knife through acrylic paint.

"Excuse me!" a woman's voice called from behind her.

Emily's hand jumped, and she smoothed down the paint she'd disturbed before turning to see who was there. She was far enough from the public trail that she hadn't expected to encounter any hikers. "Yes?"

A woman emerged from the trees, dressed in capri-length black athletic pants and a matching tank top. She strode toward Emily with such authority that Emily almost wondered if she'd accidentally wandered onto someone's private property and was about to be told off for it. But no, she was definitely in the state park, and on second glance, the woman's flushed and sweaty face indicated *she* might be the one in trouble.

"I hope you can help me," she said, seeming to confirm Emily's theory.

Emily gave her an encouraging smile. "Sure."

"I seem to have lost the trail," the woman said, embarrassment flickering over her features. "And I'm out of water, so I'd really appreciate it if you could point me toward the parking area on East Mountain Road."

"Which trail were you on?" Emily asked as she placed her knife on the palette next to her canvas. She reached into her bag and pulled out an unopened bottle of water, which she offered to the woman.

"Oh my God, you're a lifesaver." The woman practically sagged with relief as she accepted the bottle. Despite her authoritative stride when she'd walked out of the woods, Emily noticed subtle signs of strain: the way she couldn't seem to catch her breath, the sweat glistening on her skin, and that ruddy flush on her cheeks and chest, marring her otherwise pale complexion. She twisted the cap from the bottle and took several greedy gulps. "I was on the Crescent Peak Summit Trail."

Emily gaped. "That's an expert-level trail."

"I *am* an expert," the woman said, a hint of exasperation in her tone.

"Oh." Emily gave a skeptical look at the woman's obviously brand-new boots and gear.

"Well, maybe I haven't hiked in a while, but I'm a quick study and in excellent shape, so it shouldn't have been a problem for me."

Emily tried to hide her amusement at the woman's cocky overconfidence. "It's not just a matter of physical fitness. That trail is extremely technical, and Vermont's topography can't be underestimated. It gets *steep* on this mountain. I've been hiking here my whole life, and I still haven't made it to the summit."

She felt a tug of something like jealousy at the way this woman had stormed out here today with the utter confidence that she'd be able to conquer it on her first try, without any experience. What Emily wouldn't give for a little of that swagger...

"Well, I..." The woman paused and took another hearty drink from the water Emily had given her. "Apparently, I misjudged." Her gaze drifted to the easel behind Emily. "And I'm interrupting your day. If you could point me in the direction of the trail?"

"You're nowhere near it." And Emily could see the way

the woman's legs trembled with fatigue, despite her bluster. "I'll walk you out. It's a much shorter hike from here to where I parked, and then I'll drive you to your car."

"Oh, but...you don't even know me." She looked genuinely bewildered by Emily's offer. *Must be from the city.* Emily couldn't imagine living anywhere so unfriendly.

She extended a hand. "Emily Janssen."

"Diana Devlin." She took Emily's hand and gave it a firm shake.

"Nice to meet you, Diana. There, now we know each other."

"You're sure you don't mind?" There was still something hesitant in her demeanor.

Emily had the feeling Diana didn't often need to be rescued. "Not at all. Just give me a minute to pack up."

"You can finish first, if you like. I'm not in a hurry." Diana's gaze traveled over Emily's canvas. "It's beautiful."

"Thank you." Emily's cheeks warmed at the compliment. "I was just putting on the finishing touches when you walked up."

"Then you should definitely finish. Don't let me interrupt you any more than I already have."

"Okay, if you're sure. It'll only take me a few minutes."

Diana waved a hand as if to say "take your time" before retreating to sit on a nearby rock. She turned to stare out at the valley before them, and Emily was distracted by the way the sun glinted off her shoulder-length hair. Emily had first thought it was golden blonde, but the sun brought out various shades of red gleaming in its depths.

Emily didn't often paint people. Flowers and landscapes were her forte. She could never get the faces quite right when she tried a portrait, but she was struck by the desire to paint Diana the way she looked right now, with the sun shining in her hair. She'd use a dab of vermilion red, some butter yellow, maybe a bit of cadmium orange too.

She's beautiful.

The thought struck Emily out of the blue, along with the realization that she was staring. She turned to her canvas and spent a few minutes defining the petals on her purple aster—still thinking about Diana's golden hair. It would go perfectly with the fall foliage in a few months. Emily added a little more paint to define the tree line in the background, and then her painting was finished.

"I didn't know you could paint with a knife," Diana commented as Emily began to pack up her supplies.

"It adds texture and helps make more vibrant colors, because you don't have to dilute the paint. I like to use a palette knife when I'm painting flowers. It adds another dimension to the painting." She turned the canvas toward Diana.

"I've never seen it done that way before," Diana said. "I love the texture and color. Do you sell your work?"

Emily nodded. "I have pieces on consignment in a few local businesses, and I have a website, where I sell most of my stuff. A lot of people prefer to buy prints since they're cheaper than an original canvas. I sell a lot of accessories like stickers and bookmarks and mugs too."

"Fascinating." Diana's gaze flicked from Emily to her canvas and back again. "I never would have thought of putting something like that on a mug."

Emily shrugged. "I sell a lot of mugs."

"I'd love to check out your store. Do you have a card?"

Emily reached into the pocket of her bag and pulled out a business card. This had to be the weirdest place she'd ever made a sale...on the side of a mountain and at least a half a mile from the nearest trail. "No pressure to buy just because I saved you from wandering around lost out here." She offered Diana a crooked smile as she handed her the card.

Diana's eyes danced with amusement. "It's hard to pressure me to do something I don't want to do."

Emily didn't doubt that for a moment, and her heart was beating a little faster under the intensity of Diana's gaze. Was Diana checking her out? Emily had never had the best gaydar. Growing up in a small town probably had something to do with that. She rarely got to meet a stranger and stare into her eyes, wondering if Diana's heart was starting to race too.

Flustered, Emily turned away. She packed up the last of her supplies and attached the canvas to her backpack with the straps she'd installed for this purpose, so the paint wouldn't smudge on the hike down.

"You painted the flower on that rock I noticed on my way up the trail, didn't you?" Diana said suddenly.

"Yep. The park service commissioned me to paint several rocks along the public trails as a natural art installation."

Diana nodded, rising to her feet. She seemed a lot more composed now than she had been when they first met, no longer flushed or out of breath, and now that Emily had started to pay attention, she couldn't help noticing Diana's lean, athletic frame. She'd said she was in good shape, and she hadn't been exaggerating.

"Are you here on vacation?" Emily asked as she began to lead the way down the mountain toward where she'd parked.

"Work." Diana fell into step beside her. "I'm up from Boston, but my business meeting isn't until tomorrow, so I decided to see some of the local scenery. Guess I got a bit overly ambitious."

"Guessing it's not the first time." Emily couldn't resist the jab, grinning at Diana.

Diana's chin went up. "I'm afraid I've given you an inaccurate first impression. I'm usually successful at even my most ambitious ventures."

There was that confidence again. This was a woman who believed she could do anything she set her mind to, and Emily couldn't deny she found it irrationally sexy. "So what kind of business brings you to my little corner of the world?"

"I'm the vice president of independent purchasing for Devlin Hotels."

"Devlin Hotels," Emily repeated as the penny dropped. "Diana Devlin. Holy shit, you're...oh, you're a Devlin. Your family owns this huge hotel chain, and wow, I'm rambling."

"Yes, my family owns a hotel chain." Diana's tone seemed to say that she had no doubt she would have been just as successful even if she had a different last name, but she was proud of her family's legacy regardless. "I'm in charge of purchasing boutique hotels and inns around the country to bring under the corporate umbrella."

"So you're here to buy a hotel?"

Diana nodded.

Emily wasn't sure she liked the idea of any of the local hotels being bought by a corporate chain. Part of what made Crescent Falls and its neighboring towns so special was the uniqueness of the local businesses. Tourists came here to have a one-of-a-kind experience, not to stay at a Devlin Hotel.

But that was beside the point, because the true heart and soul of Crescent Falls—for Emily at least—was her grandmothers' beloved Inn at Crescent Falls, and it wasn't for sale. So, whatever hotel Diana was here to buy wasn't really Emily's concern. Diana was probably a lot wealthier and more successful than Emily had realized, though.

"You live in town?" Diana asked.

"On the outskirts," Emily told her. "I like the mountain views, if you hadn't noticed."

Diana smiled, her features softening. "I noticed. So why haven't you made it to the summit yet? It can't be *that* hard, can it?"

Emily dropped her gaze to the path ahead. "It's not. I mean, it's hard, don't get me wrong, but most of my friends have made it to the top. I belong to a group of local outdoor enthusiasts, and they do a group hike to the summit every fall, but I just...I don't know. Something always gets in the way for me."

"Hmm." Diana gave her an inquisitive look, no doubt wondering what exactly Emily meant by that, but she wasn't about to get into anything that personal with a woman who was essentially a stranger.

"Maybe this fall," Emily mused. Meeting Diana today had reminded her how important it was to push herself. She'd been coasting the last few years, watching her friends get promotions and start families and move forward with their lives while her own life stagnated.

She wanted to make it to the top of the mountain. She wanted to grow her business so she could support herself fully with her artwork. And she'd like to find that special someone too. Maybe this was her wake-up call, a sign from the universe that it was time to go after her dreams.

"So what else does your adventure group do?" Diana asked.

"Lots of hiking. Vermont is full of trails and landmarks to explore. Waterfalls, covered bridges, you name it. In the wintertime, we do a lot of skiing and snowshoeing. And..." She paused, deciding to test the waters. "We're a queer group, so we have a big outing every year to Burlington Pride."

Diana had no visible reaction to this, much to Emily's chagrin. "Sounds like fun."

"You must not get to do much outdoor adventuring, living in Boston."

"No, but I travel fairly often, and sometimes I get to do some exploring then...like today."

Emily wanted to check in and make sure Diana was holding up okay. She'd been under such strain when Emily first met her. Clearly, Diana had bitten off more than she could chew with her hike today, and while she seemed okay now, some people didn't know their own limits and would push themselves to the point of collapse before admitting they needed a break. She suspected Diana would bristle if Emily inquired, though, so she didn't.

Instead, she kept her pace a little slower than she would have otherwise. She also took extra time to point out some of her favorite flowers and trees as they passed, partly because she loved sharing beautiful things and also to give Diana a chance to catch her breath without bringing attention to it.

Fifteen minutes later, they came out at the spot where Emily had parked, and she knew she didn't imagine Diana's sigh of relief.

"That seemed *much* easier coming down than it was going up," Diana said.

"Because it was. I brought you down an entirely different way."

"How far are we from my car?"

"About a ten-minute drive," Emily told her.

"I really appreciate this," Diana said quietly, the

earnestness of her tone betraying just how scared she'd been before she found Emily.

"No problem at all." Emily was glad she kept her car clean, because apparently she cared what Diana thought of her. She stowed their gear in the trunk and then gestured for Diana to open the passenger door.

Emily slid into the driver's seat and started the car. A loud moan came through the speakers, and Emily blushed when she remembered she'd been relistening to one of her favorite audiobooks during the drive over, a steamy sapphic romance. Diana's eyebrows lifted.

"Skye's hands slid over Lucy's skin, warm fingers cupping her breasts in a firm hold," the female narrator intoned in a breathless voice.

Emily twisted the volume down to zero, but not before it was more than obvious what she'd been listening to. "Um...sorry about that."

"Nothing to apologize for," Diana said as she fastened her seat belt. "I enjoy audiobooks too. Not sure I'd have chosen that exact spot to leave the car, though." She turned, giving Emily a slightly wicked grin.

"Oh, I...well, it's a reread, so I know what happens next, but yeah...it's a good scene." Emily was rambling again. She shut up and started driving, guiding her car over the twisting mountain road to the main parking lot where Diana had set out from. She wasn't at all surprised when Diana guided her toward a shiny silver Lexus. "Nice car."

"It's a rental. I don't need one, living in the city. Usually, I fly when I'm scouting new properties, but Vermont's so close, it was easier to just rent a car and drive up."

"Ah." Emily was a little disappointed that it was time to say goodbye.

Diana held her gaze for a moment, nothing but the soft hum of the engine filling the car. "I'm staying at the Beaumont Hotel. Perhaps you'd like to meet me at the bar later so I could buy you a drink? My way of thanking you for saving me on the mountain today."

Emily felt a tingling sensation in the pit of her stomach, because *yes*, she very much wanted to have a drink with Diana tonight. Of course she was staying at the fanciest hotel around, and if she wanted to buy it, the Beaumont actually seemed like a good fit for the Devlin brand. "Yeah, I'd like that."

TWO

Emily entered the bar a few minutes before seven that evening. She'd wanted to arrive first so she could settle and order a drink before she saw Diana, and when she swept her gaze around the space, it seemed like she'd achieved her goal. She wasn't sure why she'd felt like she needed to get here first. Maybe because she felt vaguely intimidated by what Diana might be like on her own turf, and this gave her a measure of control.

The bar area of the Beaumont Hotel was a lot more understated than she'd expected after seeing the porter in white gloves who'd held the door open for her and the elaborate chandelier in the lobby. The placard out front boasted that the hotel had been around since 1846, and that history was evident in the ornate touches on the woodwork around her.

The bar was a sleek black surface that ran along the back wall, staffed by a man in a crisp white button-down shirt. Soft jazz music played, and the lighting was low enough to be soothing, but not so low that it felt too intimate to meet someone here when she wasn't quite sure if this was a date. Was Diana even queer?

There were a dozen or so other people in the room, mostly couples except for a lone man sitting at the end of the bar. Not wanting to give him the wrong impression by sitting nearby, Emily ordered a glass of merlot and brought it to an empty table for two by the window.

She pulled out her phone, unsurprised to find a string of new messages in the Adventurers group chat. Emily had texted them earlier about her unexpected rescue on the mountain, and now they were blowing up her phone in their excitement. They knew as well as anyone how long it had been since she'd dated and were fully in favor of her living it up tonight.

> **ALEXIS BELL**
>
> Have a drink for me!
>
> **TOM BELLAMY**
>
> Have more than a drink, my dear. I want you to have a wild time – do absolutely everything I would do
>
> **TALIA MICHAUD**
>
> Be true to YOU, Em (but also have funnnnnn)
>
> **ALEXIS BELL**
>
> If you couldn't tell, we're all living vicariously through you tonight…

Emily found herself laughing under her breath as she read the messages from her friends. Before he met Maddie, Tom had been quite the player. If he had rescued Diana back then, he'd undoubtedly have taken her back to her room and made good on his words. Or the bartender. He was Tom's type too. But Emily? She wasn't known for one-night stands. She wasn't known for anything particularly adventurous, despite being part of this group.

Maybe that would change tonight. Emily had joined the Adventurers to push herself out of her comfort zone, but after meeting Diana today, she realized she hadn't really done that yet. So maybe, if the opportunity presented itself tonight...maybe she'd find the courage to be adventurous for once.

"Is this seat taken?"

She looked up to find the man who'd been sitting alone at the bar now standing at her table. Irritation bubbled up. Seriously? She'd obviously chosen this table because she wanted to be left alone. "Yes, it is."

"It is *now*," he quipped, setting his beer on her table. "Are you from around here?"

Emily sighed. Men like him were exhausting. "Born and raised, and that seat really is taken, so if you don't mind..."

"Aww, come on. I'm just trying to get to know you." His dark hair was a little too greasy to attribute the look to gel. She cringed internally. "Can't I keep you company until your boyfriend arrives?"

Of course he assumed she was waiting for a man. Emily sighed again. She'd been clear that she wasn't interested, but she wasn't really the kind of person to be pointedly rude.

"I'm Matt."

Emily's gaze shifted behind Matt. Diana was striding across the room in tailored black slacks and a sleeveless off-white top, her strawberry-blonde hair loose so that the tips just brushed her shoulders, and *good God*. Emily had had a vague idea when she met her earlier that Diana would clean up nicely, but as she crossed the bar, radiating a kind of poise Emily could only dream of, Emily almost swallowed her tongue.

Diana Devlin might be the most gorgeous person she'd ever seen.

Her eyes were locked on Emily's, sharp as diamonds and even more intense now that they were highlighted by impeccably done makeup. Emily wanted to shove greasy Matt away from her before Diana got the wrong idea about his presence, but before she could think of a way to get rid of him, Diana had reached the table.

She walked straight to Emily without even glancing at Matt, sliding an arm around Emily's waist as she leaned in to press a kiss against Emily's cheek. "There you are, darling. Sorry I'm late."

God, she smelled as good as she looked, some kind of lush floral perfume, and what was happening right now? Emily could only blink at her out of lust-drunk eyes, her brain having apparently combusted at the touch of Diana's lips to her cheek.

Matt swore under his breath before picking up his beer and heading back to the bar.

"Mission accomplished," Diana said, watching him go. Her arm was still around Emily's waist, their bodies so close together that Emily's side brushed against Diana's breast every time she inhaled.

That wasn't doing anything to clear the haze from Emily's brain, but she was starting to catch up anyway. "Did you just—"

"It was effective, wasn't it?" Diana turned her head to meet Emily's gaze. "I wouldn't have if you hadn't been so clear about your sexuality earlier. I would never out anyone, even as part of a ruse to get rid of an unwanted man."

"Oh." Emily couldn't stop staring into Diana's blue

eyes. "You didn't say anything earlier when I told you I was queer."

"It wasn't relevant then." Diana shrugged, dropping her arm, and Emily missed the warmth of her touch immediately. Diana stepped around the table and sat in the chair opposite her. "I suppose it is now."

"Feels pretty relevant." Emily hoped she didn't sound as breathless as she felt. Her fingers were touching the spot where Diana had kissed her. When had she raised her hand like that? She drew in a cleansing breath as she lowered her hand to grip her wineglass.

"Then we're on the same page." Diana's soft smile made her eyes sparkle in the bar's low lighting.

"Yes. Do you want a drink?"

Diana raised a hand, catching the bartender's eye in a move much smoother than anything Emily was capable of, and he nodded, then ducked out from behind the bar and approached their table.

"What can I get for you, ma'am?"

"Whiskey, neat. Something Irish, please."

"Coming right up."

Diana thanked him, then leaned forward to rest her elbows on the table as she fixed her gaze on Emily again. "I looked up your website. Your artwork is impressive."

"Oh, thank you." Emily swallowed, her skin flushing with warmth. Diana was radiating so much sapphic energy right now, Emily had no idea how she'd missed it earlier. Maybe she'd been afraid to notice, or maybe Diana was turning on the charm now in a way she hadn't while they were on the mountain. Either way, Emily had fallen completely under her spell.

"Do you only paint landscapes?"

"Mostly, yeah. Sometimes I'll digitize individual flowers

to go on stickers and things like that. Nature is my muse, I guess."

"You're talented."

Emily's cheeks grew even warmer. "Thank you."

The bartender arrived with Diana's drink, and as Emily sipped her wine, she wished she'd gotten something stronger. Diana's whiskey looked so sophisticated...like Diana herself. Emily knew why she was here tonight. She was wholly intrigued by Diana and increasingly attracted, but what did someone like Diana see in Emily?

"That's a very intense look," Diana observed, sipping her whiskey. "Penny for your thoughts?"

"I just..." How to verbalize it without putting herself down? "I can't help feeling like you and I never would have ended up having a drink together if I hadn't rescued you today."

Diana's eyebrows went up, and she stared at Emily for a moment of loaded silence. "Isn't that true of any two people? That you might not have met if not for whatever random circumstance brought you together. I think what you're really asking, though, is would I have approached you if I met you in this bar instead of on that mountain?"

Emily blushed and shrugged. *Busted.*

Diana's gaze never wavered. "The answer is twofold. Would I have been intrigued if I first spotted you across the bar here tonight? Yes, definitely. It's easy to see that you're intelligent and interesting and someone I'd like to get to know. However, generally when I approach a woman in a bar, my interest doesn't extend past a single night, and you don't necessarily strike me as the 'one night' type."

"Oh." Emily took another sip of her wine as a weight settled in her stomach. That was a lot more honest than she'd been expecting. Diana saw Emily as most people did:

someone who played it safe. But she didn't want to play it safe tonight.

"In this case, I'm only in town for the night, so even if I wanted more than a night with you, it's not in the cards." Diana lifted her whiskey for another sip. "But I meant it when I said you're someone I'd like to get to know. I didn't invite you here for a hookup. I'm happy to spend my evening with you, even if we go our separate ways in the lobby."

Emily's next sip was more of a gulp. "And if I don't want to part ways in the lobby?"

Diana's eyes blazed with undisguised heat. "Then I'd be very lucky indeed."

HALFWAY THROUGH HER SECOND WHISKEY, Diana was pleasantly buzzed. Relaxed enough not to notice the sore muscles from her ill-advised hike, and more than a little bit intrigued by the woman sitting across from her.

Emily had on a knee-length dress colored like the sunset: a vibrant mixture of red, orange, and purple. Her chestnut-brown hair framed her face and hung in loose waves down her back. Somehow she managed to look as sweet as the flowers she painted while simultaneously being one of the sexiest women Diana had ever seen.

It was a good thing Diana lived almost two hundred miles away, or she might be in trouble. Emily was captivating, and not just because of her beauty. Diana didn't often date. She was too focused on her career to have time for a love life. Instead, she satisfied herself with the occasional one-night stand or meaningless fling.

But Emily was different, someone who took time to

enjoy the beautiful things in life that Diana tended to march straight past. Emily reminded her that if she met the right woman, Diana was capable of wanting more. She'd always assumed she'd get married at some point, but here she was, forty and far more preoccupied with her next promotion than finding a woman to settle down with.

"It's so hard to meet new people living in a small town when you're queer," Emily was saying. "I feel like I've already dated every queer woman in the area."

"Even the ones in your adventure group?" Diana asked.

Emily scrunched her nose. "Well, no, but dating friends gets messy, and some of them feel almost like family at this point, you know? A few of us have known each other since we were kids. I'm bi, so that opens up my possibilities, but honestly, there aren't many men I connect with for more than a night or two, and as you pointed out...that's not exactly my style."

Diana grinned. "I knew I had you pegged."

"Yeah." Emily ducked her head. "You're good at reading people."

"I try to be, anyway."

"And extremely modest," Emily teased, catching Diana's eye.

"Women in general are too modest, especially in business. You don't see successful men downplaying their talents. They own their strengths, and so should we."

"You're right." Emily looked thoughtful. "I hadn't thought of it quite like that, but I know I'm my own worst enemy when it comes to conquering the hurdles in my life."

"Like what?"

"Like...making it to the top of the damn mountain, like growing my business or putting myself back in the dating game."

"Did you get your heart broken?" Diana asked, ire rising at the idea of someone taking advantage of Emily's generous nature.

"Once, yes, and it was awful, but that was years ago." Emily sighed. "My last few relationships were just...disappointing. Underwhelming, really. So I haven't put much effort into finding someone new."

"Dating is hard," Diana agreed. "The higher I climb on the corporate ladder, the more difficult it is to find time for a personal life. My ten-year plan involves running the entire company, so that's been my priority. I haven't paid much attention to my love life lately, I'm afraid."

"Your ten-year plan is to run the whole company," Emily repeated, looking somewhat dumbstruck.

"Yes. My father will be retiring, and I hope to become the next CEO of Devlin Hotels."

Emily whistled softly. "Damn. You really dream big, and I'm so fucking impressed with you. I'm sitting here trying to convince myself to hike up the mountain, and you're making plans to run a Fortune 500 company."

"It's always been my goal," Diana told her. "As I mentioned earlier, I currently run the independent purchasing division. I scout boutique hotels to bring under our corporate umbrella, and I absolutely love it, but I'm hoping for a promotion to COO within the next year or two. That will be the final step to prepare for my role as CEO."

"Wow." Emily paused to thank the bartender as he brought her a fresh glass of wine. "Is it in the bag, then? Or do you have some competition to contend with?"

Diana pursed her lips. In her mind, it was a done deal, but she knew that wasn't reality. "It's down to two of us."

"Do tell." Emily leaned forward, a strand of brown hair brushing against the tabletop. Diana wanted to reach out and see if it was as soft as it looked. Maybe, if the night played out the way she hoped, she'd get to find out.

"It's between me and my brother." Diana knew her sigh revealed too much about her feelings on the subject, but she didn't mind Emily knowing the truth. That was the freedom of sharing a few drinks with someone she wasn't likely to see again.

"Wow, Devlin Hotels really keeps it in the family, huh? So your father has to pick between his kids? That sounds impossible."

"The board will vote on whether or not to approve my father's choice, so it's not solely up to him, but regardless." Diana pushed her shoulders back. "I've been laser focused on my career path since I was in college. My brother... hasn't. And I don't mean to speak ill of him. He's a good businessman, but between the two of us, the decision—to me, at least—seems like an easy one."

"And does your father agree? Do you know?"

"I think he would rather see Harrison in the position, but...I hope he'll be reasonable when the time comes. I have an advanced degree in hotel management. I've brought millions of dollars of revenue into the company through these boutique hotels. I'm an excellent problem solver with strong leadership skills. My brother is more likely to be found on the golf course."

"Well, you have my vote." Emily had leaned in even more now, close enough for Diana to see that her eyes were the color of whiskey, a rich golden color that was darker around her pupils. "I knew the moment I laid eyes on you this morning that you're a leader. You were lost and dehydrated and still came marching out of the woods like you owned the place."

Diana chuckled. "I appreciate the vote of confidence. I

was honestly starting to panic before I spotted you, and I don't panic easily, I can assure you."

"I believe it." Emily stared pensively into her wine for a few seconds before raising those honeyed eyes to Diana. "I'd love to know what it's like to have that kind of confidence. You seem so effortlessly in control and sure of yourself."

"Want to know a secret?" Diana gave her a wry smile. "Sometimes I wish I could let someone else take control for a little while, but the business world doesn't work that way, especially for a woman. Show them a moment of weakness, and they'll eat you alive."

"That sounds exhausting. I bet you look forward to these scouting trips."

"I love them," Diana told her honestly. "And this one in particular." She let her leg bump into Emily's beneath the table, the bare skin of their ankles brushing together.

Emily sucked her bottom lip between her teeth.

Diana was just buzzed enough that even that simple touch left her aching. It had been a while since she'd connected with someone the way she had with Emily, a connection that was equal parts sexual and intellectual. That intersection had always been Diana's downfall.

"Hey, Diana?" Emily's voice was lower now, almost as smoky as the whiskey in Diana's glass.

"Yes?"

"I don't want to part ways in the lobby."

THREE

The door closed behind them with a solid thump, and almost immediately, Diana had Emily pressed against the wall. She claimed Emily's mouth with a hunger that surprised her, feeling greedy as she tasted the rich, spicy flavor of Emily's wine on her lips.

"Finally," Diana murmured as she kissed her again.

Emily's gentle laugh became a moan when Diana placed a hungry kiss below her jaw, on the sensitive skin of her throat. "You just met me."

Diana felt the vibration of Emily's words beneath her lips. "Doesn't feel like it."

"Yeah, I know what you mean." Emily's hands settled on Diana's waist, pulling her closer. Her fingers tugged at the silky fabric of Diana's blouse, untucking it from her pants, and Diana heard her own rough inhale when Emily's warm fingertips brushed the bare skin at her waist.

"Before this goes any further, have you been tested recently?" Diana asked, because she took these things seriously.

Emily nodded. "My annual checkup was a few months ago, and it was all clear. I haven't been with anyone since."

"Good...and same." With that out of the way, Diana pressed forward, slipping a thigh between Emily's as she brought their mouths back together. She'd been buzzed earlier, but now she felt drunk with desire, her mind spinning as she felt the warm length of Emily's body pressed against hers.

Diana rolled her hips, pinning Emily more firmly against the wall. She delighted in the shiver that shook Emily's form at the contact. Tonight was going to be memorable. Diana was sure of it. She placed her hands on either side of Emily's face as she kissed her, slowly familiarizing herself with Emily's lips before her tongue slid into the hot depths of Emily's mouth. She left no doubt as to how badly she wanted her or how thoroughly she intended to ravish her. Diana could hardly fucking wait.

She didn't want to move quickly, not tonight. She wanted to take her time and see how many more of those breathy little moans she could elicit from Emily's throat, if she could make her scream with pleasure. Diana wanted—

"Wait," Emily gasped, and suddenly, her hands were on Diana's, fingers gripping her wrists.

Diana took a step back to return some space between them, eyebrows raised in silent question.

"You said..." Emily's tongue darted out to wet her lips, and she didn't look like a woman who wanted to stop. Her eyes were so eager, they made Diana's pulse jump to an even faster tempo. "You said sometimes you wished you could not be in control for a little while, and I said I wanted to know what it felt like to have that power, so...what do you say if we swap roles tonight?"

Diana swallowed roughly, surprised by the hot thrill

that raced down her spine at Emily's words. She could feel herself getting wet. Diana loved being in control. She *always* took control in the bedroom. She had a forceful personality, so it usually wasn't even a question. Consequently, she was shocked to realize that just the thought of letting Emily take control tonight was turning her on. More than that, she was throbbing in anticipation.

"Would you like that?" Diana's voice was a growl. "You'd like being in control? Telling me what to do? Making me beg?"

Emily let out a whimper when Diana said *beg*. That fire was still gleaming in her eyes, and there was something more intense about her gaze now, something almost...dominant. Emily surged forward then, hands on Diana's shoulders as she spun them so Diana's back hit the wall. Just as quickly, Emily's thigh was pressed between hers as those whiskey eyes blazed into Diana's. "I'd like it, yeah. The question is...would you?"

"Yes." Diana's voice came out sounding hoarse, her throat gone dry in anticipation. She hadn't known, had never suspected she'd be so unfathomably aroused by the act of surrendering control. She wouldn't do this with just anyone, but Emily seemed too inherently kind to take advantage, and Diana never had to worry about seeing her again after tonight. So, her act of submission would be her own private—and hot—little secret.

"If we're doing this, I think we should go all the way with it." Emily leveraged her position to press her thigh against Diana's pussy, right where she ached for her.

"All the way?" Diana tried to keep her voice steady when she could feel the warmth of Emily's thigh against her clit through the various layers of their clothing. But now, a frisson of doubt had snuck in, because she had no idea what Emily meant by her last statement. It was a reminder that they didn't really know each other, and Diana wasn't into anything too kinky. She had no qualms about saying no if Emily was about to take this beyond her comfort zone.

"If we're role-playing tonight, let's make the most of it," Emily said as her hands slid down to cup Diana's ass, pressing her more firmly against Emily's thigh. "Tell me your most illicit fantasy, and I'll try to make it come true."

"Oh." Diana's eyes fluttered shut, and she felt another rush of arousal in her core. Her most illicit fantasy? She didn't even know where to start, but her body was obviously onboard with the idea. She ran her mind back over her last few sexual encounters. They'd been a little too perfunctory for Diana's taste, more of a wham, bam, thank you, ma'am than anything approaching passion.

The last woman she'd been with had barely spent five minutes on Diana, as if giving her the quickest orgasm possible was the goal. But rushed orgasms were underwhelming. Diana missed having someone take their time with her, working her up until she was so turned on, she was about to lose her mind.

Emily leaned in, ghosting a kiss against the shell of Diana's ear. "I'm waiting." Her warm breath made Diana shudder with pleasure.

"I want to go slow," Diana told her. "I want you to worship my body, tease me until I can't take it anymore... and then tease me a little bit more."

"Oh, I can definitely do that." Emily pressed a hot, open-mouthed kiss to the delicate skin below Diana's ear, and already this was so much better than any of her recent hookups.

"And you?" Diana asked, turning her head to nip at

Emily's full lower lip. "What's your fantasy? I'm damn good at wish fulfillment."

Emily inhaled, a startled look passing across her face as if she hadn't considered her answer to her own question. After a moment, her cheeks darkened, and she dipped her head, as bashful as she'd been assertive a moment before.

"Tell me," Diana urged. "No judgment, I promise you that."

"I...I think I'd like to be marked. Nothing too wild, just a hickey or scratches, something I have to cover up in the morning. I want to feel like I've been ravaged, not the soft, gentle sex I'm used to." She blinked at Diana, her cheeks pinker than ever. "I want that reminder to take home with me. I want to know what's under the scarf, you know?"

"Oh yes." Diana immediately dipped her head, dragging her teeth along the curve of Emily's exposed collarbone. "I do know, and I approve wholeheartedly, both of the ravaging and of the marks left behind as a souvenir."

Emily brought their mouths back together, and for several delicious minutes, they just kissed, slow and deep and so intense, Diana's body felt heated from the inside out, centered in the ache between her thighs. This was what she'd been missing, this kind of unrushed pleasure, not to mention a woman she liked for more than the satisfaction her fingers could provide.

Then Emily tugged her forward, guiding Diana toward the king-sized bed. It was still neatly made, and Emily nudged her onto it so that she ended up seated on the white duvet, still fully dressed. Emily leaned in for a kiss before trailing her lips over Diana's jaw to her shoulder, left exposed by her sleeveless top.

Diana's breath hitched. Had anyone ever kissed her shoulder before? It was surprisingly sensitive. Emily lifted

Diana's arm, kissing her way along Diana's skin, paying special attention to the delicate skin near her wrist, a place where Diana had always been especially sensitive. As Emily swirled her tongue, Diana could hear her own loud, rasping breaths in the otherwise quiet room.

"Scoot back for me." Emily nudged Diana's hips, urging her to slide further onto the bed.

Diana kicked off her heels before she complied, letting Emily push her flat on her back as she crawled on top of her. Emily's body was warm on hers, their breasts pressed together, legs threaded. Emily's hips rocked gently as she kissed Diana, and *oh*, she could get lost in this kind of pleasure...

Time seemed to lose meaning as they kissed and touched, hands exploring while the heat between them grew. Emily's fingers skimmed up Diana's sides beneath her top. She palmed Diana's breasts over her bra before retreating to run her hands up and down Diana's thighs over her pants. All the while, her mouth devoured Diana's in an endless, ravenous kiss. At some point, Diana's thighs had parted, and Emily rested between them now, her warm weight pressing against Diana's center in a most delightfully frustrating way.

And she'd had about enough of being flat on her back. Diana rose up on her elbows, using the leverage to roll Emily beneath her. Emily's dress had bunched around her thighs, exposing so much smooth, tanned skin. Diana trailed a hand up the inside of Emily's thigh, sliding past the orange fabric gathered there until her fingers met the soft material of Emily's panties.

"Oh," Emily gasped, parting her thighs as much as the dress allowed, which wasn't very much, but it was enough for Diana's purposes. Her fingers skimmed over Emily's underwear, which was already damp with her arousal. Diana rubbed with increasing pressure, feeling the fabric become wetter as Emily's hips rocked up to meet her.

Carefully, Diana pushed the fabric to the side so her fingers met Emily's bare flesh. She coated her fingers in Emily's arousal before bringing them to her clit. Emily began to grind against her hand, a low groan escaping her throat, and Diana decided to make this first time hard and fast. Emily looked like she needed it.

There would be plenty of time afterward to ravish Emily the way she had requested, and Diana couldn't wait for that part. Her pussy throbbed in anticipation. By her own request, she likely wouldn't have any relief for a while yet, so in the meantime, she'd live vicariously through Emily.

And as much as a small part of her wanted to announce that she'd changed her mind, that she didn't want to wait, not when her underwear was already soaked through, her clit aching impatiently, a larger part of her knew she was going to enjoy every moment. The anticipation was already killing her in the very best way.

Somewhere deep down, Diana *did* like to be teased.

Emily seemed to be getting close. She ground herself more vigorously against Diana's hand before throwing her head back with a harsh gasp. Her hips jerked before going still, and then she tugged Diana down for a sloppy kiss.

But Diana was already pushing at Emily's dress, eager to get her out of it. She wanted to see her. Emily had a lithe, athletic build, and Diana wanted to explore every inch.

Emily chuckled, still breathing hard from her orgasm. She reached down to grasp Diana's hands. "Not so fast. I'm in charge tonight, remember?"

Diana grinned. *Busted.* Being submissive in the

bedroom didn't come naturally to her. "Your choice, then. Either strip me, or strip *for* me."

In response, Emily sat up, sliding out from beneath Diana. She gripped the hem of her dress, lifting it up and over her head in one slightly wriggly movement. Beneath the dress, Emily wore a black satin bra and matching seamless panties. As Diana watched, she popped the clasp to release her bra and then shimmied out of her panties.

Diana swallowed hard as she took in Emily's naked form. The muscles in her thighs and calves were well-defined, presumably from a lifetime of hiking the mountain that had bested Diana earlier that day. Two small scars stood out on her lower abdomen, and when Diana dragged a thumb over one of them, Emily responded, "Appendix when I was twelve."

Diana slid her hands up and down Emily's sides, letting her nails drag against her skin until Emily let out a little gasp of pleasure. Her breasts were small and firm, just enough to fill Diana's palms. "You're beautiful."

Emily's lips quirked, and then she scooted forward. She toyed with the clasp on Diana's pants without unfastening it, then traced a finger up and down the seam of Diana's zipper. Diana hissed, arching her hips to meet Emily's touch.

Emily cupped her over her pants and pressed down, drawing a surprised gasp from Diana's lips. Emily's fingers wiggled slightly as she leaned in, bringing her lips against Diana's left ear. "I can feel how wet you are through your pants."

Diana was not surprised by this information. "What are you going to do about it?"

Emily cocked her head to the side, pretending to consider this. Meanwhile, her fingers remained frustratingly still. Then, with a slightly wicked smile, she removed her hand altogether. "I think I'm ready to kick this teasing up a notch."

And with that, she popped the clasp on Diana's pants and began to slide them down her legs. Diana lifted her hips to help her, annoyed with herself for her excessive eagerness to get out of her clothes. Truthfully, she was more aroused than she'd expected to be at this point. She was going to have to be patient tonight, which wasn't always her strength.

With Emily's help, Diana slid out of the rest of her clothes, then lay naked on the bed, flat on her back as Emily stared down at her with heated eyes. Diana was trying to let her take the lead. She really was. But in her impatience to get some relief from the tension building in her core, Diana brought a hand between her own thighs, sighing with relief as her fingers made contact with her clit.

Just as quickly, Emily had pushed her hand aside. That dominant look was back in her eyes as she pinned Diana's hands to the bed. "Ah-ah, not so fast. I'm the only one who gets to touch you tonight, Diana. Your hands are for my body only. Got it?"

Diana gulped as a fresh rush of arousal burned through her, causing her core to clench. And then she was nodding. "Yes."

EMILY HAD NEVER FELT MORE powerful than she did with Diana pinned beneath her, nodding her submission. It was hard for her, Emily could tell. Already, Diana's commanding nature had come into play a few times, but that only made things more interesting, as far as Emily was concerned. It was a battle of wills tonight, of the very hottest kind.

Honestly, Emily couldn't believe they were really doing this. She'd had second thoughts almost as soon as she'd suggested it. Topping Diana? It seemed like a fantasy Emily would fail at in reality, and yet, Diana had embraced her submissive role tonight. She even seemed to be enjoying it. Emily had never suspected she had a dominant streak, but she was loving every moment.

Diana's chest heaved, her eyes blazing into Emily's. She'd asked to be teased mercilessly, and despite her seeming impatience, Emily saw only heat, not frustration, reflected back at her in the azure depths of Diana's eyes as Emily held her hands against the duvet, preventing her from touching herself.

"You need a little something, hm?" Emily hardly recognized her voice, it had gotten so low and husky, almost sultry.

In response, Diana squeezed her eyes shut, arching her back so her breasts pushed toward Emily's. The neatly trimmed patch of golden hair between her thighs glistened with her arousal. In her current position, head thrown back so that her hair flowed to the duvet beneath her, Diana looked like something out of an erotic painting.

Emily released Diana's hands so her own could get busy. She cupped Diana's breasts, carefully working her nipples into hardened peaks, but it didn't take her long to realize Diana's breasts weren't overly sensitive. She leaned into the touch, but she wasn't writhing with pleasure, which was what Emily wanted.

This was all part of exploring someone new, finding out which places she most liked to be touched. Emily remembered the way Diana had trembled when she'd kissed her wrist earlier, and sure enough, when Emily dipped her head to kiss the delicate skin there, Diana whimpered, hips shifting beneath Emily.

Good to know.

Emily filed that information away as she continued her exploration of Diana's body. She ran her hands over Diana's stomach and down her thighs, bypassing where she knew Diana most wanted her touch. This close, she could smell Diana's arousal as her hips shifted restlessly against the duvet.

Making her wait was an unexpected turn-on. As Emily slid her fingers over Diana's velvety soft inner thigh, drawing a faint whimper from her throat, Emily felt a surge of arousal in her own core. She followed her fingers with her mouth, kissing her way up and down Diana's thighs until she trembled, her muscles taut beneath Emily's lips.

"You're so hot when you're this turned on," Emily murmured against her skin. "I mean, you're always hot. You took my breath away when I first saw you in the bar earlier tonight, but you're like...*exceptionally* hot right now."

"Sweet talker," Diana mumbled.

"That's me." Knowing Diana must be desperate for some friction on her clit—Emily sure would be by now—she slid up to claim Diana's lips as she brought a hand between Diana's thighs.

Diana groaned into her mouth, her hips jerking as Emily's fingers parted her, finding the little nub that was surely begging for her attention. Emily circled it with her fingers, trying to judge how close Diana was, not wanting to send her over the edge yet.

But Diana seemed relatively composed as she rocked her hips into Emily's touch, kissing her hungrily, her hands fisted in Emily's hair. Emily began to stroke her, keeping her rhythm as slow as she could, and Diana matched her, thrusting her hips in time with Emily's fingers. She was sticking to her own rules, not trying to rush things.

Emily had never been very good at postponing her own pleasure. Case in point, her clit was throbbing so fiercely, she wasn't sure how much longer she could wait to be touched, and she'd already come once.

They kept at this torturously languid pace for several long minutes, until Diana's breaths grew unsteady, her hips beginning to push more insistently against Emily's hand, her thighs slick with her own arousal.

Emily gave her several hard and fast strokes, enough to have Diana panting, and then she removed her hand altogether. Diana gulped, closing her eyes. Her hips kept moving—perhaps without her even being aware of it— seeking a friction they could no longer find.

For a moment, Emily thought this would be the end. Diana would grab her hand and demand that she finish what she'd started. After several deep breaths, Diana pounced, but instead of grinding herself against Emily as she'd expected, she rolled Emily beneath her and shimmied down the bed until her head was between Emily's thighs.

"Do you want this?" Diana's voice was a growl, her breath hot against Emily's clit. "Do you want to feel my mouth on your pussy?"

The heat from those words made Emily throb. "Yes. God, yes."

"Tell me how much you want it." Diana's fingers traced tantalizing patterns on Emily's thighs as she pinned her with her gaze. She might have given control of her own pleasure to Emily tonight, but there was no mistaking who was in control right now.

"So much I'm about to lose my mind." Emily gulped,

hips arching toward Diana's mouth. "I know you're going to make me come so hard."

"Damn right, I am." Diana brought her mouth against Emily's clit.

"Fuck," Emily gasped. Her thighs fell open in silent encouragement. Diana flicked her tongue back and forth until Emily was panting, shamelessly grinding herself against Diana's face.

Just as quickly, Diana pulled away. "Not so fast, darling."

Diana lifted her head, and Emily saw her eyes—pupils blown with lust—and her chin glistening with Emily's arousal, lips quirked in the kind of grin that let Emily know she was in for a taste of her own medicine. She whined in protest.

Ignoring her, Diana started kissing her way down Emily's leg. She paused, sucking at a sensitive spot on Emily's inner thigh, then nipped at it with her teeth, hard enough that Emily suspected it would leave a mark.

Oh.

Emily trembled. Okay, that was nice. *Really* nice. Diana soothed the spot with her tongue before continuing the onslaught of her mouth. She kissed and nibbled her way over Emily's thighs until she was a whimpering mess. Diana's bites stung, but it was the kind of pain that left Emily wanting more.

She squeezed her eyes shut, trying to savor the anticipation the way Diana seemed to, but the ache in her core was overpowering. "Now, Diana. Please."

Diana slid forward, her mouth covering Emily where she ached for her. Emily cried out in pleasure, writhing against the duvet as Diana unleashed the full force of that talented mouth on her clit.

Her tongue did some kind of twirly thing that had Emily chanting, "Yes!" in a breathy voice. Diana pressed two fingers against Emily's entrance, meeting her eyes with a questioning gaze. Emily nodded frantically. Diana began to thrust with her fingers, her mouth still ravishing Emily's clit, and it was perfect, so perfect. Emily came in a hot rush, pleasure rolling languorously through her body. "God, you're good at that," she gasped.

"Why, thank you, darling," Diana murmured as she pressed tender kisses to Emily's thighs. Then she swiped the back of her hand over her mouth before scooting up to lie beside Emily. She wore a smug grin as she swept her gaze over Emily's limp, satisfied body. Emily felt boneless, blissed out, drunk on endorphins.

Beside her, Diana was flushed and breathing hard. Her eyes were bright, and as Emily watched, her hand drifted to the juncture of her thighs. Emily opened her mouth to reprimand her when Diana snatched her hand away as if she'd only just realized it was there.

"You've been very patient," Emily said, meeting Diana's lust-glazed eyes. "And you deserve a reward for your patience."

And then Emily rolled over and buried her face between Diana's thighs.

FOUR

Emily hadn't known how much she would love this. Being in control—let alone being in control of a woman as powerful as Diana Devlin—was one of the headiest things she'd ever experienced. She kissed her way over Diana's soaked flesh, loving the way she tasted and the quiver of her thighs beneath Emily's palms as Emily brushed her tongue against Diana's clit.

Diana didn't beg. Emily was starting to think Diana never begged, although she'd mentioned it during their flirty banter when they were laying out the rules of their fantasy role play. She'd asked if Emily wanted to hear her beg.

It turned out that she did.

So Emily used her tongue to drive Diana wild, never quite giving her enough pressure to come. She never spent more than a few seconds on Diana's clit before retreating to less sensitive territory. Teasing. She was teasing her mercilessly as her own arousal grew.

Diana was remarkably cooperative, hips moving against Emily's mouth, but never trying to grind against her the way Emily had done when Diana went down on her. Emily licked and kissed her way over Diana's skin, noting which places she liked best. The spot to the left of Diana's clit seemed particularly sensitive, drawing a ragged gasp when Emily kissed her there.

When Emily chanced a peek at her face, she saw that Diana had her eyes tightly closed, her lips pressed together as if to keep herself quiet. Her hands were fisted in the duvet, the muscles in her abdominals clenched tight. Despite the tension straining her body, there was something almost Zen about her appearance, as if she'd given herself over to the pleasure of Emily's mouth, no matter how long she had to wait for release.

Emily had to hand it to her. Diana's self-control was impeccable.

And Emily wanted to see her break. She wanted to hear her beg, to see her writhe and lose every bit of that flawless control. Emily dipped her head, nipping gently at Diana's clit, rewarded by a buck of her hips. Then she flicked her tongue back and forth against it the way Diana had done, paying special attention to that sensitive spot to the left of her clit. Diana made a strangled sound, her hips beginning to squirm, but still she held herself back.

This was too tame. Emily grinned as inspiration struck. "I'm ready to turn up the heat in here. New rules: I need you to tell me when you're getting close, and don't you dare come without my permission. Got it?"

She lifted her head, watching with satisfaction as Diana nodded.

"Do you want my fingers?" Emily asked as she trailed a hand up Diana's inner thigh.

Diana nodded again, her throat bobbing as she gulped for air.

This is more like it. Emily pushed two fingers inside,

and Diana's body gripped her greedily. Emily stroked leisurely as she began to kiss her way over Diana's folds. She dragged her tongue over Diana's clit, loving the way Diana's hips moved in response. Gradually, she increased the intensity of her actions until her tongue was a whirlwind, her fingers pumping in and out of Diana's body.

Diana's breathing grew ragged. Each inhale shook, a whine caught in her throat. Her knuckles gleamed white where her fists were clenched in the duvet.

"Don't forget the rules," Emily murmured.

"I can take a little more." Diana's voice was breathy and high-pitched, nowhere near as composed as she'd sounded a few minutes ago.

Emily grinned against her skin, and then she gave her what she'd asked for. She ravished Diana with her mouth, ignoring the ache in her jaw as she gave her everything she had. Diana gasped and panted, her thighs beginning to shake. Her hips moved faster, and suddenly, her hands were on Emily's shoulders.

"C-close," she whispered, her voice breaking on the S, dragging out the sound in a way that made Emily's clit throb.

She retreated immediately. Diana let out a tortured groan, but hey, she'd asked for this. She'd asked Emily to keep going, to bring her right to the edge, and she wasn't complaining even now. She sucked in deep, shaky breaths, her thighs pressed together now that Emily no longer rested between them.

Emily kissed her way over Diana's stomach as she gave her a chance to compose herself. She swirled her tongue over Diana's breasts before moving the attention of her mouth to Diana's wrists. She licked and kissed, loving Diana's gasps of pleasure.

After she'd worshipped each of her wrists, Emily lay with her face on Diana's stomach, just watching her, captivated by the rosy flush on Diana's cheeks and chest, the way her pupils still eclipsed the blue of her eyes as she returned Emily's gaze. Her breathing had slowed, her body less tense beneath Emily's.

As their gazes held, Diana's thighs parted, allowing Emily to slip between them, her stomach pressing into Diana's hot, wet center. "More?" Emily asked.

Diana nodded, pinching her bottom lip between her teeth.

So Emily dove in for more, licking and kissing as Diana's temporary calm dissipated. She didn't last as long this time. It only took a few minutes before she was panting and shaking, clearly approaching the edge.

"Close," she gasped, her body so tense, Emily knew it wouldn't take much for her to break.

Emily stopped, but didn't retreat this time. She held perfectly still, tongue pressed against Diana's clit, waiting to see how she'd react. If she'd beg. Diana wriggled beneath her, breathing raggedly. Her hands came to Emily's shoulders, nails biting into her skin.

This is it.

Emily smiled in anticipation.

The next thing she knew, she was on her back with Diana on top of her, eyes blazing into Emily's as she brought a hand between Emily's thighs, testing her before she plunged two fingers inside. Emily gasped. She was so wet that Diana's fingers entered her with almost no resistance.

Diana watched her for several seconds, and the look on her face could only be described as *feral*. Emily's core clenched around Diana's fingers as her arousal grew. Then

Diana moved, her mouth finding Emily's neck as her hand kept moving, fucking Emily hard and fast. As much as she had control of herself when Emily teased her, Diana was wild when it was her turn to ravish Emily. This was where she let herself lose control.

Emily could only hold on for the ride as Diana sucked several beautifully painful hickeys onto her neck while her fingers moved at a frenzied pace, bringing Emily to the edge in record speed. Diana's teeth sank into her neck as her thumb pressed against Emily's clit, and she was flying, tumbling into her third orgasm of the night.

As she regained her senses, she was aware of Diana's body pressed against hers. Diana's hips rocked against Emily's thigh as if she could no longer keep herself still. Emily rolled her to her back, straddling one of Diana's thighs so that her own thigh pressed into Diana's core with every movement of Emily's hips.

Diana let out a little whimper of frustration. And yet, her eyes—glazed as they were—still radiated pleasure. She was enjoying this, damn her.

Emily rocked her hips, drawing another whimper from Diana. She threw her head back, again surrendering to Emily, and it gave her an unexpected jolt of arousal. She hadn't been sure she could come again, let alone this soon after her last orgasm, but teasing Diana was impossibly hot, so...

Emily moved her hips slowly back and forth over Diana's thigh, teasing them both. She watched her closely, loving the way pleasure played across Diana's features. Her hips bucked beneath Emily, seeking more, and then she growled, her hands flailing against the duvet before gripping her own hair as if she didn't know what to do with them.

"I told you not to touch yourself." And maybe Emily was having a little too much fun with this.

Diana yanked her hands from her hair, but instead of returning them to the duvet, she gripped Emily's hips with bruising pressure. "Please. I can't wait any longer."

Emily froze. After all this time, when Diana finally begged, she hadn't even seen it coming. "Oh," she gasped, her hand automatically reaching between their bodies, finding Diana's swollen clit. But then she remembered Diana's words while she'd had Emily pressed against the wall what felt like hours ago. *I want you to tease me until I can't take it anymore...and then tease me a little bit more.*

She withdrew her hand, ignoring Diana's growl of protest. "Oh, I think you can wait just a little bit longer."

FIVE

"I think you can wait just a little bit longer…"

Diana surged beneath Emily, her body automatically protesting those whispered words, but just as quickly, she felt herself breathing deep, pushing back the overwhelming need to come. She hadn't thought she could wait another second, but now…

Emily was giving her exactly what she'd asked for, and Diana couldn't remember ever feeling this exquisitely aroused. Her pulse pounded, her clit throbbed, and her core clenched, but she was in control.

There was only one outlet available for the tension coiled inside her, and she unleashed the full force of it on an unsuspecting Emily, who let out a startled gasp as Diana pressed her against the bed, covering her with her body. But she quickly realized this wouldn't do. She couldn't press her hips against Emily without surrendering to the need to grind against her, not when she'd been denied an orgasm for so long.

Holding in a groan, Diana lifted her hips from Emily's. She pressed her thighs together in a fruitless attempt to ease the ache there as she dragged her hands down Emily's back roughly enough to leave scratches.

Diana was driven so wild by her own need that there was no holding herself back where Emily was concerned, and her lack of finesse would give Emily exactly what she'd asked for: marks she'd have to cover up with her clothes tomorrow. Diana sucked a hickey onto her neck, then scraped her teeth over her collarbone until Emily cried out, her thighs parting beneath Diana.

Diana scooted down to settle in the space Emily had created for her. She covered Emily with her mouth, scratching her fingernails over Emily's thighs as she licked and sucked with an almost punishing force.

Within minutes, Emily was writhing against her mouth, coming with a shout of pleasure that sent a hot jolt straight to Diana's clit. She could feel her hand trembling as she wiped her mouth and crawled onto the bed beside Emily.

Desperate to get some friction where she needed it, she pressed herself against Emily's side, whimpering with relief as her clit made contact with Emily's warm skin. Technically, she was sticking to Emily's rules. She hadn't touched herself, but her willpower was waning.

"You need to come?" Emily asked, her voice oddly calm as she brought her hands to Diana's hips, stilling her movements.

Diana bucked against Emily's grip. "Yes."

"Beg me for it."

"Please," Diana responded without hesitation, feeling nothing but a surge of arousal as the word left her lips. "Please, Emily. Please let me come." Her hips were still moving, and she couldn't have stopped them if she'd tried. Her pulse pounded in her ears and between her thighs, but still, Emily didn't react. She just stared, seemingly mesmerized by Diana's desperation.

"Please." Diana felt herself grow impossibly wetter every time she said the word. "Please, please, please..." Her voice broke, her hips pushing more insistently against Emily's thigh.

"Yes," Emily said finally, licking her lips. "Yes, Diana. God, you're going to come so hard."

As she spoke, she rose onto her knees, separating their bodies. "But first, take a few breaths, okay? Because I want you to last long enough to enjoy this."

And those were the magic words. Diana immediately went still, sucking in a deep breath to steady herself. She was in a fog of arousal, her senses overtaken by the insistent ache in her core, the tension coiled so tightly that if she didn't get some relief—and soon—she might actually snap.

Emily positioned herself with her body hovering over Diana's, kissing her fiercely before she brought the pleasure of her mouth to Diana's neck and down to her collarbones. Diana could hear herself breathing, rapid and harsh, seemingly unable to bring enough oxygen into her lungs. It was all good, *so* good, and yet, not enough.

She'd been teased to her breaking point, and as Emily's tongue swirled over her nipple, Diana could barely feel it over the urgent throbbing in her core. She closed her eyes, breathing through it, focusing on the way it felt to be so exquisitely aware of her body and the pleasure it could provide, so *alive*.

Emily kissed a wet trail over Diana's stomach, and Diana wasn't even trying to hold herself back now. Her hips bowed upward, seeking contact with any part of Emily they could find. She didn't care if she only lasted five seconds once Emily put that wonderfully talented mouth on her. It would be worth it, *so* worth it.

Emily pushed Diana's hips against the duvet, at the same time settling between her thighs. Her hot breath reached Diana's overstimulated flesh, and she writhed, anticipation boiling over into agony. Then Emily's tongue was against her clit, and Diana let out the most outrageous sob of relief. Any other time, it would have embarrassed her, but not tonight.

She ground herself shamelessly against Emily's mouth, any semblance of control long gone. She could hear herself talking, an endless stream of "Yes!" and "Fuck" and "More!" Vaguely, she was aware that Emily was trying to slow her down, trying to transfer the attention of her mouth to less sensitive parts of Diana, but her body screamed in protest as Emily's mouth left her clit.

"No. Please. Don't stop." Diana realized she had a fistful of Emily's hair clenched in her right hand as she tried to drag her back where she wanted her. "Sorry," she mumbled, trying to disentangle her fingers from Emily's hair.

Emily looked up and caught her eye as she used her free hand to push Diana's fingers more firmly into her tresses. "Don't apologize. I like it."

"Oh." Diana's fingers clenched.

"Hold on tight," Emily whispered, and then she proceeded to devour Diana with all the urgency she'd been craving. Her mouth was all-consuming, everywhere Diana needed her, and her tongue...

It whirled and flicked and pressed, distilling Diana's existence to the areas it touched. Her hips moved frantically as the orgasm that had been building inside her for what felt like hours finally crested. For several long seconds, she hung on the precipice, swearing profusely as pleasure swelled inside her, centered in her clit.

Perhaps sensing how close she was, Emily began to suck, her tongue continuing its relentless movements. Diana's body went rigid as she broke. The orgasm rolled through her with a scorching intensity, centered in her core as the tension there finally found its release. *Yes. Oh God. Yes yes yes...*

She let out a moan that was more like a scream as her system filled with the most wonderful sensation in the world, so much pleasure, her body tingled with it, so much pleasure, she almost couldn't handle it, her limbs thrashing against the duvet. She'd known her orgasm would be powerful from having waited so long, but this...*God.*

Eventually, the intensity ebbed, and she was aware of Emily still gently moving her tongue, helping Diana wring every bit of pleasure from her release. She flung a hand over her eyes, breathing hard as her body finally relaxed, after-shocks still twitching in her core.

"Goddamn," she managed, her voice low and raspy. She wasn't sure she'd ever come that hard before. And yet, she still didn't feel entirely sated. Even as pleasure buzzed through her veins, there was still an undercurrent of arousal in her core. Her clit still throbbed against Emily's tongue, and she didn't want her to stop.

She pushed her hips more firmly against Emily's mouth, letting out a long, low moan, and Emily took the hint. She kept going, kissing her way over Diana's flesh, exploring her folds as she gave her a chance to catch her breath.

Diana breathed slow and steady, limp with relief and yet still unbearably needy, her hips soon finding a steady rhythm that matched Emily's tongue. Arousal rose inside her until, almost before she'd prepared herself for it, she was coming again, grinding her hips against Emily's mouth as pleasure pulsed from her core.

This one was less intense than the first, but it seemed to last forever, wave after wave of bliss that had her moaning, wondering if she'd ever known so much pleasure. She basked in it. This feeling...it was worth every moment she'd waited. It was pure ecstasy. She never wanted it to end... until suddenly, it was too much. Her clit became so sensitive that she pushed Emily away.

"Good?" Emily asked, looking up at her with flushed cheeks.

"Fuck." Diana flung her head back against the bedding, so boneless, she wasn't sure she'd ever move again. Warmth still radiated from her core, her body tingling with aftershocks. "That was so fucking great, I'm not even coherent enough to tell you how good it was."

Emily slid up to lie beside her, eyes gleaming with happiness. "I didn't know you were a sweet talker."

Diana felt as though she'd melted into the duvet in a blissfully sated puddle. "Because I'm not. I just tell it how it is."

She hadn't come to Vermont looking for a hookup. Emily had caught her by surprise in so many ways, and now, she found herself hoping that this earth-shattering night was a sign of more good things on the horizon.

EMILY WOKE to the unfamiliar sound of someone breathing beside her. Her eyes popped open to take in Diana's sleeping form, barely visible in the darkened room. *Oh.* Memories of the night before flooded in, flirty drinks followed by the hottest night of Emily's life.

That really happened.

She grinned. Faint amber light filtered through the window, more likely a streetlight than the sun. Emily had the impression it was still dark outside. She squinted at the clock on the microwave, which told her it was just past five.

Emily had to be at work at eight, which meant there probably wasn't any point in trying to get back to sleep since she needed to head home soon to get ready. What was the protocol for a morning after like this?

Had Diana even meant for Emily to stay the night? After who-knew-how-many orgasms, they'd both kind of passed out without having a conversation about it. Emily couldn't bear it if anything happened this morning to dampen the magic of last night. Maybe she should just go and save them both any awkwardness.

That way, last night would remain a perfect memory.

Decision made, Emily slipped out of bed. She fumbled through the darkness to find her underwear and dress, then put them back on. She had to pee, but didn't want to wake Diana by flushing the toilet. It was only a thirty-minute drive home. She could wait. Suddenly, she was desperate to be out of Diana's hotel room, terrified Diana would wake up and be annoyed to find her still here.

Emily grabbed her purse and slipped into the hall, closing the door quietly behind her. She blinked against the brightness in the hall, running a hand over her sleep-mussed hair as she hurried toward the lobby. A different white-gloved porter was there this morning, nodding politely at her as she stepped outside.

Emily walked to her car and headed home. As she pulled into her driveway a half hour later, the sun was just peeking over the treetops. First order of business, she needed a shower. Then she needed to check on Jack, who would be eager for some attention after over twelve hours alone. She let herself into her cottage, tossing her purse on the table inside the door on her way toward the bedroom.

Already, she could hear excited chirping from the direction of the porch. Since the weather was nice, she'd left Jack's cage on the screened-in porch last night so he could chat with the wild birds in the woods behind her house. "Be right there, Jack!" she called, and his twittering grew even louder.

Emily smiled as she entered the bedroom, already stripping out of her dress. *What a night.* If she'd known a one-night stand could be that hot, that *intimate*, maybe she'd have been having more of them, but Emily wasn't generally a casual dater. She was looking for a serious relationship, especially now that she was thirty-five. Not to mention, the one-night stands she'd had in the past hadn't in any way compared to what she'd shared last night with Diana.

Last night had been *perfect*.

Meeting Diana had shaken her. It made Emily realize how long it had been since she'd pushed herself out of her comfort zone. Now it was up to Emily to keep that momentum going.

She used the bathroom and then spun before the mirror, feeling a hot thrill as she saw the purple marks on her neck, the red scratches down her back, the imprint of a mouth on her inner thigh. She'd have to wear a scarf at work today, and she was going to love every moment. No, she wouldn't be forgetting last night any time soon.

After a quick shower, she dressed in her Inn at Crescent Falls staff shirt and black pants, grateful her grandmas weren't the kind of people who'd mind if she added a gauzy scarf to her outfit to hide the marks on her neck.

Mary and Eva—or Grandma and Gram to Emily—had

met over forty years ago, and, as Mary told the story, it had been love at first sight. Eva maintained that she'd had to work to catch Mary's attention in those early days.

They'd been living in Georgia at the time, both in their thirties. Eva was recently widowed by a man who'd been more of a friend than a lover, while Mary had been out since she was a teen. It wasn't easy for them as an interracial lesbian couple in those days, but they'd found their sanctuary here in Vermont, running and eventually owning the inn.

In 2009, when Vermont became one of the first states to legalize gay marriage, they'd hosted their wedding right here on the grounds, and the inn, which had always been a popular local spot for weddings and events, soon became known as one of the most sought-after gay marriage locations in the area.

Eva and Mary had always run a queer-friendly establishment, and it was now a haven that many queer couples and families sought out for their vacations and special events, a place where they would not only be tolerated but celebrated, a place where queer was normal, where a rainbow flag waved proudly on the front porch and guests had the option to list their pronouns when they booked their registration.

Emily couldn't be prouder of the Inn at Crescent Falls or her grandmas. After her mother left her behind to chase her dreams—or a man, which was the same thing for Violet Janssen—when Emily was ten, Mary and Eva had taken her in, raising her in their apartment at the inn, much as they'd taken Violet in a decade earlier when she'd shown up in town as a pregnant teenage runaway.

After college, Emily had moved into this cottage, which had once belonged to the groundskeeper, back when that was a job that required living on-site. It was perfect for Emily, though, a cozy little house all her own. She was out of sight of the main inn, but still close enough to walk to work on the days when she staffed the front desk.

Emily couldn't imagine living anywhere else. The inn and its grounds were home. Once she was dressed, she fixed herself a cup of coffee and a bowl of cereal and brought her breakfast to the back porch to spend a few minutes with Jack. He was a song sparrow, with pretty brown feathers and stripes on his chest. She'd found him a few months ago when she was painting in the field behind the inn, just a fledgling who had survived some kind of animal attack.

The local wild-bird rescue couldn't take him due to an outbreak of avian flu, but when Emily refused to give up on him, they'd given her supplies to help her rehabilitate him herself. He was fully recovered now, except for a balance problem that caused him to fly in wobbly circles and would prevent him from ever being released into the wild.

For now, he lived in a cage on her back porch, but eventually, he would need more. Other birds to socialize with. Emily hoped the aviary would be able to take him once the flu outbreak was under control, much as she hated the idea of letting him go. She'd grown pretty fond of her sparrow.

"Hey there, my little pirate," she crooned as she opened the door to his cage.

Jack chirped loudly as he hopped to the doorway, spread his wings, and began to spiral across the porch. It made her dizzy watching him fly, but he didn't seem bothered by his disability. He chirped and sang as he soared around her, stretching his wings.

While he was out, she changed his cage liner and refreshed his food, adding a raspberry—his absolute favorite treat—to the bowl. Then she sat with him while she enjoyed her breakfast, telling him about her night while he twittered happily in response.

"Sorry for the quick visit, buddy, but I've got to go to work. I promise to spend more time with you this afternoon, okay?" She walked to where he was perched and held out her finger.

He hopped on and allowed her to transfer him back to his cage.

She washed her hands, grabbed her bag, and set out along the path that led to the inn, whistling her imitation of one of Jack's favorite tunes as she walked. It was a gorgeous June morning, warm and sunny, and while Emily enjoyed working the front desk, today she couldn't wait to get home and relax, maybe do some painting on the back porch with Jack.

She was tired from her adventurous night, sore in a few interesting places that made her blush just remembering. If the desk was slow today, she'd text her friends and fill them in. She knew they must be dying for an update after she left them hanging last night. The inn came into view ahead, its white façade standing out in sharp contrast to the lush green trees behind it.

An American flag flew out front, swaying gently in the breeze, right next to the Pride flag, and it was one of the new Progress flags that included stripes for trans rights and people of color. The inn itself was a classic colonial style with white paint, black shutters, and a porch that wrapped around the far side of the building, providing guests with views of the mountains beyond. Emily jogged up the front steps and pushed through the door.

She stepped behind the desk and booted up the computer, then took down the sign that hung on the desk overnight, containing the emergency number for guests to call if they needed anything after hours. The inn had forty rooms, which was fairly large for the area, but it wasn't large enough to justify staffing the desk overnight. Staff took turns being on call for the after-hours number, which received a handful of calls a week, usually from guests needing extra towels or late-night medicine for a sick kid.

Emily stowed her purse behind the desk and logged into the system. The inn was completely booked this week with a group of accountants who were here for a conference, meaning her Wednesday morning promised to be unusually busy.

Her grandma—Mary—breezed through the lobby a few minutes later, looking summery in pale-blue linen pants and a matching blazer, her short silver hair freshly styled. "Morning," she called.

"Good morning," Emily responded. "You look fancy today."

"Oh, I have a meeting later, wanted to look the part." Grandma touched the button on her jacket, then gestured to Emily's scarf. "You're looking rather fancy yourself."

Heat traveled up Emily's neck, but as close as she was to her grandma, she drew the line at talking about her sex life. "Thanks."

"Dinner after your shift? Gram's roasting a chicken."

"You got it." Emily smiled at her grandma before reaching for the telephone on the desk, which had started to ring. "Front desk, this is Emily. How may I help you?"

"Hi, Emily," a male voice said. "The toilet in room 102 is running constantly. I tried fiddling with it, but I can't get it to stop."

"I'll send maintenance right up," she told him. "Thanks for letting us know."

Emily ended the call and dialed the handyman who

handled weekday maintenance requests. Then she settled on her stool and pulled out her cell phone. She'd barely had time to glance at it yet today, and unsurprisingly, there was a flurry of activity in the Adventurers group chat.

TOM BELLAMY

DYING for an update. LITERALLY DYING.

DREW NGUYEN

Don't interrupt her, Tom. What if she's still with the woman from last night?

ALEXIS BELL

Pretty sure Em works this morning

TALIA MICHAUD

Emily, send us an emoji if you're alive!

I'm going to send out a search party if we don't hear from you soon

jk but also not

Emily grinned as her fingers began to tap out a quick reply.

You guys are so dramatic!

my night was <flame emoji><flame emoji> <flame emoji>

TALIA MICHAUD

Yassssss girl! Get it!!

ALEXIS BELL

wooooooooooooooo!!! We need DETAILS

TOM BELLAMY

EMILY

I AM SO PROUD

TOM BELLAMY

> I knew you had it in you!

Thanks, guys

> I'll tell you all about it at trivia night tmrw!

Emily texted with her friends for a few more minutes before things at the front desk started picking up. She checked out a family who'd been in town to hike to the falls...although they hadn't been so naïve as to attempt the summit trail. Her lips quirked as she remembered Diana's unbridled confidence, despite having never hiked a technical trail before.

From there, she directed a conference attendee with a sore throat to the nearest urgent care, handled a report of a raccoon behind the toolshed, and helped the morning's speaker get her laptop connected to the screen in the conference room.

All in all, a hectic morning, and while Emily wasn't complaining, she was tired. She hadn't gotten enough sleep last night. Now that she'd returned to reality, her time with Diana almost felt like a daydream. Could Emily really keep tapping into the bolder version of herself that she'd discovered last night?

When she was younger, she'd dreamed of traveling the world, painting the sights and supporting herself with the proceeds from her art. She'd never thought she would still be working the front desk at the inn at thirty-five. What had happened to her ambition and her sense of adventure?

Emily had just finished a phone call with a panicked woman who'd accidentally booked her reservation for the wrong night when she heard the swish of the front door opening. She glanced up, polite smile already in place to greet whoever had entered. The woman was looking down at her phone, but her hair immediately captured Emily's attention, that distinctive blend of blonde and red. Her white silk blouse and maroon skirt hugged a familiar figure. What...?

Diana straightened to meet her gaze, her eyes widening as that confident stride faltered, just for a moment. "Emily? This is a surprise."

Emily's heart was racing, a warm tingly heat spreading through her system. She was irrationally pleased to see Diana, even if she had no idea *why* she was here. Diana's gaze dipped to the scarf at Emily's throat, and her skin grew even warmer.

This felt like a moment right out of a movie. Had Diana tracked her down because she wanted to see her again? *Oh, wow.* Emily was already swooning. But on second glance, Diana had on business attire, a sleek black briefcase in her right hand. She looked ready for a meeting. And just like that, the penny dropped.

"You're in town to buy a hotel." Emily's voice came out weak and shaky. Her grandmothers weren't selling the inn. It wasn't for sale. Diana couldn't just...take it, could she?

Diana nodded, watching Emily carefully.

"This inn?" Emily managed, as everything inside her that had been warm turned ice cold. "You're here to buy *my* inn?"

Diana's chin went up, just slightly, as if she were squaring off for a fight. "If this is your inn, then yes."

SIX

"But...I don't understand."

To be honest, neither did Diana. The last person she'd expected to see behind the front desk of the Inn at Crescent Falls was Emily. She was sure she hadn't heard Emily's name before yesterday. Diana would never have knowingly had sex with someone connected to an inn she was buying. God, the things she'd let Emily do to her last night...

She and Emily had shared something special. Memorable. Diana had been irrationally disappointed to wake up this morning and discover that Emily had left without saying goodbye. Now she was wondering if she'd somehow misread the entire thing. And what in the world did Emily mean by calling this "her" inn? "I thought you were an artist?"

"I am. I work here part-time to help pay the bills." Emily looked as bewildered as Diana felt.

"Okay, well, I have an appointment with the owners, Mary and Eva Chambers-Benoit."

"My grandmothers," Emily said. "I thought you were here to buy the Beaumont?"

Diana shook her head slowly. "It's not for sale. I only stayed there last night because this inn was fully booked."

"But this inn isn't for sale either!" Emily's voice rose, her expression indignant. Her eyes gleamed with hurt...and anger.

The inn *was* for sale, though. Diana didn't know why Emily was unaware, but she wasn't about to get in the middle of whatever messy family dynamic she'd stumbled into. "I think you should have a conversation with your grandmothers."

"Did you know?" Emily practically hissed. "Last night?"

"I promise you, I had no idea you were in any way connected to this inn when I met you yesterday, and if I had, last night would never have happened." Diana kept her voice pitched low, not wanting anyone else who happened through the lobby to overhear their conversation.

"Well, I...grrr." Emily fisted her hands against the counter, glaring at Diana. She wore a pink-patterned scarf at her throat, and Diana's eyes kept drifting to it, refusing to let her forget what lay beneath. Not that she *could* forget, not when her own body was sore in some rather interesting places today.

Surely this was the least professional start to any business meeting she'd ever had. Diana had half a mind to turn around and walk back out the door, but she'd never let her personal life interfere with business before, and she wasn't about to start now. She cleared her throat. "I'm very sorry that we've found ourselves in this unfortunate situation."

"Probably not as sorry as I am," Emily said with a deflated sort of sigh.

Before Diana could figure out how to respond, two

older women—one white, one Black—entered the lobby, both smiling in Diana's direction.

"Diana Devlin, I presume?" the white woman asked.

Diana slipped her professional smile into place, doing her best to shelve her discomfort. "I am," she said warmly as she clasped the woman's extended hand and shook.

"Mary Chambers-Benoit, and this is my wife, Eva."

"It's a pleasure to meet you both," Diana said, turning to shake Eva's hand as well. All the while, she was painfully aware of Emily's wounded eyes as she observed the exchange.

"Our office is right this way." Eva gestured toward the hallway behind the desk where Emily stood. Eva was a tall, slender woman, wearing a colorful, whimsical dress that made Diana wonder if Emily had gotten her fashion sense from her. Eva wore her hair in thin braids that hung halfway down her back.

By contrast, Mary was a head shorter than her wife with a rounder figure, her silver hair cut in a short, no-nonsense style. She wore a light-blue linen suit. Together, they made a striking couple.

Diana followed them down the hallway, doing her best to walk normally despite the pain in her quads and calves from yesterday's ill-fated hike, a problem only made worse by her heels. They entered a small but bright office. Diana was here today to see if this inn was up to Devlin's standards with a personal tour, to meet the owners and discuss any concerns they might have about a potential sale and, if all went well, to lay the groundwork for that sale.

Prior to bumping into Emily in the lobby, she'd been reasonably sure this acquisition was going to work out. She loved what she'd seen of the inn so far and suspected it would be a great addition to the Devlin portfolio. If only she hadn't gone and fucked the owners' granddaughter...

"We thought we could talk business first and then take you for a tour," Eva said, gesturing to a round table to Diana's left.

"That sounds perfect," Diana told her.

"Coffee? Tea? Water?" Mary asked.

"Water would be great. Thank you." As much as Diana could use some extra caffeine after her late night, she was feeling vaguely jittery after her run-in with Emily.

Why hadn't Mary and Eva told Emily they were selling the inn? Perhaps this family was as cutthroat as the Devlins, a thought that put Diana even more on edge. She liked living under the illusion that these small inns were as warm and welcoming behind the scenes as they appeared from the outside.

Mary returned with three cups of water, and they all took seats around the table.

"The first thing we want to make clear is that we're still very hesitant about selling to a large corporation like yours, no matter how much money you offer, *if* you make an offer," Eva said. "So we'd like to find out more about what your vision for our inn would entail."

Diana nodded. That was a disappointing way to start the meeting, but she wasn't entirely surprised. Inn owners were often hesitant to sell to a larger company, and Diana was excellent at explaining the benefits of the sale to them. "I understand. That's what I'm here for."

She reached into her briefcase and pulled out two portfolios, passing one to each of the women. Sometimes, she presented her data digitally, but she tried to tailor each presentation to the client, and something told her these two women would prefer to hold the data in their hands.

"I suspect your concerns lie in how the inn will be managed after the sale, once it's part of the Devlin Hotels portfolio," Diana began, "so let me reassure you on that point: your guests will not even notice the change in ownership. Current management and staff can remain in their existing positions, to the extent that those positions remain unchanged. They'll be given the appropriate orientation as Devlin employees and qualify for all our employee benefits, which you'll find are quite generous."

Mary nodded. Her expression had become less hesitant, more curious, as Diana spoke. Eva, by contrast, remained difficult to read. She watched Diana intently, her face impassive.

"We don't purchase boutique inns like yours with the intention of turning them into a Devlin Hotel. The Inn at Crescent Falls is a local landmark, and we don't want to change that. We simply streamline your operations with the resources available to us as a Fortune 500 company and boost your visibility through your affiliation with our brand. People do seek out the Devlin name, so having that seal on your materials can only help, not to mention the advertising dollars we invest."

Diana spent the next fifteen minutes running through her usual presentation, explaining to Mary and Eva what the sale would mean for their inn.

"That all sounds nice," Eva said when Diana had finished. "But as you mentioned, our inn is a local landmark, so I'm curious what guarantees you can make us on that front. We're known for hosting same-sex weddings and for being a welcoming and inclusive space for the queer community and other marginalized people. Can you promise that won't change? Because I'll be honest with you...we aren't desperate to sell. Yes, we're ready to retire, but we're also willing to be patient until we find the right buyer."

Diana nodded. "We never intend to change the aspects of an inn that have made it unique in the first place, and as a lesbian myself, I assure you the last thing I'd ever want to do is make one of our hotels *less* inclusive. However, we do have certain brand standards that every property in our portfolio needs to adhere to. I can't promise that you'll approve of every decision made after you retire, but if you have any specific concerns, I'd be happy to address them with you now."

"Can you promise that the Progress flag will stay out front?" Eva asked. "And the display case in the lobby showing all the same-sex couples—including Mary and me —who've been married here?"

"I can't see any reason why they would be removed," Diana assured her. "I scouted your inn because of its unique legacy, not in spite of it. I can't promise the flag will stay, but please don't take that to mean we would come in after the sale and immediately take it down. It's just not corporate policy to make guarantees on the appearance of the property."

Privately, this was probably Diana's least favorite part of her job. She regretted that she couldn't do more to reassure owners. She'd lost sales due to her inability to promise not to remove a certain painting or policy, things that were trivial to the Devlin brand but would go so far to reassure owners that their legacy would remain intact. But this was the reality of working for a larger corporation. The Devlin brand standard came first.

"I understand," Eva said, although she didn't look very reassured. She exchanged a frustrated look with her wife.

Diana held in a sigh. Her gut said she'd lost the sale, and

while it might be for the best after what had happened with Emily, Diana genuinely loved this property. She wanted it more than she'd wanted any of the other hotels she'd scouted this year. Not to mention, she hated to lose. Her mind was already scrambling to come up with another way to ease Mary and Eva's worries about selling to Devlin Hotels.

"We have a lot to think about," Mary said, then stood from the table. "Now, how about that tour?"

WHEN DIANA ENTERED her Back Bay brownstone later that afternoon, she knew almost immediately that she wasn't alone. The well-worn men's sneakers inside the door were her first clue, although at least he'd remembered to take them off before tracking dirt all over her hardwood floors this time.

Diana followed the hollow clicking sound of a gaming controller toward the living room, her lips quirking into an affectionate smile as she found her nephew sprawled on the couch, headphones on, his face a mask of concentration as he battled the monster currently displayed on her TV.

"Carter," she said, waving to catch his attention. When he still failed to notice her, she called him again, louder this time. "Carter!"

He jumped, hands flailing upward as the monster on the screen lunged. His character fell to the ground as Carter paused the game, then pulled off his headset and turned toward her. "Aunt DD! I didn't hear you come in."

"Clearly," Diana said, her tone droll, but she wasn't upset, and they both knew it. She'd given Carter a key a few months ago, although this was only the second time he'd used it. Things had been tense for him at home since he came out to his parents last year, although it had gotten better while he was away at college. Now that summer vacation had begun, she feared things had grown strained again.

"Uh, sorry for just barging in on you..." He drifted off, not quite meeting her eyes.

She held in a sigh, not because she was upset with Carter, but because she wanted to strangle her brother for whatever he'd done this time. "It's fine. That's why I gave you a key. I told you that you're always welcome here, and I meant it."

"Thanks." He looked down at the controller in his hands.

She left her rolling suitcase in the doorway and came to sit beside him. "Anything you want to talk about?"

"Yeah...um, so...Mom and Dad kicked me out." He looked up at her then, his expression heartbreakingly vulnerable. At twenty-one, Carter was a man, and Diana generally thought of him as such, but right now, he was a boy, hurt by the rejection of his parents, and Diana was *definitely* going to strangle her brother.

"Oh, Carter," she murmured, resting a hand on his shoulder. He'd never been much of a hugger. "I'm so sorry. What happened?"

"I told them I'm not going back to school in the fall." He ducked his head again, perhaps fearing she wouldn't take this news any better than his parents had. "And Dad said I can't just expect a free ride. If I'm not in school, I'm on my own."

She exhaled, taking a moment to sort through her thoughts before she spoke. Her knee-jerk reaction was to scold Carter for being so immature and rash as to throw his college career away like this. But he'd already heard that from his parents. "Why did you drop out? Did something happen?"

"It was just...bad." His knee started to bounce. "I hated all my classes, and I wasn't good at any of them, and I just...I couldn't do it."

Diana felt her brow pinch. This didn't make sense. Carter was incredibly smart and had never struggled in school before. "What changed?"

"It's never been easy for me. I always feel like I have to work harder than everyone else to keep up, but lately...it's all gotten to be too much." He was fidgeting, refusing to meet her eyes, his body practically vibrating with tension.

"Okay." Diana still didn't understand, but she could see from Carter's agitation that now wasn't the right time to push. "We'll talk about this more later. Do your parents know where you are?"

"No."

She exhaled. "We need to let them know that much, at least. I'm sure they're worried."

He gave her a sharp look. "Are they, though? I didn't run away. Dad kicked me out. If he cared where I was, I'd still be at home."

She sighed. "Sometimes people say things in the heat of the moment that they don't really mean."

"Aunt DD, please don't defend him. Not right now."

Diana opened her mouth, but no words came to her. She and Carter had always been close, especially since he came out, but she was also painfully aware that she wasn't a parent. She didn't know how to handle this situation, nor did she have much experience disciplining Carter. As the fun aunt, she didn't have to deal with some of the things his parents did. But she couldn't imagine kicking her child out of the house, no matter what they had done, especially not if they looked as distraught as Carter did right now.

"I just need a place to crash for a few nights." He was staring at the controller still clutched in his hands. The TV screen, which had been frozen on the attacking monster, had gone black.

"And where will you go in a few days?" she asked.

"Dunno. Dad reminded me that I need a college degree to access my trust fund, so I'll have to get a job or something." He fiddled with the controller. "And an apartment."

Oh, this sweet, naïve man-child. As if he could find a job—or an apartment—that quickly. Rent here in Boston was astronomically high, much too high for him to afford on whatever minimum-wage job he might pick up on such short notice. "You can stay here until you've got enough money saved up for an apartment."

His whole body slumped in relief. "Really?"

"Of course. You can stay here as long as you need. Take a week or two to decompress." Because she knew the signs of anxiety and panic when she saw them. Perhaps this was something else they had in common. "But then I do expect you to start seriously looking for a job or, better yet, rethink your decision about college. There are options, you know. Just because you've hit a rough spot doesn't mean you have to quit."

"I can't—"

"Carter," she interrupted. "You're welcome to stay here as long as you need. I support you, okay? We'll talk more about the other stuff later."

"Thanks," he mumbled.

Diana had never seen him like this, so anxious, so... defeated. This was obviously about more than his grades. She'd get to the bottom of it, but not today. "I need to change and unpack and check in at the office, but then let's order some dinner—Indian, maybe?—and see if I can keep up with you in Borderlands. I've been practicing, you know."

She'd bought the Xbox last year, primarily for Carter's use. It had given her a reason to invite him over when things were difficult at home, something for them to do together when he needed a safe outlet for his frustrations. And somewhere along the way, she'd realized she enjoyed playing it too, although she preferred the adventure-type games like *Life is Strange* to the shooters that were Carter's favorites.

Diana retrieved her suitcase and carried it upstairs to the master bedroom, noting the black duffel bag on the guest bed across the hall. She closed the door to her room and changed into jeans and a T-shirt, then unpacked her things from Vermont. Memories of Emily bloomed both from her hiking ensemble and the clothes she'd worn to the bar last night.

It irked her that their electrifyingly perfect night had been tarnished by what happened this morning at the inn. With a sigh, Diana dumped her dirty clothes into the hamper, groaning at the pain in her legs. Her sore muscles had grown even more stiff during the car ride home. She'd need to stretch later.

It took only a few minutes to unpack, something she always did right after she got home rather than letting her suitcase sit around. Once it was empty and stowed in her closet, she sat on the bed and pulled out her phone, hoping against hope that her brother would have gotten in touch.

No such luck.

Well, she had a few things to say, since Carter was safely downstairs, no doubt absorbed in a game with his headset on. She brought up Harrison's name in her phone and dialed.

"So he went to your house," her brother answered without preamble.

"He's here," Diana confirmed.

Harrison grunted. "I expressly told him *not* to run to you."

The fingers of Diana's free hand clenched in a fist. "I don't think you get to dictate where he goes after you kick him out. Why shouldn't he come here?"

"You know why." His tone hardened, and Diana *hated* where she thought he was going with this. "You've already put enough silly ideas in his head."

"And by silly ideas, you mean..."

"He looks up to you, Di. First you convinced him he's gay, and now you're going to give him a free ride when he's decided to drop out of college?"

Hot sparks popped under Diana's skin, her fist now digging into her thigh. "I did *not* convince him...you know what, I'm not even going to dignify that with a response. Your son is struggling right now. I don't know what's going on, not yet, but I've never seen him so rattled. He's hurting, and instead of trying to help, you just kicked him out!"

"He's an adult, for Christ's sake. When I was his age, I'd already secured my postgraduation position in the finance department to start my career track."

"You don't have to tell me about career tracks. I *know*, and God knows how hard I've worked to get where I am. Your son needs you, Harrison. You need to stop with this 'he's too young to know what he's saying' nonsense when it comes to his sexuality, especially when you turn around and call him an adult the first time he runs into trouble at school."

"He wants to be treated like a man, he's going to have to start acting like one."

Diana wanted to scream in frustration. Harrison was going around in circles, lashing out at Carter about his college decisions when it boiled down to the fact that he was uncomfortable with his son being gay. "I think we're finished with this conversation. Your son is safe. You know where to find him if you want to talk."

SEVEN

"Ready for dinner? I think we need to talk." Mary gestured to Emily after she'd handed over front desk duties to Mariah that evening. Obviously, her grandmothers had noticed how upset she was and realized she'd learned about the sale.

Emily nodded. At this point, she was more hurt than angry, and behind that...she was scared. Somewhere over the course of the day, she'd started worrying that Gram's breast cancer was back. They hadn't mentioned selling the last time she was sick, but if the news was bad enough...

Emily's heart was racing as she followed her grandma to the apartment at the back of the inn where she and Eva lived, the apartment where Emily had lived from ten to eighteen after her mom left her here.

"Wine's open," Gram called from the kitchen as they walked in. "We're going to need it tonight."

Emily couldn't argue with that. They spent a few minutes pouring wine and fixing their plates, and once they were seated together at the table, Emily jumped right in, because her mind had been spiraling all day and she couldn't wait another moment for answers. "Why didn't you tell me you're selling the inn? Is it because...Gram, your health?"

"Your gram is absolutely fine and cancer-free," Mary said emphatically.

"But my cancer is what first put the idea in our heads," Eva added. "We're ready to retire. This inn is so important to us, and we've loved every moment we've spent here, but we're getting older. We want to travel, relax, enjoy our golden years."

Emily took a bite of chicken, her emotions rampaging in a dozen different directions. "How long has it been for sale?"

"Almost a year," Gram told her as she speared a roasted carrot with her fork. "And now, it sounds like we were trying to keep a secret from you, but I promise, it wasn't like that."

"How was it, then?" She couldn't quite keep the petulance out of her tone.

"We didn't tell anyone when we listed it," Grandma said. "We're in no hurry to sell, and we were afraid...well, we didn't want you to feel like you needed to save the inn."

Emily stabbed another piece of chicken. "You don't think I could do it?"

"I have no doubt you could, but at what cost to your own life, Em?" Gram asked. "You're an artist. That's what you've always wanted for your career. We know how much you love this inn, and how seriously you take family obligations. We figured, if we could find the perfect buyer—someone who would preserve our legacy the way we want—then we could tell you that we're selling when the story already had a happy ending."

"But what if I want to buy the inn?"

Gram quirked an eyebrow. "Do you, though?"

Emily sighed. "No." Her grandmas were right. She was an artist at heart. All she'd ever wanted was to stay home and paint for a living. "So you think Devlin Hotels is the answer?"

Grandma held up a finger. "We didn't say that. They were the first potential buyer we've had, so we decided to hear them out. We haven't made any decisions."

"And I'm not at all sure we're going to sell to them," Gram added.

"We like Ms. Devlin a lot, but it doesn't sound like she'd have much to do with the inn after the sale. Any ongoing decisions would be handled by other departments, which is a lot less personal than we'd hoped."

"It sounds like getting swallowed by the corporate beast," Gram said with a frown. "We'll consider her offer when—and if—it comes, but I don't think it's likely we'll be selling to Devlin Hotels."

Emily's emotions went for another spiral at the mention of Diana's name. Certainly the night they'd shared was affecting Emily's judgment here, but mostly...mostly she was hurt that her grandmas hadn't kept her in the loop from the beginning.

"You look upset," Gram observed.

"I feel blindsided," Emily admitted. "I can't believe you didn't tell me you were selling. I just...I don't know how to get past that."

"Put yourself in our shoes," Grandma said. "We don't want to get in the way of you living your own life. You have this...this guilt over the way your mom left, like you feel like it's on you to keep the rest of the family together. We didn't want you to feel responsible for the future of the inn. We're going to find the right person to buy it. Your cottage will still be yours. You can still work the desk if you want. But we want you to focus on your art."

"That should have been my decision to make." Emily was still hurt, but she also heard the truth in her grandma's words. Emily knew she sometimes had a tendency to fall on her own sword. She'd have done anything to save the inn, even if she didn't want to own it. She just wanted...she wanted things to stay like they were. She hated change. "But I want you guys to be happy. I didn't know you wanted to retire."

"Gram's breast cancer was sort of a wake-up call for us," Grandma said. "We aren't getting any younger, and while this inn has meant the world to us, there's so much we want to see and do with the years we have left. Please don't be upset with us, Em. I realize in hindsight that it feels a little patronizing the way we handled it, but we were only trying to make this as easy as possible for you."

Emily looked down at her plate. "I get it, even if I still feel kind of shitty about how I found out."

"How *did* you find out?" Grandma asked, and Emily realized belatedly that she'd walked right into that one.

Luckily, the truth didn't have to be the *whole* truth. "I met Diana yesterday. She'd gotten lost on a hike, and I helped her find her way out. She mentioned she was in town to buy a local inn for Devlin Hotels, but I had no idea she meant *our* inn until she walked into the lobby this morning."

"I'm truly sorry you found out that way." Grandma reached over and covered Emily's hand with her own. "We thought it would be better to spare you the 'what's going to happen' and tell you after we'd found the perfect buyer. But obviously, that backfired, and I apologize."

Emily felt her hurt and anger deflating. "Thank you.

This is still such a shock...I just, I can't imagine the inn not being ours."

"I know," Gram said. "We feel the same way, but at the same time...we're in our seventies now. It's time."

"Where will you go?" Emily asked. "Are you leaving Crescent Falls altogether?"

"No way," Gram said with a laugh. "This town is our home. No, we'll look for a small house of our own with the proceeds from the sale and use the rest to travel."

Emily's heart warmed as she pictured it. "I love that for you. I really do."

"But you're still sad, I know. These things take time to get used to, and change has always been hard for you."

Emily moved a piece of chicken around on her plate. "But if you force change on me, I'll learn to adapt." And she realized that was exactly what they'd done by waiting to tell her until they had a buyer. They'd tried to take the stress of the change out of the equation for her.

When she got back to her cottage that evening, Emily sat on the back porch for hours, just staring at the distant mountains as Jack fluttered around, singing his happy tunes. Her grandmas had promised to keep things as much the same for her as possible, but Emily couldn't help feeling like everything was going to change.

THE FOLLOWING EVENING, Emily sat at an oversized table near the back of Maude's Tavern, sipping a beer as she filled her friends in on the latest developments in her life. They met here every Thursday for trivia night, and it was always one of the highlights of Emily's week.

"Damn," Talia said with a frown. "I can't believe your grandmas are selling the inn."

Drew shrugged. "I can. I mean, they're old. They want to retire. Good for them. My grandparents basically had to start over when they emigrated here from Vietnam, and they ended up working almost till the day they died. So I think it's great if Em's grandmas can quit while they're still young enough to enjoy it."

"When you put it that way..." Emily gulped from her beer. "I feel bad for being upset about this."

"Just trying to put it in perspective," Drew said with another shrug.

"You can feel sad about it while still wanting your grandmas to enjoy their retirement." Alexis wrapped an arm around Emily and gave her a squeeze. "It's a big change."

"I haven't even told you guys the craziest part yet," Emily said. "You know the woman I hooked up with the night before last? It turns out she was here to buy the inn. She works for Devlin Hotels. She...she's a Devlin. Diana Devlin."

Tom whistled. "Hot damn, Em. When you decide to have a one-night stand, you go all out. You fucked the woman your grandmas are selling the inn to?"

"And a hotel heiress?" Tom's wife, Maddie, asked. "Is she rich?"

"Well, she's definitely not poor." Diana certainly had money, but she also seemed hardworking and ambitious, not a woman content to live off her father's success. No, Diana wanted to run the whole company. "I don't think my grandmas are going to sell to her, though. They're worried about getting lost in the shuffle as part of the Devlin brand. They're probably going to keep looking for a better buyer."

"Makes sense," Talia said. "Glad they're being picky."

"I'm glad too. Mary and Eva won't let you down," Tom said. "Now let's get to the good stuff. You used three flame emojis yesterday. We want to know *everything*."

Emily's cheeks felt like a flame emoji right now. She didn't generally kiss and tell, but for once, the person she'd slept with didn't live in town. None of her friends would ever meet Diana, so why not share a little? Suddenly, she was *bursting* to share. "It was probably—*definitely*—the hottest night of my life."

"Emily! Get it, girl!" Tom exclaimed. "I'm getting bossy vibes from what you've told us about this woman. Did you let her dominate you in the bedroom or what?"

"Actually, um..." Emily's face had achieved three-flame-emoji status now. Her skin was *burning*. "While we were at the bar, getting to know each other, she said sometimes she wished she wasn't in control for a little while, and I said I wanted to know what that kind of control felt like, so when we got to her room, we kind of...swapped roles."

For a moment, they all stared at her, mouths hanging open.

Emily was so flushed, she was starting to sweat. She had on a sleeveless ribbed top with a high neck to hide the hickeys still visible there. Would her friends notice?

"So *you* dominated *her* in bed?" Tom exclaimed. "This is exciting new territory for you, Em, I mean...not that I've ever been in your bed." He glanced at his wife, who elbowed him playfully. "But you're always tentative when we're out adventuring, and you seem that way in your career and relationships too."

She exhaled, reaching for her beer. "*Tentative* is a good word to describe me. Diana brought out this whole other side of me, and...I really liked it."

"Hottest night ever, huh?" Alexis gave her a high five. "Good for you."

Emily ducked her head. "Thanks. It got me thinking, though. Like, I want to keep the momentum going, keep pushing myself out of my comfort zone, you know? And with my grandmas retiring, it feels like another push. Maybe it's time to really focus on my art so I can quit working the front desk."

"I am one-hundred-percent onboard with that," Talia said. "I can't tell you how many people have commented on the paintings in our nursery. I've given out at least five of your cards since Colette was born."

Emily looked around the table, her cheeks still warm. "I really appreciate you guys...you know that, right?"

This group had seen her through some of the best—and worst—moments in her life. She couldn't actually remember life before Alexis. They'd met in kindergarten, not that either of them remembered meeting. Emily and Alex had just always known each other. By middle school, they were best friends, and nothing had changed in the years since.

Emily had known Talia nearly as long, although since Talia was a few years younger, they hadn't been in any of the same classes. Last year, Talia and her wife had welcomed a baby girl, and the whole group was loving their status as honorary aunts and uncles to the first Adventurers baby.

Tom was the oldest member of their group, and also the newest to Crescent Falls. He'd moved here in his early twenties, looking for a fresh start after he transitioned. When Emily first met him, Tom was a bit of a wild man, partying most nights and hooking up with an endless stream of random people. Then he fell in love with Maddie, and the rest was history. These days, he was a happily married man who spent most evenings at home with his wife.

Drew was the baby of the group at twenty-three. Emily had known him since he was a kid—she'd even babysat for him once or twice—so it still sometimes boggled her mind to sit at the pub and share a beer with him, but she loved how diverse their group was. It kept things interesting.

None of them had commented on her unusual shirt choice, though. It hadn't occurred to them that she might be hiding hickeys. They didn't think she had it in her, and somehow that made her even more determined to keep pushing herself, to be less predictable, more adventurous.

Alex looked at her phone and frowned. "Crap. Frankie's home early. I might have to miss trivia."

"Oh, come on," Drew protested. "Team Gay All Day needs you."

"Invite her to join us?" Emily suggested, already knowing it wouldn't work. Alex's girlfriend rarely joined them for trivia night, even though she was always invited. More often, she convinced Alex to leave early instead.

"She's tired after a full day at the shop. I should probably go." Alex polished off her beer, put down some money, and stood. "Kick ass on my behalf, okay?"

"Will do," Emily said, but she doubted they'd win without Alex. Tom and Maddie's team was hard to beat even when Emily's team wasn't outnumbered.

"Actually, I need to head out early too," Talia said apologetically. "Colette's teething, and she's been miserable all week. Neither Chantal or I have gotten much sleep, so I promised her I wouldn't be out late tonight."

"Falling like flies," Tom said. "No problem. Go give that teething baby a kiss from the Adventurers."

"Will do. Look at this brand-new tooth, though. She's

looking like such a big girl all of a sudden." Talia held up her phone, showing them a photo of a smiling baby with warm brown skin just a shade lighter than Talia's and a curly mop of black hair. A tiny sliver of white tooth was visible on her bottom gum.

"Oh my God, she does look bigger," Emily exclaimed. "Will you bring her on our hike this weekend? I need a baby fix."

"Definitely. Chantal needs a break, and Coco loves being outside. See you guys then." Talia left cash for her meal and followed Alex toward the front door.

"And then there were four," Drew said, gesturing to the bartender for another beer.

"Let's team up," Tom suggested. "Adventurers versus everyone else tonight."

Drew placed a hand dramatically over his heart. "That means Em and I actually have a chance of winning for once."

"Hey," Emily protested. "We won a few weeks ago."

"And *we've* won three times since," Tom teased. "Just for tonight, I'll bring you under my wing..." He swept a hand dramatically across the table, almost knocking over Maddie's beer.

"Can you believe this guy?" Drew asked Emily, eyebrows raised.

"Just for that, I think we should keep our teams separate," Emily told him. She adored Tom, but he was insufferable about his winning trivia team.

Tom rolled his eyes. "Oh, come on."

"Nope," Drew said. "Emily and I will kick your ass all on our own."

"Yeah," she bluffed. "It's bad luck to change up the teams at the last minute anyway. You've told us that before."

"She's got you there," Maddie said.

"Fine, fine," Tom agreed. "Get ready to lose, then."

He was probably right, but Emily didn't care. Keeping their usual teams was the safe move, and Emily always played it safe. She was trying to change that—especially now—but change was hard.

Change could wait until tomorrow.

EIGHT

The bad luck that befell her during her trip to Vermont seemed to have followed Diana back to Boston. Over the next few weeks, nothing went her way. Despite making a generous offer to Eva and Mary Chambers-Benoit to purchase the Inn at Crescent Falls, they turned her down, preferring to wait for a noncorporate buyer.

Not willing to admit defeat, Diana made a second, higher offer, which they also declined. She'd even called to see if there was anything else she could do to change their minds, but they wouldn't be swayed.

Carter was still living with her, but as far as she could tell, he hadn't spent as much time looking for a job as he had playing video games. He continued to shut down her attempts to get to the bottom of his problems at college, and she was tired of him moping around her town house. She loved her nephew, but he needed to get his act together.

As she arrived at the office on the Monday after the Fourth of July weekend, Diana was determined to get things back on track. Her team had narrowed down a list of five potential new hotels for acquisition, and she was ready to start her own research to see which one she'd scout for purchase next. She couldn't afford to let her department's performance record slip, not with her next promotion on the line.

She stepped into the elevator, already thinking through her plan of attack as she stabbed the button for the twenty-second floor.

"Diana!"

She turned at the booming voice to see Vance Wagner, a senior member of the board and longtime friend of the family, crossing the lobby. With a smile, she pressed the button to hold the elevator for him. "Good morning, Vance. How are you?"

"I can't complain. Missed you at dinner on Saturday."

She kept her smile firmly in place. Yes, she'd declined dinner at Harrison's over the weekend, a dinner he'd invited several board members to. She hated having to take sides in this situation, but when forced, she had taken Carter's. "Next time."

Vance made a sound of agreement as the doors slid shut and the elevator began to climb. What was he doing here today? He only came to the office when there was a board meeting, but she would have been informed if that was the case.

Wouldn't she?

"Is there a meeting today?" she asked, keeping her tone curious instead of tentative.

Vance nodded. "Between you and me, Harv's retiring at the end of the year."

"Wow." Diana's mouth formed the word, but the sound got stuck in her throat. This was news to her. *Big* news. Harvey Iverness was Devlin Hotels' chief operating officer, a title she hoped to claim after his retirement. "That's sooner than expected."

"I hear Mary's not doing well," Vance said, his expression pinched with concern. "Early onset dementia."

"Oh no, I'm sorry to hear that." Harv's wife was only in her fifties, far too young to be dealing with dementia.

"Very sad," Vance agreed.

It was sad. Tragic, even. Diana's heart went out to her, even as her mind started racing. Harvey hadn't been expected to retire for another five years or so. If he retired this year...

It meant there would be a new COO soon. The board was here for a meeting she hadn't been invited to. Was her father proposing his choice for the next COO today? Her chest tightened, and her eye twitched. She could be announced as Harv's successor *today*, a move that would virtually guarantee her path to CEO.

This was supposed to have been years down the line. Suddenly, her end game felt tangible in a way it never had before. She could almost taste it. After all these years, all her hard work, it was finally happening.

"Have a good day, Diana," Vance said as the doors to the elevator opened on the executive floor.

"You too, Vance." She waved as he turned right, headed toward the boardroom. She went left, spotting two more board members as she headed to her office. Definitely a board meeting. Diana pushed a hand into her bag and gripped her keys, her thumb automatically moving over the calming strip. She focused on the textured surface until her breathing had slowed.

"Good morning, Diana," her secretary, Nancy, greeted her from the atrium outside Diana's office. Nancy was in her midsixties, more focused on her upcoming retirement than on office gossip, so Diana knew better than to ask her about the board meeting.

"Morning," Diana said.

"Your father scheduled a meeting with you at eleven," Nancy told her. "I've added it to your calendar."

"Thank you." Diana continued through the door into her office. A meeting with her father. Surely this had to do with the COO position. It was really happening. She would find out *today*.

Diana set her laptop on the desk before placing her bag in its usual drawer. Then she took a few minutes to tend to the plants on the shelf by the window. She carefully pinched off dead leaves and tested the soil to see which of them needed water. The dragon tail and the peacock plant also liked to have their leaves misted to combat the dry office air.

She loved her plants. Caring for them was relaxing, a good way to ground herself during a hectic or stressful day. Plus, they brightened her office and arguably improved her air quality.

Once the plants were watered, Diana sat at her desk. She lost herself in the reports her team had sent with the next round of hotels to consider acquiring. None of them excited her the way the Inn at Crescent Falls had, but one of them would have to do. The strongest contender seemed to be a mountain lodge in Montana.

That would be an interesting trip. Imagine the hiking she could do in Montana... Briefly, her mind drifted to an image of Emily on a mountainside in Vermont, painting purple asters. Shortly after she returned from Vermont, Diana had purchased that painting from Emily's online store, a beautiful reminder of a memorable day.

She'd been enamored with the painting from the

moment she'd first seen it, but after the awkward way she and Emily had left things, Diana had asked Nancy to complete the purchase for her so her name wasn't on the receipt. Maybe she'd been afraid Emily would refuse to sell it to her, or maybe Diana didn't know how to handle the fact that she was still thinking about her one-night stand weeks later.

She yanked her thoughts back on track, going over the financial records for the lodge in Montana. Before she knew it, her phone dinged with a calendar alert, letting her know the meeting with her father was in ten minutes. The morning had flown by, as it often did.

Diana locked her laptop and stood, rubbing at the tension headache building between her eyes. By now, the board would have met and possibly even voted to approve a new COO. Suddenly, her body was a mess of nerves, her skin prickling with anxiety. What if her father had chosen Harrison for the job instead of Diana?

Her ears started to buzz, and her fingertips tingled. She closed her eyes, focused on her breathing to avoid a panic attack. She'd been preparing for this moment her whole adult life. She'd done the work. Now she had to trust her father to make the right choice. Emotions firmly under control, she set off for her meeting.

Edward Devlin's office was at the other end of the executive floor. Diana greeted his secretary, who waved her past. "Go on in. He's ready for you."

"Thank you, Sarah."

Diana knocked before pushing the door open. Her father stood with his back to her, staring out at the city. The wall behind his desk contained floor-to-ceiling windows, offering a panoramic view of Boston, a more impressive view than her own since his office faced downtown while hers looked toward the airport.

She closed the door behind her. "Good morning, Dad."

He turned to face her, hands in the front pockets of his slacks and an easy smile on his face. His hair had faded to white now, but it had once been the same reddish blonde as hers. Diana took after him in both looks and ambition. "Ah, Diana, come on in and have a seat."

She sat, clasping her hands over her knees to keep from fidgeting.

"I'll get right to it," he said as he sat behind his desk. "You probably saw that the board was here this morning. Harv is taking an early retirement."

"I heard," she said. "That was unexpected."

"Indeed. So, as you've probably also guessed, I called a meeting this morning to vote on the next COO. I won't be making a formal announcement for a few more days, but I hope you'll join me in congratulating Harrison."

"Harrison," she repeated with numb lips. Harrison would be the next COO. For a terrifying moment, her mind emptied of everything except static, the sound of her dreams being extinguished. "I don't understand."

He sighed. "Diana."

"Why not me?" She gazed at him expectantly, her face a polite mask despite how she felt inside, like she'd been kicked in the stomach, like the ground had shifted beneath her feet.

"It was a tough decision," he said finally. "I don't have to tell you how much I value your work here, Di. You're a remarkable woman and a vital asset to this company, but ultimately, I felt that Harrison is the right man for the job, and the board agrees."

She refused to flinch or crumple in her seat, no matter how badly it hurt. "So Harrison is in line to be CEO."

"Yes."

Her scalp prickled as hurt burned into anger. "You know how hard I've worked for this. My record in the independent purchasing division is exemplary, and Harrison—"

He held up a hand. "Harrison is the eldest, and he's put in the time to build an invaluable network of connections. He's well respected, Diana, and I don't mean to say that you're not. But he's more of a big picture thinker than you are, which is critical for a future CEO. You've done an outstanding job overseeing our independent purchasing division, but you spend a lot of time on the road. You're less visible. Around the office, people wish you'd be a little bit...softer."

"Oh?" Her fingers were clenched around the edge of the chair. "And do they wish Harrison would soften up a bit too? Or you? No? Just me, because I'm a woman?"

"You know what I mean." His tone was overly patient, and it made her want to scream. "This isn't a bad thing. You'll be promoted to COO after Harrison takes my place. Devlin Hotels will be in excellent hands with the two of you leading it."

"Harrison spends more time on the golf course than I spend scouting hotels," she said with forced calm. She'd never lost her temper in front of her father—not at work, anyway—and she wasn't about to start today. "I've streamlined operations to the point that independent purchasing is the most profitable division in the company. Imagine what I could do as CEO!"

His expression remained frustratingly patient. "You're a confidant woman, and I'm extraordinarily proud of everything you've accomplished here. But there's more to being

CEO than business acumen. Optics are involved. Harrison is a family man. He's well liked, and he's made personal connections with so many of our vendors and subsidiaries that, frankly, you haven't taken the time to nurture."

"A family man," she repeated, unable to keep the edge out of her voice. "You know he recently kicked Carter out of the house, right?"

"Carter is an adult, and that has nothing to do with Harrison's suitability as CEO."

"Hey, you're the one who just listed 'family man' as one of the reasons he'd make a better CEO than me," Diana snapped. "Lesbians need not apply?"

"Please don't make this about something it's not." Her father's tone finally hardened. "We value you here, Di. You're an important part of the Devlin team, but I had to choose who I thought would be best for the top job, and I chose Harrison."

"Understood." She nodded briskly, rose from her chair, and strode down the hall to her office. Nancy smiled politely as she passed. Diana packed up her things and returned to Nancy's desk, noting the way her receptionist minimized the beach condo she'd been looking at. She'd be retiring at the end of the year, and she and her husband were planning a move to Florida. Clearly, Nancy's mind was already there. "I'll be working from home this afternoon. Please hold my calls unless there's anything urgent."

"No problem," Nancy said, not asking any questions about why. Maybe she already knew, or maybe she just didn't care. Not for the first time, Diana wished Nancy was more of an ally. Diana sure could use one right now.

Devlin Hotels was more than a job for Diana. This was her family, her legacy, her whole world. And now she'd been dealt a crushing blow. She needed to get out of here. She needed privacy to tend to her emotional wounds.

Diana opened the rideshare app on her phone and requested a car, knowing she didn't have patience for the subway. As she stepped into the elevator, she looked down at her hands, surprised to see that they were shaking. Her whole body felt like it was vibrating. Anger. Hurt. Betrayal. Bewilderment. She wasn't entirely sure what she was feeling, but the cocktail of emotions had shaken her to her core, and she needed some time to process.

Thankfully, her car arrived not long after she reached the street. Hopefully, Carter would be out, because she really needed to be alone this afternoon. Actually, she needed to vent, but this wasn't something she could complain about to him.

Diana had a sudden, overwhelming urge to spew the whole ugly story onto a sympathetic shoulder. If only she were better at cultivating friendships...or relationships. But she'd prioritized her career over everything else. She had only casual acquaintances, no close friends. No girlfriend to hold her while she cried. Diana was alone in a tower of her own making.

She'd given almost twenty years of her life to Devlin Hotels on the assumption that one day, she would run it. Now, she had no idea what to do with herself. Sure, COO was an excellent job, one she'd been looking forward to on her way to CEO. But to stall there? To always be second fiddle to Harrison?

That sounded unbearable.

Becoming the CEO of Devlin Hotels was the only career trajectory she'd ever considered for herself. How could she have been so naïve? Now she had no idea what to do. The tightness in her chest was almost unbearable. She felt like she might actually explode from all the pent-up emotion she was holding inside.

To her immense relief, the town house was empty when she arrived. She went straight upstairs to her bedroom and changed into athletic gear, then headed out for a punishing five-mile run. The sidewalks were annoyingly crowded on this July afternoon, disrupting her stride as she had to continually dodge pedestrians.

Back home, she guzzled a bottle of water, showered, and then poured herself a generous glass of whiskey, which she took with her onto the back patio. Her backyard was little more than this patio. When she bought it, the patio had been bordered by an unsightly chain-link fence, but she'd hidden it from sight behind the lush greenery she'd planted, turning the backyard into her own private oasis.

She stretched out on a chaise lounge, gaze fixed absently on a flowering purple lilac. It reminded her of the flower Emily had been painting when they met. She had no idea how long she'd been out there, sipping whiskey and stewing in her thoughts, before she heard the glass door slide open behind her.

"Hey, Aunt DD." Carter plopped onto the chaise beside her, wearing jeans that looked like they'd been chewed up by machinery, although she suspected he'd bought them that way. He held a beer in his left hand, and at her startled look, he grinned. "I'm twenty-one now, remember?"

"So you are." She'd never shared a drink with her nephew before. How odd.

"I had a job interview today." He leaned forward so his elbows rested on his knees.

"Not dressed like that, I hope." She allowed her lips to quirk so he knew she was teasing.

"Changed when I got home."

Home. If he realized he'd just referred to her town house that way, he gave no indication. Diana, by contrast, felt a curious burst of warmth in her heart at his word choice. "Tell me about it," she said. "What kind of job?"

He looked down at the beer in his hands. "You know that all-natural store down the street? They need a weekday sales associate."

"Selling herbal soap?" She heard the incredulity in her voice. "Carter, you're an engineer."

"No, I'm *not.*"

Diana startled at the unexpected vehemence in his voice. Carter's jaw was clenched, his shoulders hunched. His gaze was locked stubbornly on the beer in his hands. He'd completed three years of his engineering degree, had been on that career path since he was sixteen or so, when he'd first interned at Devlin Hotels in their architectural design division.

"What do you mean, you're not?" she asked.

"Forget I said anything." He sounded like the petulant teen he'd so recently been, but this was the tone he usually directed at his parents, not Diana. She found she didn't like being on the receiving end of it. "You wouldn't understand anyway."

She purposefully gentled her tone. "Try me."

"Engineering was the career Dad picked for me. I thought it was okay when I was like fifteen, but now I hate it, and the classes are so hard. I can't keep up. It's not for me."

"I had no idea." Diana took another sip of her whiskey. "I'm sorry if I took part in pushing you toward a career you didn't want."

Carter grunted. "Whatever."

She rolled her eyes. Moments like these, she was reminded how young he still was. Not a child, but not a fully mature man yet either. "What do you want to be, then? What's *your* chosen career path? No judgment from me, whatever it is. I promise."

"I have no idea. I can only tell you a bunch of stuff I hate."

Neither of them spoke for a few minutes, both of them sipping their drinks and pondering where their lives had gone wrong. Well, that's what Diana was thinking about, anyway. She'd lost the only job she'd ever wanted. At least Carter was still young enough to chart a new course for himself. What was she going to do?

"Your father was promoted to COO today. Did you know?" she asked finally.

Carter made a scoffing sound. "Finally, huh? That's all he's talked about for as long as I can remember: COO and then CEO."

Diana's stomach clenched painfully. "That's all I've talked about too. I guess you and I both find ourselves at a career standstill."

"Fuck," he exclaimed, and hearing her nephew swear was almost as disconcerting as sharing a drink with him. "I never put two and two together before. You and my dad were shooting for the same job."

"We were," she confirmed.

"That sucks," he mumbled. "I'm sorry."

"It does, and thank you."

"My dad will be CEO? That's what this means? And you won't?" He looked at her then, his eyes wide and concerned.

"That's what it means."

Carter darted another glance at her. "You should quit."

It was her turn to scoff. "Carter, just because I supported you when you dropped out of college doesn't mean I condone it as a solution to your problems or that I have any intention of doing the same. I don't quit, even when things get hard."

"That's not what I mean," he said. "I mean, not exactly. Like, you're really passionate about buying these independent hotels, right? That's always been your thing?"

"I am, yes." She didn't have to ask how Carter knew this. He'd spent one of his summer internships in her office, traveling with her to get a feel for the independent purchasing division. It had been a fun summer.

"You're meant to be running things, Aunt DD. You'll never be happy working for my dad the rest of your life, and you're really good at the boutique hotel thing. What if you start your own company? Be your own boss."

She inhaled. "It's not that simple."

"Why not?"

"Well, I..." She faltered, mind spinning. Why not indeed? "I don't know."

An unexpected burst of laughter came from the chaise beside her. "I don't think I've ever heard you say those words before."

"What words?"

"'I don't know.'" He snickered again. "You always have the answer. Always. You're probably the smartest person I know."

"Oh." Her throat tightened. "Thank you."

"You could call it DD Boutique Hotels, or something like that. Hey!" He sat up straight. "I could work for you! I could do your website—I took a class on that last year, and it was pretty cool—and I could answer your calls, and whatever else you need. We could really do this."

"Don't get ahead of yourself, Carter." She kept her tone neutral. "There's a *lot* more that goes into starting a business than building a website."

"Like what?"

"Not to blow your mind twice in one night, but…I don't know." She tossed a gentle smile in his direction. "I've never started one or even considered it."

"I could help you research. I mean, I've got some free time on my hands…"

"That you do." And she couldn't help noticing that Carter looked more animated right now than she'd seen him in months, maybe years. There was a light in his eyes that she hadn't even realized was missing.

More, she felt a glimmer of that light inside herself too. What if…?

"I didn't hear a 'no' yet," he pressed, grinning at her.

"You didn't, but you haven't heard a yes either."

"What does that mean?"

"It means you've given me something to think about. This is not a decision to be made lightly or after the amount of whiskey I've had tonight." She held up her empty glass. "But here's one 'yes' I'll give you: you're welcome to spend some of that free time researching the logistics."

He bounced again. "Got it. You won't regret this, Aunt DD."

If only she believed that was true.

NINE

Diana couldn't concentrate at work. Now that the official announcement had been made, the whole office was buzzing about Harrison's upcoming promotion. And while Diana had seen a few sympathetic glances tossed in her direction, for the most part, the mood at Devlin Hotels headquarters was celebratory.

"Harrison will make an excellent COO," Mike Franzini, the director of research and development, had said. "Just last weekend while we were golfing together, he told me..."

That was where Diana tuned out. She didn't want to hear any more about Harrison. He would be a good COO. She could have been a great one. On that sunny July afternoon, she sat at her desk, fighting a growing sense of discontentment. If there was one thing Diana was *not* good at, it was stagnating in place. Answering to Harrison for the remainder of her career sounded unbearable.

She opened the email Eva and Mary Chambers-Benoit had sent when they declined her offer, rereading their reasons for turning her down. "We're concerned that the

Inn at Crescent Falls might lose its way if someone from the Devlin Hotels' marketing department who's never even seen it in person was making decisions about its future."

If Diana ran her own company, she could have given the Chambers-Benoits the reassurances they needed. She could have closed the sale.

Was she really thinking about this? She'd mostly been humoring Carter when he first brought it up, but the more she thought about it, the more she realized her nephew might be on to something. She'd be more of a small business owner than a corporate CEO—at least, at first—but she'd be her own boss.

She could build a company from the ground up, make it into exactly what she wanted it to be. She wouldn't have to work within the constraints of a company founded and run by men. She could focus exclusively on what she loved most: independent, unique hotels.

It could be a dream come true.

Or she might fail spectacularly.

When she got home that evening, Carter was waiting for her with the results of another day of research. He was more focused and productive than she'd ever seen him. Over the last few weeks, he'd prepared charts, spreadsheets, and even an estimated budget. He'd even called her lawyer —with her permission—and talked through the legal aspects of forming a new company.

In short, she was beyond impressed with him. And she was having an increasingly difficult time not saying yes to his idea. It could be amazing. It could be perfect. It could crash and burn and leave her broke and unemployed at forty.

As driven as Diana was, she had trouble pivoting. She chose a path for herself and didn't stray from it, no matter what distractions came along. Now that she'd reached a dead end on her chosen path, she was having an exceedingly hard time choosing a new direction.

"Come on, Aunt DD. Let's do this," Carter said, giving her an impossibly hopeful smile. "You know you want to. Let's make it official already."

She sat at the kitchen table, head in her hands. "I want to, but..."

She'd considered her options a dizzying number of times. She could accept her position as number two at Devlin Hotels while Harrison became CEO. She could look for a position at a rival hotel chain, which might prove difficult given her last name and the noncompete clause in her contract. Or she could grab hold of the parachute Carter had given her and leap...hoping she stuck the landing.

The possibility of landing flat on her face was unacceptably terrifying.

"I'm scared, Carter. If I do this and fail, I could lose *everything*."

She'd never dipped into her trust fund. She hadn't needed it, had always had more than enough money to support herself on her salary at Devlin Hotels. The money in her trust fund, plus an inheritance from her grandparents, would be enough collateral to launch a new business, but she would be investing everything she had into the venture.

Not to mention, she would drive a wedge between herself and her family.

"Don't forget your mantra," Carter said. "The one you've been telling me for as long as I can remember..."

"Feel the fear and do it anyway." As Diana said the words out loud, something clicked into place inside her. *Fuck fear.* She exhaled as a smile stretched her lips. She thrived on a challenge. She could do this. Now that she'd let go of the fear and made a decision, it felt like that metaphorical weight had been removed from her shoulders. She could breathe again, and it felt amazing. "You're right. Let's do this."

Carter clapped his hands with a whoop. "For real? You mean it?"

She arched an eyebrow. "Am I in the habit of saying things I don't mean?"

"Nope. Wow, okay. We're really doing this."

"We are." She walked to the liquor cabinet and pulled out her most expensive bottle of whiskey, then poured a generous amount into two tumblers. "This calls for a toast."

"Fuck, yeah."

She handed him a tumbler of whiskey. "I'm going to call my new company Aster Boutique Hotels." Inspired by the flowers in the painting on her wall. Inspired by Emily. "And my first purchase will be the Inn at Crescent Falls."

"Damn, when you make a decision, you're all in." Carter clacked his tumbler against hers. "Cheers to Aster Boutique Hotels."

"That's right." She'd done her own research and planning, even when she hadn't been sure she'd go through with it. She tossed her whiskey back in a single gulp, feeling the burn all the way to her toes. Her body blazed with renewed confidence, the sudden certainty that she could do this, that it might even be better than running Devlin Hotels.

It was time to hand in her resignation.

"IS THIS A JOKE?" Edward Devlin held her letter of

resignation as his blue eyes—so similar to her own—drilled into her.

"No, it's not." Diana sat in the guest chair before his desk, hands clasped loosely in her lap, back straight. Her stomach was in knots, but he didn't need to know that.

"Of all the ridiculous..." He trailed off, looking at the letter again and then back at her. Apparently, she'd rendered him speechless. For a long minute, neither of them said anything. Then his lips twisted as if he'd tasted something bad. "This is your reaction to Harrison's promotion? I expected better from you, Diana. Honestly, this is an embarrassment."

His words landed like a physical punch, knocking the air out of her. "I'm sorry you feel that way."

"The first time things don't go your way, you quit? I raised you better than this."

Diana lifted her chin. "You raised me to want what's best for myself. You're one of my biggest inspirations, Dad, and that's why I've decided to launch my own business."

"That's so incredibly foolish and naïve. Do you know how hard your grandfather worked to build the Devlin brand? How many new businesses fold in the first two years? You could have been second-in-command of the entire company!"

"And that's the problem." Diana met his gaze unflinchingly. "I want to be the CEO. I hope that in time, you'll come to respect my decision."

His expression was stony. "I wouldn't count on it. From where I'm sitting, you're disrespecting me and tarnishing the family name."

"That's truly not my intention. I just need to take my career in a new direction. I have to look out for myself." Diana stood, brushing her hands over the front of her skirt as she worked to keep her expression neutral. "I've given two weeks' notice. I trust you'll be able to fill my position in that time."

Without waiting for his response, she strode from his office. Her heart was racing, a mixture of exhilaration and anxiety. She'd done it. She'd quit. There was no changing her mind now. The reality of what she'd done was starting to catch up with her, though, and she detoured toward the restroom.

Inside, she rested her hands on the counter and took several deep breaths. She wished she had her key chain with its calming strip, but in its absence, she rubbed her hands over the fabric of her skirt, letting the slight roughness of the weave provide the sensory feedback she needed. She couldn't have a panic attack right after she handed in her resignation. How would that look?

Like she was running scared.

Diana was *not* afraid. She was fearless, or at least that was the image she upheld at work. She drew in another slow breath, then wet a paper towel and pressed it against the back of her neck.

And then she left the restroom with her head held high.

Luckily, she'd had the foresight to schedule the meeting with her father at the end of the day. When she reached her office, she packed her briefcase to go home, aware Nancy was at her desk just outside Diana's office. She ought to tell Nancy the news before she heard it from someone else, but maybe it could wait until tomorrow morning.

Diana was too anxious to do it now. Her body twitched with restless energy, making it difficult to hold herself still. Briefcase slung over her shoulder, she headed for the elevator. Five minutes later, she had donned a face mask—because if the pandemic had taught her anything, it was that public transportation was germy as hell—and boarded the subway.

Ordinarily, she didn't mind the noise or the close quarters, but right now...she was wound too tight. Her anxiety was spiking. She needed fresh air and a few minutes alone to decompress.

So she got off a stop early and headed for the Fens, a nearby nature preserve. It wasn't much to look at, originally having been little more than a salt marsh, but there was a nice park with a fountain and benches where she sometimes liked to sit. It was also one of her favorite spots to go for a jog, but she wasn't dressed for that today.

Her mind drifted to the scenery in Crescent Falls, the peace she'd felt when she sat on that rock on the mountainside, overlooking the valley. This felt like a poor substitute in comparison. She removed her mask and settled on an available bench, sensory key chain in hand, and let the tinkling sound of the fountain soothe her nerves.

After a few minutes, her muscles began to loosen. That twitchy feeling receded, and she blew out a long, slow breath. She'd quit her job. Not just any job. She'd walked away from a career where she had been poised to become second-in-command of a Fortune 500 company, not to mention the financial security that came with it. That was a big fucking deal.

As she blew out another measured breath, she realized why she'd come to this park instead of going straight home to celebrate with Carter. Yes, she was excited about her new venture. Hopefully, it would be everything she'd dreamed of, but first...first, she needed this moment to grieve what she'd given up.

Suddenly, the sense of loss was almost overwhelming. She pressed a hand against her chest, gasping through it.

Her eyes were dry, but her heart wept for the way her father had treated her today. It hadn't been unexpected, but God, it still hurt. She wasn't sure their relationship would ever recover.

A dull buzzing in her ears alerted her that she was starting to hyperventilate. Using a technique her therapist had taught her, Diana breathed through her nose, counting a full five seconds on each exhale, until the fuzziness had receded from her brain.

Then she sat straighter on the bench. Eyes on the future from here on out. As soon as possible, she would send a new purchase offer to Eva and Mary Chambers-Benoit. If all went well, Diana would return to Vermont. And to Emily, although this time, everything would be different.

TEN

August arrived with an abundance of warm, breezy days, prompting Emily to spend as much time outside as possible. She'd been restless for the last few months, probably since the night of her earth-shattering one-night stand. Maybe the exposure to Diana's fearless confidence had opened Emily's eyes to all the ways in which she was the opposite of fearless or confident.

She stared at the trail marker ahead, marking the split where the trail divided. To the right, the Blossom Trail meandered along a scenic hillside, while the Crescent Peak Summit Trail veered left, headed for the top of the mountain. Beside her, Alexis pulled out her water bottle and took a long drink.

"I'm going to do it this year," Emily announced as she and Alexis took the fork onto the Blossom Trail. "I'm going to make it to the summit. This is going to be my year."

"Cool," Alex said. "But I don't know why you care so much if you make it to the top. It's just a mountain."

"Because it's not that hard. I should be able to do it." She gazed toward the peak. "The rest of you have done it more than once. The only thing holding me back is myself. It's a hurdle I really want to conquer."

"If it's that important to you, then yes, you should do it. Let's get you ready to make it to the top. What do you think would help?"

Emily pondered that as she and Alex walked to a large rock and sat to take in the view. With most people, she danced around her fears or changed the subject, but Alex was her closest friend and one of the least judgmental people she knew. "Confidence. That's what I need."

Alexis gave a brisk nod, as if this didn't surprise her. "Is there a particular part of the trail that's intimidating you?"

"Several of them," Emily said. "I psych myself out at the ravine, and also the cliff." The spot where hikers had to leap over a two-foot-wide chasm that dropped about ten feet was nerve-racking for many hikers, as was the part near the summit where the trail narrowed as it hugged the side of a cliff with a steep drop on one side.

But those were technical challenges. They weren't what was truly holding her back.

"I have a mental block where the summit is concerned," Emily admitted. "I'm afraid to push myself to the top. I don't know why."

"Okay." Alex didn't sound surprised by this either. "Do you think it's because your mom hiked to the summit without you when you sprained your ankle that time? That was right before she left town, wasn't it?"

"It was the last hike we ever took together," Emily admitted. "She was—and still is, I guess—so stubborn when she puts her mind to something. Nothing was going to stop her from making it to the top that day."

Alex's lips twisted to the side. "Not even helping her injured daughter."

Emily wished she could say she'd encouraged her mom to keep going without her, but that wasn't true. She'd been in so much pain and so afraid she'd broken her ankle. She'd been in tears when her mom went on without her, promising she'd be back before Emily knew it.

She'd known it. She felt like she waited forever, ankle throbbing, tears drying on her cheeks, waving off concerned hikers who stopped to help, wondering why a ten-year-old was alone on a trail that difficult. Finally, Violet had returned, euphoric over her success as she'd shown Emily photos from the summit.

A month later, Violet had followed her boyfriend du jour to Paris, leaving Emily with her grandmothers. Violet came back to Crescent Falls every now and then for the occasional visit, but as the years passed, those visits had become increasingly awkward. Seeing your mother and realizing you don't know her anymore was almost worse than not seeing her at all.

It had been close to a decade since her last visit, when she'd breezed into town, having booked a room at the inn so she and Emily could spend time together. Emily had tried her best, but she'd been in her midtwenties then, and her mother was little more than a stranger. After a couple of uncomfortable dinners, Violet had done what she did best and left.

These days, she occasionally tagged Emily on Facebook with captions like "Wish you were here!" which was even more awkward because she obviously didn't. She'd never actually invited Emily to visit her.

Maybe Alex was right; maybe her mom's abandonment was part of Emily's mental block when it came to reaching the summit. *Ugh*. Thinking about her mother filled Emily with all sorts of uncomfortable feelings, so she tried not to whenever possible.

"Anyway." Emily hugged her knees against her chest. "I want to do the hike."

"Good for you," Alex said. "Seems like this is about more than making it to the top of the mountain for you, and I'm all for pushing ourselves to do hard things, especially when we have besties there to support us."

She gave Alex a grateful look. "Besties make everything better."

"I need to push myself too, I think," Alex said. "I took this job at Frankie's store to tide me over while I looked for something better, and now I've been there for two years."

"It's not a *bad* job," Emily said.

"No, but I'm not using my degree. I'm not doing what I love." Alex had been so proud of her culinary degree when she graduated. She dreamed of opening her own bakery someday, but in the meantime, she'd taken a job at a restaurant in town. The reality of life in a kitchen, though, was that Alex had worked a lot of nights, weekends, and holidays—the opposite of her girlfriend, Frankie, who owned a shop downtown that sold local art and home goods.

Emily was fond of that shop. Frankie sold some really unique things there, and she kept a selection of Emily's paintings on consignment. In fact, Frankie's shop was responsible for a significant portion of Emily's local sales.

Alex's and Frankie's opposing schedules had caused friction in the relationship, though, so when the restaurant where Alex worked went out of business, she'd taken a temporary job working with Frankie at her shop. Two years later, Alex was still working there.

"It's hard living *and* working with Frankie." Alex

shrugged. "Sometimes, I think it would be nice to have one part of our daily lives that's separate, you know?"

"Totally. Have you applied for any other jobs?"

"Not in a year or so," Alex admitted. "I haven't even looked."

"Okay. You help motivate me to get to the top of the mountain, and I'll help you dust off your résumé and get back out there. Deal?"

Alex grinned, tapping her knuckles against Emily's. "Deal."

When Emily got home later that afternoon, she was somewhat surprised to find a text from her grandma, asking her to stop by when she had a chance. Grandma had followed the text with a sunflower emoji, which was code for "nothing's wrong." It had started during Gram's cancer treatments, when every text sent Emily into a panic that they'd received more bad news. A sunflower emoji meant Emily didn't need to worry.

Even now, the presence of that cheery flower after a text was a source of reassurance. Still, their definition of "not bad news" might differ slightly from Emily's if this had anything to do with the inn. For the last two months, Emily had been waiting with bated breath for an update to the news they'd blindsided her with earlier that summer.

After a quick shower, Emily walked over to the inn. Already, she could feel a crispness in the evening air that hadn't been there a few weeks ago. Soon, fall would arrive, and that was when Vermont really dazzled. Emily had never lived anywhere else, but she could still appreciate that she lived in a beautiful state. The foliage was truly spectacular, and she couldn't wait to paint it. Her foliage paintings were always highly anticipated among her customers.

At the inn, she bypassed the front door and circled

around back to the patio that marked the private entrance to Grandma and Gram's apartment. A rainbow-striped suncatcher winked against the glass, casting bursts of light across the white-painted wood beneath her feet. Emily smiled as she knocked.

"It's open, honey," Gram called from inside.

Emily went in, shutting the door behind her. "Hi."

"We're in the kitchen," Grandma answered, and Emily followed the scent of something savory as she crossed the living room and entered the kitchen. "Stew's almost finished. Want to join us for dinner?"

"I'd never say no to dinner I don't have to cook or your stew. So what's up?" Emily sat at the kitchen table.

"We won't keep you in suspense." Gram gathered her braids in one hand, pulling them back from her face as she sat across from Emily. "We've sold the inn."

"Oh." The word came out almost like a gasp. Emily swallowed hard. "That's...congratulations. It must be a big relief for you."

"Aww, honey, you should see your face." Gram gave her a sympathetic look. "This isn't going to be as big of a change as you think, except that Grandma and I won't be living in this apartment. We've got our eye on a little house just a few miles down the road, though, but that's a story for later."

Emily's smile felt more natural then. Grandma and Gram would only be living a few miles away? That wasn't so bad. "So who's your buyer? Anyone I know?"

"In a manner of speaking. We've sold to a brand-new company, Aster Boutique Hotels."

"I love the name," Emily enthused. Asters were one of her favorite flowers, so cheerful.

"I do too," Gram told her. "They're a company who buys and oversees independent, boutique hotels around the country, and the Inn at Crescent Falls will be their first purchase. The owner was able to give us all the assurances we've been looking for, that our queer legacy won't be touched. Our staff will remain unchanged with the exception of a new manager who will replace your grandma and me. We're going to sell the cottage to you separately for a few hundred bucks, whatever's legal, so the deed is yours. No one can mess with your home."

Emily fiddled with her bracelet. "That sounds great, except that they're a brand-new company. What if they go out of business and the inn ends up in bankruptcy or sold to someone who'll change things?"

"The owner doesn't seem like she's accustomed to failing," Grandma said, joining them at the table. "In fact, as Gram mentioned, you've met her: Diana Devlin. She's left Devlin Hotels and started her own company."

"Holy shit!" Emily blurted, then slapped a hand over her mouth. "Sorry, but wow...that's...*wow*." She gave her head a quick shake. Diana had awed Emily with her ten-year plan to run Devlin Hotels. How had she gone from that to this? What could have changed so drastically in such a short time?

"Why is that so surprising to you?" Gram asked.

"Because when I met her, she told me about her plan to become CEO of Devlin Hotels. She had it all mapped out. It was honestly one of the most impressive things I've ever heard, so now I'm wondering...how did her plans change so suddenly? Maybe she's all talk. Maybe you ought to be cautious accepting her offer." It was hard to imagine Diana not being every bit as competent as she seemed, but then again, she'd bitten off more than she could chew with her hike. What if that was a more common occurrence for her than Emily had thought?

"It's a risk we're willing to take," Grandma said. "Her plan is solid, Em. We feel confident about it. Since we're her first acquisition, she's going to come up and manage the inn herself during the transition, so Gram and I can start our retirement immediately."

"She's coming here?" Emily cleared her throat to cover the slight squeak in her voice. Diana was coming back to town. Oh boy...

"Yes. She'll be here for two months or so, until she's hired a full-time manager," Grandma said.

"We've booked a month-long cruise around the Mediterranean." Gram's eyes were glowing now, excitement radiating from her so powerfully, Emily felt it in the pit of her stomach. "We leave mid-September."

"Oh, that's...really soon." Emily's eyes stung, but she wasn't going to cry about this. It was just...why did everyone she loved eventually leave her to go travel the world? First her mom, then Jenny—the woman she'd fallen head over heels in love with about five years ago—and now her grandmothers. "So the sale is a done deal, then?"

"It is, honey," Grandma told her. "We got the price we wanted, and Ms. Devlin has given us every assurance we asked for. If her company goes belly up in ten years, well, who's to say the same wouldn't have happened to us? We can't control everything. We can only do our best, and this seems as close to perfect as we could hope for. Your job and home are secure, the inn's legacy is secure, and we get to retire while we're still young enough to enjoy it."

"We're going to drink wine in Florence, Em." Gram's voice was awed. "We're going to dip our toes in the Mediterranean and have real champagne in France and tour the Sistine Chapel."

"That does sound amazing." Emily smiled despite the

lump still lodged in her throat. Unlike her mom, Gram and Grandma were coming back, and they deserved an amazing trip like this more than anyone she knew. "I'm sure I don't have to remind you to take lots of pictures?"

"We'll create an album on Facebook," Grandma promised. "And update it every night."

"Unless we're too busy having fun," Gram added.

Emily laughed. "I'm really happy for you both. You deserve this."

"And you're okay with the sale of the inn?"

"I mean, I'm as okay with it as I'm going to get." Emily decided to go for full honesty...well, at least about the inn. "Change is hard for me. You know that, but I know I'm just being selfish, and I'll get over it."

"Oh, honey." Gram wrapped her arms around Emily and hugged her tight. "You're not selfish, and I think that, in the long run, this is going to be good for all of us. You'll see."

"I hope so." Emily tasted salt on her lips and realized she'd lost the battle with her tears. "Mostly, I'm just so glad that you're going to have this amazing retirement together. Now, tell me more about this little house a few miles down the road?"

ELEVEN

"You have arrived," the voice from her phone's GPS app announced.

Diana slowed her car and peered into the woods, looking for any sign of her rental house, but there was nothing visible in any direction except trees. She rolled the car slowly down the dirt road, eventually spotting the entrance to a driveway. Hopefully that was it. She hadn't realized the house Carter had rented for her was in such a remote location.

A black mailbox stood at the entrance to the driveway, bearing the number 235. This was it, Diana's home for the next two months. Carter had shown her photos of the house's interior before he booked it, but she hadn't looked at a satellite view. It was truly in the middle of nowhere. Supposedly, the inn was only a ten-minute drive from here, though.

"Cute," she said out loud when the house came into view. It looked like the log cabin out of a classic children's story, something she hadn't realized still existed in modern times. It certainly wasn't someplace she would have ever imagined herself living.

Diana stopped her car in the driveway. There wasn't a garage, but that was fine since she'd be gone before there was any snow on the ground to worry about. She shut off the car and reached in back for one of the plants she'd brought with her. She'd left most of them at home under Carter's care, but if she was going to be here for two months, she needed a few of her favorite plants for company.

Of course, she had all the plants she could ever want right outside her door. The house was surrounded by lush green trees and bushes, endless forest in every direction. She couldn't even see the road from here. Diana stepped out of the car and approached the house, entering the code she'd been given into the keypad on the front door.

Inside, the cabin looked like...well, it looked like a real log cabin. The walls were constructed from wood beams. It gave the room a warm feel, and even though it wasn't her style, she thought it suited the area. More importantly, the house had plenty of modern amenities, including a hot tub out back.

Diana walked to the kitchen table and set down her polka dot plant. She'd find a better place for it soon, but this was a good enough spot while she unloaded the car. It took her about fifteen minutes to bring in her bags and unpack everything.

The master bedroom was just off the living room. In fact, the cabin was only a single level, which was new for her. She was used to living vertically in her narrow Back Bay town house. The window in the bedroom looked straight into the forest. No sweeping mountain views here, but the trees were pretty enough.

Diana spent the next few minutes rearranging her plants, finding windowsills and sunny spots for them around the cabin. Then, as it was approaching dinnertime, she turned her attention to the empty kitchen cabinets. That was a problem, and a quick Google search revealed that the nearest grocery store was about twenty minutes away.

Maybe she should go into town tonight and have dinner at one of the local restaurants. First, she texted Carter to let him know she'd arrived and ask if he'd been able to fix the bug that had broken all the images on her new website that morning.

All fixed, he replied, with several emojis and a link to the website, which indeed seemed to be working perfectly now.

That was a relief. While she was in Vermont, she had proposals to write for two more hotels she hoped to purchase before the end of the year. It was an aggressive start, but the numbers supported her actions, and she would reap the reward next year as each hotel began to bring in revenue.

Vermont was quiet. Diana paced her living room, unnerved by the absolute silence outside. No cars. No people. She didn't even hear a plane in the sky. She couldn't believe she didn't have any neighbors.

Her stomach rumbled, reminding her about the empty pantry. Diana pulled up Google maps and drove into town, where she had dinner at a local bistro. She was surprised to find herself looking for Emily while she ate, wondering if she might have decided to go out for dinner tonight too. Diana almost wished they hadn't slept together, so she might have a friend here in town, but she couldn't bring herself to regret their night together.

Heat spread over her skin every time she thought about that night.

Diana had thought about it entirely too often over the last few months, so often that she worried she would have trouble keeping things professional between them now that she was back in Crescent Falls. Hopefully, Emily had gotten over her bitter feelings about Diana buying the inn, because while Diana could handle her hostility, she'd much rather be friendly with her.

Whatever happened, though, she wouldn't get involved with Emily again now that she owned the inn. No, from here on out, their interactions would be purely professional.

Back at the cabin, Diana spent a few hours looking over her plans for the Inn at Crescent Falls. She had so many things to go over with Mary and Eva before they officially retired. Diana's first week at the inn would be their last.

Once they moved out of the apartment in back, Diana would have it cleaned and renovated so it would be ready for the next manager. She closed her laptop and rubbed her eyes, suddenly exhausted. It was still too quiet in this cabin. Diana could hear herself breathe. That was weird. She was out of her element here, and she hated that feeling. She'd been at the same job in the same building for almost twenty years, and now...everything had changed.

For the first time in her life, she was truly the boss. She owned her own company. It was exciting. Thrilling. And...terrifying.

No matter that the odds were against her. Diana would *not* fail.

She stood, deciding to call it an early night so she'd be well rested for her first day at the inn. She washed up in the bathroom and then turned off the light, plunging the cabin into darkness.

"Fuck," she mumbled, frozen in the bathroom doorway. She couldn't see the bed. She couldn't even see her hand in front of her face. She blinked a few times, waiting to see if her eyes would adjust. This was *too* dark. Weren't there streetlamps in Vermont? Frowning, she put the bathroom light back on and walked to the living room, where she turned on a small lamp that would hopefully provide enough ambient light for her to sleep.

She climbed into bed and lay there, blinking up at the ceiling. The lamp from the living room was a little too bright for her taste, but she was too tired to get back up and turn it off. The only sound in the bedroom was a faint rushing noise that she finally identified as the wind blowing through the trees outside her window. It was oddly unsettling.

Well, that, and she could still hear herself breathing. And now that she was thinking about her breathing, it quickened. Anxiety had her sucking in rapid breaths, and she scowled at herself. Here she was in this adorable little cabin in the woods, probably the most objectively peaceful place in the world, and she was too anxious to sleep.

An eerie noise came from outside, not quite a howl, but definitely an animal sound. Diana's neck and arms prickled as her hair stood on end. She sat up, realizing as she did so that the curtains on the bedroom windows were wide open, revealing the endless darkness outside. She felt suddenly hyperaware that she was alone in a house in the middle of the woods.

No one would hear her if she screamed. A shiver shook her shoulders.

"You're being ridiculous," she murmured, just to hear the sound of her voice. Objectively, she knew it was true. Crime was nearly nonexistent in Crescent

Falls. She'd researched the area before she purchased the inn. This was one of the safest places in America. And yet...

The darkness outside was impenetrable. She got up and shut the curtains. At least now she didn't feel like the creatures of the forest were watching her. There was that sound again. Was it an owl? Yes, it did sound like a hoot, now that she was thinking about it. Owls were harmless, no matter how spooky they sounded.

She scrambled back into bed and picked up her phone to text Carter.

> This cabin you rented is too far out in the woods! It's creepy.

CARTER DEVLIN

> Aunt DD r u afraid of the dark?

> You would be too if your room was so dark you couldn't see your hand in front of your face.

> And it's too quiet.

CARTER DEVLIN

> Want me to come up? I'm loud!

> In a few weeks, once you've got the home office established.

CARTER DEVLIN

> OK well ur too old for a nightlight but maybe install a white noise app

> Night

> Good night.

She hadn't even realized white noise apps existed, but of course they did. The wonders of modern technology. She searched the app store, downloaded one with good reviews, and chose the option for city sounds.

"That's more like it," she muttered as the faint sound of cars rumbling and other engine noise filled the room. She exhaled, willing her body to relax. Tomorrow, shit got real. She'd be managing the inn. And she'd see Emily. Diana had prepared for this. She would pull Emily aside to address their personal history and reassure Emily that it wouldn't affect their new working relationship. Simple enough. Diana was a professional. It would be fine.

She closed her eyes, rolled onto her side, and waited for sleep to come.

———

EMILY WAS DISCREETLY READING an e-book on her phone when the front door to the inn slid open. She quickly turned off the screen, but her smile froze the moment she spotted Diana's familiar form coming through the door. Yes, Emily had known Diana would be here today, but she had hoped she'd be helping a visitor when Diana arrived, too busy to say hello.

Now here she was, alone in the lobby with Diana, who looked goddamn amazing in black slacks and a royal-blue top. It set off the red tones in her hair beautifully, and if she'd been standing a little closer, Emily was sure the color really made her eyes pop too. Emily's skin tingled, and her stomach pinged. She inhaled sharply.

Oh no. Where had *that* come from?

She hadn't been around Diana long enough in June to know if she was really attracted to her or if it had just been a spur-of-the-moment thing. Emily had been too upset the morning after their one-night stand to feel anything but hurt when she realized Diana was trying to buy the inn. She had expected to feel something similar today, and instead...this.

Heat spread across her chest and up into her cheeks as she faced Diana. "Hi."

Diana's smile was polite, gracious even. Those blue eyes locked on Emily's, something intense sparkling in their depths that Emily wasn't sure how to read. "Good morning."

"My grandmothers are waiting for you in their office. You can go on back," Emily told her. "You remember where it is, right? Or I could show you, because I—"

"I remember," Diana interrupted her nervous rambling, her expression softening. "Have a nice day, Emily."

And with that, she strode down the hall like she owned the place. Well, she *did* own the place now, didn't she? Emily had mixed feelings about Diana being back in town, but she'd made peace with her grandmas retiring. They'd bought the little house down the street that they'd had their eye on and would be moving in next week.

It would be weird here without them, but Emily could still pop by for dinner or just to hang out, and their new house had the prettiest little pond out back. She could hardly wait to set up her easel there and paint it.

Knowing Diana owned the inn, though? That made Emily extremely uncomfortable. She had been so impressed with Diana when they met, and now she couldn't trust anything Diana said. Maybe she was all talk. Maybe she dreamed big but didn't have what it took to follow through. Until she knew for sure, Emily would be watching Diana closely to make sure the inn was in good hands.

A hint of Diana's floral perfume lingered in her wake, and Emily hated the memories it stirred. It sucked knowing what your new boss looked like naked, how she sounded when she came. How her voice trembled when she begged. It sucked that Emily's body still overheated in her presence.

Did Diana feel the same? There had been *something* on her face when she looked at Emily just now, but she might just have been eager to get started here at the inn. Diana probably hadn't thought about her night with Emily since she left Vermont the first time.

Ugh.

Emily tapped the screen on her phone, bringing up her e-book, but she couldn't focus on reading anymore. Instead, she sent a message to the Adventurers group chat, lamenting her situation. Immediately, her phone began to ping with responses.

> **ALEXIS BELL**
>
> Whatever you do, don't kiss your hot boss
>
> **TOM BELLAMY**
>
> I mean, maybe kiss her if she looks like she'd be into it...
>
> she's not your boss permanently anyway
>
> **TALIA MICHAUD**
>
> No kissing. That way lies heartbreak, Em
>
> > I don't think she even wants to kiss me again, so no worries there
> >
> > Just sucks having to see her every day
>
> **TOM BELLAMY**
>
> Let's find you a new hookup then!
>
> **ALEXIS BELL**
>
> I met a nice girl at my yoga class last week, def queer vibes

Emily was grinning when a guest came into the lobby

needing her assistance. From there, her morning picked up. She kept reasonably busy until lunchtime, when she made the five-minute walk back to her cabin to heat up leftovers from the pizza she'd made last night.

Maybe she was afraid she would bump into Diana if she ate in the break room as she usually did, but the weather was nice, and she never minded walking home for lunch. She took her pizza onto the porch with Jack, watching him spiral from perch to perch for a half hour until it was time to head back to work.

She was only on until three today, and just as she was handing the desk over to Mariah, Diana entered the lobby, headed straight for her.

"Oh good. I was hoping to catch you before you left," Diana said, and Emily's traitorous heart sped at her words before she registered Diana's professional veneer. She wanted to ask her something about work. *Duh, Emily*.

"Can I help you with something?" She gave Diana what she hoped was a politely indifferent smile, but it felt weird on her face.

"I'm trying to catch up with all the staff today, just to introduce myself..." Diana's lips quirked as she shrugged, acknowledging that they already knew each other. "And to check in with how things are going and what you might want or need professionally."

"Oh, okay."

"Great. I won't take up much of your time." With that, Diana turned and strode down the hallway.

Emily followed her to the break room, somewhat surprised when Diana shut the door behind them. This was more private than she'd expected. They sat across from each other at the table.

Diana clasped her hands on its wooden surface. She

looked tired, Emily realized suddenly. Her makeup didn't quite hide the dark shadows beneath her eyes, and her shoulders were rigid, as if she was trying not to let herself slump. "As I mentioned, I'm checking in with all the employees today, but before I start my usual speech, I want to address the elephant in the room."

"Oh." Emily hadn't expected this either. Somehow, she'd assumed Diana would try to avoid talking about their night together.

"I know we're in a tricky situation here, given our personal history," Diana said. "But I don't want it to be awkward. That night is in the past, and I'm sure we can both be professional about it now. Not to mention, I'll be hiring a full-time manager in the next month or so, and as soon as I do, you'll report to that person instead of me. Are you comfortable with that?"

"Sure," Emily agreed, staring at her hands instead of meeting Diana's gaze. Truthfully, working for Diana sounded awkward as hell, so Emily hoped she found a new manager quickly.

"Great. So, I've been meeting with all the employees today to get to know them and see what they're looking for from the new management. More responsibility? Less? Shift changes? Suggestions for improvement? That kind of thing."

Emily shrugged. "I'm fine as I am. Like I mentioned when we first met, I just work here a few days a week to help pay the bills."

"And you're not looking for any changes?" Diana asked, professional as ever, but there was still that tension in her shoulders, as if maybe she wasn't quite as comfortable around Emily as she was pretending to be.

"Nope, no changes. I'm good." Emily realized she was

drumming her fingers against the tabletop and moved them to her lap instead.

Diana gave her a questioning look. Emily was being weird. She knew she was, but she didn't know how to act around Diana anymore.

After an awkward pause, Diana continued. "As your grandmothers probably told you, I'll be here for the next two months, making sure the transition is a smooth one. I've got a few renovations planned, nothing drastic, more like a general freshening up."

"Oh?" Emily heard the skepticism in her tone, but she didn't want any more changes to the inn. Diana's presence was overwhelming enough.

"Fresh paint, a new computer system to better manage online reservations, picnic tables under that grove of trees over there." Diana gestured out the window, indicating the tree line on the far side of the back lawn. "That sort of thing."

Emily exhaled, trying to relax. "Picnic tables sound great, actually, and our computer system is a beast."

"A total dinosaur," Diana agreed. "My nephew is good with computers, and he's found a new system that should be a big upgrade. He'll be up in a few weeks to help get it installed."

"Does he work with you, then?" Emily couldn't help asking, trying to imagine Diana working with some young techy guy, keeping it all in the family even though she no longer worked for the family business.

"Yeah, he's my first employee." Diana's expression filled with unmistakable affection for her nephew.

"What happened to your old job, if you don't mind my asking?" Emily blurted, surprising herself and probably Diana too. But suddenly, she needed to know. She *had* to know if Diana was as competent as she seemed. "Because you were all set to become the next CEO of Devlin Hotels, and now...well, now you've started your own company, and frankly, I'm confused."

Diana straightened, those eyes that had been so warm a moment before cooling behind what Emily could only imagine was her CEO mask. "My circumstances changed."

She obviously didn't want to talk about it, but how else was Emily ever going to trust Diana to run this inn? "How, though? Because I was so impressed with your ambition and your confidence when we met. You had me completely convinced you were going to be the next CEO of Devlin Hotels, and now you don't even work there anymore. So I can't help wondering, are you really committed to this inn or are you just going to run off when the next shiny thing catches your eye?"

Diana's nostrils flared, and a muscle beside her eye twitched. "Whatever you saw in me then is still here, I promise. I've always been passionate about boutique hotels, and now they're my exclusive focus. This inn is important to me, Emily. I'm committed to its success. I'm not going to abandon it and chase after the next shiny thing that catches my eye, as you so eloquently put it."

Emily did feel a little bad for saying that, but she wouldn't apologize for airing her concerns. Diana had been so singularly focused on her path to CEO of Devlin Hotels when they met. Why had she changed her mind? Managing boutique hotels had to feel like small potatoes by comparison. Who was to say she wouldn't get bored here?

"Do you have any other concerns? If not, I'll let you get home." Diana tilted her head, awaiting Emily's answer.

"Nope, that's my only concern." And Diana hadn't

done much to allay it, nor had she answered Emily's question about why she'd left Devlin Hotels.

"All right, then. Have a nice evening, Emily." Diana stood, giving Emily a smile that didn't seem quite as genuine as the one she'd worn when she first saw Emily that morning.

Had Emily hurt her feelings with her questions? Emily deflated, uncomfortable with the idea that she might have hurt Diana. She'd just needed reassurance that the inn was in good hands. Maybe she should apologize.

But Diana was already out the door.

TWELVE

Why couldn't she sleep in this freaking town? Diana thumped a fist against her pillow in frustration. She'd been in Crescent Falls for a week now and had yet to get a decent night's sleep. The white noise app helped a little, but sleep was no longer her friend.

Just as Emily no longer was. Not that Emily had ever been her friend, per se. But they'd shared a profound connection when they first met. Now Emily had closed herself off, despite Diana's attempts to set things right between them. Diana had been relentlessly friendly to her all week, and Emily had been nothing but stilted and awkward in return. It hurt more than Diana would have anticipated.

Emily didn't trust her. She was concerned that Diana was all talk and no follow-through, which chafed like ill-fitting underwear. The very idea that Diana didn't know how to run the inn properly...it was preposterous! But she also couldn't entirely blame Emily for doubting her. Maybe Diana should have just told her why she left Devlin. At the time, it hadn't entered her mind, but in hindsight...she wondered.

Diana had been raised to keep certain things to herself to avoid causing embarrassment for the family. It was why she'd never talked about her anxiety with anyone but her therapist, and the events that led to her leaving Devlin Hotels fell solidly in the same category. She didn't necessarily agree with her parents' policy, and yet, she found herself upholding it anyway. Apparently, there were some things she just didn't know how to talk about.

In the long run, it didn't matter. She didn't need Emily's approval. Diana knew she would do a good job, that she would improve the inn in ways its former owners would be proud of. Sooner or later, Emily would come around and see it, and if she didn't, well...Diana would just keep pretending she didn't care.

With a sigh, she rolled to her back. She knew every beat of the city sounds that played on a loop from the white noise app by now, her mind unconsciously anticipating what came next. Behind the white noise, she could hear the wind rushing through the trees, a sound that had become slightly less ominous now that she'd been here a week.

Fatigue burned her eyes and weighed down her body, so why couldn't she sleep?

As if in answer, her limbs twitched with suppressed anxiety. It hadn't been this bad in years. When she got back to Boston, it might be time to see her psychiatrist and get a new prescription. She'd been on SSRIs for most of her twenties, but a combination of cognitive skills learned in therapy, regular exercise, and the security that came with her appointment to vice president of independent purchasing had allowed her to keep her anxiety under control without medication for over ten years now.

Of course, she should have anticipated that her recent career upheaval would throw her off-kilter. She'd spent the last week working with Mary and Eva to make the transfer of ownership as seamless as possible. Tomorrow, Diana would be running things on her own.

She was operating without a safety net for the first time in her life. Yes, her new business was insured, but she no longer had the financial security of her personal nest egg...or the certainty that her family would bail her out if she needed help. Being on her own was exhilarating, but also scarier than she'd expected.

Being a Devlin came with a certain level of privilege. She knew that and had never taken it for granted. Her family's wealth and reputation had given her advantages in life, both personally and professionally. Now, it was time to build her own future.

She had such big plans for this inn, and tomorrow, she could start implementing them. She wanted it to be perfect, a flawless first day as the inn's official owner. So naturally, her body was sabotaging her. Diana sighed, her legs shifting restlessly between the sheets.

Maybe she should do more hiking. She hadn't been on a hike since that day in June. Surely that would help burn enough energy to calm her down. Plus, she needed to take advantage of the mountain scenery while she had it. All too soon, she'd be back in the city. She'd seen a few yellow leaves outside her windows this morning. Soon, the foliage would really start to turn, and it was supposed to be extraordinary up here.

Diana sat up. Now that she'd acknowledged the anxiety prickling beneath her skin, she had a few tools available to help calm it so she could sleep. It was too late for exercise, but she had CBD drops she sometimes took on nights like this. She padded to the kitchen and dabbed a few drops on her tongue, then washed them down with a glass of water.

She could also try meditating for a few minutes to clear her head. She could already tell her thoughts were too chaotic for that tonight, though. Rather than getting back into bed, she walked to the window and stood staring out into the darkness. When she'd been here in June, she hadn't realized how dark it got out here in the mountains. Thanks to Emily, she hadn't even left her hotel that night. Hadn't even looked out her window.

She'd been too busy letting Emily edge her to one of the most powerful orgasms of her life. *God.* She was throbbing just thinking about it. And maybe that was another reason she was wound so tight lately. She hadn't been with anyone since. She'd been so busy getting Aster off the ground, she'd barely taken care of her own needs. Plus, she'd had Carter in the room next door.

But she was alone now, and orgasms were great for stress relief. Her hand slipped inside her sleep shorts, and she hissed as her fingers made contact with her clit. She rubbed a few circles around it, surprised at how aroused she already was. Her fingers dipped lower, sliding through her wetness as her mind helpfully replayed the way Emily had teased her, fingers ghosting over her until Diana had begged for more.

She swayed forward, her free hand slapping against the window to support herself, but...she couldn't do this in front of the window. Even though she knew there was no one out there—her current isolation was part of the reason she couldn't sleep, after all—she still felt exposed, on display for the creatures of the forest, if nothing else.

She hurried to her bed and crawled onto it, lying on her stomach so she could thrust her hips against her fingers the way she liked. Her vibrator would be better, but somehow she hadn't thought to pack it. Her fingers moved almost frantically as her need grew, but every time Emily's face surfaced in her mind, she forced it away.

Yes, she'd masturbated to the memory of her night with Emily several times since June, but she couldn't do that now that Emily was her employee. She searched her brain for someone else to fantasize about, scrolling through her mental inventory of hot actresses, but nothing seemed to help.

"Need a little something more?" Emily's voice murmured in her head.

"Yes," Diana panted, stroking faster, but *no*. Not Emily. She groaned in frustration. Why couldn't she do this without thinking of Emily? Purposefully, she cleared her mind, focusing on the sensations in her body, the needy ache between her thighs and the heat crawling over her skin. Her breath caught as she pressed her fingers more firmly against her clit.

She braced her knees against the quilt, thrusting harder against her fingers. She was almost there...

"I think you can wait just a little bit longer..." Emily whispered in her head.

Diana ignored her, grinding against her fingers. Tonight, any orgasm would do. Her wrist was starting to ache, and she was so tired. So goddamn tired. "Just finish already," she muttered to herself, frustrated as she switched to her left hand. She rubbed and rubbed, but she could feel herself losing steam now.

Her arousal plateaued as her frustration grew. She was starting to get sore, and yet her orgasm remained frustratingly out of reach. With a groan, she flopped onto her back in defeat. Her core still ached for release. She was out of breath, her muscles coiled even tighter than they had been before she started.

Fuck. Me.

That night, she slept worse than ever, arriving at the inn on Monday morning sleep-deprived and grumpy. As she entered through the back door, she bumped into Emily, who seemed to have also just arrived for work.

"Good morning." Diana gave her a cheerful smile that in no way reflected her current mood.

"Morning." Emily barely glanced at her.

"Got any fun plans this week?"

Emily looked vaguely annoyed that Diana was still talking to her. "Just working. Celeste, our events manager, is visiting her mom in Connecticut this week, which...obviously you know that, but she usually covers for me when I take lunch, so I've got a couple of extra-long shifts coming up."

"Oh." Diana *had* known that Celeste was out of town, but not that Emily wouldn't have lunch coverage. "I'd be happy to cover for you. It would give me a good opportunity to get some experience with the front end of things."

But Emily shook her head. "That's not your job. It's fine, really."

Diana forced herself to keep smiling when she really wanted to groan in frustration. She *hated* this awkwardness between them. "Really, I want to."

"You do?"

"Of course." She was trying to win Emily over, but also, she *did* want to familiarize herself with running the inn from the ground up.

"Well, okay. Thanks."

"No problem. Have a nice day, Emily." She headed down the hall to her office, which Eva and Mary had vacated on Friday. Grateful for the privacy, Diana set up her laptop and got to work. She had a contractor coming that afternoon about the picnic tables, and she needed to get a job listing posted for the new general manager position.

She hoped to fill it by the end of the month so she had plenty of time to train the new manager on the day-to-day particulars of running the inn. Once everything was running smoothly, she could return to Boston, and right now, that moment couldn't come soon enough. She felt like one of the wilted leaves she plucked from her plants, a brittle, dried-out husk of herself.

After a quick call with Carter, she turned her attention to finalizing the job description for the new general manager. To combat the fatigue that seemed to have infused every cell in her body, she poured herself a cup of coffee from the pot behind her desk.

By lunchtime, the job was posted, and the coffee pot was empty. Diana had had a surprisingly productive morning, all things considered. A routine call to the bakery that supplied the inn's continental breakfast had turned into an hour-long conversation as the chatty woman on the other end of the line initiated a brainstorming session on ways to improve their breakfast service, ideas that Mary and Eva had apparently suggested she save for the future owner.

It was an extremely informative call. Diana had jotted several pages of notes on all the new options she wanted to implement, but for the past thirty minutes or so, she'd been ignoring increasingly urgent distress signals from her bladder after drinking so much coffee.

"Thank you so much, Vera. I'll definitely be over to visit the bakery in person soon and talk more about this," Diana said.

"Absolutely! I can't wait to meet you. I'm here every morning."

"Perfect. If I don't make it over this week, next week for sure," Diana told her.

She ended the call, shifting impatiently in her seat as she finished jotting down her notes, not wanting to forget anything. She'd learned long ago that it was worth the extra effort to write her thoughts down while they were fresh. Then she closed her notebook and stood, her knees wobbly from a combination of exhaustion and overcaffeination.

Tonight, she *had* to sleep, dammit. She strode toward the door, slamming straight into Emily, who had just crossed the threshold into Diana's office. For a moment, nothing registered but the warm press of Emily's body against hers, heat spreading like a flash fire through Diana's system as her body reminded her of what she hadn't finished last night. Just as quickly, she stepped backward, jaw clenched in irritation at herself.

Emily stared at her. "I, ah..."

Diana crossed her arms over her chest, resisting the urge to tap her foot against the floor. Now that her senses weren't intoxicated by Emily's body touching hers, she remembered how badly she had to pee.

She was also painfully aware of something else. In her single-minded determination to buy the inn and get her new business up and running, she'd failed to consider what it would be like to work with Emily after the night they'd shared. It hadn't just been sex. It was really intimate sex. Diana had let herself be vulnerable that night. She'd *begged*.

And now she had to act as if it meant nothing. She had to stand here as if her armor wasn't dented, as if it didn't feel like Emily was poking at her weak spots every time she looked at Diana with those mistrustful eyes.

She reeled in her spiraling thoughts and cleared her throat. "Yes?"

"Um, there's a disgruntled guest at the front desk demanding to see the manager."

"Lovely," Diana muttered. "And what is their grievance?"

"He swears he booked his room—one of the luxury suites upstairs—for $99 a night. Those rooms don't *ever* go that cheap, certainly not in the fall. The rate on his booking is $259, and even that's a pretty good deal for that room. The system isn't wrong, but sometimes people try this, hoping they can convince me to give them some ridiculously cheap rate just because they said so."

"I see, and he's waiting at the front desk?"

"Yep. The reservation is up on the screen. You know how to use the system, right?"

"Of course." And with that, Diana turned and strode toward the lobby.

EMILY KEPT a polite smile in place as Diana dealt with the belligerent man at the desk, reluctantly impressed with her customer service skills, even if things had been weird for a moment there in her office. Diana had been nothing but friendly since she returned to Vermont, but she'd jumped away from Emily just now like she couldn't stand touching her. Or was it that she was afraid to touch her, given their history?

Emily couldn't be sure. She wasn't sure of anything where Diana was concerned. The easy rapport they'd shared in June was long gone. Now, things between them were polite at best, and Emily knew it was her fault. She'd been throwing up barriers since Diana's return, uncomfortable with her owning the inn and reluctant to trust that Diana knew what she was doing.

She seemed different now from the way Emily remembered her when they first met, polite and reserved and... tired. Emily couldn't help noticing that Diana had looked exhausted ever since she arrived. Maybe this career change had been harder than she wanted to admit.

"As you see here, the rates on the room you booked vary from $159 to $399, depending on the season, so it's not possible that you booked it for $99," Diana told the belligerent customer with all the poise that had made Emily swoon for her in the first place. She was firm but charming, somehow convincing him that he'd made a mistake after all.

"I guess I might have been remembering a price I saw at the hotel down the street," he finally admitted.

"That hotel does book more cheaply, but they don't have our views or amenities," Diana assured him, sounding as if she'd worked here for years. "Here's a gift card for $50 off your next stay, to make up for the misunderstanding."

"Oh," the man's wife said, eyes lighting up as she accepted the gift card. "Thank you."

"Is there anything else I can help you with?" Diana asked, hands clasped loosely behind her back, and Emily quickly yanked her gaze back to Diana's face before she was tempted to stare at her rose-colored skirt or the shapely ass it covered.

"No." The man still looked somewhat disgruntled, but his face had lost its ruddy color.

"I hope you have a safe and comfortable trip home," Diana told him, her expression warm and gracious.

"Yeah. Thanks." He turned and headed for the front

door, his wife giving them an apologetic look over her shoulder as they left.

"That was impressive," Emily blurted as soon as the door had closed behind them. "I was sure we'd have to end up giving him the lower rate just to get him out the door without causing more of a scene."

Diana raised her eyebrows at Emily. "Still doubting my qualifications?"

"No," Emily murmured, somewhat ashamed that Diana had called her out on her skepticism.

Diana touched her shoulder with a soft smile, then headed down the hall, heels clicking on the hardwood floors. Emily turned, not even fully aware she was watching Diana walk away until she noticed Diana had turned right at the end of the hall, away from her office. Toward the bathroom.

And now Emily remembered that Diana had already been on her way out of her office when Emily slammed into her in the doorway. Emily had terrible timing, as usual. But Diana hadn't complained, not today or a single time since she'd bought the inn, although she was obviously under stress and Emily had inadvertently been making things harder for her.

Emily still didn't trust her completely where the inn was concerned, but the truth was, she probably wouldn't have trusted *anyone* to love this inn the way her grand-mothers had. Her distrust was her own problem, though, not Diana's, and Emily was going to try harder to be nice from here on out.

She glanced at her phone to check the time and noticed a Facebook notification from her mother. Emily flinched, discomfort squirming in her stomach. Still, she clicked on it to see a picture of her mom with her current boyfriend, posing for a selfie on the Vegas strip. She'd tagged Emily with her usual "Wish you were here!" followed by a bunch of random emojis.

Emily was never sure how to react. It was so awkward, so superficial. Eventually, she hit the Like button, her standard response. The phone at the desk began to ring, and Emily suppressed a sigh as she reached for it. "Front desk, this is Emily. How may I help you?"

"We need more towels in room 205," a woman said. "Could you send some up?"

"Absolutely," Emily said. "Someone from housekeeping will be right up with fresh towels for you."

Emily dealt with that and then spent a relatively quiet final hour of her shift. As she handed the desk over to another employee, Jeremy, for the afternoon, Emily was craving the peace she found with a paintbrush in her hand. The black-eyed Susans were blooming in the field behind the inn, and she was going to take a canvas down there and see where her muse led her.

She gathered her things and began the walk home. As her cottage came into view, Emily saw a green Subaru Outback in her driveway, and her step quickened. Why was Alex here? And more importantly, why hadn't she called to let Emily know she was here?

Since Alex didn't have a key, Emily walked around back and found her friend on the porch, playing with Jack. "Hey," Emily called. "Why didn't you come up to the inn and say hi?"

Alex looked over, and Emily's stomach dropped. Her eyes were red and swollen, and as Emily opened the screen door to join her, Alex released a shuddering breath, her diaphragm hitching with the aftereffects of tears. A *lot* of tears.

"Frankie and I had a fight." She wrapped her arms around her knees, staring at her feet. "A stupid fight, but it was a big one."

"Aww, sweetie, I'm sorry. Do you want to stay here tonight?"

"Maybe," Alex whispered, releasing another shaky breath.

"I have a bottle of white wine in the fridge. Why don't I bring it out here, and you can tell me everything?" Emily suggested. "And then we'll put on a scary movie or something utterly *non*-romantic and eat ice cream."

Alex's shoulders slumped with what looked like relief, and she nodded. "That sounds good."

"Okay. Give me one sec." Emily headed toward the door to the house, pausing to whistle at Jack, who was fluttering insistently around her head, chirping at the top of his lungs. "Wine for the humans and a blueberry for you, okay?"

Behind her, Alex snorted with laughter.

Emily went inside and set down her bag, then uncorked the wine and grabbed two glasses plus a blueberry for Jack, and headed back to the porch. She sat beside Alex and filled both glasses nearly to the brim before handing one to her friend. "Vent away."

Alex sighed. "We were at the store, and she saw me looking at job listings on my phone. There's a bakery in Manchester that's looking for a pastry chef, which I thought might be a good fit for me, but Frankie got so mad, said I was sneaking around looking for new jobs behind her back. She wants me to keep working with her at the store. Things are going so well, why would I want to ruin it? You know how she gets sometimes..."

Emily did. Alex and Frankie had been together for about five years, but they'd been off and on for most of that time, and they fought a *lot*. Sometimes, Emily thought they were in love, and sometimes she wondered why the hell they were still together. When they fought, Frankie would say things that made Emily want to throttle her because Alex was the sweetest human ever. Inevitably, things would blow over, and they'd go back to normal.

"So we yelled at each other, and someone came into the store while we were yelling, and then Frankie got even more mad because we'd made a scene in front of a customer. She managed to make the sale and then went back to yelling at me, and I just...walked out in the middle of my shift and came here."

"Fuck, I'm so sorry." Emily wrapped an arm around Alex, giving her an awkward half hug while they balanced their wineglasses.

"I hate when we fight." Tears shone in Alex's eyes, which were still red and puffy from all the crying she'd done before Emily got home.

"I'm super pissed that she got mad at you for looking at jobs. There's nothing wrong with you pursuing your own career, Alex. I know you two have fun working together at the store, but you deserve more than that."

Alex nodded, her bottom lip trembling. "Of all things to fight about! She's always been supportive before, or at least I thought she was? I guess I haven't actually looked for a culinary job since we got back together this last time."

"Sounds like you need to have a serious conversation about it, once you've both calmed down."

"Yeah." Alex took another gulp of wine.

"In the meantime, girls' night." Emily tapped her glass against Alex's, glad to be the one giving comfort this time. Alex had held her while she sobbed endlessly after Jenny—the woman Emily had thought was the love of her life—left her for a job in New York City a few years ago. Emily had been a wreck for weeks.

She and Jenny had been together for two years when Jenny was offered her dream job doing graphic design work for one of the television studios in Manhattan. Jenny had asked Emily to come with her, but when Emily refused to leave Crescent Falls, Jenny prioritized the new job over her girlfriend.

Emily was still friends with her on social media, and Jenny was thriving in the city, always posting stunning pictures of herself and her graphic design work. She'd also recently gotten married. She'd moved on while Emily was still spinning her wheels, wondering why her little hometown was never enough to satisfy the people in her life.

"Don't suppose you have any chocolate ice cream in your freezer?" Alex asked, the hint of a smile tugging at her lips.

"You know me. I've always got an emergency stash."

They finished the bottle of wine, then went inside and got out the ice cream. They were halfway through *The Woman King*—and the carton of ice cream—when Alex's phone rang. From the look on her face, Emily knew it was Frankie. She paused the movie as Alex accepted the call.

"Hey," she said in a subdued tone.

Emily got up to put away the ice cream, then dawdled in the kitchen for a few minutes to give Alex some privacy. When she returned to the living room, Alex was saying, "I'm sorry too." A pause. "Yeah, okay. I'm at Emily's." She ended the call and gave Emily a sheepish look. "She's going to come pick me up...since you got me pretty tipsy on wine."

"Are you sure you don't want to stay the night? Or at least for the rest of the movie?"

"I'll come back and finish the movie, promise. But Frankie and I should probably talk things through now that we've both calmed down."

Emily nodded. "I hope you get it all worked out, and if you're still upset later, don't hesitate to come back, 'kay? I'm always here for you." She pulled Alex into a hug.

She hugged Emily back. "Always. What are best friends for, right?"

"Exactly. But, you know, fun stuff too."

Alex laughed as she sat back. "Luckily, fun stuff more often than sob fests."

They sat and chatted while they waited for Frankie, and fifteen minutes later, Alex was on her way home. Emily contemplated her choices for the rest of the evening. She was too tipsy to drive now too, not that she'd been planning to go anywhere tonight. Actually, she'd planned to paint, before she got home and found Alex on her back porch.

It wasn't too late to do that. She wasn't particularly hungry for dinner after all that ice cream, and there were still about two hours before sunset. Decision made, Emily gathered her portable easel, a canvas, and her painter's bag and set out for the hill behind the inn.

In the distance, she could just make out the summit and its distinctive stone tower. A tug of longing hit Emily. Someday, she'd make it up there, hopefully someday soon. As she looked around for the perfect spot to set up her easel, she noticed that someone was in one of the lounge chairs near the tree line.

She didn't want to disturb a guest—or have her painting

solitude disturbed—so she started to head toward the other side of the lawn before she noticed a strand of distinctive golden hair. "Oh, hi—"

Her words died on her lips as she rounded the chair and saw that Diana was fast asleep in the lounger. She'd curled on her side, one hand propped beneath her chin, and Emily's heart gave a funny little double beat, because Diana looked equal parts adorable and gorgeous. This was the first time Emily had seen her relaxed since she'd returned to Crescent Falls.

And there was no way she was going to wake her. She'd noticed Diana's exhaustion earlier today. She needed the sleep, however unconventional her current location. Emily wouldn't disturb her, but she'd keep an eye on her while she slept, just to be safe.

Emily set up her easel a few feet away and sat down to paint.

WHAT WAS SO *BRIGHT*? Diana squeezed her eyes more tightly shut as she drifted awake. Bright light glared on the other side of her lids, but where the hell was she? Her eyes popped open to the disorienting image of Emily painting in a grassy field as the setting sun blazed above the treetops.

What in the world...?

It was like something out of one of Diana's most private fantasies. She'd had a dream like this once, where she'd come across Emily painting while she was on a hike, but this time, instead of Emily leading her to safety, they'd fucked on the mountainside.

But this didn't feel like a dream. Diana was groggy with

the aftereffects of sleep, which meant she was awake. She sat up, horrified to realize she'd nodded off in one of the loungers behind the inn. And if the position of the sun was any indication, she'd slept for hours.

And Emily was really sitting there a few feet from Diana's chair, painting.

Diana must have made a sound, because Emily turned to smile at her.

"Hi," she said brightly, which was even more disorienting, because Emily hadn't been this friendly to Diana since she'd bought the inn.

Diana ran her hands over her clothes, trying to ascertain how much of a sleep-rumpled mess she was. Her skin pricked with discomfort for Emily to see her this way. Diana had been trying so hard to win her over, to convince Emily that she was going to elevate the inn—not harm it— and now she looked unprofessional and sloppy.

"I came out here to paint the black-eyed Susans." Emily gestured to the canvas in front of her, where she'd painted a lush landscape with pretty orange flowers. "I didn't want to disturb you since you looked like you needed the sleep, but I also didn't want to leave you by yourself out here in case you slept until after dark or something."

That was incredibly thoughtful of her. It caused a constant ache in Diana's chest that this sweet, caring person no longer trusted her. "What time is it?" Diana managed to ask.

"Almost seven. I was going to wake you if you were still asleep when I finished painting."

Seven. Diana had come outside after she'd finished work a little after five. She'd been asleep in full view of whatever guest happened to walk by for almost two hours. Heat rose in her cheeks. "Thank you for keeping an eye on me."

Emily beamed. "Any time."

Diana turned to rest her feet on the ground, still gathering her wits. She felt almost drunk. After a week of sleep deprivation, she was deliriously tired, and she couldn't tell yet whether this nap had helped or hurt her cause. Right now, she felt like her brain was operating at half speed.

"You seemed tired earlier." Emily spoke cautiously, as if she were afraid of overstepping any bounds.

Diana stared at her, noticing the way the sun brought out golden highlights in her brown hair. Emily had on a pink-patterned dress that looked amazing against her tanned skin, and Diana's defenses were low enough right now that she had to clench her fingers around the edge of the chair to keep from reaching out and touching Emily.

For a dizzying moment, Diana couldn't think of anything except how much she wanted to kiss Emily. She wanted to fall asleep in Emily's arms the way she had that night. She'd slept so well her first night in Vermont with Emily in her bed.

But that was in the past. Now, Diana's longing was replaced with embarrassment that Emily had noticed how tired she was. "I've had trouble sleeping at my rental. It's... too quiet. I'm used to the city, I guess."

Emily nodded thoughtfully. "A lot different out here, I bet. Where are you staying?"

"A rental cabin on Shady Farm Road."

"Oh yeah, it gets pretty remote out there."

"It's so dark at night," Diana heard herself saying. "How do you *sleep*?"

"Um." Emily giggled. "You don't like it to be dark when you sleep?"

"Not so dark that I feel like I'm in a tomb. I'm used to ambient light, I guess."

"Well, in that case, wait for the full moon. It'll be nice and bright outside then."

"Really?" Diana couldn't keep the surprise out of her voice. "You can see by the light of the moon?"

"Oh yeah," Emily said. "I can see clear across my yard when the moon's full. It's really cool looking too, like silver. You've got to see it."

"Hmm." Diana ran a hand over her hair, smoothing it into place. The sun was in her eyes as it neared sunset, causing her to squint at Emily. "I should really get home."

"At this point, you should stay for the sunset," Emily said. "I was planning to."

Diana would love nothing more than to stay here and watch the sunset with Emily. God, how she wanted to. But that sounded romantic and...intimate. If she stayed, it would be torture not to kiss her, and while Emily was being unusually friendly right now, a kiss definitely couldn't happen. Diana stood, wrapping her arms around herself. "I really need to go."

"Okay. Suit yourself."

"Bye, Emily." Diana turned and started walking back up the path before she could talk herself out of it. She'd already locked up her office before she came outside, so she avoided the inn entirely now, circling around the building to the spot where she'd parked her rental car. She sat with a groan, wishing she didn't feel even more tired now than she had before her nap. She cranked the radio for the drive home.

After a quick stop at the general store to pick up a sandwich for dinner, she pulled into her driveway just past seven thirty. This evening, she was going to treat herself to some self-care in hopes of setting herself up for a better night's sleep, because God knew she needed it.

Although she was starving, she put her sandwich in the fridge and changed into athletic gear, determined to get in a quick run before it got too dark. Regular exercise had always been a great counterbalance to her anxiety. She headed out, jogging down the dirt road she lived on, which was heavily wooded. The canopy of branches overhead made it seem darker than it actually was.

A car approached, tires crunching over the small rocks covering the road. Its driver raised a hand as he passed, and Diana automatically waved back. The first time it had happened, she'd thought the driver must have mistaken her for someone they knew, but she'd been waved at enough times now to realize this was just something Vermonters did, a friendly gesture.

She completed the two-mile loop that had become her after-work routine and took a quick shower. Then, wearing her favorite blue robe over her silkiest pajamas—she loved the way they felt against her skin—she sat at the kitchen table to eat dinner. Afterward, she poured herself two fingers of whiskey, put on a soothing playlist, and wandered through the cabin to care for her plants. She watered them and misted their leaves, relieved that they all seemed to be getting enough sunlight, since her cabin was mostly shrouded by the surrounding forest.

With her plants tended to, Diana walked to the back window. Her mind drifted to the way she'd stood here last night and the frustrating experience that followed. It had been foolish not to bring a vibrator with her on a two-month trip, but she'd been so focused on work as she packed.

Well, this was an easily remedied problem, at least. She walked to the kitchen to get her cell phone, navigated to the website of her favorite brand, and started browsing. She quickly added a wand to her cart like the one she'd left at home, but then a clitoral suction device caught her eye. She'd been meaning to try one of those. So, she added that to the cart as well and selected expedited shipping during checkout, because she was in urgent need of a good orgasm, and since she couldn't have Emily, she'd take the next best thing.

THIRTEEN

The sunshine was calling her name. Emily stood behind the front desk, gazing dreamily out the window. She'd already decided to take her lunch break outside so she could soak in the sun. It was mid-September now, her absolute favorite time of year. The air outside was cool and crisp. The leaves were starting to turn, but the flowers were still blooming. It was perfect.

This year, it was a little bittersweet, because her grandmas had just left on their month-long Mediterranean cruise. Yesterday, they'd posted photos of themselves in Barcelona before the cruise ship departed. Emily missed them already.

The front door slid open, and Tom, Drew, Talia, and Alex walked into the lobby. What in the world? "What are you guys doing here?" Emily asked. It wasn't totally unheard of for her friends to show up while she was at work, but it was unusual.

"We're headed out for a quick hike this afternoon and thought we'd stop by and have lunch with you first," Tom said, holding up a large bag from the deli in town.

"That's extremely random, but thank you." Emily stared at her friends, still suspicious, because Tom had a distinctly mischievous glint in his eye. He kept glancing down the hall toward the offices in back. "This wouldn't have anything to do with me mentioning that Diana would be covering the desk while I took lunch today, would it?" She kept her voice pitched low, although it was still ten minutes before her lunch break and she hadn't heard the distinctive click of Diana's heels in the hall yet.

"Total coincidence," Tom deadpanned while Talia giggled behind him. Drew was shaking his head like he couldn't believe he'd been talked into this, and Alex just gave Emily a guilty shrug. "Okay, fine. We've all been *dying* to meet this woman, and Alex mentioned this potentially golden opportunity, so I insisted we crash your lunch break. But we brought your favorite pastrami!"

"I appreciate the pastrami...and the company, even if you're here for stalkery reasons." Emily rolled her eyes at her friends. She was glad to see them even if she simultaneously wanted to shove them back out the door because any minute now, Diana would come down the hall and stumble right into this setup.

"Sorry, but after you carried on about the best sex of your life and how this one-night stand changed you as a woman, you can't blame us for absolutely having to meet her," Tom said.

"Okay, first of all, keep your voice down, like...*way* down." Emily raised her eyebrows at him, because not only did she not want Diana to hear any of this, but there were guests around too. "And secondly, I don't remember saying anything about being a changed woman."

"Maybe not those exact words, but you did say something to that effect," Tom insisted. "You definitely *looked* like a changed woman when we went out for drinks that night."

"I mean, you did," Talia agreed. "You'd definitely had your world rocked."

"It was just sex," Emily whispered. "Really great sex, but just sex, and now she's my boss for the next month or so, so I expect you all to be on your best behavior when she comes down that hall, okay?"

Tom lifted three fingers. "Scout's honor."

"It's weird without your grandmas here, huh?" Alex said, changing the topic. She glanced around the lobby as if looking for evidence of the new ownership.

"So weird," Emily agreed. "I keep waiting to hear Gram's laugh or see Grandma come through the front door."

"How are they enjoying retirement so far?" Tom asked, resting his hands on the desk.

"They're loving it," Emily admitted with a rueful smile. "I wish I'd known how ready they were. Maybe I could have helped them get started sooner. They've been busy settling into their new house, and yesterday, they left on their Mediterranean cruise. They can't wait to see the world."

"I want to see the world," Talia said, her tone wistful.

"Maybe we should expand our adventuring and have a big trip somewhere each year?" Drew suggested. "Because I'd like to travel more too, but I don't have anyone to go with for anything other than my annual trip with my parents to visit relatives in Vietnam. I'd like to see new places too."

"I'm in," Tom agreed.

"Me too," Talia said. "Let's start somewhere warm... maybe with a beach. Family friendly would be a plus too, so Chantal and Colette could come with me."

Emily pressed her lips together as her friends began

talking over each other, excitedly planning their international adventure. She'd never been past the states that bordered Vermont—New York, New Hampshire, and Massachusetts made up the sum total of her travel experience. The thought of going farther, of seeing the world...it felt overwhelming somehow, like she might not find her way back home, like there was an invisible string tethering her here, a string she was afraid to break.

While Talia talked about zip-lining through the rainforest and Tom advocated for them to learn how to scuba dive, Emily's attention diverted to the unmistakable click of heels against the hardwood floors. *Behave, please,* she silently begged her friends, because it was too late to say it out loud.

Diana came down the hall in maroon pants and a matching blazer that brought out the red highlights in her hair. She paused when she caught sight of the group gathered at the reception desk.

"Hi," Emily said as Diana stepped beside her behind the desk.

Diana glanced at Emily's friends, her brow slightly pinched as if she was trying to decide if these were guests and if so, why they were all hanging around the reception desk, talking about international trips. "Everything okay?" Diana murmured, that piercing gaze now focused on Emily.

Before Emily could answer, the raucous conversation around them ceased, everyone falling comically silent as they caught sight of Diana. *Way to make things awkward, guys.* They were all watching Diana now with barely disguised curiosity.

"My, um...my friends stopped by to take me to lunch," Emily said. Diana was standing so close beside her, it had

Emily's heart racing. Her cheeks were probably bright pink by now, and she was never going to hear the end of this.

"Hi," Tom said, extending a hand. "I'm Tom, and that's Alexis, Drew, and Talia. We're all in an outdoor adventure group with Emily."

"The Adventurers," Diana said with a polite smile as she shook Tom's hand. "Diana Devlin. It's nice to meet you."

"You too," Tom enthused. "Hey, you're welcome to join us on a hike or something while you're in town. We go out almost every weekend. I think you'd fit right in." He tapped the mini Progress flag on the front desk, not so subtly hinting at Diana's sexuality, which he'd only know if Emily had told him about their night together, and she was definitely going to give him hell for this. She'd been trying to smooth things over with Diana, and this surely wasn't the way.

"I do enjoy hiking." Diana darted a glance at Emily, her expression guarded. "But I'm pretty busy right now with the inn."

"I bet you are," Tom said. "We were just saying how weird it is not having Emily's grandmas around. They left you some pretty big shoes to fill, huh?"

"Alas, my shoes are quite small," Diana quipped, glancing down at her feet, which were as petite as the rest of her, "but I spent all last week working with Eva and Mary to ensure the future of the inn will be what they envisioned. I'm confident I can continue their vision while also implementing a few new ideas to further the inn's success."

"I'm sure you can," Tom said, and Emily knew him well enough to tell he'd been impressed with her answer. "Mary and Eva wouldn't have left you in charge if they didn't have faith in you. This inn's special around here, you know?"

"I do know." Diana nodded, hands resting on the counter. "It's important to me too. That's why I made it my first purchase under the Aster Boutique Hotels brand."

"Okay, I think we like you," Tom said with a grin, drawing laughter from the rest of the group. "Have you gotten to see much of the town yet? Emily's lived here her whole life, you know. She's a great tour guide if you need one."

"I've seen the basics," Diana said, sidestepping the second half of his comment.

Emily's heart was racing, embarrassment heating her skin. Surely by now, Diana realized that Emily's friends knew about their night together, and Emily could only hope Diana wouldn't be upset with her about it. But Diana's expression remained polite. If she'd caught on to why the group was here, she gave no indication.

"You should come to the fall festival," Talia suggested. "It's the first weekend in October. It's super fun and a great way to meet people in town."

"We'll see," Diana deflected, but it sounded like a no.

Emily would be at the fall festival. She looked forward to it every year, and now that she was thinking about it, she wanted Diana to go. A lot of the local vendors who supplied the inn would be there, people who had expressed concern about the inn's ownership changing hands, worried that a businesswoman from Boston was all wrong for the job.

Most people in Crescent Falls had been here their whole lives, and they tended to be distrustful of outsiders. This could be a good opportunity for Diana to build rapport and show she was dedicated to the community. Plus, Emily had been looking for an opportunity to smooth things over with her, and this could be just the thing.

But it was a conversation for another time. Right now,

Emily was starting to sense something defensive behind Diana's cool veneer. She probably felt ambushed by Emily's friends, uncomfortable that they knew about her history with Emily. The best thing Emily could do was get them out of here before anyone said or did anything to make things worse.

"Come on, guys." Emily stooped to grab her bag from its spot under the desk. "I've only got thirty minutes. Let's get going."

Luckily, her friends took the hint and started moving toward the door. Emily paused to look at Diana. "You good?" It was only the second time Diana would be watching the desk for her, and while she seemed at ease with the booking system, Emily imagined it had been some time since Diana had worked a frontline job like this.

Diana nodded, making a shooing motion with her hand. "Go and enjoy lunch with your friends. In fact, take the whole hour. I can use the opportunity to spend a little more time seeing how things run on this end."

"Oh...are you sure?"

"Positive. The best way to understand what needs changing is to get hands-on experience."

Emily smiled. "Thank you."

"You're welcome." Their eyes held for a moment, and Emily felt it in the pit of her stomach.

Oof.

Her attraction to Diana just kept growing, no matter how hard she tried to deny it. Suddenly aware that she and Diana were still standing close while her friends watched from the doorway, Emily turned and walked away.

"ENJOY YOUR STAY," Diana told the young couple in front of her as she handed them their room keys. They'd had their arms around each other since they entered the lobby and kept sneaking kisses while Diana checked them in. Usually, she found that kind of public show of affection grating, but today, she felt an uncharacteristic tug of longing.

One of the women reminded her of Emily, which led Diana to imagine herself checking in to a hotel somewhere with Emily for a romantic weekend together. Now she was frustrated with herself for becoming increasingly smitten with Emily when she was supposed to be doing the opposite. These feelings were beyond inconvenient.

If she were anywhere else, Diana would visit the local gay bar and find someone to hook up with, a surefire way to get Emily off her mind. But Crescent Falls and its surrounding towns were too small to have a gay bar, and anyway, small towns weren't suited to discreet one-night stands. She'd learned that lesson back in June.

Her stomach growled, reminding her that she should have eaten something before she covered Emily's lunch break. She glanced at her watch, surprised to see that it had already been forty-five minutes since Emily left. The time had passed more quickly than she'd expected while she'd been busy dealing with guests. She'd also jotted down several ideas to run past Carter while he was building the new website with its upgraded reservation system.

The front door slid open with a whoosh, and Diana's polite smile became a genuine one when she saw that it was Emily. Even when things were awkward between them, Diana was always glad to see her. Emily was like a ray of sunshine in Diana's day.

"Thanks for covering the desk for me," Emily said,

holding out an insulated cup. "Alex brought fresh cider from her parents' orchard. I thought you might like some. It's honestly the best cider you'll ever have. I look forward to it every year."

Diana took the cup, not sure if she'd ever had fresh cider before. "Thank you. That was thoughtful."

"Any time. I want you to get a flavor of Vermont while you're in town. This is the absolute best time of year here. Actually, you should really come to the fall festival that Tom was telling you about. It would be a great chance to meet some of our vendors and reassure other local business owners that you're committed to the inn and its legacy, you know?"

"Why should I have to reassure them?" Diana frowned. Eva and Mary had sold the inn to her. Why did anyone else's opinion matter?

"They're mistrustful of outsiders. I'm sure they want to give you the benefit of the doubt because my grandmas vouched for you, but they don't like big companies coming in and buying up local businesses. And I realize that's not exactly what you did, but it kind of looks like it on paper. Anyway, don't be a Jacqueline Norwood. Just make an effort around town, that's all."

"Who's Jacqueline Norwood?" Diana asked.

"She used to be a famous ballerina, I think, moved here with her football-player husband about ten years ago. Rich as hell, both of them, and they never showed their faces in town. A lot of rich people retire here. As long as they don't act like they're better than us, we get along fine, but these two..." Emily shook her head. "He died a few years ago, and now she's living in this big mansion all by herself, and she *still* hasn't made any effort around town. You'd think she'd want to be involved in the local ballet company or something at least, right? From what I've heard, she's stuck-up as hell, and before you say that's just gossip...you're right. It *is* gossip, but the point is that the town has made its mind up about her now. Don't give them a reason to feel the same way about you, you know?" Emily shrugged. "Anyway, if you come to the fall festival, it's a great way to get to know people. Plus, it's a lot of fun."

Diana lifted one shoulder noncommittally. She wasn't the festival type, although she did see the value in Emily's suggestion to be seen around town. Surely she could do that by visiting local businesses instead of attending this festival, though. "I'll think about it."

Emily nodded as she slid in beside Diana behind the desk. She was still several feet away, and yet, Diana felt her presence in every cell in her body. To distract herself, she lifted the cup and took a sip. Flavor exploded on her tongue, the sweet taste of apples with a rich spiciness she hadn't expected.

"Wow, this is really good."

Emily beamed at her. "I'll tell Alex you said so. She worked in that orchard every year while she was growing up. She's the one who suggested that her parents add a hint of maple syrup to the recipe, and I'm convinced that's what makes it the best."

"Mm."

"Anyway, thanks for letting me take a long lunch with my friends."

"No problem." But the embers in Diana's chest cooled as she remembered how uncomfortable she'd felt when she realized Emily's friends knew about their history, that they'd clearly come here today to meet Diana because of it. Her stomach rumbled again, and she backed out from behind the desk, still holding the cup of cider. "I'm heading out for a bit, just call my cell if anything comes up."

Diana stopped in her office to get her purse, then headed to her car in search of lunch. With Emily's words echoing in her head, she decided to go to the café downtown instead of grabbing a sandwich to go from the general store as she usually did. If Emily thought Diana needed to be seen around town, well, that was something she could easily accomplish.

Her father had mentioned her failure to nurture business relationships as one of the reasons he'd passed her over for CEO. Diana never made the same mistake twice.

At the café, instead of taking a quiet table in back, Diana sat at the counter, chatting politely with a young waitress named Summer, who told Diana that her mother owned the place. The next thing Diana knew, she was being introduced to the owner.

"Cheryl O'Malley." The woman shook her hand with a firm grip. "So you're the woman who bought the inn. I was glad to hear Mary and Eva finally retired. Are you staying in town?"

"For a few months," Diana told her. "Until I've hired a full-time manager at the inn. I've just started a new company—Aster Boutique Hotels—that will manage independent hotels across the country."

"Oh yeah? You should stop by our local women-in-business group. We meet the second Monday of every month." She rummaged around beneath the counter and handed Diana a business card.

"I'd love that," Diana told her. "I'll put your next meeting on my calendar."

"Great. See you around, Diana."

As she turned her attention to the bowl of soup in front

of her, Diana decided that her outing had been a success. She was extremely curious to attend the next women-in-business meeting. Her phone buzzed with an incoming email, which turned out to be a notification that the toys she'd ordered were out for delivery.

Thank God. She really needed an orgasm she didn't have to think about, the kind of release where she could just close her eyes and let the vibrator do all the work. The tension in her shoulders said that release couldn't come soon enough. She hadn't tried again on her own, knowing her anxiety was so high right now that she'd probably end up frustrated.

After lunch, she spent a quiet afternoon at the inn. Things had started to settle down now that she'd been here a week and a half. The initial bumps caused by the shift in ownership were beginning to level out. Just after five, she checked in with Jeremy, who had taken over the front desk from Emily a few hours ago, and then she headed for her car.

As she drove to her cabin, thoughts of a luxurious evening began to take root. She had a bottle of wine she could open, a hot tub she hadn't yet used. Any minute now, that package would be delivered, and she'd be ready to indulge. There were benefits to living out here in the woods: no one to interrupt her evening of self-care.

This road was a dead spot for cell service, so as she pulled into the driveway, her phone began to ding with notifications as it connected to the cabin's Wi-Fi. Diana had turned to grab her purse from the passenger seat when she saw movement. For a moment, her eyes couldn't make sense of what they were seeing, a large black animal strolling across the driveway toward her car.

That was not a dog.

"Bear," she whispered as adrenaline flooded her system, making her stomach swoop and her scalp prickle. There was a bear in her driveway. A *huge* bear.

Frantic, she jabbed a finger against the automatic lock button on the door. Of course, the doors were already locked, but she jabbed it several times just to make sure. She'd heard stories about bears breaking into cars...did they do that while people were inside them?

The bear glanced over its shoulder at her, and their eyes met, or at least that was how it felt to Diana. Despite her fear, she felt a bit awed in the presence of such a magnificent creature. She'd never seen one in person before. Big as it was, it didn't seem aggressive...not that she was likely to get out of her car anytime soon...or *ever*.

As Diana watched, the bear crossed the driveway and ambled into the forest. She sat there, breathing hard. What should she do now? The trees around the house were so thick that she lost sight of the bear almost immediately. Had it kept walking, or was it watching her now, stalking her from the protection of the forest, waiting for her to leave the safety of her car?

Her phone began to ring, its cheery tune making her jump. Without looking away from the spot where the bear had entered the woods, she fumbled with her free hand until she'd grabbed it. A quick glance revealed Carter's name on the screen.

"Carter, help," she said as she connected the call. "I've been cornered by a bear in my car."

"What? A bear? Where are you?" His voice rose, sounding more excited than alarmed.

"I'm in the driveway of the rental cabin, I just got home from work, and there was a bear in the driveway."

"Holy shit. That's so cool! Did you get a picture?"

"No, I didn't, and did you miss the part where I'm trapped in my car?" She rolled her eyes, slumping in her seat. The whole thing felt a little less scary with her nephew on the other end of the line.

"What's it doing?" Carter asked, definitely sounding excited now. "Is it standing outside the car? Take a picture! I want to see."

"It walked into the woods. I can't see it anymore."

"Oh. Then why are you trapped?"

"Because it might be stalking me from the trees, I don't know. People get attacked by bears! Do we have grizzly bears in Vermont? This one was huge. Looked more black than brown, though."

"Hang on. I'm googling."

While he did that, Diana scanned the trees around her, looking for any sign of the bear. As far as she could tell, she was alone, but the trees were too thick to be sure.

"Okay, it seems like you only have black bears in Vermont, and they aren't generally aggressive toward people. It says not to approach them...like, duh." He laughed. "But if this one walked away and went into the woods, you're probably fine."

"All the same, I'll wait a few minutes before I get out of the car. Were you calling for something specific or are you just lonely there in my town house by yourself?" She put a teasing note in her voice.

"I wanted to let you know you got a package and also, I'm going to come up and join you around the middle of next week. I should have the system ready to start testing by then."

"Great." Internally, she heaved a sigh of relief. Carter had turned out to be a bigger asset than she could have imagined, taking over all the technological aspects of the business. Diana didn't consider herself a dinosaur when it came to technology, but she couldn't have set up this new online-reservation system on her own. "There's plenty of room for you here at the cabin, so just rent a car when you're ready and let me know when to expect you."

"Awesome. I can't wait to see Vermont."

"You should be just in time for the foliage," she told him.

"Eh, leaves don't excite me, but I'm sure I'll find something to entertain myself."

"You mentioned a package?" Diana asked.

"Oh yeah. I don't know what it is. It's pretty small. The return address label just says 'shipping department,' no company name."

Oh no. A warm flush rose in her cheeks as she realized what Carter was holding, with its famously discreet packaging. In her rush to place the order a few days ago, she'd forgotten to update the shipping address. The toys had gone to her town house instead of coming here to her rental. "Oh. Um..."

"Want me to put it aside for you or is it something you need? I could bring it with me next week."

"No," she said quickly. "No need to bring it. It's just, um—" She fumbled, trying to think of something he wouldn't be tempted to open. "It's a toiletry item, but I don't need it urgently." She hoped he misinterpreted her awkwardness to mean he was holding a box of tampons so he'd immediately put it aside and never mention it again.

It seemed to work. She heard the muffled clatter of him putting it down. "Okay. I left it on the end table for you."

"Thank you." She let out a sigh as she panned the woods again. There would be no battery-assisted relief for her tonight, and she wasn't sure she felt comfortable sitting in the hot tub now that she knew there were bears in the area. Her evening of self-care was a bust.

And, now that she was thinking about it, she *did* need to buy tampons soon. Perhaps some of her recent irritability and difficulty sleeping could be chalked up to PMS.

"Are you still in the car?"

She sighed again. "Yes."

"Come on, Aunt DD. The bear is long gone. You can go inside now."

"Will you stay on the line with me, just to be safe?"

He snorted with laughter. "Not sure what help I can be from two hundred miles away, but sure."

"You could at least call 911 on my behalf if you hear me being mauled," she said dryly.

"You aren't going to be mauled. Go on. I'll stay on the phone."

"Thank you." Summoning her courage, she shut off the car and picked up her purse. Her heart gave a nervous kick as she stepped out of the car, half imagining that the bear would rush at her from the woods the moment she was exposed, but nothing happened.

She speed walked to the door and let herself in, locking it securely behind her.

FOURTEEN

Diana couldn't deny she was relieved to see Carter's rented SUV pull into the driveway the following Wednesday. Since the incident with the bear, she'd been so jumpy on her daily jogs that she finished each one more anxious than when she'd started. Consequently, she was sleeping worse than ever.

And then there was Emily. Working with her every day was more difficult than Diana had anticipated. Whenever she saw her, Diana's palms got damp, and her focus slipped. She'd never felt this way about a woman before. Ironically, Emily seemed completely unaffected by Diana's presence, which only increased Diana's discomfort.

So, she was glad to have a familiar face around the house for a few days. She enjoyed Carter's company, and maybe he could even be a buffer between her and Emily at the inn while he installed the new system.

"Hey, Aunt DD," he called as he stood from the car. "You weren't kidding when you said this cabin was in the middle of nowhere."

"Not even a little bit." She smiled, holding the door open for him.

He lifted his backpack out of the car and followed her inside. "I mean, I looked at it on Google maps when I booked the place, but it's not really the same as seeing it in person. Not sure I've ever been this far off grid. I don't even have a signal on my cell phone!"

"No, you'll need to connect to the Wi-Fi and make sure you've enabled calls over Wi-Fi too."

"Got it." He dropped his backpack on one of the kitchen chairs and looked around. "Cool place. Looks just like the pictures. Seen any more bears?"

"Luckily, no."

"I want to see one." Carter walked to the back window and looked out. "But from, like, inside the house where it can't eat me."

"This from the person who reassured me last week that the bear wasn't going to attack me," Diana teased.

"I know, I know, but I still don't want to come face-to-face with one."

"That makes two of us." She already felt more relaxed, having him here. Maybe she'd actually sleep tonight, knowing there was someone else in the house. When had she become a person who preferred having company to living alone?

"I'm starved," Carter said dramatically. "Can we have lunch before we head to work?"

Diana nodded. Since he'd told her to expect him around noon, she'd come home on her lunch break, anticipating his request. "There's a café on the way to the inn that has good soups and sandwiches."

"Great. Just give me a minute to get ready." He took his backpack to the guest room, and then went into the bathroom. When he came out, his hair was neatly combed and the stubble that had been on his cheeks when he arrived was gone.

She felt a tug of something almost maternal as she saw the effort he'd made to look professional. He'd been consistently impressing her since she hired him. She still thought he'd made a mistake dropping out of college, but she could also see that he was happier now, looking more confident and mature every day. Maybe it wasn't the end of the world if he helped her get her business off the ground before he went back to school. And there were options, once he was ready to discuss them. Perhaps he could complete his degree part-time or online.

A few minutes later, they were in the car.

"I had no idea places like this really existed," Carter exclaimed as she drove. "Look at that, an actual red barn! And okay, I guess I see why people get excited about fall leaves, because wow...yeah. That's pretty." He talked all the way to the café.

Diana smiled more than she had in weeks.

Inside, they ordered sandwiches and sat at one of the tables in back to wait for their food. The table beside theirs was occupied by a young man of Asian descent who looked vaguely familiar. He wore a T-shirt emblazoned with the name of an electrical company and was halfway through a roast beef sandwich. Diana stared for a second too long, trying to place him. By the time she'd remembered that he was part of Emily's adventure group, it was too late to look away. He'd seen her and was smiling.

Please don't let this be awkward.

"Diana Devlin, right?" he said, standing from his table.

She nodded. "That's right. I'm sorry. I didn't catch your name when we met last week."

"Drew Nguyen." He extended a hand, his gaze shifting to Carter.

"Nice to officially meet you, Drew," Diana said as she shook his hand. "This is my nephew, Carter. He's my admin and IT guy with the new business."

"Hey, Carter." Drew turned to shake his hand too.

"Hi." Carter gave him a shy smile. It was remarkable to Diana how mature he seemed one minute and how young the next. Twenty-one was such a transitional age.

"How long are you in town?" Drew asked him.

"Through the weekend," Carter said. "Maybe longer, depending how long it takes me to get the new system installed."

"Cool," Drew said. "A bunch of us are going out after work tomorrow. It's trivia night at the pub, which is a lot of fun. You're welcome to join us." He swung his gaze to Diana. "You too, Diana. Emily will be there."

"Yeah, that sounds awesome," Carter enthused. "I'd love to come."

"Great." Drew's smile widened. "Can I get your number? I'll text you the details."

Diana pursed her lips. She was fairly sure Drew was just being friendly, but the Adventurers were a queer group. Despite her hesitance to send her nephew off with a group of people she barely knew, trivia night might be a good experience for Carter. He'd led a rather sheltered life in her brother's home. As far as she knew, he'd never had a boyfriend. Maybe he needed some queer friends.

Drew tapped Carter's information into his phone and returned to his own table.

"Who's Emily?" Carter asked her as soon as they were alone again. "Have you met someone here in Vermont?"

Diana dropped her gaze to her hands. "No, Emily works

at the inn. Her grandmothers used to own it. She's part of this adventure group that does a lot of hiking around the area, which is how I met Drew."

He gave her a skeptical look. "You, hiking?"

She huffed. "For the record, yes. I did go hiking when I first came up here, but lately I've stuck to jogging on the roads near the cabin, although even that's been questionable since I ran into that bear. I'm not part of their adventure group. They came to see Emily at work one day last week, and she introduced us."

"Okay," Carter said. "I think I want to go to trivia night. It sounds fun."

"Sure." As much as Diana wanted him to have new experiences, she also felt a tug of melancholy. She'd been looking forward to having him around for a few days. Now he'd been in Crescent Falls all of five minutes, and he'd already made a friend and plans to go out, while Diana had been here for weeks and had no friends or plans.

Carter would probably prefer if she didn't go to trivia night, and that was probably for the best. The last thing she needed right now was to spend time socially with Emily.

And if she was a little bit disappointed to stay home alone tomorrow night, she would never admit it to anyone, not even herself.

———

EMILY WAS COUNTING down the minutes until her shift ended. Working the front desk at the inn just wasn't the same now that her grandmas no longer owned it. Sure, the inn *looked* the same, but it didn't feel like home in quite the same way. She didn't realize how much she'd enjoyed being able to sneak back to their apartment on her break and share a cup of tea with Gram or go for a stroll around the grounds with Grandma.

Things were still strained between Emily and Diana. If she wasn't mistaken, Diana was avoiding her as much as possible, which had prevented Emily from having the opportunity to undo the damage she'd caused when Diana first arrived. At this point, Emily just wanted to quit her job and paint.

Heels echoed down the hall, and Emily's body did its familiar dance of confusion as she prepared to face Diana... her pulse quickening while her shoulders tightened, a combination of excitement and discomfort that seemed to take over whenever they were in the same room.

She pasted what she hoped was a casual smile on her face as Diana approached the front desk with a man at her side. Who was that? He wore black jeans and a long-sleeved tee that somehow managed to look both casual and expensive, and he was younger than she'd initially thought, maybe not much over twenty. There was something familiar about him...

"Emily, I'd like you to meet my nephew, Carter," Diana said. "He's here to oversee the installation of the new website and reservation system."

Her nephew. Of course. Emily's mood lifted as she took in Carter's shy but hopeful expression. He was probably fresh out of college on his first real job.

"Hey, Carter. It's great to meet you," she said enthusiastically. "So, you're updating our system?"

He nodded. "I'll be rolling everything out tomorrow morning, just getting familiar with your local software this afternoon."

"Great. It can certainly use an upgrade. Let me know if there's anything I can help you with. I've been using this software for years, and I know the town really well too, if you're looking for things to do while you're here."

"I actually just met one of your friends while I was at lunch with Aunt DD, and he invited us to trivia night tomorrow?" Carter darted a glance at his aunt, who was drumming her fingers against the edge of the counter, watching their conversation.

"Oh yeah? Which friend? Trivia night is super fun. You should definitely come. You too, Diana." She tossed the invite out there, hoping Diana might take it, hoping it might be a way for them to find common ground, or maybe they were doomed to spend the rest of Diana's time here in Vermont tiptoeing awkwardly around each other.

Also, she was inexplicably swooning over the way Carter called her Aunt DD. Was DD her nickname or just something he called her? Emily had so many questions. If only she and Diana were friendly enough for her to find out the answers.

"Drew," Carter said, just as Diana said, "I'm busy tomorrow evening."

Emily bit back her disappointment. It might have been fun to see Diana at the local pub, but then again, Emily wasn't sure she could imagine Diana in a weathered booth, drinking a beer. The mental image was smokin' hot, though. Diana in jeans and flannel? Okay, she had to stop this line of thought, especially while she was standing in front of Diana's nephew.

"Definitely come, Carter," Emily said. "We'll have a lot of fun."

THE FOLLOWING EVENING, Emily found herself sitting next to Alex at a booth in Maude's Tavern, with Drew and Carter across from her. Frankie hadn't been able to make it tonight...or so she said. Frankie rarely joined them at trivia night, but it had left them with an open spot on their team, which Carter had filled.

"Did you graduate this year?" Emily asked while they waited for their burgers. She was curious to get to know him. He seemed a lot more laid-back than Diana, but there was something hesitant about him too, like maybe he hadn't quite adjusted to life after college.

At her question, Carter dropped his gaze to the beer in front of him. "I, um, didn't graduate. I'm taking some time off to rethink my options."

"Good for you," Drew said. "We're so young when we pick our majors. It's so easy to get stuck in the wrong track before we're old enough to figure out what we actually want to do with our lives. I have a biology degree I'll probably never use now that I'm working as an electrician. But hey, I finally found something I'm good at and that I enjoy."

"Yeah...that's...that's it exactly." Carter nodded, as animated now as he'd been subdued before. "I let my dad push me into an engineering track when I was a teen. We have, I mean...my family owns Devlin Hotels, so it was always a given that I'd work there too, and my dad thought this would be a good fit for me, but it wasn't. I was terrible at it, and the further I got into college, the more I realized how miserable I was."

"Sounds like you needed a break to figure things out," Alex said.

"Well, my dad thinks I'm a total failure." He ducked his head again. "He kicked me out of the house. I mean, things had already been strained between us, but this was the final straw, I guess." He looked simultaneously devastated and also like someone who'd finally found a friend to vent to about something that had been weighing on his mind for a long time.

"That's tough." Emily's heart went out to him.

Carter took a big swallow of his beer. "Yeah."

"So you're working for your aunt while you figure things out?" Emily asked.

He nodded. "Living with her too. She basically saved my ass after my parents threw me out. It turns out that it's a lot harder to find an affordable apartment in Boston than I thought, and there aren't many good paying jobs for college dropouts."

Emily's heart filled with warmth to know that Diana had been there for him when his parents hadn't. Emily had spent a lot of time with Carter today while he got the new system up and running, and she had noticed the easy rapport between him and Diana. She seemed softer around him, almost maternal, a side Emily wouldn't have suspected Diana had.

"It's hard. I hear you." Alex gave him a sympathetic look. "I have a degree in culinary arts, but I work in my girl-friend's gift shop. My situation is sort of the opposite of yours, though. I always wanted to be a chef, and somehow I just never made it happen."

"Being an adult is hard," Carter said with such a dramatic sigh that the whole table burst out laughing.

"Well, I'm glad you've got a job with your aunt for now," Drew said. "You'll figure the rest out. That was the biggest thing I realized after I graduated last year. Like, there's so much pressure to decide your career when you're eighteen, but really, you've got your whole life to figure it out. People change careers all the time."

"That's so true," Emily agreed.

Their burgers arrived, and they chatted about lighter topics while they ate. This weekend, they were all going apple picking at Alex's parents' orchard, and Carter agreed to come too. Emily hoped he could convince Diana to join them. She kept wondering what it might have been like if Diana were here at the pub tonight. Would she have had a good time? Would it have been anything like the time she and Emily shared drinks at the Beaumont?

Talia, Tom, and Maddie were in the next booth and kept leaning over the seat backs to exchange conversation. The whole thing was loud and chaotic and everything Emily loved about her Thursday night tradition.

"Five minutes until trivia begins," Megan the bartender called. "Team captains, see me for a scorecard."

"Any good at trivia?" Drew asked Carter, whose eyes rounded at being put on the spot. "Because we'd really like to kick those guys' asses tonight." He jabbed an elbow toward the booth behind them.

"I heard that," Tom called, "and you haven't got a chance. We're unbeatable."

"Humble too," Alex called, but she was grinning.

Emily went to get a scorecard from Megan, but as she slid back into her booth, she paused before writing their team name at the top. "Uh..." She glanced at Carter. "We're usually Team Gay All Day, because...well, the Adventurers is a queer group, but, um...we could use a different name tonight if it makes you more comfortable?"

Carter did his best impression of a deer in headlights, and Emily wasn't sure how to read his expression. Honestly, she had no idea of his sexuality. Surely he wasn't homophobic, not with how close he and Diana seemed to be, but not every young straight guy wanted to be on a trivia team called Gay All Day.

They sat in a moment of awkward silence while Emily tried to think of a less flamboyant team name. Then Carter cleared his throat. His neck had gone a bit splotchy. "Um, that's fine. The team name, um, applies to me too, so…"

Something about the way he said it made Emily think he hadn't come out to many people yet, that this was a big deal for him. That Emily's and her friends' reactions might be a formative part of his coming out experience. She broke into a huge grin just as Drew slapped him on the shoulder, saying, "Right on! I had a hunch when I invited you to join us tonight."

Carter's blush had spread across his cheeks now, but he was grinning at the reception to his news, looking almost giddy. Suddenly, Emily remembered that he'd said things were strained between him and his parents even before they kicked him out, and she could only hope that didn't have anything to do with him being gay.

Thank God he had Diana.

"Between these two booths, we have all the letters in LGBTQ," Emily told him. "So you're in good company here with us."

"Cool," Carter said, his voice hoarse with emotion. "That's really cool."

"Did I hear you mentioning letters?" Tom called over the seat.

"Officially welcoming Carter into the group," she called back.

Tom's face appeared over the seat. "Oh yeah? You're one of us?"

"Yeah." Carter smiled at him, confidence growing by the minute. "I'm gay."

"Pansexual trans guy here." Tom gestured to himself. He pulled out his phone, and Emily knew without asking what he was going to show Carter. It was a photo from last year's Burlington Pride. The five of them had their arms around each other, wearing matching rainbow tie-dye shirts. Alex's shirt was emblazoned with a big L, then Drew with G, Emily with B, Tom with T, and Talia wearing Q. Emily had a framed copy at home. She was pretty sure they all did.

"I love that." Carter was beaming now. "We didn't have anything like that at my college. This is...awesome."

"You're welcome to join us next year," Emily said. "We can always use two Gs."

"When I'm around, we have two Bs," Maddie said.

"And my girlfriend Frankie makes two Ls," Alex added.

"I'm only here for a few days, but maybe I can visit again," Carter said. "I'd love to have more queer friends."

"You're welcome any time," Alex told him warmly. "We'd love to have you."

"All right, folks," Megan's voice echoed through the bar, amplified by her microphone. "It's trivia time. We've got five teams playing tonight, so it should be a lot of fun. Our first category is geography. Everyone ready?"

A round of cheers went up. Based on the exuberant energy in her booth, Emily thought Team Gay All Day might actually have a shot at winning.

FIFTEEN

Diana paced the cabin. Why wasn't Carter home yet? Maybe she should have gone to trivia night. It didn't sound like her scene. The very thought of people shouting trivia questions through a crowded bar made her anxiety spike, not to mention her discomfort around Emily's group of friends. By now, they probably knew she knew they knew, and...she didn't like any of it. But she liked Emily, no matter how much she wished she didn't.

Now, Diana just wanted Carter to come home. It was a little after ten, which probably wasn't late for a twenty-one-year-old, but it was bordering on late for her on a work night. Not that she'd fall asleep any time soon, even if she tried. Something about Vermont didn't agree with her once the lights were out. She had yet to achieve an eight-hour night here.

She fought the urge to text Carter, knowing the true cause of her discomfort had little to do with him being out past ten. It was the thought of him being out with Emily and her friends that was driving her crazy. Apparently, somewhere deep down, she wished she were there with them. Maybe she liked the thought of snuggling up to Emily in a booth at the bar, no matter how loud and chaotic their surroundings.

She was good at trivia too, dammit.

Diana paced to the back window, staring into the black void behind the cabin. What if Carter had gotten turned around on the roads after dark? There were so many spots without cell service. What if his GPS had lost signal and he'd made a wrong turn? These rural roads all looked the same after dark. Had he been drinking? Surely he knew better than to drink and drive, but as his aunt, she'd never actually had that conversation with him.

She should have gone to trivia night.

Gravel crunched outside, and as she spun to face the front door, she saw headlights approaching the cabin. *Thank God.*

A car door slammed. She heard muffled voices and laughter, and then Carter was coming through the front door as the car outside pulled back onto the road. Who had driven him home?

"Hey, Aunt DD," he called as he walked into the living room and plopped on the couch. "Trivia night was so much fun! You should have come."

"Oh yeah?" She sat in the chair across from him, purposefully relaxing her posture so as not to give away how anxious she'd been while she waited for him. "Did you win?"

"Nope," Carter said, not sounding the least bit disappointed. "Team Rainbow Revolution kicked our asses... that's Tom, Maddie, and Talia. I was teamed with Drew, Emily, and Alex. We came in third."

"I'm glad it was fun." She studied him. He did look

happy. Lighter, maybe. Did he not have friends at school? "Who drove you home?"

"Tom and Maddie. Tom doesn't drink, and he was worried that I'd had three beers, even though they were spread out over several hours, so I'm totally fine, but..." He shrugged.

Diana's estimation of Tom went way up. "I agree with Tom. Better safe than sorry when it comes to driving after drinking. You can always call me too, if you need a ride, you know."

He shrugged again. "Or Uber."

"I actually wonder how reliable that is up here, but in Boston, yes."

"Right?" Carter laughed. "Drew said you can't even get food delivered in Crescent Falls. There's like one place that will deliver, and only if you live within a few miles of downtown, which we definitely don't."

"I do miss the conveniences of Boston," she agreed.

"Did...did you know they're a queer group?" Carter attempted nonchalance, but there was an urgency in his tone that gave away how important this discovery had been for him.

"Yes, I did know that."

"I had no idea, and like...I've never hung out with so many queer people before. That was exactly what I wanted to find at college! But Dad sent me to Royce, where all the guys were obsessed with girls and golf and impressing their parents. If there were any other gay people there, I never met them."

"I'm sorry." Diana's heart went out to him, but this was another thing they had in common. Most of the family had attended Royce University, which was as preppy as its name suggested. The students were primarily wealthy, white, and at least pretending to be straight. "I sympathize completely. In fact, I didn't even dare come out until after college."

"I really hate our family sometimes." Carter looked down at his lap.

She let out a surprised laugh, which sounded a lot more bitter than she had anticipated. "Yeah, I know that feeling too."

"Anyway, the Adventurers are really cool, and they said I'm welcome to hang out with them anytime. I'm going apple picking with them this weekend. They said they'd invited you too?"

Diana straightened, feeling that tug of longing in her chest again. Apparently, she *wanted* to go apple picking. Or maybe she just wanted an excuse to see Emily outside work. This could be a good opportunity for her to make local connections as the new owner of the inn, though. Yes, that was the reason she should attend. "They did."

"So, are you going?" he asked.

She was almost afraid to meet his gaze, afraid of what she'd see. Did he want his aunt to tag along, or would he rather hang out with his new friends without her? But when she finally looked into his eyes, his expression was hopeful. She exhaled. "Yeah. I'll go."

And so, on Saturday, Diana and Carter joined the Adventurers to go apple picking. She stood near the entrance, gazing out over rows of apple trees that spread as far as she could see, with the mountains as a backdrop. It was lovely.

In front of her, Emily, Alex, and Talia giggled as they posed for silly photos behind a panel that had been painted to look like cows grazing in a field, with cutouts for their faces. Emily stuck her face through the opening for the baby cow, laughing, as the rest of the group snapped pictures. When they'd finished, Carter, Drew, and Tom took a turn behind the display. Diana had declined to join them, but now she felt...not excluded since it had been her choice not to participate, but somehow she still felt a little bit left out.

Turning, she approached an older couple who stood by the barn, greeting customers. She assumed these were Alexis's parents, the owners of the orchard. "Mr. and Mrs. Bell?"

"Yes," the woman replied with a warm smile. "Are you a friend of Alex's?"

"I've only just met her, actually. I'm sort of tagging along with the adventure group today," Diana explained. "I'm the new owner of the Inn at Crescent Falls. Diana Devlin." She held out a hand, which Alex's mother took readily.

"It's so nice to meet you, Diana. I'm Kathryn, and this is my husband, Doug."

"Great to meet you both," Diana said as she shook their hands. "I've only been here a few weeks, but I'm already so charmed by Crescent Falls." It wasn't just a line either. There was something unexpectedly appealing about this town, despite her inability to sleep here. Diana spent a few minutes chatting with Kathryn and Doug before Emily came to get her.

They all took bags from a table in front of the barn and set out to pick some apples. Each row of the orchard was labeled with what kind of apple tree grew there, and Diana was surprised to realize how few apple varieties she recognized.

"What kind do you recommend?" she asked Emily.

"That depends. Do you like sweet or tart apples?"

"Oh, tart, I think."

Emily nodded. "You'd probably like McIntosh. They're

tart and delicious. You might like the Cortlands too, although they're a little sweeter."

"I do like McIntosh," Diana said. "I've had them from the grocery store."

Emily grinned. "Wait until you try one fresh from the tree. You won't believe how much better it tastes. Come on." She led the way down a path between trees toward a different section of the orchard, populated by larger trees with knobby branches. Emily carefully considered the tree in front of her before plucking a large, red-and-green apple from a lower branch. "See?"

Diana followed her example and soon had a handful of ripe apples in her bag. When she looked over to see how Emily was doing, she found Emily at the other end of the row, holding a squealing toddler. Diana had been introduced to the little girl, Talia's daughter Colette, when they first arrived at the orchard.

Emily twirled Colette, causing another squeal of laughter. Talia and her wife, Chantal, stood nearby, taking photos. Alex, Tom, and Maddie were gathered at the tree beside them, while Carter and Drew walked off together toward another part of the orchard.

Diana turned away, clenching her jaw. She'd never been very good at making friends. She spotted an apple overhead that was perfectly round and red, one of the prettiest she'd seen yet, but when she reached up, it was a few inches past her grasp. That seemed to be the theme of her morning.

"Need a hand?"

Diana turned to find a petite blonde woman beside her, holding up what almost looked like a lacrosse stick. The woman used the net at the end of the stick to snag the apple Diana had been trying to reach, then handed it to her.

"Thank you so much. I'm Diana Devlin, by the way, the new owner of the Inn at Crescent Falls." She extended a hand.

The woman took it and shook. She was a little older than Diana, late forties maybe, and refined, as if she came from money. She was the type of woman Diana would have expected to meet at one of her parents' parties, not in an apple orchard in Vermont. "Jacqueline Norwood."

"Nice to meet you, Jacqueline."

"You too, Diana." With a polite wave, Jacqueline continued down the path.

Why is that name familiar...?

Diana had just figured it out when Emily reappeared at her side, cheeks flushed from the cool mountain air.

"Oh my God, do you know who you were just talking to?" she whispered.

"Yes. She introduced herself," Diana said. "She hardly seems like the villain you made her out to be."

Emily rolled her eyes. "Not a villain, just a stuck-up snob."

Diana bristled, certain she'd been described that way a time or two herself. "She seemed nice enough, even helped me reach an apple. Maybe people are judging her harshly because she's an outsider?" *Like me?*

Emily sighed. "It's possible, although I've heard so many stories, it's hard not to think at least some of them are true. Anyway, let's try that tree over there. It looks like it's bursting with ripe apples."

OH NO. *No no no...* The word scrolled on repeat in Diana's brain as her alarm went off on Monday morning.

She swallowed, whimpering at the sharp pain in her throat. Her nose was congested. There was a deep ache in her bones and a shivery sensitivity on her skin that suggested a fever.

She didn't have time to be sick. *For fuck's sake.* She'd felt a little achy and rundown as she was getting ready for bed last night but had hoped she would sleep it off...not that she'd slept well enough to give her immune system a fighting chance.

Groaning, Diana slid out of bed and wrapped herself in her warmest robe. She did what she could to freshen herself up in the bathroom and then shuffled toward the kitchen. Her joints hurt. Her head hurt. Her throat hurt. She *hated* being sick, dammit. She'd never had the time or patience to take a sick day, but she couldn't go to the inn like this. She was probably contagious, not to mention she felt like absolute shit.

Speaking of contagious...

She rummaged through the pantry until she came up with the box of Covid tests she always kept handy. Holding back a sneeze, she swabbed her nose and started the test, then looked around for anything she had on hand that might help with her symptoms. The owner of the rental cabin had left her an assortment of teas, which might feel good on her sore throat. And she had ibuprofen, which would help with her fever.

Beyond that, she was screwed. She already knew that food and grocery delivery services were nonexistent here in rural Vermont, since she'd tried to coordinate deliveries for herself to help with her busy schedule. Now, she'd have to either suck it up and manage with what she had on hand or rally the energy to go out later. Hopefully she could at least schedule curbside pickup.

She eyed the bag of apples on the counter. It was practically the only food she had in the house, and well, maybe that saying about an apple a day keeping the doctor away had some merit. Right now, she wasn't the least bit hungry, though.

She hovered near the kitchen counter until the test revealed a negative result, and then she exhaled with relief. Not Covid. This was probably just a nasty cold, then, but she'd take another test later to be sure. It seemed a bit early in the year for the flu, but maybe flu season started earlier this far north.

Carter had left yesterday afternoon, but they'd spent most of the weekend together. She should check in with him and ask if he was sick too. Hopefully she hadn't given him whatever she had. *Ugh.* She rubbed a hand over her aching forehead. Every inch of her hurt, from her scalp to her toes. She really, *really* hated being sick.

Worse, she'd likely brought this on herself. She'd been running around Vermont for almost a month with her anxiety levels sky-high and barely sleeping. She'd run herself into the ground, and it had affected her usually robust immune system. It wasn't the first time this had happened.

Grumbling with annoyance at herself, she washed down two ibuprofen with a glass of water—wincing every time she swallowed from the pain in her throat—and made the executive decision to work from home. Given the foggy state of her brain, she couldn't remember what she was supposed to do at the inn today anyway.

She would be more productive here, and she could keep from spreading her germs too. She eyed her laptop grumpily. It was only seven. Surely she could take a nap before she got to work. Decision made, Diana crawled back into bed.

————

UNKNOWN

Hi this is Carter

Got ur # from Drew

EMILY STARED at the text messages in surprise. Why in the world was Diana's nephew texting her?

Hey! What's up?

CARTER DEVLIN

I'm worried about my aunt

She's sick w flu or something, she doesn't sound good and idk if she's got medicine or food at the rental house

She'll probably kill me for this but I think someone should check on her and maybe drop off cold meds and soup or whatever

Consider it done!

I didn't even know she was sick – thanks for the heads-up!

Emily pressed a hand against her heart, hating to think of Diana all alone in that rental house while she was sick. Carter was a good egg, recruiting someone to drop off a care package for her. And...Emily was irrationally glad she could be the one to deliver it. When it came down to it, Emily cared about her, and she wanted to make sure she was okay.

Her gut said Diana wasn't good at looking after herself when she was sick. And while Emily didn't have much experience at caretaking, her grandmas had certainly fussed over her enough times while she was sick to give her a good idea of what Diana might need. Emily pulled up the website for the café on her phone and dialed their number.

"Hi, are you serving chicken noodle soup today?" she asked once the call had connected.

"Yep," the teen on the other end of the line responded. "Chicken noodle, harvest squash, and minestrone today."

"I'd like to order a large takeout container of the chicken noodle, the biggest size you have, and I'll take a container of the harvest squash too," Emily said. "Do you have fresh bread?"

"Yep," the teen said again. "We have loaves of French bread, whole or pre-sliced."

"I'll take two loaves, pre-sliced," Emily decided. Simplicity was key when you were sick. "Can I pick that up in forty-five minutes?" Because she had another stop to make on the way.

"Sure," the teen said. "Can I get a name for the order?"

"Emily Janssen."

"Got it. See you then."

"Thank you." Emily hung up, grabbed her favorite flannel to ward off the cool air, and headed for the grocery store to pick up some cold medicine and other supplies.

An hour later, she arrived at Diana's rental cabin, loaded down with shopping bags. Diana's car was in the driveway, which was a relief. Emily knocked, waited a few moments, and knocked again. She had both hot and cold items with her that couldn't be left on the front porch, so hopefully Diana wasn't sleeping or in the shower.

Emily peeked through the front window, but the cabin was dark and quiet inside. Her arms were beginning to ache from all the bags. Emily knocked again, louder this time, and then—in case Diana thought it was a salesperson at her door and was ignoring her until she went away—she called out, "Diana? It's me, Emily."

That did the trick. She saw movement in the living room and then Diana approached the door, wrapped in a thick, rose-colored robe. Emily held up the bags so Diana could see them.

Diana opened the door, and *oh boy*, she really did look sick. Her cheeks were flushed with fever, but behind it, she was pale. Her hair was unkempt, her eyes red and watery. Before either of them could say anything, Diana turned to the side, covered her face in the crook of her elbow, and released a rattling cough.

Emily's heart clenched. It brought out something unexpectedly protective in her to see Diana this way. "Hi. Carter told me you're sick, so I brought some supplies."

"Thank you," Diana said, her voice hoarse. "That was... really nice of you." The look she gave Emily was almost shy and definitely embarrassed. "I can't believe Carter called you."

"I'm glad he did. You don't look like you're in any shape to go shopping."

"I'm not," Diana admitted. She already seemed droopier than she had when she first opened the door, as if her energy was waning. "I hate to put you out, though, especially on your day off."

"That's what friends are for," Emily told her with a bright smile. "Now, why don't you get back to the couch, and I'll fix you a bowl of soup? It's hot from the café."

"That sounds—" Diana turned her head to cough again. "I really appreciate you bringing me soup, but I don't want to get you sick. You should probably just leave it here on the porch."

"Nonsense. Here, I've got a mask." Emily put down her bags and pulled out the mask she always kept in her purse. She put it on and then gestured for Diana to go back inside. "Don't worry about me. Just let me take care of you for a few minutes, okay?"

Diana crossed her arms over her chest. "I don't think—"

"Please?"

Diana stared at her for a moment, seemingly at a loss for words, and then she turned and led the way inside, her movements stiff and sluggish.

Emily brought her bags to the kitchen. First things first, she needed to get the cold items into the freezer. "I brought popsicles," she told Diana. "They'll feel great on your throat later."

"Thank you," Diana responded, coughing. She stood awkwardly in the living room, still looking like she wanted Emily to leave. Had no one cared for her when she was sick before?

"Have you taken any medicine? I brought Dayquil and Nyquil and also cough drops."

Diana exhaled in what looked like relief. "Dayquil sounds wonderful. I had some ibuprofen when I woke up, but I didn't have anything else here to take."

"One dose of Dayquil, coming right up. You go sit." Emily filled the little cup that came with the bottle and brought it to Diana, who gulped it gratefully. Now that Emily was standing over her, she saw that Diana was shivering. Her hand trembled where it held the cup.

"Thank you," Diana whispered as she handed the cup back, then drew her robe tighter around herself.

"No problem. How does chicken noodle soup sound? I also have harvest squash."

Diana hugged herself, looking absolutely miserable, but

when she looked up at Emily, there was gratitude in her eyes. "That sounds good, actually. I haven't eaten today. Either is fine."

Emily's heart melted on the spot. If she hadn't been so sure Diana would hate it—and that she was probably super germy—Emily would have given her a big hug, because Diana sure as hell looked like she needed one. "You got it."

Emily settled for giving her hand a quick squeeze before she returned to the kitchen. She noticed two Covid tests sitting on the counter, both negative. Thank goodness for that, at least. Chicken noodle was a staple when you were sick for a reason, she decided. After rummaging through the cabinets to find what she needed, she fixed Diana a bowl of soup and wrapped a napkin around several slices of bread, then brought it all to the couch.

"Mm. Thank you." Diana took the soup gratefully, balancing the bowl on her lap. She took a spoonful, wincing as she swallowed. Her nose was running, and she sniffed ineffectively.

Emily went to the kitchen for the tissues she'd bought. As she walked back to the living room, she swept her gaze around the interior of the cabin. "I've driven past this place before, but I've never been inside. It's so cozy. Does the owner expect you to care for their plants or what?" Because there were several well-tended houseplants in the windows, more than she would expect to find in a rental property. She placed the box of tissues on the table in front of Diana.

"They're mine," Diana told her, pausing to cover another cough. "I brought them with me."

"Oh, that's so cool." Emily looked at the meticulously tended plants with fresh eyes, imagining Diana wandering about the cabin, watering and caring for them. They meant enough to her that she'd brought them with her from

Boston, and that was…well, it was adorable, and it made Emily feel all warm inside. "You must really love plants, huh?"

Diana nodded. "I find it calming, having them around."

Interesting. "I love that. Unfortunately, I have a black thumb. I can't seem to keep anything alive."

"Ironic, given how much you love to paint them. You probably aren't giving them the proper care." Diana sounded like hell. Looked like it too, but her voice was as authoritative as ever. "You need to look up the care requirements for each plant—what kind of soil they prefer, if they need direct sunlight, how often to water them, that kind of thing. If you spend a minute getting to know them, they'll fare a lot better."

Emily thought that advice was probably applicable to more than just plants, and right now, she was *loving* this insight into who Diana was outside the office. "Maybe sometime you could recommend a good plant for me to start with?"

Diana nodded. "Sure. Spider plants are always a good bet, but let me think about it."

"Great."

They kept talking while Diana ate. Well, mostly Emily kept the conversation going. Diana was putting on a brave face, but she obviously felt awful. Her cheeks were still flushed, but her eyes looked a little less fever bright now, as the medication started to kick in. Her hands shook, and she couldn't go more than a few minutes at a time without coughing.

When she'd finished her soup, Emily took the bowl from her. "Now, why don't you go take a shower while I finish putting things away? Trust me, you'll feel *so* much better after."

Diana frowned, as if the effort of getting off the couch required more energy than she had at the moment.

"Go on." Emily made a shooing motion with her free hand. She'd had the flu last winter, and she remembered how much she'd dreaded showering every time until she was in it. "Once you've been in the steam for a few minutes, blow your nose. The shower will loosen everything up, and you'll be able to clear out your sinuses enough to get a good nap after."

"Really?" Diana perked up at that. "I'd love a good nap."

"Trust me. The steam will work wonders."

"Okay." She stood, looking at Emily. "Are you heading out then?"

"I'll stick around until you're settled if that's okay?" *Please don't kick me out.* Emily was surprised to realize she really, really wanted to stay.

"Okay," Diana agreed quietly.

Emily waited until she heard the distant sound of the shower, and then she went into the kitchen to finish putting away the supplies she'd brought. She had also intended to clean up any dirty dishes that Diana hadn't felt up to, but the kitchen was spotless.

Emily put the leftover soup in the fridge, along with a selection of sports drinks. Her grandmas always insisted Emily drink those when she was sick to maintain her electrolytes. She took one bottle out of the pack and brought it to the living room, placing it on the coffee table next to the bag of cough drops and the tissues.

Then her curiosity got the better of her and she wandered the room, checking out Diana's plants. What did it say about her that she'd brought plants with her from Boston? Emily wasn't sure, but she loved it regardless.

Unsurprisingly, Diana's plants were in excellent health. Emily didn't see so much as a dead leaf anywhere. She was particularly drawn to a plant in the back window with pink spots on its leaves. Emily snapped a quick picture of it with her phone. Maybe she'd paint it later. She could always use new inspiration for her art, and plants were her signature.

Actually, she'd been a little low on inspiration lately. She lived in such a beautiful location in a beautiful state, and yet...she'd been painting the same flowers and vistas her whole life. She needed something new to inspire her.

As she took more photos of Diana's plants, Emily started envisioning a set of stickers and prints highlighting various houseplants. After she'd looked at all the plants, she sat in the chair next to the couch and messed around on her phone until Diana returned from the shower.

"You're still here," Diana murmured as she walked into the living room. She had on purple plaid flannel pajamas that looked super warm and cozy, her hair wet and wavy around her face. Her cheeks were pale, and her eyes were clearer than they had been before her shower. The medication seemed to have kicked in and lowered her fever.

"I was just admiring your plants. I took some pictures for painting inspiration if that's okay?"

Diana nodded, a soft smile curving her lips. She settled on the couch, tucking her feet under herself. "Of course. I can't wait to see what you paint."

"This one's my favorite." She held up her phone, showing Diana a picture of the pink-spotted plant.

"I like that one too. It's called a polka dot plant. Well, it has a scientific name, but I can't remember it right now." She rubbed a hand over her forehead.

"Feeling any better?"

"Much," Diana told her. "I would have dragged myself

to the grocery store at some point, but your delivery has been a lifesaver. I really appreciate it."

"My pleasure. It must be hard to get sick when you're away from home, without your things and the usual people you'd call on."

"Especially up here in rural Vermont, where I can't just use one of my apps to arrange a delivery." Diana's gaze landed on the cough drops and sports drink Emily had left for her on the coffee table. "Oh, you really *are* a lifesaver. My throat feels like I swallowed glass, and I'm probably dehydrated too."

"Drink up. My grandmas swear by sports drinks to help get over a cold or flu. That and homemade chicken noodle soup."

"Both of which I now have, thanks to you." Diana reached for the bottle, which contained a bright blue liquid. She took a long drink, then unwrapped a cough drop and pulled the throw blanket from the back of the couch around herself.

"And thanks to Carter for letting me know."

Diana's expression grew fond. "Yes. I called him this morning to see if he was having any symptoms since we'd spent the weekend together, but he's still healthy, thank goodness."

"I'm glad."

Diana was curled up against the end of the couch now, her eyes starting to droop.

"I should probably let you rest," Emily said reluctantly. She didn't want to leave, but Diana looked so much more comfortable now, and she didn't want to overstay her welcome.

"I think I'm going to try to take that nap you suggested," Diana said hoarsely. "The cough drop is helping."

"Good." Emily stood and walked toward the front door. "I put the rest of the soup in your fridge, plus a bunch of sports drinks. And don't forget about the popsicles."

"I won't. Thank you, Emily."

Emily hesitated by the front door, wishing they were close enough that she could stay and care for Diana until she was feeling better. "If you need anything else, just call or text me, okay? Everyone needs a little caretaking when they're sick, and I...I like you. A lot. So let me help if I can. Please?"

Diana swallowed, her expression hard to read. She opened her mouth, then closed it again, her eyes never leaving Emily's.

Please ask me to stay.

But Diana only smiled, her eyes soft, almost affectionate. Finally, she nodded.

"Okay, then. Bye, Diana. Hope you feel better soon."

And with that, Emily slipped out the door.

SIXTEEN

I like you. A lot.

Those words had lived rent free in Diana's brain since Emily showed up on Monday with enough provisions to see Diana through her illness. The truth was, she liked Emily a lot too. She liked Emily so much more than a one-night stand or even a friend, but even if she wanted to explore the possibility of a relationship with her—which she could admit to herself that she definitely did—she didn't know if Emily felt the same way.

She *did* know Emily would never leave Crescent Falls, and Diana would never leave Boston, so the whole thing felt doomed anyway. If Diana could just keep her feelings to herself, soon enough she'd be back at home, far away from Emily and all the inconvenient things she made Diana want: affection, friendship, a hand to hold...not to mention the scorching hot sex.

By Wednesday, Diana felt well enough to go outside for a short walk. Her fever had subsided, and she was much less congested today. The inn was running smoothly without her, which boded well for its success after she went home.

Next week, she would start interviewing candidates for the manager's position. Once that person was hired and trained, Diana would return to Boston, hopefully by the end of October.

Except a little part of her dreaded leaving Vermont. Because Emily liked her. A lot. And every time Diana replayed those words in her head, she felt a warm flutter in the vicinity of her heart. She'd been so sure Emily wanted her to leave, that Diana was the only one catching feelings, and now she had to wonder...what exactly did Emily mean when she said she liked her?

Surely she was just talking about friendship. Even that sounded wonderful. Diana could use a friend. She longed to be part of the adventure group. How had Carter jumped into it so easily? Maybe Diana would have too if she'd gone to trivia night.

She was driving herself crazy cooped up at home, thinking about Emily.

After her walk, Diana called her psychiatrist to set up a virtual appointment. Getting sick had been a wake-up call. Obviously, she had reached the point where she needed help managing her anxiety. It was starting to control her life the way it had in her twenties, and it was probably time to go back on medication, at least temporarily.

With that accomplished, Diana was still feeling restless, so she decided to take a drive to the local garden store. She wanted to buy Emily a plant as a thank-you. It seemed like the perfect gift after Emily had been so interested in Diana's plants. She wasn't sure yet what she'd choose for her, definitely something bright and colorful, something that reflected Emily's personality and might help inspire her art.

When she got to the garden center, Diana put on a

mask to be safe, although she was pretty sure the virus had left her system. Today, she was just tired and had a lingering cough. As she wandered through the greenhouse, Diana passed over the rows of colorful mums and other fall blooms. She was looking for something Emily could enjoy all year long.

Her gaze caught on a selection of gerbera daisies, and right away, she knew she'd found Emily's first plant. Gerbera daisies were relatively easy to care for and extremely colorful. Diana spent a minute researching them on her phone to know what kind of soil to purchase and what tips to give Emily for their care.

Then she perused the available daisies. Her attention focused on a smaller plant in the middle of the display with bright orange petals that faded to yellow as they approached the eye of the plant. Its coloring reminded her of the sunset, and she'd noticed that Emily favored those colors in her clothing and her art.

Diana fetched a rolling cart for her purchases, then placed the daisy plant on it, followed by a bag of potting soil and a red ceramic pot that would be the perfect finishing touch. She also got a bottle of plant fertilizer for Emily.

Satisfied with her purchases, Diana went home. She repotted the plant, pleased with the way it looked in the red pot. It was too bright for her taste, but she thought it suited Emily perfectly. And then, exhausted but satisfied, Diana went to bed early.

The next morning, she showered and dressed for work, relieved to feel mostly back to normal except for some lingering fatigue. She placed the cheerful potted daisy inside a box and set it on the floor of her car so it would stay put during the drive.

Instead of parking in the staff lot behind the inn, she

took the little road that led to Emily's cabin. She'd never actually seen Emily's home up close, only from a distance, as it wasn't included in the sale with the rest of the inn's grounds.

It was a small, white-paneled cottage with royal-blue shutters and an assortment of ceramic pumpkins on the front porch, all painted with brightly colored flowers. Diana smiled at the sight, wondering if Emily sold her painted pumpkins. She wouldn't mind having one for her front steps back in Boston.

The cottage was situated in the middle of a sizable grassy yard that sloped downhill until the forest took over. Emily didn't have a view of the mountains here like the rolling vista behind the inn, but she did have privacy, and with the grassy yard surrounding the cottage, it felt less closed in than Diana's rental. Sometimes she felt like her cabin was about to be swallowed by the forest, whereas this cottage felt open and inviting.

Diana parked beside Emily's SUV. After retrieving the plant, she walked to the front door and knocked. While she waited, she admired Emily's painted ceramic pumpkins up close. Her favorite was one of the smaller pumpkins, covered in a variety of maroon, lavender, and white flowers.

The door opened to reveal a smiling Emily. "Diana? This is a surprise."

"A thank-you for your help when I was sick, and also because you said you wanted a plant." She held out the pot of daisies.

Emily gasped, clapping her hands in delight. "Oh, they're beautiful! I love daisies. Thank you so much." She stepped back, motioning for Diana to follow her into the house.

"I don't want to intrude if you're busy," Diana hedged,

because she wasn't entirely sure it was wise for her to go inside Emily's house. Although Emily seemed to have moved past her hurt feelings, this felt more personal than anything they'd shared since Diana bought the inn.

"You're not intruding. I was about to have a cup of tea and sit on the back porch with my sparrow."

"Your...sparrow? As in, a bird?"

Emily grinned. "Yep. I found him on the hill behind the inn this spring. He'd been attacked by some kind of animal, but the local wildlife rescue couldn't take him because of an avian flu outbreak, so I nursed him back to health myself."

Somehow this didn't surprise Diana in the least. "Are you going to keep him, then?"

"He can't be re-released because his balance is wonky from his injuries. You'll see when you meet him." Emily took the pot from Diana and set it on the coffee table in front of her sofa. "I want them here where I can look at them every day. So pretty." She smiled at the pot of daisies. "Anyway, once the avian flu outbreak is under control, I'm still hoping to bring him to the sanctuary so he can have more room and other bird friends, but for now, he's my buddy."

"That's sweet."

"That's me." Emily led the way toward the kitchen. "What kind of tea do you like? I was going to have pumpkin spice."

"Is that caffeinated?" Diana asked.

"Yeah. It's flavored black tea."

"Perfect. I'll have that too. I'm still a little tired from being sick, so extra caffeine can't hurt before I head into work."

"Good thinking." Emily lifted a tea kettle from its

warming plate and filled two mugs with steaming water. She added a tea bag to each mug and handed one to Diana. "I've got sugar and honey too, if you want some, but I find this blend to be sweet enough on its own."

"I don't like overly sweet tea, so I'll skip the sugar."

Emily led the way toward the back of her house. "It's gorgeous outside this morning. I just love fall. Come and meet Jack."

"Jack Sparrow?" Diana couldn't fight her smile.

Emily snapped her fingers, looking pleased. "You got that quicker than most of my friends. Yes, Jack Sparrow. I left him out of his cage when I answered the door, so just watch out for him when you go onto the porch."

"You have a screened-in porch or does he just stay nearby?"

"It's screened. I wish I could let him fly outside, but he'd be such easy pickings for any predator." Emily held the door to the porch open, and a small brown bird flew straight toward her, chirping loudly, except he wasn't flying straight at all. He kind of swooped and spiraled as if he wasn't sure which way was up.

"Did he have a brain injury?"

"Something like that, I think." Emily cooed to the sparrow as he landed on her shoulder. "He's completely uncoordinated, but he seems happy, so I guess he'll still have a good life, especially if he gets to go live with the other nonreleasable birds at the sanctuary."

They sat in chairs that faced each other as Jack twittered and flapped around the porch. Diana gave her teabag a swirl and looked out at Emily's backyard. The trees were an enchanting mix of fall colors, yellow and orange and red mixed in with the green.

Emily blew on her tea. "Glad you're feeling better."

"Me too. It knocked me on my ass for a few days, that's for sure."

"'Tis the season for getting sick, unfortunately."

Diana stared into her tea. It smelled delicious, like pumpkin pie. "I've been under a lot of stress lately, probably took a toll on my immune system."

"Because of the new job?" Emily asked.

Diana nodded. "Among other things."

Emily was watching her closely now. She leaned forward in her seat. "Will you tell me what happened? Why you left Devlin Hotels?"

Diana felt her hackles going up, and she blew on her tea, making a concerted effort to push them back down. Emily deserved the truth, even if it was hard for Diana to speak it. "Shortly after you and I met back in June, I learned that my father had chosen my brother—not me—to replace him as CEO. Rather than see my career stall beneath him, I decided to branch out and start my own company."

"Oh damn." Emily sagged in her seat. "That really sucks. I'm sorry."

Diana shrugged stiffly. "It is what it is, but it's a bit of a sore subject for me, not something I enjoy talking about."

"I understand. Thank you for telling me." Emily's expression was remorseful. "I...I'm sorry for doubting you when you first bought the inn."

"You had every reason to doubt me. It's fine."

"Still." Emily took a tentative sip of her tea and grimaced. "Way too hot. I wish I had trusted my gut where you're concerned." Then her eyes went wide. "Wait, is Carter's dad the brother who got the CEO job?"

"Yes, he is." And she was glad Emily knew the truth

now, even if Diana was increasingly uncomfortable with the topic at hand. It was hard to share these things. Her parents would call it airing the family's dirty laundry, something they avoided at all costs. Diana wanted to do better, though. She wanted to *be* better.

She and Emily fell silent for a few minutes, sipping tentatively at their tea. It felt like a comfortable silence, though, at least to Diana. She was mesmerized by the brightly colored trees surrounding Emily's porch. Every gust of the mountain breeze sent yellow and red leaves swirling through the air. "I thought we had nice foliage in Massachusetts, but Vermont really takes it to a new level, hm?"

"That's what I hear. I've never lived anywhere else, so I'm spoiled with all the natural beauty around me. Hey, speaking of fall stuff, are you coming to the fall festival this weekend?"

"I wasn't planning to."

"Oh, please come. One of our friends from out of town is coming up for the weekend, so we're doing the fall festival on Saturday and a foliage hike to the falls on Sunday. The weather's supposed to be perfect. It could be a great chance for you to show your face around town if you want a work-related reason to go, plus it's just a lot of fun."

"Isn't the festival more geared toward families?" Diana couldn't imagine what a businesswoman like herself would do at a fall festival, nor did she think it was a good idea for her to hang out with Emily and her friends. She hadn't exactly fit in with them last time.

"Earlier in the day it is, but my friends and I go around dinnertime and stay late. That's when all the adult fun happens. Even Carter's coming!"

"I know. I can't believe he's driving back up for the weekend."

"Because he knows it's going to be fun. Come on, I'll make sure you have a good time. What do you say?" Emily's pleading face was her undoing.

Diana sighed. "Okay. I'll come."

THIS WAS A MISTAKE.

The grass beneath Diana's feet had been trampled flat. Food trucks were lined up to her left, their generators adding a diesel hum to the ambient sounds of the evening. A row of porta-potties stood to her right, and in the distance, she could just make out the green expanse of a cornfield. She was surrounded by families with children toting pumpkins and ice cream, shrieking as they chased each other over the grass.

This was not Diana's scene. Absolutely nothing here appealed to her in any way.

"Drew said they were meeting up by the Maple Madness truck," Carter said.

Diana pressed her lips together, wondering if he would be upset if she feigned a work emergency and bailed. It was six o'clock, and the festival was as loud and crowded as she'd feared. Already, she could feel her anxiety building. "Maybe I should—"

"Nope." Carter interrupted before she could get the words out. "I know what you're thinking, but this will be fun, Aunt DD. At least go say hi to the group and see how you feel afterward."

"Okay," she relented. Carter was right. She should at

least say hi to everyone before she made her excuses and left.

"I really want to try one of these maple creemees I've been hearing about. Or maybe an apple cider donut. Maybe both?" He grinned, motioning toward one of the trucks.

Diana looked toward the maple-themed food truck he had indicated, and her gaze landed on Emily, who stood beside the truck, wearing a flannel shirt in shades of orange and burgundy and matching, burgundy-colored jeans. She was laughing about something with Alexis, and Diana felt a punch of adrenaline in her stomach. Okay, so there was at least one thing at the festival that appealed to her.

Carter was already walking in that direction, so she fell into step behind him. She hadn't been sure what to wear and didn't want to ruin her running shoes if the field was muddy—they'd had some light rain yesterday, after all—so she'd worn black jeans, her thickest sweater, and the hiking boots she'd bought back in June for her ill-fated attempt to reach the summit of Crescent Peak.

Emily waved as they approached. "Hi, guys! So glad you came."

"My aunt is super skeptical right now, so you've got probably five minutes to convince her to stay," Carter joked.

Diana bristled to have her insecurities laid out like that. It made her sound snobbish. Diana didn't talk about her anxiety. She'd been raised to keep this kind of thing to herself, and while she was trying to do better, it was hard to break old habits...especially when she was already feeling anxious.

"Those burgers are calling my name. Catch you later." Carter jogged off to join Tom, Maddie, and Drew in line for one of the food trucks.

Emily turned to Diana, amusement twinkling in her eyes. "Why am I not surprised this isn't your scene?"

"Because you once saw me get lost on my way up a mountain?" Diana returned, surprised to feel her lips twitching with the urge to smile.

"You got an A for effort that day, though. Okay, lucky for you, I've been coming to this festival my whole life, so you have the absolute best guide for the evening. We're going to have fun. I promise."

Diana bit her lip. She rarely did things because they were fun. She sought out activities that were productive, or relaxing, or even pleasurable...like a one-night stand. But fun? She couldn't remember the last time she'd done something with that particular goal in mind.

Her gaze settled on a gaggle of children running by with half-melted ice cream cones in their hands. It wasn't that she didn't like children. She'd always been a doting aunt to her nephew, but if she could choose an enjoyable way to spend a Saturday evening, it didn't involve being surrounded by kids who'd had too much sugar and were shrieking at the top of their lungs. The noise prickled between her shoulder blades, increasing the tension there.

Emily tsked. "No judgments. Not yet. There's a reason we waited until six to come. The families have had their fun and will be leaving soon. The adult portion of the evening starts after dark."

"Really?" Diana hadn't imagined being here after dark. What could they possibly do here that late?

Emily nodded, hooking an arm through Diana's as she led her toward a purple food truck. "First, we're going to enjoy some amazing food and local cider. There's a live band starting at seven. Maybe some dancing?" Emily glanced at her, and Diana's pulse kicked at the thought of dancing with her out here under the stars. "And once you're a little tipsy, the real fun begins."

"Real fun?" Diana already felt tipsy from being this close to Emily.

"Mm-hmm. There's moonlight pumpkin picking, and if you're really feeling adventurous, my personal favorite: the haunted corn maze."

"Why would anyone want to go pumpkin picking in the dark?" Diana asked. It made no sense. The whole point of pumpkin picking was to choose one you liked the look of.

"Because it's fun," Emily told her, as if this made perfect sense. "We use flashlights, and someone inevitably gets spooked by a weird shadow, which honestly makes it even more fun. And in the morning, you get to see what your pumpkin actually looks like. I've gotten some really weird ones, and some really awesome ones."

"I don't need a pumpkin. The inn's already fully decorated for fall."

"But you should go moonlight pumpkin picking anyway, Diana, because it's *fun*." Emily smiled, looking so happy and carefree, Diana imagined she *would* have fun if she stayed with her for the evening, but was that a good idea? She was trying so damn hard to keep her attraction under wraps, and if she got tipsy and stumbled around a darkened pumpkin patch with Emily...well, she'd probably either end up kissing her or having a panic attack.

Before she could decide how to respond, they were in front of the purple food truck, which boasted the best Asian fusion cuisine in Vermont. Ten minutes later, Diana had a curry bowl that smelled delicious, while Emily had gone with stir-fry. Then they were on their way to the next truck, where they each got a hard cider.

Emily led her to a picnic table near what Diana now

saw was a stage where a band was currently setting up. Tom, Maddie, and Carter were already at the table, burgers and drinks in hand. Carter was laughing at something on Tom's cell phone, and Diana's chest warmed to see him making friends and looking so happy.

He was undeniably more confident and energized since he dropped out of college. Maybe he really *had* needed a change. Maybe none of the adults in his life had realized how unhappy he was. She could look back now and see the signs of strain, but she hadn't realized how serious it was at the time.

"He looks happy, huh?" Emily said, obviously having noticed where Diana's attention had drifted.

"He does." She sat next to Emily, placing her food and drink on the table.

"He seems to fit right in here," Emily commented before taking a sip of her cider. "Too bad he's not staying longer."

"I'm sure he agrees with you," Diana said. "He's completely taken with Crescent Falls."

"Unlike you." Emily shot her a look before taking a bite of her stir-fry.

"That's not fair." Diana sipped her cider. It was just a little bit tart, but bursting with rich apple flavor, and she felt the warmth of alcohol as she swallowed. Delicious. "There's a lot I like about Vermont, but there's a lot I miss while I'm here too. I'm a city girl at heart."

"I'm going to try to change your opinion tonight." She gave her a smile so sunny, Diana was already convinced, at least where Emily was concerned.

"You're welcome to try," she responded.

"Challenge accepted." Emily's smile turned slightly naughty then, and it made Diana's heart beat so fast, she felt flushed under her sweater.

Drew sat across from them. "Em, is Alex coming tonight?"

Emily nodded. "She and Frankie will be here after they close the store at seven."

"Cool." Drew popped open the paper container he'd brought with him, revealing a cheeseburger and fries. "Hi, Diana."

"Hi, Drew."

Talia and a brunette Diana didn't recognize joined them at the table. "Hi, guys. Diana, this is Margo. She's visiting from Chicago. Margo, Diana's the new owner of the inn."

"I've heard all about you. Nice to meet you, Diana." Margo extended a hand, her expression warm and friendly. "Alex and I were college roommates, so she keeps me up to date with what's going on in town."

"Ah." Diana shook her hand. "Nice to meet you, Margo."

Emily turned to Talia. "Ready to terrify us?"

What in the world did that mean?

At Diana's obviously confused expression, Talia laughed. "I'm working in the haunted corn maze later. I'm not allowed to tell you what my role is, but let's just say... there's a chain saw involved."

"A chain saw?" That sounded a lot more intense than what she'd been imagining.

"Awesome," Emily said enthusiastically. "I have yet to get through the maze without screaming. What do you think, Diana?"

"I think not." No way did she want to be chased by someone with a chain saw, even if she knew the person behind the mask was Talia.

"Oh, come on. At least stay for a dance?" Emily gave

her another of those smiles that were always Diana's undo-ing. Maybe she could stay just a *little* bit longer.

"Maybe," she relented.

"How about this: I'll take you around and introduce you to everyone you should know as the new owner of the inn, and then you'll let me have a dance before you leave?"

How could she say no? "Okay. Just one dance."

SEVENTEEN

The band was playing one of her favorite songs. Perfectly tipsy after two ciders, Emily had already been dancing on the grass in front of the stage for a little while. Alex, Frankie, and Margo were with her, while Tom, Maddie, Drew, and Carter were attempting a game of cornhole, laughing uncontrollably when none of them could see well enough to get a sandbag in the hole. The sun had set thirty minutes ago, and it was getting dark fast.

As Emily spun to the beat, her gaze settled on Diana, seated alone at the picnic table where they'd eaten dinner. Diana was sipping from a cup of cider and watching Emily dance. She wore a gray sweater and black jeans that looked just the slightest bit preppy, and it made Emily want to ruffle her up even more than usual.

Despite her buttoned-up attire, Diana had been more relaxed with Emily tonight than she had been in the weeks since she'd returned to Crescent Falls. They seemed to have softened around each other in general since Diana was sick, and Emily was determined to use the festival as an excuse to press the growing closeness between them.

She approached the picnic table. "Dance with me."

Diana's lips thinned. She'd probably only ever danced in formal ballrooms in fancy clothes, and Emily thought that was all the more reason to see her cut loose in this grassy field as the stars began to pop out overhead.

Emily reached for her hand, giving it a gentle tug. "Please? I'm awfully impressed with you tonight, you know."

"You are?" Diana's brow wrinkled adorably. She downed the rest of her cider and stood, her hand still clasped in Emily's.

Emily nodded. She'd been floored when she took Diana around to introduce her to various vendors in attendance tonight, only to hear variations of "Great to see you again, Diana," from every single person. As it turned out, Diana had already taken Emily's advice. She'd ingratiated herself to all the right people in town. They knew her. They liked her.

And Emily had underestimated her. Diana had taken her concerns seriously. She'd done the work. She was every bit as competent as Emily had first thought her to be. She hadn't given up on her dream of being the CEO of Devlin Hotels. It had been taken from her, so she'd created a new path for herself.

She was so fucking impressive, and Emily was so fucking smitten.

"I tried to introduce you to all the right people tonight, and they already knew you."

Diana stepped closer, her eyes locked on Emily's. "You gave me a challenge. I met it."

"You always do, don't you?"

Diana's next step brought her so close, they were almost touching. "I told you that when we met."

"Yes, you did." Emily could hardly breathe. She still held Diana's hand, and it was all she could do not to yank Diana in and kiss her. She'd wasted so much time doubting Diana, making everything awkward between them, and now...

"Emily?" Diana sounded hoarse, and her pupils were blown.

Oh.

Oh.

Diana wanted her too.

Oh God, what was Emily supposed to do with this information? "Dance with me?" she managed over the pounding of her heart.

Diana nodded, allowing Emily to lead her to the makeshift dance floor. "I've never danced on grass before."

"The grass makes it more unpredictable and therefore more fun." Emily flung her hands in the air and moved her hips to the beat, profoundly aware of the electricity still crackling between them. "I love this song."

After watching her for a few beats, Diana started to move. She looked a little stiff, but she was out here, and she was dancing, and that was already a win in Emily's book, because she knew this wasn't easy for an uptight person like Diana.

The song ended, and Emily recognized the opening strains of Carly Simon's "You're So Vain." This band really had great taste in music.

Diana's eyes crinkled with a smile. "And this is one of *my* favorite songs."

By the time the band reached the chorus, people were shouting the lyrics as they danced. Caught up in the moment, Emily threw one arm around Alex, the other around Diana as she sang along at the top of her lungs.

Diana gave her a startled look but didn't pull away. If she was singing, Emily couldn't hear her, but she was at least mouthing along with the lyrics.

Emily would take it.

Alex broke free to wrap her arms around Margo, the two of them singing as they spun each other across the grass. Then it was just Emily and Diana with arms around each other's shoulders. Emily turned, and their bodies bumped. For a moment, their faces were so close, they were practically kissing, but before Emily could give in to temptation, Diana stepped away. She turned to face the band, dancing a little more freely than she had at first.

A few minutes later, Emily saw flashlights beginning to move through the pumpkin patch, and she seized her opportunity. Waving goodbye to Alex, Frankie, and Margo, she motioned for Diana to follow her as she led the way toward the pumpkin patch.

"I'm not sure I agreed to this," Diana muttered, although she followed Emily willingly enough.

"You have nothing to lose," Emily said. "If you don't like it or don't want to risk picking a pumpkin in the dark, you can just watch me pick mine, and then we'll go get some dessert and maybe another cider. Deal?"

"I suppose." Diana looked over, her expression mostly hidden by the dark, but Emily still felt the heat of her gaze.

Something was happening between them tonight, and Emily wanted it so badly, even if she knew it would break her heart to kiss Diana and then watch her leave in a few weeks. But God, how she wanted to kiss her...

She greeted Mrs. Dubois, who gave them vine clippers and a quick rundown of where the best pumpkins were and how to gesture with their flashlights if they needed someone to come over with the cart to carry a larger pumpkin for them.

Then they were on their way into the patch, illuminating the ground ahead of them with the flashlights on their cell phones. The air had cooled now that the sun had set, and even in her warmest flannel, Emily was chilly. Soon, she might need to get her jacket out of the car.

Or take Diana's hand, because any contact between them tonight lit her up like a wildfire.

"For the record, I still think this is weird," Diana said quietly.

"That's what makes it fun. You can pick pumpkins during the day anywhere, but this is the only place I know of where you can pick them in the dark."

There weren't many people in the pumpkin patch yet. A few scattered flashlights bobbed in the distance, but no one was close by. All around them, pumpkins shone a dull gray in the moonlight, giving them a spooky vibe that Emily dug. As her gaze roamed around them, she stopped suddenly, her brain tripping over her feet as an idea formed.

"Okay?" Diana asked, stopping beside her.

Emily nodded. "Sorry. I just thought of this year's spooky painting. I want to paint a pumpkin patch by moonlight like this one, using blues and greens and grays instead of the usual fall colors. I can do a big full moon overhead, dramatic shadows..."

"I like it," Diana said. "Will you be able to paint it from memory?"

"Maybe." Emily turned off the flashlight on her cell phone and opened her camera app, aiming it at a pumpkin in front of her. She snapped a few quick pictures to see how it came out. Grainy as hell, but the vibe was there. "This will work."

"Good." Diana had shut off her flashlight too, and now they were bathed in moonlight. Diana's gray sweater must have some silvery threads in it because it had a vaguely iridescent quality under the light of the moon, just the slightest bit shimmery.

Emily lifted her phone and snapped a picture from behind as Diana stood admiring the pumpkin patch before her. It didn't come out great—way too dark and lacking all the iridescence Emily had just been admiring—but again, the vibe was there. Diana looked cool, sophisticated, and just the slightest bit glamorous even standing in the middle of a darkened pumpkin patch.

Diana turned her head, and Emily put her phone away before hurrying to stand beside her. For a few seconds, neither of them said anything. They just stood with their shoulders touching, staring across the darkened rows of pumpkins. Emily could still hear the band, although the music was muffled, just stray notes and a rhythmic beat.

It felt like they were separate from the festival, isolated in their little bubble of darkness. This was so different from Emily's usual pumpkin patch experience, when she and her friends would laugh and goof around with their flashlights, trying to freak each other out and competing to see who could find the funniest-looking pumpkin.

This was...unexpectedly romantic.

Diana turned her head, her eyes glittering in the moonlight, and Emily forgot to breathe. That electricity was even stronger now. She wanted Diana to kiss her. She wanted it so badly, her whole body flushed with heat, her pulse thrumming in her ears. Her gaze dropped to Diana's lips, remembering the way they felt on hers. She'd felt those lips all over her body, a fact her body was reminding her of pretty intensely right now.

Emily had been holding herself back. She'd convinced herself she needed to make sure Diana was trustworthy, that she would do what was best for the inn. She'd held herself back because she was convinced Diana had gotten what she needed from their one-night stand, that there was no way she felt this too. She'd held herself back because she was afraid of getting hurt.

They had all been excuses. Flimsy, stupid excuses.

But just as Emily had made up her mind to go for it, Diana stepped away. She sank her hands into the back pockets of her jeans and walked a little farther down the row of pumpkins. Emily swallowed her disappointment. It was probably for the best, but...now that she knew Diana wanted her too, Emily's self-control was slipping.

"I've found my pumpkin," Diana called, glancing back at Emily.

"Really?" Emily hurried to her side, eager to see what Diana had chosen. She was pointing at a small pumpkin that was perfectly proportionate, its skin an even, pale color in the moonlight. Emily smiled. It was *so* Diana. "I love it."

Diana stepped closer and looked down at it. "How do we pick them? I've never actually taken a pumpkin off the vine before."

Emily pulled out the cutters Mrs. Dubois had handed her. She knelt and snipped Diana's pumpkin free from its vine, careful to keep enough stem that the pumpkin should last through the season...or at least through Diana's stay in Vermont.

"Thank you." Diana lifted her pumpkin, her face scrunching with displeasure as she likely discovered it was wet underneath from yesterday's rain.

Emily hurried down the next row. Now that Diana had chosen a pumpkin, Emily didn't want to make her stand around holding it. They were heavier than they looked. She found a lopsided pumpkin about the same size as Diana's, one side bulging comically while the other side was flat. Even in the moonlight, she could see its uneven coloring, but something about it looked happy, a little quirky even. She snipped it and held it up.

Diana's amusement was plain to see. "Perfect."

Emily walked over, bumping their shoulders together. "Admit it. This was more fun than you expected."

Diana exhaled, her gaze again finding Emily's in the darkness. "Yes, it was."

———

DIANA SIPPED from a new cup of cider and relaxed in her chair. Before her, flames snapped and popped. She hadn't noticed the enormous firepit at the center of the field until someone lit a fire in it. Now, she and Emily were seated in front of it, a bag of apple cider donuts between them, still warm from the oven.

Surprisingly enough, Diana was having fun. She'd even survived a visit to one of the porta-potties after she and Emily returned from the pumpkin patch, which hadn't been nearly as awful as she'd feared. Now she was cozied up by a warm fire with good food and drink, listening to the band and wishing the night never had to end.

Something had shifted between her and Emily tonight. They were relaxed and flirty with each other in a way they hadn't been since that first night. All this time, Diana had thought she was the only one who still felt anything, but the chemistry between them tonight was mutual. She was sure of it.

But no matter how much she wanted to kiss Emily in

that moonlit pumpkin patch, she wouldn't. Not while Emily still worked at the front desk, maybe not even if she didn't. Diana was only here another month. They'd had their one-night stand. If they got back in bed with each other now, it would lead to messy complications.

The fire emitted a loud pop, and a burst of sparks shot upward, glittering overhead before the chilly night air extinguished them, leaving only ash to drift toward the ground. And it *was* chilly. If Diana had realized she was going to be here this late, she'd have brought a jacket. Her sweater was warm, but still, she shivered as she took another sip of her cider.

It filled her with the sensation of warmth, even though she knew alcohol actually did the opposite. Right now, she'd take even the illusion of warmth. Any other time, she'd have used the temperature as an excuse to leave, but she wasn't ready to go. Somehow, the fall festival had cast a spell over her and Emily, and she wanted to hang on to this flirty closeness between them for as long as possible, because she had a feeling the spell would break when she went home.

She wasn't even sure where Carter was. He'd been off with Tom, Maddie, and Drew for most of the evening, and she was glad to see him having fun. Diana leaned forward in her chair, bringing herself closer to the fire.

Beside her, Emily picked up the bag of donuts, snagging one for herself before offering the bag to Diana. Emily had insisted that a dozen mini donuts weren't too many for the two of them to share, and she might have been right. They'd already polished off more than half the bag. The little donuts, covered liberally in cinnamon sugar, were *delicious*.

Diana took one, and they shared a smile. She was starting to understand why lesbians loved flannel so much, because not only did it look amazing on Emily, but she also looked very cozy in it. Maybe Diana would buy some flannel before she left Vermont. After all, she was her own boss now. She could dress however she wanted when she wasn't seeing clients, especially while she and Carter were still running their office out of her town house.

"You look like you're having deep thoughts," Emily said before popping the donut in her mouth, cinnamon sugar clinging to her lips.

It took every bit of Diana's willpower not to lean over and kiss it off. "Actually, I was admiring your flannel."

"Yeah?" Emily licked her lips, removing the sugar.

Diana really needed to stop staring at her lips. "It looks good on you."

Emily tugged the flannel more tightly around herself. "I wish I could say I was a queer-girl stereotype, but everyone wears it up here. It's practically the state uniform."

Diana shivered again, distracting herself from the chill by eating her donut.

Emily gave her a shrewd look. "Ah. I see you weren't only admiring my flannel for sapphic reasons. I should have realized you were cold in that sweater, especially after you just got over being sick. Honestly, I'm getting cold too. I've got a jacket in my car. Actually, I might have two? I tend to throw lots of warm layers in there during the colder months so I've always got something when I need it."

"I'm okay. We're sitting in front of a fire, after all," Diana deflected.

"Let me go see what I have. I need to take our pumpkins to the car anyway. I'll be right back." Emily handed her the bag of donuts, picked up their pumpkins, and walked off in the direction of the parking lot.

Diana resisted the urge to watch her go. She loved the way Emily's ass looked in those jeans but didn't want to be caught looking. Instead, she focused on the dancing flames in front of her, lost in her thoughts. The fire was oddly mesmerizing. Maybe she should add a fireplace to her repertoire of calming techniques, because her earlier anxiety seemed to have dissipated.

When she looked up, she spotted Carter on the other side of the field, near the corn maze. He and Drew were standing close, and as she watched, Drew leaned in and kissed him.

Oh.

She frowned, trying to decide how she felt about that. On some level, she'd seen this coming, and she wanted Carter to be happy, but he was still so newly out, so inexperienced when it came to relationships. She didn't want him to get hurt.

"Here you go," Emily said, standing next to Diana's chair with a black jacket in her hand. She'd swapped her flannel for a jacket too, but hers was purple.

"Thank you." Diana stood, shrugging gratefully into the jacket. She rubbed her hands up and down her arms, already feeling warmer. "This is much better."

"I'm glad." Emily sat and grabbed another donut.

"You've known Drew awhile, right?" Diana nodded toward the two men, who were still kissing over by the cornfield. "Do you trust him?"

Emily followed her gaze. "Aww, look at them. I had a feeling they were into each other. And yes, I've known Drew since he was a kid. I used to babysit him, actually. He's a great guy. A bit of a goofball sometimes, but mature in the ways that matter. I don't think you have anything to worry about."

"He's older than Carter."

"Not by much," Emily said. "He graduated last year. I think he's twenty-three?"

"Younger than I thought," she mused. Two years wasn't much of an age difference, but Carter still seemed so immature sometimes...

"I think they're adorable together," Emily said.

"They are," Diana agreed. "I just...well, I worry about him. He's supposed to be in his senior year of college right now, and I think he's doing well working for me and making new friends in Vermont, but..."

"You're a really good aunt, you know that?" Emily reached over and took her hand. "He's lucky to have you in his life."

She gave her head a quick shake. "I just want what's best for him, and I'm trying not to let my rigid ways of thinking get in the way of that. If he's happier working for me this year than finishing college, maybe that's all right, but...what will happen long term? Surely he'll want something more from his career eventually."

"Just because he's not in college right now doesn't mean he'll never go back. It sounds like he'd gotten stuck, and now he's taking some time to figure out who he is and what he wants. This might end up being great for him long term."

"Yeah." Diana watched as Carter and Drew headed toward the entrance to the haunted corn maze. "I guess sometimes I have trouble seeing him as an adult who works for me and makes out with people at the fall festival."

"I bet he was doing that in high school, honestly," Emily said with a laugh.

"Actually...he's been kind of a late bloomer when it comes to dating. I think he's known for a while that he's gay but didn't feel comfortable acting on it. My brother thinks it's a phase, and worse, an idea I've planted in his head."

"Well, that's just good old homophobia. You and I know better, and I can also imagine how much it's meant to him having you in his life, not only as a gay role model but someone who gives him a safe place to be himself." Emily was still holding her hand, her fingers warm and soft in Diana's, and she was enjoying it more than she'd ever admit.

She couldn't believe she was sharing these things with Emily. Diana could practically see her mother's disapproving glare, but at the same time, it felt good to confide in a friend. "I had hoped he'd have a better coming-out experience than I did. My parents reacted almost exactly the way my brother and his wife did with Carter. Honestly, I think that, at least on some level, my parents *still* think it's a phase, that eventually, I'll come to my senses. We're civil with each other, but I don't know how they'd react if I ever brought a woman home to meet them and forced the issue."

Emily inhaled sharply, turning to look at Diana in the firelight. "You've never introduced a girlfriend to your parents?"

She shook her head. "I haven't had many girlfriends, to be honest, and those I've had...well, there's never been anyone serious enough to bring home. I've been focused on my career." Her chest ached as she acknowledged to herself that part of the reason she'd never settled down was the ingrained knowledge that it would lessen her chances of taking over Devlin Hotels, that a single career woman was more palatable to the board than a married lesbian. The realization shamed her, and she ducked her head, focusing on what remained of her cider.

"And here you are, running your own business. I know it's not what you'd imagined for yourself, but I think in the long run, this will be better. You get to build this business from the ground up, make it yours inside and out, create a brand you can be proud of." Emily gave Diana's fingers a squeeze.

Diana smiled. "Thanks. Sorry for getting all maudlin over here."

"You've had a tumultuous year. You're entitled to feel however you feel about it."

"Thank you." They were sitting too close now, and Diana was staring at Emily's lips again, almost overwhelmed by the urge to kiss her.

"You're welcome." Emily's voice was little more than a whisper. She'd leaned in too, clearly on the same train of thought.

It would be so easy to close the gap and kiss her…

A scream pierced the night, followed by the buzz of a chain saw. Diana jumped, inadvertently ruining the moment. Over the last half hour or so, they'd heard various screams, yells, and roars from the haunted corn maze. Rationally, she knew what they were by now, but still, she startled easily when it came to fake sounds of terror, apparently.

Emily cleared her throat, then stood, and Diana's heart sank. She wasn't ready for their magical evening to end. "On that note," Emily said. "I think it's time for us to go through the haunted corn maze ourselves. Ready?"

Not even a little bit, but if the alternative was saying good night… "Ready."

EIGHTEEN

Cornstalks rustled around them, the only sound Emily could hear as she and Diana ventured into the maze. The music and laughter of the festival had been muted by the stalks surrounding them. Overhead, the moon shone nearly full, bathing everything in its pale, silvery light. The maze was cloaked in darkness, but Emily knew from past experience that certain spots would be illuminated—usually in shades of purple or red—to keep them on track.

"I don't like this," Diana murmured. She'd zipped the jacket, hiding her sweater, so there were no shimmery strands to catch the moonlight this time.

"Nothing scary has even happened yet," Emily said with a laugh. "Afraid you're gonna scream louder than me?" She nudged Diana with her shoulder, receiving an amused smile in return.

"I don't scream."

"No? I seem to remember—" Emily cut herself off as she realized what she'd been about to say, the way Diana had lost control that night when Emily finally let her come.

"For fuck's sake." Diana jumped to the side as if something unexpected had touched her, which it probably had, given where they were.

Before Emily could respond, something cold and feathery brushed against her cheek, and it was her turn to yelp, cringing away from the touch even as she felt a nervous giggle building in her throat. It was fun to be scared when she knew there was no real danger.

She and Diana approached the end of the long path that had led them into the heart of the maze. "Left or right?" Emily asked.

"Left," Diana decided, and they started walking again. A vicious growl came from the cornstalks, and Diana lurched away from it with a startled yelp. "What is that?" she hissed.

"A sound effect." Emily seized the opportunity to take her hand. "The maze is full of them."

"What if it's not? What if there are coyotes in here? Or...or a bear? I saw one, you know, right in my driveway. It was *enormous*." The growl came again, closer this time, and Diana quickened her pace, half dragging Emily down the path away from it.

Emily giggled as she hurried after her. "No animal would come in here with all the screaming and monster sounds. Only humans enjoy this stuff. You didn't tell me you saw a bear."

"We weren't all that friendly at the time. Oh my God." Diana stopped so suddenly that Emily bumped into her from behind. She peered over Diana's shoulder to see a person dressed as a ghoul approaching them, talon-like hands extended in front of them. "I know that's probably someone you know, but..." Diana sidestepped as the ghoul approached her.

"Remember what they told us before we entered. The actors aren't allowed to touch us."

Diana backed up until she was pressed against the cornstalks, then darted past the ghoul, still dragging Emily behind her. Emily yelped as the ghoul swiped at her, claws missing her by inches.

They darted around another corner and directly into a giant spiderweb. Cold, damp, cottony strings wrapped around them. Diana swore, swatting at the mess, while Emily said, "Ew, ew, ew!" until they'd worked their way out of it. *That* was new this year.

The next stretch of the maze was impenetrably dark, only the faintest outline of cornstalks visible, and even so, they bumped into the dry, scratchy plants multiple times as they crept down the path. They both walked with their hands out in front of them to keep from face-planting into any more unfortunate surprises.

Noises echoed around them, ghostlike wails and the sound of something thrashing around in the corn. A high-pitched scream came from their right, and Diana jumped, bumping into Emily, who let out an inadvertent scream in response. The look Diana gave her was hard to read—especially in the low lighting—but she didn't seem upset. On the contrary, she almost looked like she was having fun.

They headed down a wider path lit with flickering purple lights that illuminated various ghostly hands reaching toward them from the cornstalks. They hurried through that section, temporarily blinded as they made a right and entered an unlit path after their eyes had adjusted to the purple lights.

Emily put her hands out in front of herself. She was walking so quickly that she didn't have time to react when she heard the rustling sound of Diana bumping into cornstalks as she reached the end of the path. Diana spun, and Emily walked right into her, instinctively gripping Diana's shoulders to steady herself.

"Oh," Diana murmured. Her chest rose as she inhaled sharply.

They'd already had so many near misses tonight, and Emily just...reacted. Her arms were around Diana almost before she'd realized what she was doing, her face tilting forward so their lips met. Diana froze for a moment, and then she released a little growl as she kissed Emily back. Her lips were cool from the night air, but her mouth was hot as her lips parted, her kiss bold and all-consuming and everything Emily had missed since the last time she kissed her.

Right now, she was exquisitely aware of how much she'd missed it, how much she still wanted Diana. Emily pressed forward, sliding her hands down to Diana's ass as the chemistry between them ignited. Emily felt more alive than she had in months.

The night was dark and endless around them. Stars twinkled overhead. Cornstalks rustled in the breeze as Diana sank her hands into Emily's hair, tugging just enough to make Emily gasp with pleasure. They were wrapped up in each other, kissing almost frantically, and Emily's body burned with need. She wanted more.

She wanted everything. She wanted Diana naked beneath her, right now.

A sharp scream split the air, and they jumped apart. Adrenaline tingled in the pit of Emily's stomach. For a minute, she'd completely forgotten they were in the middle of a haunted corn maze. Maybe Diana had too. She was staring at Emily with glassy eyes, the nuances of her expression hidden by the darkness.

For a long moment, neither of them said anything.

Another scream split the night air, and they both startled. Diana reached up to smooth back her hair, and Emily wondered what hers looked like. Was her lipstick smeared? When they exited the maze into the better-lit part of the festival, would it be obvious to her friends what she'd been doing in the corn maze with Diana?

"Come on. We'll talk about it later." Diana took Emily's hand, and they walked back through the dead-end path they'd ended up on, hustling past the flickering purple lights and groping hands until they found another path to try. A large scarecrow stood in the moonlight before them, button eyes staring sightlessly in their direction. Emily was still processing everything that had happened in the last few minutes. Her mind was spinning. A cool breeze caressed her tender lips, and she smiled as she hurried after Diana.

That happened. They kissed.

The scarecrow lunged toward them, raggedy hands just missing Diana's jacket, and she let out a little yelp that was almost a scream, stumbling backward into Emily. Diana glared at the scarecrow as she passed it, and Emily giggled. Diana was adorable when she got flustered, and maybe it was the cider talking, but Emily felt like that kiss had uncorked everything she'd bottled up since June.

And then some.

Because now she knew Diana so much better, and she liked everything she'd learned in the month since Diana returned to Vermont. This was a woman she could actually fall for...except for the unfortunate fact that Diana was returning to Boston in a few weeks. That realization sobered Emily's romanticized thoughts pretty quickly.

The man running toward them in a Scream mask finished waking her up. She squealed, jumping behind

Diana as the man passed them, disappearing into the cornstalks.

"Are we almost finished?" Diana asked, her voice tinged with frustration and something else Emily couldn't quite identify. "Surely we must be almost to the end."

"I think so." They turned another corner, walking past several glowing skeletons that chased after them and a bubbling cauldron that smelled vaguely like cotton candy. There was enough light here for Emily to see the tension in Diana's posture. Either she was kicking herself for kissing Emily, or she was really ready to be done with the maze.

Emily didn't like either possibility. As they entered another darkened stretch on the path, she hauled Diana up against her and kissed her again. "For the record, no regrets on my part."

Diana softened against her. "Me either, but—"

The distinctive buzz of a chain saw cut through the night air, and Diana pulled out of her arms. A figure clad in ripped, blood-soaked clothing rushed at them from the stalks, and Emily squealed before remembering who it was...and what she might have just seen.

Emily grabbed Diana's hand and sprinted down the path, because the chainsaw-wielding madman was always at the end of the maze. Sure enough, the exit loomed ahead, and she and Diana dashed onto the lamplit path that would lead them back to the main field.

Before they reentered the more crowded part of the festival, Emily tugged Diana to a stop. "I know it's complicated, and maybe we shouldn't do it again, but I meant what I said when you were sick. I really like you, Diana. I don't know how to resolve the fact that you're leaving in a few weeks, but..."

Diana stepped closer, her expression fully visible now,

and it was tender, even affectionate. "I like you too. I always have. I like you too much to hurt you, and I'm afraid that's exactly what would happen if we started something now."

Emily knew she hadn't been able to disguise the disappointment on her face.

"I mean, Boston's only a three-hour drive," Diana said. "I'm willing to try things long distance, but I'm not exactly the committed type, and you're completely committed to your life here in Crescent Falls."

Emily sighed. "If circumstances were different..."

Diana pressed another kiss to Emily's lips. "If circumstances were different, you'd already be in my bed."

———

IF CARTER WEREN'T HERE, Diana would have bailed on the foliage hike the following morning. Emily had been right about one thing: Diana had fun at the fall festival. She'd enjoyed herself a lot more than she'd expected to, so much that she'd lost her senses and kissed Emily in the middle of the corn maze.

So much that last night, she'd slept better than she had in weeks. Diana was rested and refreshed this morning, and hopefully, the new prescription she'd just received from her psychiatrist would help her keep the momentum going, but a hike with Emily and her friends? That felt a lot like playing with matches.

"I'm not that into foliage or anything," Carter said as he carried a mug of coffee out of the kitchen, "but the hike sounds fun."

"Or a certain person you'll be hiking with?" Diana asked as mildly as she could. She hadn't broached the topic last night, exhausted and distracted by her own romantic problems, but now she wanted to check in with him about Drew.

Carter sipped his coffee and gave her a knowing look. "I heard I wasn't the only one kissing someone last night."

Diana flinched. "Um…"

"Talia was the chainsaw murderer who interrupted you and Emily, you know."

Diana *had* known that, although she'd tried to convince herself that maybe Talia hadn't seen anything, or if she had, that she'd keep it to herself. Diana had never discussed her sex life with her nephew before. What was appropriate here? "Emily and I…well, it's complicated."

"Because you're going back to Boston soon?"

"Mostly, yes. What about you and Drew?"

Carter shrugged. "I don't know. It's all new, and Boston's not that far away, so we'll see. But I like him. I *really* like him." His cheeks went pink with the admission.

"Carter, I'm thrilled for you." She gave his hand a quick squeeze. "And I'm here if you want to talk about anything."

"Okay."

She looked down at her coffee, feeling more like a parent than she ever had before. But Carter was inexperienced, and his parents were still in denial about his sexuality. "You'll be safe, right? I mean, if things go that far…you'll need condoms."

"I know that, and we only kissed for the first time last night." His cheeks were even pinker now, and his tone had grown defensive, or maybe just embarrassed.

She rubbed a hand over her forehead. "I'm sorry. I'm not trying to make things awkward, I just…sex education isn't always LGBTQ inclusive. I didn't have anyone to talk to about these things when I was younger, and I want to make sure you do, okay?"

He fiddled with his mug, pointedly not looking at her. "Yeah, uh, okay."

"No judgment, whatever it is, I promise."

He nodded again. "Thanks. Now can we get ready for the hike?"

She held in a sigh. There was no getting out of it now. And besides, she did want to see the foliage. She also wanted to see Emily. As she put her empty coffee mug in the sink, her gaze fell on the pumpkin she'd picked last night. In the light of day, it was a pale creamy color, almost white. She never would have chosen it, but now that it was hers...she kind of liked it. It was different, just like her life in Vermont.

Everything in her life these days was different, and she liked it all.

An hour later, she was on a leaf-covered trail with the rest of the adventure group. Carter and Drew were walking together, talking quietly, as were Margo and Alexis. Tom, Talia, and Emily were chatting, while Diana brought up the rear.

She focused her attention on the foliage overhead. The leaves around her were mostly a mix of green, gold, and brown. Here and there, she saw pops of red, but apparently, they were heading toward one of the best vistas in the area for viewing foliage.

"Hey."

Diana turned to find Emily walking beside her, and her heart sped, flooding her chest with warmth. "Hey, yourself."

Emily's smile was more sweet than sexy, and yet, it only made Diana yearn for her even more. "Having fun?"

Diana nodded. "I had fun last night too...just like you said I would."

Emily's smile broadened. Her brown hair was in a high

ponytail, and she had on another flannel, this one in shades of blue and purple. Diana loved her in flannel. "I'm glad, especially after...you know."

"Apparently, word traveled fast about that." She gave Emily a meaningful look, still annoyed that the whole group knew her business.

Emily's expression turned bashful. "Yeah, sorry about that. Talia saw us, and she told Drew, and I'm guessing Drew told Carter, if it got back to you."

"It did." She exhaled, already a bit winded. Again, she'd underestimated how strenuous it was to hike in Vermont. "I guess it was unavoidable, but I don't like gossip."

"Neither do I," Emily said, "and my friends aren't gossips. Well, Tom is a little bit, but he means well. They just want me to be happy."

Diana wasn't sure how to respond to that.

"I think..." Emily pressed her lips together and then exhaled slowly. "I think we should stick with friendship since you're leaving so soon, but I *do* want to be friends. I hate the way we were tiptoeing around each other the last few weeks. I don't want to do that anymore. Let's hang out, grab lunch together at work, that kind of thing. I'd love it if you came on more of our group activities...you and Carter both. I enjoy spending time with you, Diana."

Diana heard the truth in Emily's words, even as her stomach dropped. She was already breathless from the hike, and she *knew* she had no business kissing Emily again. It was entirely inappropriate now that Diana owned the inn and especially with her leaving town soon. But somehow, in the middle of that cornfield last night, she'd started thinking maybe...maybe she could have it all. "You're right. I'm sorry for kissing you last night."

"Oh, don't you dare apologize," Emily said, sounding

vaguely outraged. "First of all, *I* kissed *you*, so if anyone should apologize, it's me, but...I loved every moment. Kissing you in the middle of a haunted corn maze? Once in a lifetime."

"It was pretty great," Diana admitted. "And I'd like to give it a try as friends. I could use a friend here in Vermont."

"Yay for friends." Emily grinned. "Is this only your second time hiking here?"

"Yeah. I've been running every day on the roads near my rental, but I haven't gotten back out on the trails."

"Well, we do group hikes almost every weekend if you want to join us. This is a really gorgeous time of year to hike." She swept an arm around them, and she wasn't wrong.

The trees around them were decked out in various fall shades. Some were still bright green. Others contained a mixture of yellow and orange, and a few were bright red. The forest floor was carpeted in fallen leaves that crunched underfoot as they walked. In front of them, Alex had picked a bouquet of brightly colored leaves, and Margo was taking pictures of her holding it.

"I think I'd like to go on more hikes with your group." Diana was enjoying this one, especially now that she and Emily had cleared the air between them. They hiked for about thirty minutes before they arrived at their destination at the base of Crescent Falls. The waterfall roared in front of them, while to the right, the valley beckoned, bursting with color.

Diana couldn't get over the way the distant mountain-sides looked this time of year. There was so much red! They took a variety of group selfies, and Emily even convinced her to take a selfie of the two of them together. Emily had also taken a lot of pictures of the leaves for painting inspiration. Diana made a mental note to ask to see them once she was finished. Maybe one of these fall vistas could find its way home with her.

Once she was back at her rental cabin, she started thinking about dinner. She'd worked up an appetite on their hike. She looked in the fridge to see if there was anything she could cook for her and Carter before he headed back to Boston.

"I'm going out for a while," Carter called from behind her.

Diana straightened, closing the refrigerator with a frown. "But you have to drive back to Boston tonight."

"Well, I was thinking about that." He gave her a sheepish look. "I brought my laptop and everything with me this weekend because...what if I work from Vermont this week? I mean, surely I'm more help to you here than two hundred miles away at your town house."

She stared at him for a moment in silence. He'd caught her off guard, and she hated that feeling. "You want to stay here for the week?"

"Yeah." He shrugged. "Why not?"

"Is this because of Drew?" she couldn't help asking.

Carter's expression hardened. "That's none of your business. I'm an adult, Aunt DD."

She crossed her arms over her chest. Oh, she wasn't going to tolerate that attitude. "You're living under my roof, and that means I get to be a little bit involved in your life. It was just a simple question."

"Was it, though? You automatically assume I'm being irresponsible, that I'm making all my decisions because of a guy, instead of considering that maybe I like it here. I have friends here, not to mention *you're* here, and you're my boss, so why should I be in Boston by myself?"

"Carter..."

"Ugh, whatever. You're as bad as Mom and Dad some-times." He grabbed his keys and his jacket off the kitchen counter and headed for the door. "I'll be back late. Don't wait up."

NINETEEN

Emily approached Diana's office door on Wednesday morning with a spring in her step and butterflies flapping in her stomach. When Diana had asked on Monday if Emily would be interested in helping her interview candidates for the new manager position, she'd been floored. And thrilled. And...overwhelmed.

She'd just gotten used to having Diana here at the inn, and already it was time to hire her replacement. Still, it meant a lot that Diana was letting her help. It showed that Diana still wanted Emily's family to have a voice even though they didn't own the place anymore.

The office door was open, and Diana looked impressive as hell in a royal-blue blouse and dark gray slacks, eyes squinting slightly as she stared at the laptop in front of her. Emily knocked on the doorframe to get her attention.

Diana looked up, a warm smile softening her features. "Perfect timing."

Emily looked around the office that her grandmothers used to share. It had sometimes felt a bit cramped then, but it seemed almost spacious with just one desk in it. Diana had added a couple of guest chairs, and Emily moved toward one of them.

Diana shook her head. "We'll go to the break room so we can sit around the table together. I've got five candidates coming today. They're my top five after conducting phone interviews, and I'm fairly confident we'll find our new manager in this group, but I have a B list to consider tomorrow if not."

Emily nodded. "Sounds good, but I bet you've got a winner in these five."

"I hope so." Diana stood and handed Emily a manila folder. "Résumés. I've also added notes from the phone interview after each one."

"Of course you did," Emily said with a little laugh.

"What's that supposed to mean?" There was a slight edge in Diana's tone, as if she'd taken offense. She seemed to have embraced the decision they'd made during the hike on Sunday and had been even more friendly with Emily than before while keeping things completely platonic between them, but this was a reminder that some tension still lurked beneath the surface.

"It means you're super prepared as usual, and I think you're very impressive," Emily told her, loving the way Diana softened in response.

"Oh. Thank you."

"You were right when I met you, you know," Emily said. "You're meant to be a CEO. It suits you."

"I don't feel like much of a CEO yet," Diana said as she came out from behind her desk. "Only a small business owner, but this is just the beginning for Aster, I'm sure."

"I'm sure too. Now let's go find our new manager."

Three hours later, Emily sat beside Diana in the break room as the second candidate left. The next person wasn't scheduled to arrive until after lunch. She looked at Diana. "What did you think of Eric?"

"He's not the right fit," Diana responded. "I hope you agree."

"I do. He's qualified enough, but he just...I can't put my finger on it."

"It was his attitude." Diana stood, smoothing a hand over the front of her slacks where wrinkles had gathered over the course of the morning. "He seemed more interested in profit than in preserving the character of the inn. He hid that from me on the phone, but his body language today gave him away. His heart wasn't in it when I brought up the inn's LGBTQ legacy."

"His heart wasn't in it," Emily mused. "Yeah, I think that's exactly it. My grandmas were right to sell to you, Diana. You're going to do them proud."

Diana's eyes sparkled. "Thank you."

"Want to grab lunch together?" she asked. Mariah was covering the front desk today, while Emily helped Diana with interviews, so she was free to go out for lunch if she wanted.

"I'd like that," Diana agreed.

They drove to the café, where Emily ordered a cup of corn chowder and a BLT while Diana got a salad with local smoked trout and goat cheese.

"I was surprised to see Carter in town yesterday," Emily said after the waitress had taken their orders. "Is he staying in Vermont until you leave?"

Diana sighed, lifting her water for a sip. "I think he might. He...we had a disagreement on Sunday night."

"Really?" Emily felt her eyebrows go up. She'd always been so impressed with how well Diana got along with her nephew, so this was totally unexpected.

"He was supposed to drive back to Boston on Sunday evening, but instead, he just announced that he was going out, that I shouldn't wait up, and that apparently, he'd brought his laptop and planned to work here this week. As if that's his decision to make."

"Uh-oh," Emily said. "Does it matter whether he works here or in Boston?"

"Of course it matters." Diana frowned. "He's researching a hotel in Maryland for me this week, which can be done anywhere, but the landline dedicated to my company is in Boston. We can dial in to the voicemail from here, but no one's there answering the phone. I have plants that need to be watered and errands that need to be run. And mostly, it matters because I'm the boss and he should have *asked* before he decided to just stay here because he met a guy he likes."

Emily flinched. "Yeah, he should have. Is it because of Drew, you think?"

"I do, but now he's defensive about it and won't talk to me." She threw her hands up in frustration. "I've never fought with him like this before. Maybe it was a mistake to hire him. Right now, I miss just being the fun aunt."

"That's hard."

"I'm glad he's met someone. I truly am," Diana said. "And he's still doing a good job for me at Aster, so maybe everything's fine. I don't know. I wouldn't accept this behavior from any other employee, but I don't work for Devlin Hotels anymore. It's just Carter and me, and the whole idea with Aster was to have a fresh start, to make my own rules."

Emily pondered that for a minute. "I think your roles have shifted, and that's probably hard for both of you. He went straight from his parents' house to yours, and now you feel a little bit like a parental figure to him at a time when he wants to feel mature and independent. I bet things will settle soon."

"I hope so. I'm going to talk to him tonight. I'm done letting him avoid me. It's childish." She wrinkled her nose.

Emily laughed. "So you're looking at a hotel in Maryland next?"

Diana nodded. "I've got four I'm considering, but I think this one in Maryland will be my next purchase."

"Cool. Will you work there for two months too?"

"No. In most cases, there will be a manager or managers already in place, so I'll only stay for a week or so during the transition. With your grandmothers in a hurry to head out and see the world, and since this was my first solo purchase, it made sense for me to step in temporarily until I'd found a new manager."

Emily's phone dinged with a notification, and when she looked, she saw that her mom had tagged her on Facebook again. She tapped it, bringing up a photo of her mom sipping from a steaming mug in an eclectically decorated coffee shop. "The colors in here remind me of your paintings, Emily," the caption read.

Emily stabbed the screen again to close Facebook, discomfort crawling over her skin. She exhaled, refocusing on Diana.

"It was great to see you at the meeting the other day, Diana," Cheryl O'Malley, the owner of the café, said with a warm smile as she passed their table.

"You too, Cheryl," Diana responded. "Thank you for the invitation."

Cheryl nodded. "Hope to see you again next month."

"What was that about?" Emily asked once Cheryl had gone in back. "What meeting?"

"Cheryl invited me to join the local women-in-business group," Diana told her. "It was really interesting and a great networking opportunity."

Emily's heart melted just a little bit more to know that Diana had done so much to ingratiate herself to the community...that maybe Diana was starting to enjoy herself in Crescent Falls. She was making real connections here.

They talked through the rest of their lunch break, and Emily was fascinated to learn more about Diana's new business and all the things she planned to accomplish over the next year. Emily hadn't been able to ask her about it before, when they were still avoiding personal conversations. Diana's business plans were as impressive as she'd expected.

Diana was as impressive as she'd expected.

After lunch, they returned to the break room to meet their next candidate. Emily had hoped the new manager might be someone local, but she'd already looked over the résumés, and all five candidates were from out of town. That wasn't necessarily a bad thing. After all, Crescent Falls was a tiny town, perhaps too small to contain the right person for this job, but it was also a town that liked familiarity. And none of these names were familiar.

The inn felt less personal to Emily with every new decision made. Maybe it was time for her to move on too. "Change can wait until tomorrow" had been her motto for entirely too long. She needed to do the work to allow herself to make a full-time living as an artist.

Mariah knocked at the doorway with a brunette about Emily's age standing beside her. "Ms. Devlin. Your next guest is here."

The brunette extended her hand. "Paige Seton. Nice to meet you."

IT WAS past five when Diana and Emily finished the last interview. Diana felt the beginnings of a tension headache squeezing her skull. The day had been long, but productive. At least, she hoped it was. "What did you think?" she asked as she stood, stretching her back. The chairs in this room weren't comfortable enough for a full day of use like this. She was sore. Hopefully, her evening jog would help.

"I know who I'd pick," Emily said as she stood as well, rolling her shoulders.

"Who?" Diana asked, hoping it was the same person she had decided on. All five candidates were qualified. She felt confident that three of them could do well in the position, but there was one who stood out in her mind.

"Paige," Emily said. "She has the experience, the enthusiasm, *and* she's queer. I know we can't hire her based on that, but it sure doesn't hurt."

"No, it doesn't," Diana said, "and she's my pick too."

Emily beamed at her. "Really?"

Diana nodded. "Which means it's an easy decision. I'll call her in the morning and offer her the position."

"Awesome. I think she's going to be a great fit," Emily said. "Thanks so much for letting me help."

Diana reached for her hand and gave it a quick squeeze, her fingers tangling with Emily's. It was surprisingly hard to let go. "I was glad to have your input."

They smiled at each other, and the energy in the room seemed to shift. Diana could still feel the warmth of Emily's skin on hers, and her mind was searching feebly for excuses to prolong the moment. She wanted to ask Emily to dinner, even though she knew it couldn't happen. The two of them couldn't go to dinner without it feeling like a date, for Diana, at least.

This was more than attraction. She'd developed real feelings for Emily, which was completely unexpected. She clasped her hands behind her back to remove the temptation to fidget...or to reach for Emily again. "I'll see you tomorrow, then."

Emily nodded before heading toward the door. "Bye, Diana."

Diana watched her go, and then she exhaled, surprised to realize her heart was pounding. When had she developed such strong feelings for Emily? Perhaps she'd mistaken her feelings for awkward tension before, but now that she and Emily were hanging out together as friends, there was no more hiding from the truth.

Nothing to do about it either. Diana was mature enough to know she'd get past this. Once she was back in Boston, she'd put her energy into moving on. Maybe this was a wake-up call, though, a realization that she *was* ready for a serious relationship now that she no longer feared career retribution. Maybe now she could focus on fully realizing her potential, both at work and in her personal life.

She'd start by addressing the conflict between her and Carter. This had gone on long enough. She picked up her phone and sent him a quick text, telling him she expected him home for dinner at seven. That gave her enough time to go for a run and fix something for them to eat. She was pretty sure she had a chicken in the fridge that she could roast.

She gathered her laptop from the table, stopped in her office to collect her purse, and then she was on her way to the rental cabin. Once there, she seasoned the chicken and put it in the oven, along with some potatoes, and then set out on her run.

She sweated through her frustration as she completed her usual two-mile loop. Her mountain stamina was definitely improving. She was panting but not exhausted when she finished. Even better, when she came out of her bedroom a few minutes before seven to check on dinner, Carter was in the kitchen carving the chicken for her.

"Hi," he said sheepishly as he placed a serving of chicken and potatoes on a plate and handed it to her.

"Thank you. I hoped we could talk over dinner."

"Yeah. I figured that was coming. Sorry for how I acted on Sunday."

She nodded, gesturing for him to join her at the table. They took a minute to collect drinks and cutlery and then sat across from each other. "I know things seem casual because it's just you and me at Aster so far, but this *is* a business. You have to talk to me before you decide to stay up here for a week. I had things I needed you to do in Boston."

"I'm sorry. I guess I didn't think it would be a big deal."

"Carter, I just left behind the security of a position that was supposed to have seen me through retirement. I've invested my life savings into a risky new business. *Everything* is a big deal to me right now."

He looked up at her, eyes wide, forkful of chicken suspended halfway to his mouth. "I...I never thought of it like that. For me, this was just a fun new adventure."

"It *is* a fun adventure, but it's also a big fucking deal. If this business fails, it could ruin me. I honestly don't know what I would do. I certainly couldn't afford to try again with something new. I'd probably have to crawl back to Devlin Hotels and beg for whatever position they would give me, which undoubtedly wouldn't be as good as what I gave up."

Carter gulped. "I get it now. I...I'm really sorry, Aunt DD."

"When I say I'm counting on you, this is what I mean, okay? I really am counting on you."

Carter's eyes had gotten shiny, his cheeks red. "I'll take it more seriously from now on, I promise."

"I appreciate that." She cut a bite of her chicken. "Things are going well for you and Drew, then?"

"It's not just about Drew," Carter said quickly. "I mean, I've been hanging out with him, yeah, but I've never had queer friends before. I've never even been *out* to my friends before. I just feel like I've finally found somewhere I fit, you know?"

Her heart clenched. She remembered how it felt to be newly out and how tightly she'd clung to the first people who accepted her, especially when she hadn't received that same acceptance at home. Of course he had done the same. "I do know, and I'm so glad you've found that with the adventure group. I hope you can find a similar group in Boston. This part of your life is just starting. You're going to find so many people who love and accept you for who you are."

"I hope so." He looked down at his plate. "I don't know anyone like that in Boston. I've lost touch with all my so-called friends from college already."

"I'm sorry."

"So can I stay as long as you're in Vermont?" he asked. "Dad still won't talk to me. I don't have anything waiting for me in Boston. I just want to be here in Crescent Falls with you and my new friends for now."

"Oh, Carter..." Her voice sounded rough from the lump that had risen in her throat. "Of course you can. But from now on, you'll clear your work schedule with me first, okay?"

He nodded vigorously. "I won't let you down again."

TWENTY

I love your fall foliage painting. I would have bought the original from your store if someone hadn't beaten me to it.

Emily stared at the text from Diana in surprise. They hadn't texted before, although they'd been increasingly friendly with each other over the past week since the fall festival. Truthfully, it was killing Emily a little bit to spend so much time with her without being able to kiss or touch her, even if Emily was the one who'd insisted they could only be friends.

Diana was irresistible when she put her energy into something, and she seemed to have fully embraced her new role as Emily's friend. She often invited Emily to lunch, and she'd even joined the Adventurers for another hike over the weekend. And now, she was apparently stalking Emily's website.

It wasn't the first time she'd complimented Emily's art either. Maybe Emily had thought Diana was just being polite before, but now she was starting to take her seriously.

Diana might say something once to be polite, but she wouldn't send a text like this unless she meant it. She was genuine that way.

> I'll save my next canvas for you!

DIANA DEVLIN

> Or give me a heads-up to check your store the minute you upload it <winking emoji>

Emily smiled. There was no way she was letting Diana pay for it. They texted back and forth until it was time for Emily to get ready for work. Of course, that meant she'd see Diana in person soon. Diana was at the inn right now, probably training Paige, who'd started on Monday, but Emily was only working noon to four today.

She used a sunflower seed to lure Jack into his cage and then went inside to change. And then, since it was a gorgeous October afternoon and the foliage would be past peak any minute, she took the scenic route to work, meandering along the trail that ran through the woods and up the hill behind the inn, where some of the prettiest trees were.

She pulled her phone out of her back pocket and snapped a few photos. She could never get enough of the foliage, even though she lived right in the middle of it.

"Hey," a familiar voice called, and Emily spun in surprise.

Diana was seated at one of the picnic tables she'd had installed along the edges of the field for guests to take in the view. She had a half-eaten sandwich in front of her and was wearing a burgundy wool peacoat that accentuated the red tones in her hair. She looked made for October in Vermont, like she belonged here, even though she didn't.

"Hi yourself." Emily walked toward her. "Taking a scenic lunch break?"

"It's too beautiful to sit inside today," Diana said. "I spent most of the morning showing Paige the ins and outs of the property."

"How's she doing?" Emily sat at the table across from Diana, grateful she still had ten minutes before she needed to go inside and start her shift.

"Really well. I think she'll be ready to take over full-time managerial duties by the end of the month."

Emily's stomach dropped. "Which means you'll head back to Boston."

Diana's gaze was steady as she nodded. "I might be back for a day here and there if she runs into any problems, but yes."

Emily had known this. Diana had always planned to leave by the end of October, but suddenly, it all felt so much more real. So *soon*. "I guess you're ready to go home."

"I am, although I've enjoyed Vermont more than expected." Her eyes were so blue right now. That burgundy coat really suited her.

Emily's thoughts were spiraling. "I'll miss you," she blurted.

Diana's expression softened. "I'll miss you too, but you'll see me again. If for no other reason, I have a feeling Carter's going to be back up here to hang out with your friends. He's quite taken with the adventure group."

"Yeah, he is. I hope you guys do come back to visit. Carter's in the Facebook group now. You should join too. That's where you'll find the calendar with our upcoming events."

"Maybe," Diana said. "I don't use Facebook much."

"I don't either, aside from that group. And speaking of

upcoming events, Alex just scheduled our annual hike to the summit of Crescent Peak. It's on Halloween this year. People will probably hike in costumes. I...maybe this is my year. I don't know."

"It *is* your year," Diana said, sounding as confident as ever. "Let's do it together. It sounds like the perfect way to end my time in Vermont."

Emily sighed. "I used to sign up every year, but something always kept me from reaching the top. One year, we got rained out. Another year, I had a migraine. The next year, it was right after Gram's lumpectomy, and I was with her in the hospital. Eventually, I just felt like I wasn't meant to reach the top, and I haven't even signed up the last two years."

Emily heard how lame that sounded. She knew those were just a bunch of excuses, that she was letting her insecurities hold her back. "I think deep down, I'm afraid, although I'm not really sure why."

Diana reached out and took her hands across the table, staring at her with all the intensity that had caught Emily's attention in the first place, that aura of confidence she wore like a cape. "You know what I say? Fuck fear."

Emily looked down at their hands. "It's not that easy."

"I never said it would be easy, but sometimes you have to feel the fear and do it anyway. Ever since I saw that bear in my driveway a few weeks ago, I've been terrified every time I go out for a run, but I still go. I'm nervous as hell the whole time, but I refuse to give in to the fear."

"Black bears really don't want any trouble." Emily looked up. Diana was still watching her intently, and they both knew this conversation wasn't about bears. "The first time I tried to climb to the summit, I was ten. I was with my mom, and I was so excited that we were doing this together.

About two-thirds of the way up, I sprained my ankle, and she went on without me. Not long after that, she moved to Paris with her boyfriend and left me here with my grandmothers, and...I don't know. Somehow, I have a mental block about that hike now."

"Fuck," Diana murmured. "That would definitely mess with your head. She just left you here for her parents to raise?"

"And never looked back." Emily tried to shrug, but her shoulders felt stiff. "They aren't her parents, though. Mary and Eva took her in when she was sixteen and pregnant with me. She'd run away from home and had nowhere else to go. Then, after she left, they took me in too. They became my legal guardians when I was ten."

Diana's eyes warmed. "They really are special, aren't they?"

"They're the best," Emily agreed. "My mom, well...I guess she wasn't ready to be a parent. She lives in Las Vegas now, but she moves around a lot, always a new man on her arm, always convinced he's 'the one.'"

"I'm sorry," Diana said. "That's rough."

"It is what it is...but somehow, this is the result. I can't seem to get up the mountain." Or leave town. She was just stuck here, like she was still that ten-year-old with the sprained ankle, waiting for her mom to come back for her.

"All the more reason to go for it this year," Diana said. "Let it be your excuse to push yourself out of your comfort zone, the way I did when I left Devlin Hotels and started Aster. Take a risk. Aim big. Fuck fear. What do you say?"

Emily exhaled. "All right. Let's do it. Let's hike to the summit together."

EMILY WAS ALREADY REGRETTING her decision by the time she made it to the front desk. She'd made peace with not reaching the summit. If she tried again this year and failed, it would hurt even more than usual, because this year had already shaken her confidence. Her grandmas had sold the inn. Emily was pining after yet another woman who loved living in the city.

It was so much easier to stay on the well-trodden path.

She forced a smile as she greeted a happy family checking in for a much-anticipated vacation. They were already exclaiming over the foliage and asking for recommendations on the best places to take in the views. Emily loved sharing recommendations with the guests, but somehow, it felt different now.

She felt different.

She loved this inn as if it were an actual member of her family, but she didn't want to spend the rest of her life working at the front desk. Now that her grandmas had left to see the world and Diana was preparing to return to Boston, it was time for Emily to move on too. It was time to stop hiding behind the safety of this desk.

It was time to stop saying she'd focus on her art career tomorrow.

"Hi, Emily."

She turned to find Paige standing beside the desk, watching her with a thoughtful expression. "Hi, Paige. Can I help you with something?"

"Diana wanted me to spend a few hours shadowing you this afternoon to get a handle on the software and see our policies in action with the guests. I want to learn everything inside and out before she leaves."

"Oh, yeah. Perfect." Emily moved over, gesturing for

Paige to join her behind the desk. "How are you liking it here so far? You're brand-new to Vermont, right?"

"So new I'm still living out of my suitcase," Paige said with a laugh. "I'm from Saratoga Springs, New York. I'd been looking unsuccessfully for a job in hotel management there for a while. I'd just been through a breakup, and I'd always wanted to live in the mountains, so when I saw the listing for this job, it just felt like the right thing at the right time, you know?"

Emily *didn't* know, but she understood that others sometimes liked a fresh start after a breakup. She couldn't imagine ever leaving Crescent Falls. "Must have been a bad breakup."

"Not really. We just kind of grew apart, but it felt like the right time to make a change. So, here I am." Paige gestured around herself.

The right time to make a change. Emily didn't know what that felt like either, but she was still thinking about it when her shift ended at four. She'd enjoyed working with Paige. Paige was enthusiastic about the inn and seemed dedicated to learning her new job from the ground up. Emily respected that and thought it boded well for Paige's success as the new manager.

She'd have to text her grandmas tonight and give them an update. Their cruise had ended, and they were in Norway right now. Their Facebook feeds were full of stunning scenery, waterfalls and fjords and Scandinavian architecture. They were even hoping to see the northern lights while they were there.

They were making a change in their lives, just like Paige. And Diana.

And here was Emily, right where she'd started.

Fuck fear.

Diana's words came back to Emily as she logged out of the system and turned the desk over to Mariah. What would happen if Emily just...went after what she wanted? If she did the scary things she'd been avoiding, took a leap of faith the way Diana and Paige had done?

She knew what her first impulsive action would be.

Without giving herself a moment to change her mind, Emily strode down the hall to Diana's office. The door was open, and Diana sat behind her desk, squinting at her laptop as she typed rapidly on the keyboard.

"You might need glasses," Emily blurted from the doorway, then winced, because that wasn't what she'd come here to say.

Diana looked up in surprise, a smile tugging at the corner of her lips. "Is that so?"

"You're always squinting at your laptop, but...I have no idea why I just said that."

"I suspect glasses are somewhere in my near future, but I'm not quite ready to go there yet." Diana tilted her head, studying Emily. "Was there something you needed?"

"Yeah, I...I wanted to tell you something." Her heart was pounding, adrenaline tingling in the pit of her stomach. *Fuck fear.* Emily turned and shut the door to Diana's office, giving them privacy.

Diana's expression changed, all traces of her earlier teasing gone as she tried to figure out what Emily was doing. Diana rose behind the desk to face her.

Emily crossed the office, doing her best to project the confidence she'd embodied that night in June as she placed both hands on Diana's waist and kissed her. It was just a quick kiss. She released Diana's lips as soon as she'd claimed them, meeting her startled gaze to check in with her and make sure this was okay.

"That was unexpected," Diana murmured, licking her lips as her gaze explored Emily's face. "To what do I owe this pleasure?"

"I'm going after what I want, taking chances like you said earlier."

"I'm what you want?" One of Diana's hands was on Emily's ass now, the slight pressure of her fingers bringing their bodies closer together.

Emily nodded, breathless, a warm ache already growing between her thighs. She wanted Diana so much, she could hardly breathe. How had she kept her at arm's length for the past six weeks? "You're the first thing I want."

Diana's pupils dilated, a pink flush spreading over her cheeks, and her fingers were digging into Emily's ass a bit more firmly now. "What's the second?"

"I want to quit my job at the front desk."

Diana drew in an audible breath. "Fuck fear, indeed. You're going all out, aren't you?"

Emily nodded. She couldn't seem to get enough air into her lungs. Her head was swimming. "Not right away. I need to try to get my art earnings up first, but maybe I can plan to quit at the end of the year?"

"Consider it done," Diana said with a firm nod. "I mean this in the kindest possible way when I say you're easily replaceable as front desk staff. Your art, on the other hand, is irreplaceable, and I wholeheartedly support you making it your full-time career."

"Okay," Emily whispered. Tears had welled in her eyes, and she wasn't sure why. She'd come in here to seduce Diana, and somehow, she'd gotten carried away and quit her job instead. It felt right, though. Terrifying, but right.

She stared at Diana. They were still standing close, hands on each other's bodies, both breathing hard, but they'd only shared that one quick kiss right after Emily shut the door, and now she wasn't sure how to get them back on track.

"I'd like to explore this kissing thing further," Diana said as if she'd read her mind. Her voice was a little bit deeper than usual, evoking memories of their night together. This was how she sounded when she was aroused.

Emily gulped.

Diana surged forward, her hands sliding up Emily's back to tangle in her hair, bringing their mouths together for another kiss, this one as wild and hungry as the first one had been tentative and questioning. Diana's teeth nipped at Emily's bottom lip, creating a sting that was echoed by a throb of need in her core.

Just as quickly, it was over. Diana released her and took a step back, turning to shut down her laptop. "But we can't do this here, and Carter's at my rental house." She gave Emily a questioning look.

"My place is closer...and private."

Diana picked up her purse and led the way toward the door. "I'll drive."

TWENTY-ONE

Diana had only been to Emily's cottage one other time, when they'd shared pumpkin spice tea on the back porch while Emily's rescued sparrow flitted around them. Today, Diana barely spared a look around the living area before she was kissing Emily again. Sure, she noticed the brightly colored daisies on the coffee table—the ones she'd given Emily—but then her hands were in Emily's hair as their lips met, and everything else faded into the background.

She walked them forward until Emily's back was against the wall, Diana's body pressed against her everywhere she could reach. Unfortunately, her pencil skirt was too snug to let her get much leverage, but it didn't matter. She was already throbbing without being touched. She'd been fantasizing about Emily since their night together, which meant she'd had four months to anticipate this moment. Coupled with the sexual frustration she'd experienced since she got to Vermont, she probably wasn't going to last long tonight.

Nothing like last time.

"I want you to be yourself this time," Emily said. One of

her hands slid between them, rubbing over the front of Diana's skirt, and she arched her hips into Emily's touch, already eager to be out of her clothes.

"Myself?" she asked, her voice rough with need.

Emily nodded, still rubbing her over her skirt, and Diana had to bite her lip to keep from whining with impatience. "We were acting out fantasies, and you let me be in control, but tonight, I want to experience the real you. Be as dominant as you like. I want it."

Emily's eyes were dark, her hair hanging messily around her face, and she looked so beautiful, so sexy, Diana could barely speak.

She swallowed, pushing Emily's hand away as she reached below the hem of Emily's knee-length dress. After months of thinking about it, she was going to ravage Emily, and this wall looked like an excellent place to start. "I want you right here the first time."

Emily nodded quickly, her expression pleading, and Diana felt another rush of arousal as she realized she wasn't the only one feeling a bit desperate here. Her suspicion was confirmed as her fingers brushed the wet fabric of Emily's underwear. Diana hooked a finger under the band and tugged them down while Emily wriggled and kicked until they were on the floor.

"Have you thought about this since that night?" Diana asked as her fingers met Emily's wet flesh.

Emily gasped. "Yes."

"Tell me." Diana kept her touch teasingly light, refamiliarizing herself with Emily's body as she waited for her response. And suddenly, she was dying to know. Maybe because Diana had spent so much time fantasizing about that night, she needed to know if it had meant as much to Emily.

"Diana..." Emily's breath hitched as Diana brushed a thumb over her clit. "I've never felt that powerful during sex before."

"Yeah?" Diana teased a finger against her entrance. "You enjoyed being in control?"

Emily nodded, her cheeks flushed. "You're powerful. I felt it from the moment I met you. You're confident and sexy and so assertive. You know what you want, and you just go for it. So for you to let me be in control that night? Yeah, it was memorable for me. Diana, please." Her hips bucked against Diana's hand.

But Diana wouldn't be rushed. She continued her slow exploration of Emily's body, gradually working her up... and working herself up in the process. Diana's core ached. Her panties were soaked. And she was loving every moment. "Do you think about me when you touch yourself?"

Emily whimpered, her hands grasping at Diana's waist, dragging her closer. "Yes. God, yes, I've thought about you... I've fantasized about you. That night...it was the best sex of my life, okay?"

That got Diana's attention in a hurry. She froze, her body flushing hot, and for a moment, they just stared at each other.

Emily cast her gaze over Diana's shoulder, looking vaguely embarrassed. "I know I was just another conquest for you, a way to pass a random night in an unfamiliar town, but that night really rocked my world." The discomfort on her face was like a knife to Diana's heart.

She hated to slow things down when they were both already so aroused, but she couldn't bear to see that look on Emily's face. She couldn't let Emily go another moment feeling so insecure about how much she meant to Diana, not when she'd come to mean more to her than any woman ever had before.

Diana's hand had slipped to Emily's thigh, and she left it there for the moment. "Is that what you've thought this whole time? Well, you're wrong. I've never considered any woman to be a conquest, and you were never *just* anything to me, Emily. Granted, I wasn't thinking past a single night when I invited you up to my room, but surely you realized how much I enjoyed myself...how much I enjoyed *you*. I've never let anyone dominate me like that before. That night was just as memorable for me."

Emily blinked at her, eyes wide and so heartbreakingly vulnerable.

"I haven't been able to get you out of my head since," Diana admitted.

Emily gulped, those big brown eyes glossy now. "Really? I..."

"Really. You meant something to me then, and you mean even more to me now." Diana brushed her free hand over Emily's cheek. This was more than just sex for her, so much more. By the look on Emily's face, she guessed it was more than sex for her too.

"Oh," Emily whispered. "I had no idea. I..." Her back was still against the wall, Diana's body pressed against her, and she shifted now, her hips pushing forward. "Touch me. Please."

Diana brought her hand against Emily's pussy, and this time she didn't hold back. She leaned in, claiming Emily's lips for a deep, passionate kiss as she stroked Emily's clit, circling and rubbing the way she remembered Emily liked best. Emily was breathing hard as she kissed her back, hips moving to Diana's rhythm.

Beneath Diana's fingers, she grew increasingly wet, her

gasps and moans becoming louder and more urgent. Diana picked up her pace. She could hear the wet slip of her fingers against Emily's flesh. Oh, how she loved that sound.

"More," Emily gasped, hips jerking against Diana's hand.

Diana changed positions, pushing two fingers inside Emily as her palm provided necessary friction. Diana thrust into her, using her own hips for leverage. Each thrust sent Diana's fingers deeper into Emily and brought a new cry from her lips.

"Yes...God...yes...I'm going to..." Her voice went high-pitched, her hips losing their rhythm, grinding erratically against Diana.

Diana used her free hand to grip Emily's ass as she hauled her closer, positioning her the way she wanted as her fingers curled forward, rubbing that perfect spot inside her. Emily let out a strangled sound, her body clamping down on Diana's fingers and then pulsing with the waves of her release.

"Holy fuck," Emily managed once she'd caught her breath. Her hands were on Diana's waist as if she wasn't sure her knees would hold her up.

Diana held her gaze as she brought her fingers to her mouth and sucked. As Emily's sharp flavor met her tongue, Diana felt an answering surge of need in her core. God, she'd forgotten how much she loved Emily's taste.

Emily moaned, shuddering in Diana's arms. Her hips pressed forward against Diana, and that was all the invitation she needed. She dropped to her knees, covering Emily with her mouth. Diana took her time at first, teasing and exploring with her tongue as Emily recovered from her first orgasm, but Diana knew from past experience that Emily rebounded impressively fast.

Within minutes, Emily was grinding against her face, begging for more. Diana let the insistent ache in her own clit fuel her as she devoured Emily, licking and flicking her tongue until Emily started to tense against her. Sensing she was close, Diana closed her lips over her and sucked, not letting up until Emily shouted her release.

Her legs shook and quaked, and then she slid down the wall to sit in front of Diana, blinking at her in blissed-out pleasure. If Diana's skirt hadn't been so confining, she'd have straddled one of Emily's bare thighs right then. The need for friction was overwhelming, but she was glad for the forced moment of self-control too.

After months of frustration, she'd soon have all the pleasure she could handle. Emily would be worth the wait.

"TIME TO MOVE this to the bedroom?"

Emily felt half-drunk as she sat slumped against the wall, gasping for breath. Her body still tingled with pleasure. That was by far the hottest thing she'd ever done in her living room. *Whoa.* Diana's words filtered through her ears, and she nodded. Yes, the bed sounded good right now.

Speaking of Diana, she was crouched in front of Emily, still fully dressed. Technically, Emily was still mostly dressed, although her underwear was on the floor somewhere. Diana's skirt was too snug for Emily to have any fun, though, and now that her brain was coming back online, she was beyond eager to get her hands on Diana's bare skin.

She wanted to give Diana an orgasm worthy of how much she meant to her now. Last time, it had just been sex. Really, *really* hot sex, but they'd been little more than strangers. This time...it was more. This time, it was *everything*.

Emily scrambled to her feet. She reached for Diana's hand and hauled her up beside her. Diana stumbled, wincing as she released Emily's hand to rub at her knees. There was a red circle on each knee where Emily's hardwood floors had dug into her while she was kneeling.

"Come on." Emily led the way into her bedroom. Her bed was unmade, the lavender sheets rumpled from when she'd rolled out of them that morning, but she didn't care. She knew Diana well enough by now to know that—while she probably made her own bed every morning—she wouldn't judge Emily's messiness.

When she turned around, Diana was already lowering the zipper at her hip. Emily seized the opportunity to help, sliding the skirt over Diana's slim hips to land on the floor, revealing black seamless panties.

Impulsively, Emily slipped a hand beneath them, and they both gasped when her fingers met Diana's bare flesh. Diana wasn't just wet, she was *soaked*. When her gaze met Emily's, the yearning there made Emily's breath catch.

Here was irrefutable proof of how much Diana still wanted her, and she'd been pretty clear earlier that she'd fantasized about their night too. Diana didn't say things she didn't mean.

Emily wiggled her fingers, gathering Diana's wetness on her fingertips before she brought them against her clit. Diana let out a little whimper, clutching Emily against her as her hips began to move. She sounded needy enough that Emily wondered if she might come right here, still fully dressed except for her skirt, standing in her heels beside Emily's bed.

That would be hot. Emily rubbed faster.

Then again, maybe fucking Diana in her heels wasn't the best idea. One of Diana's ankles wobbled as her legs started to shake, and she lost her balance. Emily guided her so she landed on the bed, bouncing gently from her momentum. God, she looked sexy, flat on her back on Emily's bed, her blouse still buttoned while her panties were bunched low on her hips.

And the heels. Her legs dangled over the side of the bed, one heel still on, the other dangling from her toes, about to fall. She looked so perfectly debauched, Emily could hardly stand it.

"For fuck's sake," Diana muttered, kicking off the heels Emily had just been admiring.

Emily knelt beside the bed to kiss one foot, then the other. Diana's toes were painted a deep maroon, perfect for the season. Emily kissed her way up Diana's legs, pausing to pay special attention to her knees, which were still red and sore looking.

Apparently impatient, Diana wriggled against the bed, pushing her underwear down her legs. Emily caught them at her knees and pulled them the rest of the way off. Now Diana was bare from the waist down, and Emily couldn't wait another moment.

Judging by the whine in Diana's throat, neither could she.

Emily crawled forward to settle between her thighs. She looked up and caught Diana's eye as she brought her mouth against Diana's pussy. Diana's back arched, and her hands moved to cover her breasts. Then she made a frustrated sound, as if she'd forgotten she still wore her bra and blouse.

"No teasing," she told Emily in a voice that was probably supposed to sound commanding but actually sounded desperate. "Not this time."

"Not *this* time," Emily repeated, emphasizing the second word. She'd give Diana what she needed now, but later? Who knew?

"Emily, please." Diana's fingers worked clumsily at the buttons on her blouse as she shifted her hips with impatience.

Emily kissed her again, taking the time to explore with her mouth. She remembered all the spots Diana loved the most...the crease of her inner thigh, that spot just to the left of her clit. Her wrists. Emily yearned to kiss those too, but they were still covered by her blouse.

She stalled just long enough to let Diana finish undressing herself. The blouse joined her skirt on the floor, and a black bra followed seconds later. Emily was momentarily distracted by the view of Diana's perfect breasts before Diana nudged her back between her thighs as she took her breasts in her own hands.

"Please," Diana whispered, her voice catching.

Emily started working in earnest then. She pushed two fingers inside Diana, stroking in and out as she transferred the full attention of her mouth to Diana's clit. She ran her tongue beside Diana's clit in that spot she seemed to love so much as she applied gentle suction with her mouth, and Diana bucked beneath her.

"Yes," Diana moaned. "Just like that. Don't stop."

Emily wasn't planning to. She kept moving her tongue and her fingers, gradually increasing her pace as Diana grew closer to her release. Her hips pushed more insistently against Emily's mouth. Her breathing was ragged as she gasped and swore.

Emily sucked harder, and Diana went rigid against the bed.

"Oh fuck," she cried out. "Oh God. Yes...oh!"

Her inner walls spasmed around Emily's fingers as she came, and Emily kept moving, kept thrusting, kept sucking as Diana writhed and swore until she finally went limp beneath her, pushing shakily at Emily's shoulders.

Emily sat up, wiping her mouth with the back of her hand as she took in the view before her. Diana's hair was a golden halo around her head, beautifully mussed from thrashing against the sheets, her cheeks stained a dark pink, her eyes bright and damp.

"For the record, still the best I've ever had," Emily said, emboldened by the moment.

"For the record...same." Diana ran a hand through her hair, still gasping for air, and *oh wow, oh wow, oh wow*. She hadn't said that earlier. It was one thing for Emily to say it. She'd had a few relationships over the years but nothing too adventurous. But Diana? Well, she was a lot more experienced.

"Really?" Emily asked, her voice embarrassingly breathy. She yanked her dress over her head and unfastened her bra so she could slide in naked beside Diana.

"Really." Diana wrapped an arm around her, drawing her in for a kiss. "You blow my mind every time we're together, Emily Janssen."

"And you've just blown mine all over again." Emily rested her forehead against Diana's. Her arm was around Diana's waist, one leg nestled between Diana's thighs. Their naked bodies were entwined from head to foot, and this was so much more intimate than their first night. They'd barely known each other then. Now, Emily wanted to stay in this bed with her forever.

They lay together like that for a few minutes, just enjoying the comfort and closeness between them. They shared occasional kisses that gradually became more heated, hands beginning to roam, legs shifting as they sought friction.

Emily pushed a hand between Diana's thighs, groaning in pleasure when Diana returned the favor. She'd gotten pretty worked up again while she was going down on Diana, and now she ached for release. Diana's fingers began to stroke, and Emily's did too. They gasped in unison.

Diana hooked a leg over Emily's hip, giving her easier access as she brought their bodies together. Their hands bumped, getting in each other's way, but just as quickly, Diana had adjusted her position, bringing them into perfect alignment.

Their mouths came together for a sloppy kiss as they kept moving, bodies pressing more insistently against each other, toes scrambling for purchase against the sheets. Emily broke first, moaning into their kiss as the orgasm rushed through her. Her fingers lost their rhythm, and Diana rolled them so she was on top, straddling Emily's thigh.

She moved against her, head thrown back, bottom lip pinched between her teeth as her face contorted with pleasure. Emily reached for one of Diana's arms and brought it to her mouth, swirling her tongue over the delicate skin on Diana's wrist, and she whimpered, grinding harder.

Emily could watch her like this forever, lost in the throes of passion. Diana's eyes slid shut, and her lips parted. Emily gave her wrist one more kiss, and Diana jerked against her, panting and gasping as she came.

Finally, she stopped moving, sucking in deep, ragged breaths. Her hair hung in messy golden waves over her face, and a fine sheen of sweat glistened on her chest. She was stunning, perfect, and, for tonight anyway, she was Emily's.

TWENTY-TWO

Diana opened her eyes to the golden light of the setting sun. She was still in Emily's bed, still naked, although now there was a warm blanket over her...and a warm woman pressed against her. Emily gave her a lazy smile, eyes half-lidded as if she'd had a nap too.

"Sorry for conking out on you," Diana murmured, semi-embarrassed for falling asleep.

"Absolutely no apology needed," Emily said, sliding closer to give Diana a gentle kiss. "We did some hard-core exercise earlier, and the nap was great."

"It was," Diana agreed. She felt calmer than she had in months. Part of that was due to her new medication and a newly hired manager who'd taken a lot of the daily work-load off her, but Emily had helped too...both with orgasms and with comfort.

"I don't know about you, but I'm starving," Emily said.

As if it heard Emily's words, Diana's stomach let out a loud rumble of agreement that made them both laugh. "Do you have food here, or should we go out?"

"I definitely want to go out with you sometime," Emily

said. "But tonight, I'd rather stay in if that's okay? I want to enjoy this perfect evening, just the two of us."

"There's nothing I'd love more."

First, they stepped into a quick shower together, rinsing off sweat and sex. Emily lent Diana flannel pajama pants and a blue hoodie before dressing in similarly cozy clothes, in deference to the cool October evening.

While Diana opened a bottle of wine, Emily pulled a bag of shrimp out of the freezer and put it in a bowl of cold water to thaw. "Shrimp fra diavolo?" she asked. "It's basically shrimp in a spicy marinara sauce over spaghetti the way I make it. An easy but tasty dish I like to fix when I have unexpected company for dinner."

"Sounds delicious," Diana said as she looked around for a corkscrew. "Do you often have unexpected company for dinner?"

"Yeah, but it's usually Alex or someone else from the adventure group."

"Have you two known each other a long time?" Diana asked.

"Since kindergarten," Emily told her. "We were both born and raised here in Crescent Falls. We went to college together too, although we didn't end up as roommates."

"That's surprising." Diana twisted the corkscrew and popped the cork, then moved to grab two glasses.

"She roomed with Margo, who you met at the fall festival. Margo's family moved here our senior year of high school, and they became inseparable pretty quickly. At the time, I was annoyed. I felt a little left out, but that was just me being an immature teenager." She shrugged.

"Were they together?" Diana asked.

"Nope. Just friends. Really close friends." Emily paused with a box of pasta in her hands. "I did wonder at first. I think Margo wanted to be more than friends, but if she did, Alex never noticed or felt the same. Margo moved away after college, and that was the end of it."

"How long has Alex been with Frankie?"

"They've been on again off again for years." Emily frowned as she emptied the box of pasta into the pot. "Sometimes, I wish they'd end it for good, and I know that sounds horrible of me, but I don't like the way Frankie treats her. She tends to put her own interests first."

"Sorry to hear that."

"Alex has a degree in culinary arts. She's dreamed of being a chef for as long as I can remember, and she's just working in Frankie's shop, selling soaps and wind chimes."

"Speaking of jobs." Diana handed Emily a glass of wine. Now that the urgency between them had calmed, she wanted to follow up on the conversation they'd had in her office. "Did you mean to quit yours today or was that a spur-of-the-moment thing?"

Emily flinched. "One-hundred-percent impulsive."

Diana sat on one of the stools at the kitchen island and sipped her wine. "You can take it back if you want. Technically, now that Paige is managing the inn, you should give your notice to her anyway."

"I don't want to take it back. I was thinking about what you said, about not letting fear hold me back. I've always wanted to be a full-time artist, but I've never really pushed myself because I have that income from the inn to help pay the bills. And I love the inn, but it's not as special without my grandmas there. You're leaving soon too, and then I'll just be a woman in her midthirties working an entry-level job instead of doing what I love."

Impulsively, Diana leaned across the counter and kissed her. "Not at all what I had in mind when I encouraged you to fuck fear this morning, but I'm so glad you're doing this."

"What were you thinking?" Emily asked, twirling one of the drawstrings on Diana's borrowed hoodie between her fingers. "Were you hoping I'd kiss you?"

Diana smiled, shaking her head. "Believe it or not, I was just thinking about you making it to the top of the mountain. But it's all tied together, isn't it? You've been afraid to take risks, both with your career and in your personal life."

"Yeah, so...we'll see how it all works out." Doubt flickered in Emily's eyes, as if she was already regretting her afternoon of impulsive decisions.

Diana hoped she wasn't one of Emily's regrets. Sooner or later, they'd have to talk about what this meant. They'd already had a one-night stand. This was different, at least for Diana. She so rarely dated that she wasn't sure of the rules. All she knew was that she hadn't been able to get Emily out of her head for months, and now she wanted to hold on to whatever this was with both hands, even if it meant a long-distance relationship.

They sipped wine, and Diana helped her with dinner, which they brought out to the little table on Emily's back porch, where Jack fluttered around them while they ate. After dinner, they snuggled together on the love seat, a warm blanket wrapped around them as they listened to the chorus of crickets and other insects outside. It was fully dark now, and Diana was so comfortable, so relaxed, she never wanted to leave.

"Stay here tonight?" Emily asked.

"Yes," she answered immediately, because she'd like nothing more than to sleep beside Emily tonight. "But...Carter."

Emily gave her an amused look. "What about him?"

Diana scrubbed a hand over her face. She'd lived alone since college, and consequently, she was completely unaccustomed to having anyone notice or care where she spent her nights. "If I text him that I'm staying here tonight, well... he'll *know*."

Emily frowned. "Did you not want people to know? I mean, we didn't really talk about it yet, but I guess I was hoping—"

"I'm hoping too." Diana squeezed her hand. "I don't care if people know we're together—if we *are* together, which we obviously need to discuss—but telling him I'm spending the night here feels like telling him I'm having sex, and he's my nephew, and...ugh, that's so awkward. How do parents handle something like this?"

Emily was laughing now. "Don't ask me. By the time I was old enough to know what sex was, I was being raised by my happily married grandmothers. But Carter's an adult, and he's *not* your son, so I think you need to just suck it up and tell him where you are."

"I guess." Reluctantly, she left the warm cocoon of Emily's blanket and went in search of her phone. She found her purse tossed haphazardly on the couch, where she'd left it when she arrived earlier. Her phone had spilled out onto the cushion, and when she tapped the screen, she found a string of unread texts from Carter.

CARTER DEVLIN

Picking up a pizza. Want some?

Pizza's here, where r u?

Hello?

Srsly where r u?

"Fuck," she mumbled as she brought her phone to the back porch.

"Everything okay?" Emily asked.

"Carter's been texting me for an hour. I think he's worried." And she felt like an asshole.

"It's fine. You're both adults. Just text him now."

> Sorry. I came to Emily's for dinner and forgot to check my phone.

> I'm staying here tonight. See you tomorrow!

There. She'd done it, although she still felt somewhat mortified about what might be going through her nephew's head right now. She'd be perfectly happy for him to never think about her having sex.

The phone buzzed in her hand, and when she looked, he had texted back a thumbs-up emoji. Emily looked over her shoulder and laughed when she saw his response. She brushed a strand of hair from Diana's face, and her expression sobered.

"To answer your earlier question: are we together? I think yes, but...casually, I guess, since you're leaving so soon." Emily turned to look into the darkness beyond the screen.

"Casual is a good place to start," Diana agreed. She didn't have experience with anything else, but her priorities had shifted over the last few months. She was taking her own advice and going after what she wanted, even the things that scared her. "But Boston isn't that far away, so it doesn't put a definitive end to things when I leave either."

Emily turned to face her, eyes wide. "What are you saying?"

"I'm saying I'm open to a long-distance relationship. Let's enjoy ourselves for the next few weeks, and when it's time for me to leave, let's see where we are and what we want to happen next."

———————

DIANA WALKED into her rental cabin the next morning feeling a bit like a teenager who'd missed curfew. She couldn't even remember the last time there'd been someone living with her to notice she'd been out all night, and it brought a surge of discomfort that quickly morphed into impatience for Carter to get his own place. She'd hoped she could sneak into her bedroom to shower and change before she saw him, but he was seated at the kitchen table when she walked in, mug of coffee in one hand, cell phone in the other.

He looked up and grinned. "So, you and Emily, huh?"

"Yes." She dropped her purse on the counter.

"That's cool."

To her extreme annoyance, she could feel herself blushing. "Thank you."

Before her embarrassment worsened, she excused herself to shower. As she stood under the hot spray, her mind wandered to last night. She'd slept so peacefully, even without her white noise app to play city sounds. Truthfully, she'd adjusted to life in Vermont more than she'd expected. She liked it here, but she could never see herself living here permanently.

Visiting on the weekends to see Emily? That felt much more plausible. And maybe Emily could visit her in Boston too. Maybe she'd like to paint the harbor and the skyline. It sounded pretty perfect to Diana's newly smitten brain.

With Paige managing the inn, Diana spent the morning at her cabin putting together a presentation package for the hotel in Maryland that she was interested in. She hoped to schedule a visit to see it in person soon. After that, she had properties in North Carolina and Maine to look at. She was sticking to the East Coast for now, but her five-year plan involved expanding nationwide.

"Are you coming to trivia tonight, then?" Carter asked as she packed up to head to the inn after lunch. He'd gone to the local pub with the adventure group every Thursday that he'd been in town. Diana was always invited too, but she always declined. Tonight, though...

"Yeah, I suppose I could come."

And that was how she found herself in the passenger seat of Emily's car that evening on her way to Maude's Tavern, her skin prickling with anxious energy. She wanted Emily's friends to like her, wanted to move past the awkwardness she felt when she'd been around them previously.

Emily pulled into the lot behind the tavern and parked. "What's that?" She gestured toward Diana's lap.

Diana tensed. She hadn't realized she was using her calming strip until that moment, but she knew immediately what had captured Emily's attention.

"Is it a sensory thing?" Emily asked, sounding curious.

"It's nothing." Diana shoved it into her purse. Her skin felt too tight, and she was already reaching for the door handle, desperate to escape the close confines of the car.

Emily touched her shoulder gently. "Sorry. I didn't mean to pry."

Diana froze. What was she doing? She was trying to be more open, trying not to carry on her parents' bad habits. She was trying to have a real relationship with Emily, and that involved sharing things with her, even when it was hard. Diana blew out a long, slow breath. "You didn't pry. I shouldn't have gotten defensive." Another breath, then she pulled her keys out of her purse and handed them to Emily. "It's a calming strip."

"Oh cool. I've seen ads for these. Do you like it?" Emily ran her thumb experimentally over the strip and smiled.

"I do. It helps with my anxiety."

"Really?" Emily looked at her in surprise. "You don't strike me as an anxious person."

Diana took another slow breath, pushing down the instinct to deflect, to change the subject, to get out of the damn car. "That's because I've learned to hide it well."

Emily reached for her hand, eyes wide and earnest. "What do you mean?"

"I'm very driven, as you've probably noticed." She managed a small laugh. "Very ambitious, always focused on success, but that drive also makes me a bit high-strung. I think I've been anxious since I was a child. Sometimes, I'm able to manage it on my own with tools like the calming strip, but sometimes I need extra help from my therapist and even medication."

"Diana, I had no idea." Her fingers squeezed Diana's.

"That was kind of the point." She laughed again, aware it sounded strained. "These things aren't talked about in my family, so it's something I've always kept to myself."

Then Emily's arms were around her. Diana buried her face in Emily's hair and inhaled the apple-cinnamon scent of her shampoo, in the process finding another tool that helped calm her: Emily's embrace. Emily's hair had smelled citrusy back in June. If she changed her scent to suit the season, well, that was just one more thing Diana lov—liked about her.

"Thank you so much for telling me," Emily murmured, squeezing her tight. "If there's anything I can do to help or if something I do is bad for your anxiety or anything like that, please tell me. I want to be here for you."

"Thank you." Diana held on for dear life, but she was breathing easier now. "I didn't realize until after I left Devlin Hotels how rigidly I'd been forcing myself into their mold, trying to do what it took to become CEO. With Aster, I want to make time for a personal life, and...I'm trying to be more open about the things I've always kept hidden, like my mental health."

"I'm so freaking proud of you," Emily whispered. "You have all these layers I didn't know about, and every time I uncover one, I just like you more."

"You like me more because of my anxiety?" Diana heard the skepticism in her tone.

"I like you more because you're *human*. We all have things we struggle with, and I can see that it was really hard for you to open up about this. It means a lot that you shared something so personal with me."

"I'm trying to open up more...especially with you."

Emily kissed her cheek. "Thank you."

Diana closed her eyes. "Full disclosure: I'm back on meds now. Leaving Devlin, starting Aster, all this uncertainty...it really did a number on me."

"I did notice you looked tired. I'm sorry I wasn't more supportive."

"You were fine. I was the one clamming up every time I felt uncomfortable."

Emily pulled back enough to meet Diana's eyes. "Looking back, knowing what I know about you now, of course it was stressful. Leaving your family's company...that was huge, and probably very scary."

"Terrifying," Diana admitted.

"But you did it anyway. Living up to your own motto, right?" Her gaze fell to the calming strip in Diana's lap. "Wait...were you anxious tonight about hanging out with my friends?"

Diana's pulse spiked again, discomfort crawling over her skin.

"I felt that." Emily's arms tightened around her. "I felt you tense up. I guess that's my answer, and wow...again, I had no idea."

"I haven't exactly fit in with them in the past." She forced the words out. "And it's uncomfortable for me that they know our history."

"They may be boisterous and nosy, but they aren't judgmental. You could walk in there and announce that you take anxiety medication, and you'd probably wind up in the middle of a group hug. They like you, Diana. They've been rooting for us from the start."

"Have they?" She sat back, releasing Emily so she could smooth out her blouse and check her hair...fidgeting. She was fidgeting, so she reached for her calming strip, letting Emily see her use it.

Emily's smile was gentle. "They have. Some of them have taken psych meds too, you know. You're far from alone."

Diana felt an unexpected dampness in her eyes. "I'm not?" It sounded a little hoarse, a little vulnerable, and she felt herself flush but refused to give in to the instinctive shame.

Emily shook her head. "I think you'll find that a pretty high percentage of the population has dealt with mental health stuff in some way."

Diana exhaled again, sliding her keys—and the calming strip—into her purse. "Shall we go inside, then?"

Emily nodded. "I'll be right beside you if you need anything, okay?"

Dammit. Diana's eyes were damp again. She covered the moment by leaning in for a quick kiss. "Thank you."

A FEW MINUTES LATER, Diana was seated in a vinyl booth, nonalcoholic cider in one hand, the other clasped with Emily's. She could have used a good buzz tonight to help with her nerves, but her new meds didn't mix well with alcohol. Alex and Frankie sat across from them, which made the whole thing feel a little bit like a double date, but Drew, Carter, Tom, Maddie, and Talia were crammed into the booth beside them, constantly shouting over the back of the seat like they were all one big group, despite the fact they'd be separate teams once the trivia started.

Diana very much wanted to fit in, to feel like part of the group the way Carter seemed to. These were Emily's friends, and she'd like them to become her friends too, but friendship had never been one of Diana's strengths. She'd always been too focused on schoolwork and then her career to have friends. Hopefully, it wasn't too late to start now.

Frankie rested her elbows on the table. "I heard it was a big day for you yesterday, Em."

Diana bristled. Did everyone at the table know she'd spent last night at Emily's?

Emily gave her hand a gentle squeeze before she replied. "It was. I gave my notice at the inn *and* signed up for the summit hike."

Diana exhaled, annoyed with herself for jumping to the wrong conclusion and for being obvious enough about it that Emily had noticed. She was still raw after their conversation in the car. She'd scratched herself open, made herself vulnerable, and received nothing but compassion and support in return. Despite her ragged nerves, she felt closer to Emily than ever.

"Diana gave me the nudge I needed," Emily said. "Did you know that the first time I met her, she was out there hiking to the summit by herself, never having hiked in Vermont before?"

"Damn." Frankie regarded Diana with raised eyebrows. "That's either ballsy or stupid. How did it go?"

"I lost the trail about halfway up," Diana admitted. "I might have been in real trouble if I hadn't bumped into Emily."

"Emily to the rescue." Frankie laughed. "I tried that hike once. I made it to the part where you have to jump over that little ravine and noped right out. There's a reason I'm not an official member of the Adventurers group. I just tag along for the fun stuff."

"Well, I think it's great," Alex said. "You two can hike to the summit together, and then you can take one of those kissing selfies in front of the tower!"

Diana gave her a questioning look.

"It's kind of a 'thing' the locals do," Alex explained. "Kissing selfies at the summit. I keep trying to convince Frankie to try again so we can take one."

"But no," Frankie responded, jabbing playfully at Alex with her elbow.

Luckily, Diana was saved from further discussion of kissing selfies by the bartender announcing the start of trivia night.

"Just to warn you," Emily told Diana, her expression

apologetic, as Alex went to get their scorecard. "Our team always loses."

Diana lifted an eyebrow. "Not tonight, you won't."

Diana sometimes got overconfident about things, but not this. The first category of the evening was military trivia. Alex and Frankie shared a groan, but Diana smiled. She knew a lot about a lot of things. Maybe if she helped the team win, it would help her feel like part of the group.

Maybe.

"Ready for your first question?" the bartender called. "What year did World War II end?"

"1945," Diana told Alex, who held the scorecard.

"Are you sure?" Frankie asked.

"Yes."

"Okay." Alex wrote it down.

"Next question," the bartender called. "What does the acronym SWAT stand for?"

Diana tapped a finger against her lips, thinking.

"Special something? Like special ops?" Emily suggested.

The W had to stand for weapons. Diana searched her brain. "Special weapons and tactics, I think."

Alex filled out the scorecard. Over the course of the next hour, Diana drank cider and helped her team answer questions. By the time they handed in their scorecard, she was relaxed and—dare she say it?—she was having fun.

The bartender took a few minutes to tally the score-cards, and Diana seized the opportunity to visit the restroom. As she returned to their table, the bartender had just picked up her microphone. "Tonight's winner is Team Guy All Day. Congratulations, guys. See me to claim your gift card."

Someone whooped, and the next thing Diana knew, she

was being spun in a circle. Various hands were patting her back, and then she found herself being hugged by both Emily and Alex, which felt surprisingly nice.

"We did it," Alex was saying. "We really won!"

"I knew you were smart," Emily told Diana through a wide grin, "but you're like, *really* smart."

"Figures," Drew said with a good-natured eye roll, "the one night I defect to the other team, we still lose. Still happy for Team Gay All Day, though."

Everyone was in exuberant spirits as they left the bar, but no one more than Diana. She felt like she'd won a prize infinitely more valuable than a gift card to Maude's Tavern.

Emily turned to her with a hopeful expression. "Stay with me again tonight?"

Diana's pulse quickened. "Yes."

TWENTY-THREE

Emily scowled at her laptop. She'd spent the morning adding features to her online store. After hours of research, she'd signed up with a third-party vendor that allowed her to sell new products like throw pillows and earrings featuring her art—and of course she'd ordered one of each for herself because they were adorable. Now, she was setting up a monthly sticker club, something some of her customers had been asking for.

With the sticker club, she would release a brand-new sheet of stickers each month, and people could subscribe to be the first to receive them. She would theme the stickers to the month they released, with lots of fun new designs. People got really enthusiastic about stickers, so she hoped it would be a hit.

It wouldn't be a huge moneymaker, but one thing she'd learned over the years was that all these little things added up. Cumulatively, she earned more on prints and accessories featuring her art than she did on her original paintings. She needed to increase profits from her online store by thirty percent by the time she quit the inn, so she hoped these new additions would help bridge the gap.

But no matter how many times she fiddled with it, she could *not* get the subscription form for the sticker club to load correctly. Her patience was wearing thin.

"Why the scowl?" Diana asked. They were seated at her kitchen table, working together. It had been a week since they rekindled their romance—one of the best, most romantic weeks of Emily's life. They'd spent as much of it together as they could, knowing that Diana only had another week or so left in Vermont.

Already, she was spending less time at the inn and more time at her rental house, focusing on the next steps for her business now that the Inn at Crescent Falls was running efficiently without her. Emily had stayed here last night, and they'd spent the morning together working on their respective businesses and enjoying each other's company.

"I can't get this form to work right," Emily said as she shoved back from the table in frustration. "I need a break, maybe some fresh air."

Diana held up a finger. "Wait. I have an idea first." She turned her head and called, "Carter? Got a minute?"

He came out of his bedroom in jeans and a long-sleeved tee for a band Emily had never heard of. "Sure. What's up?"

"Emily's having trouble with this web form she's building, and if there's one thing I've learned about you in the past month...you're really good at figuring out web stuff."

"Yeah, sure. I'll take a look." He came around the table to stand beside Emily. "What's wrong with it?"

"Every time I fill it out with sample information to test it, I get this random string of computer code instead of a confirmation that my request was sent, and I'm not seeing the data in the spreadsheet where it's supposed to land."

"Do you mind?" He sat beside her and gestured for her to slide her laptop over.

She moved it in front of him. "Thank you. This thing is driving me nuts."

"No problem. I like finding bugs in the code. It's satisfying."

Diana gave him an affectionate look. "We could not be less alike."

He flipped her off with a teasing smile. Emily got warm fuzzies watching them interact like this, especially knowing neither of them had this kind of relationship with their own parents. Thank goodness they had each other.

"Might take me a few minutes," Carter said as he clicked a button to bring up all the code for the web form.

Those strings of code made Emily anxious. It was a language she couldn't read where one wrong letter could break everything. Rather than hover, she stood and walked to the fridge for a drink of water.

Diana came to stand beside her. "I'm leaving town tomorrow for a few days."

Emily's breath hitched. It might only be a few days this time, but soon it would be permanent. "To Boston?"

"I'll be flying out of Boston, yes, but I'm actually going to Maryland to look at another hotel. It's a bonus that I can also stop at home and check on my town house."

"Well, that's exciting. I know you've been looking at this hotel for a little while now."

Diana nodded. "Assuming all goes well with my visit, I hope to put in an offer next week."

She was moving on, buying her next hotel, keeping to the schedule she'd laid out when she first arrived in Vermont. This wasn't sudden or unexpected, no matter how much it felt that way to Emily right now. She'd always had trouble with people leaving...particularly people leaving *her*.

"Fingers crossed for you," Emily said. "My grandmas are getting home tomorrow, so if you're not around, I'll probably bring takeout over to their house and let them regale me with vacation stories."

Diana smiled. "I bet you're excited to see them."

"Understatement," Emily laughed. "I've been missing them like crazy."

"Found it," Carter called. "A whole section of the form had gotten corrupted, so I generated fresh code for that part, and it's working now. You'll just need to reinput the email address you want the forms to deliver to."

"Carter, you really *are* good at this web stuff," Emily said. "Thank you."

"No problem." He stood from the table with a shrug. "I'm heading over to Tom and Maddie's house to meet up with some people. We're going to watch a horror movie and maybe play some video games later."

"Okay," Diana said. "Have fun."

He grabbed his jacket and keys off the kitchen table. "I'll be out late, but like, give me a sign if I'm going to walk in on something I don't want to see, 'kay?"

Diana made a choking sound. "Carter!"

"What? We're all adults here." He grinned as he headed toward the door.

"I'm still your aunt," she called after him.

"And that's exactly why I don't want to walk in on you having sex," he called back as the door closed behind him.

Diana stood at the kitchen counter, cheeks pink. After a moment, she started laughing, shaking her head. "I'm equal parts mortified and amused that conversation just happened."

"It was hilarious," Emily said, "and he probably can't joke with his parents like that, right? It's great that he feels so comfortable with you."

Diana's expression softened. "I suppose you're right." She paused, looking at Emily. "So, it looks like we have the house to ourselves for the evening."

"So we do. Didn't you mention a hot tub? It would be a perfect evening for it."

Diana's lips twisted to the side. "Yes, there is one. I was excited about it when I first got here, but then I saw that bear in the yard, and...well, now I feel like I'd be a sitting duck out there in the hot tub."

Emily stepped closer, wrapping her arms around Diana. "You're adorable with your irrational fear of bears. Most black bear attacks happen when you accidentally corner one or get between a mama bear and her cubs. They're not ever going to just charge out of the forest and attack you in your hot tub."

"Really?" Diana stared at her, and the glint in her eyes said she was warming to the idea of going in the hot tub together.

"Really. We don't have any wildlife in Vermont that's going to bother you in your hot tub. So...want to?"

"Yes." Diana brushed her lips against Emily's. "Plus it means I get to ogle you in a swimsuit."

"Well, unless I go home and get one, I might have to go in wearing my underwear."

"I brought a couple with me for the hot tub. You can borrow one...in case Carter comes home early. Otherwise, I might suggest we forgo clothing entirely."

"Diana Devlin, I had no idea you condoned public nudity."

Diana laughed. "Have you seen the back of my cabin?

It's impenetrable forest out there, no one to see us but the bears."

"And we've already established that they don't care. All the same, I'll take you up on that offer to borrow a swimsuit."

Ten minutes later, Emily wore a modest black bikini while Diana was in a royal-blue one-piece that did wonderful things for her cleavage. And her legs. And... "That color looks amazing on you," Emily said, her voice slightly husky. "It really brings out your eyes."

"Thank you." Diana stepped closer, tracing her fingers over the edge of Emily's swimsuit. "I didn't know how hot it would be to see you in my bikini."

Emily felt herself blushing. There was something especially intimate about sharing clothing with the person you were dating. Emily had always loved it. "Come on, let's go check out the tub. If we hurry, we'll be able to enjoy the sunset."

"You can't see much of it from here," Diana warned as she grabbed two towels and led the way out of her bedroom. "The sky overhead sometimes turns purple, though."

"Sunset is a beautiful time of day even if you can't see the horizon." Although right now, Emily was distracted by the view of Diana's ass in that swimsuit. Daily runs had done amazing things to her glutes and hamstrings.

They went out the back door, and Diana lifted the lid away from the hot tub while Emily pressed the button to start the jets. As the water began to churn, colored lights blazed beneath the surface, pink and purple and blue, giving the hot tub a party vibe. Emily laughed. "Wasn't expecting that."

"Not a fan of the colors." Diana sat on the edge of the tub and put her feet in. "It feels amazing, though."

Emily skipped that step and slid straight into the water, settling on one of the submerged seats. Hot, swirling water buffeted her body, and she sighed in pleasure. "It's perfect, even with the cheesy colored lights."

Diana slid in beside her. "You make the same sound when I touch you."

"Do I?"

"Mm-hmm. Like this." Diana's hand found Emily's thigh beneath the water, slowly sliding up until it met the edge of her bikini. She paused there and then moved her hand to cup Emily over her swimsuit.

"That calls for more than a sigh," Emily said breathlessly.

"Yeah?" Diana began to rub, watching Emily intently.

Emily moaned, already aching from Diana's touch. She hadn't intended to have sex in the hot tub, but then again...

"I like that sound too," Diana murmured, still rubbing Emily over her swimsuit.

"Can I..." Emily pressed a hand over Diana's, stilling her. "Can I touch you first this time? You always start with me. Hardly seems fair."

"What if I told you that getting you off is my favorite form of foreplay?" Diana wiggled her fingers, and Emily gasped. "I like the anticipation." Diana's voice was low and rough, sounding every bit as aroused as Emily felt.

"I'd say...I can't argue with that logic." Emily pushed her hips against Diana's hand, encouraging her.

"Better leave this on, in case Carter comes home early. Don't want to traumatize him." Diana slipped her hand beneath the bikini bottom. The water was so hot that Diana's fingers felt almost cool by comparison when they found Emily's bare flesh.

She whimpered, attempting to grind against Diana's fingers.

"Yes," Diana murmured. "I love the sounds you make. It gets me so hot."

Emily whimpered again, still thrusting her hips, but this angle just wasn't working. Diana couldn't get the leverage she needed, and Emily was quickly getting frustrated.

"Come here," Diana said. "On my lap."

Emily spun to straddle Diana's lap, and Diana positioned her hand so that Emily could ride her. With each thrust of Emily's hips, Diana's fingers hit all the right spots. The water splashed around them, a pink spotlight illuminating Diana's arm as she worked.

"Just like that," Emily gasped, thrusting harder. She kept moving, her hips becoming almost frantic as her need grew.

"Let me see how much you love my fingers," Diana growled. "Come for me, darling."

She sounded so dominant, so *hot*, that Emily came, just like that. The orgasm rushed through her, leaving her shuddering in Diana's arms. When she'd caught her breath, she looked down at Diana. "Hot tub sex...one-hundred-percent recommend."

"Do tell." Diana's thighs were parted beneath the water, and she hissed as Emily nudged her knee against Diana's core.

"Ready? Or would you like to get me off again first?" Emily teased, her knee still pressed between Diana's thighs. "Wouldn't want to rush your foreplay."

Diana considered that for long enough that Emily thought she might actually choose the second option. She'd never met anyone who enjoyed prolonging her pleasure as much as Diana. For a moment, neither of them moved. And then Diana surged forward, spinning them so she straddled one of Emily's thighs, her hips already moving.

She ground herself there for a few minutes, as Emily watched in aroused anticipation. She *loved* watching Diana lose control. But Diana must not be getting enough friction through the swimsuit because she groaned in frustration. "Need your fingers," she gasped.

Emily pushed Diana's suit to the side so her fingers met her where she needed it, rubbing firmly against her clit.

"Yes. That's perfect." Diana ground harder against Emily before throwing her head back with a cry as she found release.

Emily gazed up at her in awe to find the sky overhead streaked with the pink hues of the sunset. It was gorgeous, every bit as lovely as the woman straddling her lap. Today had been pretty perfect. Every day since she and Diana got together had been pretty perfect.

What in the world was Emily going to do when Diana went back to Boston?

DIANA STEPPED into her Boston town house the following evening with a happy sigh. She'd been looking forward to this all week, the chance to spend an evening at home. In the morning, she'd fly to Baltimore, then drive out to visit the Cornflower Hotel. Her town house smelled stale from having been closed up for a few weeks with no one living here.

She couldn't wait to breathe some life back into it. After kicking off her shoes, she carried her bag upstairs to her bedroom, then checked on her plants. She'd hired a neighbor's teenager to water them, but she was eager to see for herself that they'd been properly cared for. She flipped on lights as she went, illuminating the empty rooms one by one.

"Damn." Her string of pearls succulent looked half-dead. Its long strands of pearl-shaped buds hung over the edge of the pot, but they were pale and mushy looking now, not their usual vibrant green. She'd worried her plants would be neglected, but this one had been overwatered. It was literally drowning in its own pot.

Diana lifted it from the mantel and carried it to the kitchen, where she spread a few paper towels on the counter. Then she gently tipped the plant out of the pot, shaking most of the soggy dirt into the trash, and settled the plant on the paper towels to dry out overnight. Hopefully, it could be saved. If it bounced back, she'd repot it in fresh soil before she returned to Vermont.

Luckily, the rest of her plants were in better shape. She pinched off dead leaves and tended to another succulent that had been overwatered before she finally turned her attention to dinner. After weeks of having to cook for herself or deal with the meager options in town, tonight, she could order any cuisine she wanted and have it delivered right to her door.

"Vietnamese, I think," she mused as she picked up her phone. She'd been craving pho, and it was perfect soup weather. She'd just confirmed her order when the phone in her hand began to ring. Her brother was calling. Diana frowned as she answered. "Hello, Harrison."

"How dare you take my son to Vermont!" he shouted in lieu of hello. "You had no right."

She flinched, grateful he couldn't see it. "I didn't take him anywhere. He's a grown man capable of going where he pleases."

"For the love of God," he raged. "I meant for him to do some soul searching after he quit college, to realize how hard life would be without a degree. I wanted him to struggle so he'd reenroll in school."

"He *has* struggled, which you would know if you hadn't kicked him out of your house."

"By taking him in and coddling him like this, you're rewarding his bad behavior," he continued as if she hadn't spoken. "I won't tolerate it. He needs to learn from his mistakes."

"He's learning." Diana kept her tone calm and level. "He's working for me, earning a paycheck, figuring out his next steps. I'm hardly known for coddling."

"The hell you aren't. This is outrageous. Tarnishing the family name, both of you. There's no coming back from this, Diana. You'll never work at Devlin Hotels again, and it's only because of Mom's bleeding heart that you're still welcome at the dinner table."

She held her breath so he wouldn't be able to hear the air whoosh from her lungs as his words landed like a punch to her solar plexus. Yes, she'd known she was driving a wedge between herself and her family when she quit, but she hadn't known it ran *this* deep. "I'm sorry you feel that way," she said once she trusted her voice to come out normally.

"You've made your bed, but I won't let my son lie in it with you. Tell him that if he keeps avoiding my calls, I'll come to Vermont and get him myself."

"I'll do no such thing—" But the phone interrupted her with a beep, letting her know Harrison had ended the call. Diana barcly restrained herself from hurling her phone across the room. Her chest was so tight, she wanted to scream, but she wouldn't do that either. Instead, she went upstairs to take a shower before her food arrived.

An hour later, she was freshly showered and seated at her kitchen table with a steaming bowl of pho in front of her. It was delicious, just what she'd wanted, but her peaceful mood had been ruined by Harrison's call. She sipped and sighed, wishing Carter and Emily were here with her. The town house felt lonely by herself.

She couldn't help picturing the scene at Emily's grandmothers' house tonight. No doubt the three of them were sitting around the kitchen table together, enjoying a livelier conversation and more laughter than had ever occurred at a Devlin family dinner.

Diana needed to talk to Carter about taking his father's calls, but it could wait until she was back in Vermont. She finished her soup, put the bowl in the dishwasher, and then read for a few hours until she was ready for bed. On her way upstairs, she noticed the box Carter had set aside for her...the one she'd meant to have delivered to her rental cabin. Now was the perfect time to try out her new toys, but she was exhausted and not feeling even remotely sexy tonight.

She set the box on her bedside table, still unopened. Once she was settled against her favorite sheets, she tapped out a quick text to Emily, wishing her good night. Then she put her phone on silent and switched off the lamp beside the bed. Almost immediately, she was annoyed by the yellowish glare of the streetlight outside her window. A car turned at the corner, its headlights slashing across her wall. It accelerated with an obnoxiously loud engine.

She missed the chirping of crickets and the warmth of Emily's presence beside her. She'd found it nearly impossible to sleep in Vermont at first, but sometime over the last two months, she'd gotten used to the sound of the mountains. Now the city sounds around her were keeping her awake.

And yes, she was aware of the irony. Perhaps she was just a fussy sleeper. She'd been so looking forward to this evening at home, but aside from the pho, she hadn't enjoyed herself at all. Now she was just disappointed and lonely.

With a sigh, she rolled over and closed her eyes, waiting for sleep to claim her.

TWENTY-FOUR

Maybe next fall, Emily would offer hand-painted ceramic pumpkins on her website. She'd received a record number of comments on the Instagram post where she shared pictures of the ones on her front porch from people asking where to buy them. She'd even brought a few over to her grandmas' last night as a housewarming gift. The pumpkins were fun to paint and not that time-consuming, but they might be a headache to ship.

Emily had been brainstorming all week, coming up with new ideas and ways to increase her income. She was determined to get her profits up by the end of the year. Maybe if she channeled Diana's confidence and decided failure wasn't an option, she'd succeed.

But she couldn't help worrying that nothing she'd done with her shop was enough, that the income from her art would remain too little to live on, that Emily would end up having to keep her part-time job at the inn to make ends meet.

With a sigh, she leaned back in the love seat on her porch, watching Jack as he fluttered from perch to perch, chattering to the other birds in the forest. Diana hadn't even been gone twenty-four hours yet, and already Emily missed her like crazy. She'd heard how lovesick she sounded last night when she told her grandmothers about the new woman in her life.

She hadn't necessarily planned to tell them—given she didn't know what would happen when Diana left town—but once she was in their kitchen, and they were begging to know everything they'd missed, she hadn't been able to hold it in. Naturally, her grandmothers were thrilled for her and already asking when she'd bring Diana over for dinner.

Right now, Diana should be at her meeting at the hotel in Maryland. Tomorrow, she'd be back in Crescent Falls, but in another week, she'd be gone for good. She'd suggested they could still see each other after she was back in Boston, but in her heart, Emily knew she wasn't meant for a long-distance relationship.

And her heart was a problem, because right now, it ached in a way that meant Diana had already claimed a piece of it. Emily was falling for her. Truthfully, she'd been falling since that night in June. At this point, she'd already fallen, and now Diana was ready to move on and conquer the next thing on her list.

She might be willing to try things long distance, but was there any hope of Diana settling in Crescent Falls someday? Because this cottage was Emily's home. It would *always* be her home. What had she been thinking, getting involved with Diana right at the end of her time in Vermont? Now it was only going to hurt even more when she left.

From the table, Emily's phone started to ring with an unfamiliar Vermont number. "Hello?"

"Hi, is this Emily Janssen?" a male voice asked.

"Yes, it is."

"Hi, Emily. This is Nikolai from the Vermont Avian Sanctuary. You've been on the waitlist to surrender a rehabilitated song sparrow. Do you still have him?"

Emily blinked in surprise. Jack flew by, twittering so loudly that Nikolai probably heard him through the phone. "Yeah, I still have him. He's with me right now, actually."

Nikolai laughed. "Thought I heard a sparrow. Well, I have good news for you. The avian flu outbreak has been contained, and we have room for him in our songbird habitat. You could bring him as soon as tomorrow."

"Tomorrow. Wow." Emily swallowed. For the last six months, Jack had kept her company on her back porch. His happy chirps were the soundtrack to her evenings. She was going to miss him so much.

"Is Monday better?" Nikolai asked.

"Yeah. Monday sounds great. Thank you."

Emily ended the call and sat dejectedly on her porch for a few minutes, watching Jack fly around the space. He deserved this. He'd be so happy at the sanctuary in a huge enclosure full of real trees and other songbirds to hang out with. No matter how much she enjoyed his company, she couldn't keep him here just to make herself happy.

Just like she couldn't keep Diana here just to make Emily happy.

Diana and Jack both deserved to stretch their wings and fly as far as they could go. If only Emily could do the same. She wanted to, just like she wanted to make it to the top of the mountain. Maybe she'd stood in one place for so long, she'd become rooted to the ground. She was terrified of what might happen if she set herself free.

What if she spent the rest of her life drifting meaninglessly like her mother?

Emily's phone rang again, this time with a call from

Diana. "Hi," Emily said as she connected it, trying to infuse false cheer into her tone. "How was the hotel?"

"It has potential," Diana said. "Overall, it was in better shape than I'd feared. It needs a lot of cosmetic work, new paint, fresh carpet in the guest rooms, that kind of thing. But the property itself has solid bones, and it's in a great location, plus the existing staff is very competent. The current owners want to stay on to manage it. They just don't want the financial responsibility of ownership any longer. I think it's a good investment."

"That's awesome," Emily said. "So you're going to make an offer?"

"I am. I'll finish putting my offer together this weekend and send it in on Monday." She paused. "Are you okay? You sound...sad."

Emily flinched. She hadn't expected Diana to notice anything was wrong. "I'm a little bummed out, yeah. I just got a call that the sanctuary is ready to take Jack. So it's great news, really, I'm just going to miss him."

"Aww, that *is* good news. Will you be able to visit him there?"

"I think so, yeah."

"Good. Listen, my cab's pulling into the airport, so I'm going to have to let you go. Call me later?"

"Yep. Safe travels."

"Bye, Emily."

She ended the call, watching as Jack landed on top of his cage, chirping at the top of his little lungs. In a week, both he and Diana would have left Crescent Falls behind. Everyone around her was succeeding, and Emily wanted that for herself too. She wanted it *so* much, but it still felt beyond her grasp.

ON MONDAY, Diana accompanied Emily to the bird sanctuary. It was an interesting facility, with various enclosures housing owls, hawks, eagles, and other birds. She'd never seen a bald eagle before and was awed by its size and elegance. Jack had fluttered right into his new cage when they arrived, already calling out to the other birds at the facility.

"He can go into the songbird enclosure after he completes a thirty-day quarantine period," Nikolai had explained. "But you're both welcome to visit the enclosure today to see where he'll be living."

So now they sat side by side on a bench inside a large building similar to a greenhouse. Trees grew throughout, and a manmade stream ran through the middle of the enclosure. All around them, birds chattered and sang. It looked like bird heaven to Diana. If a bird couldn't be released into the wild, surely this was the next best thing.

"This will be a wonderful home for him," Diana said.

Emily smiled, but her eyes were sad. "It will be. I can't wait to come back and visit him once he's in here with the other birds."

"He won't be hard to spot." Diana had never seen a bird fly in spirals the way Jack did.

Emily managed a small laugh. "No, he won't."

"And now that you don't have a bird at home to take care of, maybe you'd like to spread your wings too?" Diana asked, testing the waters. "Maybe visit me in Boston?"

"I'd like that," Emily said with a soft smile.

They sat in the bird enclosure for a few more minutes before walking back to the car. Diana kept checking her phone, even though she knew it was probably too soon to have heard back from the current owner of the Cornflower Hotel. She'd sent in her offer first thing this morning, so at any moment, she could be the owner of *two* boutique hotels.

She couldn't wait.

It had taken her some time to adjust to this new life, to mourn the dream she'd given up and embrace a new path for herself, but she'd done it. She was so excited about Aster's future, about *her* future. It might be a decade or more before Aster reached its full potential, but this would be a more fulfilling career trajectory for her than being the CEO of Devlin Hotels.

With Aster, Diana could focus on the boutique hotels she loved the most. She would create the corporate culture she wished she'd had at Devlin Hotels. She wanted to fill her company with individuals as diverse and unique as the hotels she purchased. Now that she was taking the next step, purchasing her next hotel, she felt reinvigorated.

With Emily at her side, Diana felt like taking on the world.

ON TUESDAY AFTERNOON, Diana and Emily were curled on the couch in Emily's cottage together, kissing, when Alex texted to say that Thursday's hike to the summit had been postponed because the weather forecast called for pouring rain. They probably wouldn't be able to take their group hike until sometime next week, and by then, Diana would have left Vermont.

"I'll come back for the hike," she told Emily. "I want us to do this together."

"Promise?" Emily asked, something unexpectedly vulnerable in her tone.

"Of course," Diana told her. "We're going to hike to the summit together."

Emily blew out a breath. "I just worry about what's going to happen once you—"

She was interrupted by Diana's cell phone, which was ringing with an incoming call from Andre Winters, the owner of the Cornflower Hotel. Excitement burst through Diana's system. This was it, the call she'd been waiting for. "Hang on. I've got to take this." She connected the call. "Diana Devlin."

"Diana, hi. It's Andre Winters from the Cornflower Hotel."

"It's great to hear from you, Andre." Her stomach twisted, anxiety overtaking excitement as she registered his tone, which sounded vaguely apologetic.

"I wish I was calling with better news, but I wanted to let you know that we accepted an offer that unfortunately wasn't yours."

"Oh." Her mind went blank, her skin numb. She'd thought she had this in the bag. "I'm sorry to hear that."

"To be frank, Devlin Hotels offered more money," he said.

Diana sucked in a breath. *Devlin Hotels?* She'd lost this purchase to her own family? The Cornflower Hotel should have been too small to be on their radar. She'd had no idea they even put in an offer. Was it an unfortunate coincidence, or had they done this to spite her? Harrison's angry phone call last week echoed in her ears.

"We were also concerned that your business is just too new," Mr. Winters continued. "We were afraid that in the long run, you wouldn't be able to deliver on all the things you promised. It felt risky. This hotel is important to us, and we feel more secure with a trusted name like Devlin Hotels."

"Right," Diana murmured. "Well, thank you for letting me know. I appreciate your time and consideration." She ended the call, staring blankly out the window.

"Bad news?" Emily asked.

"I didn't get the hotel in Maryland." Diana swallowed roughly. "They sold to Devlin Hotels instead."

"Oh, Diana. Goddammit, that's awful. I'm so sorry."

"Thank you." Her mind was already scrambling to come up with next steps. If she didn't secure a second property by the end of the year, she would fall significantly behind her first quarter goals for Aster. What if this happened again? What if her father's company kept swooping in behind her to offer more money?

She hadn't seen this coming. Now she felt blindsided, a feeling that had always been her undoing. This year had already knocked her down so many times. She'd been counting on this win. Her eye twitched with a level of anxiety she hadn't felt in weeks.

Diana stared at the phone clutched in her hands as if a solution would magically appear. It didn't. This wasn't a devastating setback, but it was a demoralizing one. She'd done what she always did and gotten overconfident, already making plans for the new hotel before she'd secured the purchase.

"Hey, are you okay?" Emily rested a hand over Diana's.

She nodded, then shook her head, reminding herself not to hide her feelings from Emily. "I will be. I just...I need to regroup."

"Okay."

Diana had planned to spend her evening with Emily, to

enjoy a leisurely dinner on the back porch. She'd hoped it would be a celebratory dinner, but now...she felt uncharacteristically gloomy. Irrationally disappointed. And uncomfortably unsettled. She needed to sit with her laptop and go over the data. She needed to come up with a plan to better position her business to compete with Devlin Hotels. She hadn't anticipated that they'd go after the same properties, at least not right off the bat. Of course, she'd known it might happen on occasion, but now she had to consider that her family wanted her to fail.

She stood. "I need to look over some things on my computer."

Emily nodded. "Want to do something tomorrow? Maybe a hike if it's not raining yet?"

Diana couldn't think about hiking right now. Everything in her was focused on her business and getting things back on track. "I think I may actually head back to Boston a few days early."

Emily recoiled, crossing her arms over her chest. "What about me? Us?"

Diana gave her a questioning look. "This has nothing to do with us. I already told you I'd be back next week for the rescheduled hike. In fact, I'd love for you to come to Boston with me for the weekend. Will you?"

Emily's chin went up. "I'm working at the inn this weekend."

"Then I'll see you next week for the summit hike. But right now, I need to go home and regroup. I need to sit in my office and figure out next steps."

"Please don't run away from me because you got bad news," Emily whispered, her eyes glossy.

"I'm not running away." Diana pushed a hand through her hair. She heard the frustration in her voice, but she didn't understand why Emily was making a big deal about this. Diana just needed to go home a few days earlier than planned. Right now, she was *reeling* from what her father had done. She couldn't focus on anything else. "I told you I'm coming back next week."

"What if you don't, though? I just...I thought we had more time. If you leave now..." Emily shook her head. "I'm afraid that once you're back in Boston, everything will be different. Either we'll drift apart, or we'll get frustrated trying to visit each other. I feel like you're hoping that eventually I'll decide to move to Boston, and that's not going to happen."

Now Diana felt the first prickling of anger, because she couldn't believe Emily was doing this, right now of all times. "Actually, I was never under any illusion that you would leave this town. I was just willing to take whatever part of you I could have." Her voice wavered at the end, and she clenched her jaw to keep her hurt feelings at bay. Why didn't Emily think Diana was worth the effort of at least trying to make this work? Diana was ready to fight for their relationship, and Emily was already throwing in the towel. "I never expected you to move to Boston. If we're being totally honest here, it feels like *you* were hoping I'd decide to move to Vermont to be with you, and that's not going to happen either."

Emily turned away, mumbling something under her breath as she headed for the back door.

"What was that?" Diana raised her voice. "Dammit, Emily, don't pick a fight with me and then walk away. If you have something to say, just say it."

Emily spun, her cheeks glistening with tears. "I said... maybe I was. Deep down, maybe I was hoping you'd stay, and now I realize how stupid that was."

"It's not stupid, but my life is in Boston. It always has been."

"And mine will always be here."

"Then what are we doing right now?" Diana flung her hands out in frustration. "We've only just started dating. We haven't even tried long distance yet. I love being with you, and I want to keep being with you, but you have to be willing to meet me halfway here."

"I just...I want..." Emily's voice broke, her chin quivering. "I need more than that. I think I need more than you're willing to give."

"Then I guess it's time for me to go." Pain surged in Diana's chest. Was this just a fight or were they breaking up? She didn't have enough relationship experience to know, and she didn't handle uncertainty very well. Still, she had a sense that if she pushed for an answer now, Emily would end things definitively, and Diana couldn't face that reality yet.

She took a deep, shaky breath, forcing the pain into a place she could deal with once she was at home. Then she picked up her purse and headed for the door. "Goodbye, Emily."

TWENTY-FIVE

"What happened?" Carter asked as Diana walked into the cabin.

She paused in the entranceway. "I...what? How did you know something happened?"

"You look upset. Or pissed. Or both. Um, do you want to just tell me?" He leaned against the kitchen counter, arms crossed over his chest, brow pinched in concern.

"We lost the Cornflower Hotel. They sold to Devlin Hotels."

"Fuck." He pushed a hand into his hair, leaving it sticking up in all directions. "Well, that sucks. What now?"

"That's what I need to figure out. I'm going to head back to Boston a few days early since things are basically finished here in Crescent Falls."

"What about Emily?" he asked.

She rubbed a hand against her breastbone, right over the ache there. It felt like a crack in her heart that she was desperately holding together. If she let go, let it fracture, she'd fall apart, and she wasn't ready for that to happen. She wasn't ready to acknowledge that Emily had the power to break her heart, because that meant...that meant...

Carter blanched. "Oh shit."

And Diana realized her eyes had welled with tears. She blinked them back, reaching into her purse for her calming strip, but her fumbling fingers couldn't find it. "I guess she doesn't want to try things long distance after all. I just...I'm going to pack up and drive back to Boston tonight. You should pack too. It's time to go home."

She turned and fled to her bedroom, hoping she didn't look as upset as she felt, but if the look on Carter's face was any indication, she definitely did. She shut the door behind her with too much force, flinching as it slammed. Then she pulled her suitcase from the closet and started packing. If she stopped, if she sat...she might cry, and she just couldn't deal with her emotions right now.

She'd been so sure she and Emily would make things work long distance, it had never occurred to her that Emily might be having second thoughts. Once Diana committed to something, she was all in. She planned for success, always. Now she felt like she'd missed a step and gone into free fall. She had metaphorically tumbled off the mountain, and the only safe landing place was her town house in Boston.

She'd nearly finished emptying the closet when Carter knocked on the bedroom door. Straightening, she blew out a breath, making sure she had her emotions firmly under control before she responded. "What?"

"Um, can we talk for a minute?" he asked through the door.

She sat on the bed, pushing her hands beneath her thighs to keep from fidgeting. "Come in."

The door swung open, and Carter stood there, looking uncomfortable. "Can you stay tonight? I have something I want to talk to you about, but not while you're this upset."

"I'm fine," she snapped, then flinched. "I'm sorry. I'll be fine once I'm home, I promise. I'm just ready to leave. Can you tell me what you need to tell me once we're home?"

He shook his head, his gaze dropping to his sneakers. "I, um, I don't want to go back. That's what I was going to tell you. I'm staying in Crescent Falls."

"What?" Her voice came out angry and high-pitched, and she pressed her fingernails into the backs of her thighs, trying desperately to calm herself. "I know you and Drew have something going on, but that's no reason to just move to Vermont. You don't have a place to stay here, or a job, or—"

"Aunt DD, take a breath and let me explain." He straightened, looking suddenly so much more mature than he had before. "Drew and I are just casual. I like him, yeah, but that's not why I'm staying. Actually, he's been showing me around. He took me to his old college campus—Vermont State University—and I filled out an application this morning. I want to start there for the spring semester."

She blinked, her mind spinning. "Oh. Oh, wow."

He gave her a hesitant smile. "Yeah, so...I want to keep working for you part-time if that's okay. In fact, working at Aster is how I figured out what I want to do. I really like working with computers, building websites, that kind of thing. I'm going to get a degree in web development."

"Carter, that's wonderful." There were tears in her eyes again, but this time, they were the happy kind. Then she was on her feet, pulling him into a big hug. "I'm so proud of you."

"Um, thanks." He patted her back awkwardly, and she remembered belatedly that he wasn't a hugger.

She released him and took a step back. "So you're staying in Crescent Falls to finish college?"

"And maybe longer? I don't know. I really like it here. I like being part of the Adventurers group. I feel like I fit in here in a way I never did back in Boston. I only had a year left at Royce, but it'll take me longer now that I've switched majors. We have a few days left on the rental here, and then Tom and Maddie offered me their guest room while I look for an apartment...or I might live on campus come January. I'm still figuring it out."

"Okay." She nodded, blinking back more tears, not even sure what she was feeling anymore. "How will you pay for it?"

He shrugged. "I'll take out loans if I have to."

"I'll support you however I can. I'd like you to keep working at Aster part-time, if you can swing that with your studies. I need your help, and that way you'll have a source of income since your parents aren't paying your way anymore. And on that note, you need to call your father and tell him about your plans before he shows up here, hell-bent on dragging you back to Boston. Maybe he'll even agree to pay for you to finish college here."

Carter nodded. "I'll call him tomorrow. Promise."

"Okay. You can stay with me in Boston until the new semester starts if you have trouble finding an apartment. You're always welcome at my home, Carter."

He ducked his head. "Thanks. I appreciate that."

He left her to finish packing, and when she came out of the bedroom a few minutes later with her bags in tow, she found him watching TV. He really wasn't coming back with her.

"I'll call you tomorrow," she said.

"Yep. Drive safe, and um...sorry about the hotel...and Emily."

She nodded as her throat constricted painfully. It hurt that he'd managed to find something here in Crescent Falls that she hadn't, and then she had the irrational urge to beg him to come home with her. But no, she would be returning to Boston on her own. Funny, she'd always lived by herself and always preferred it that way, and now...the prospect felt awful.

As she towed her suitcase to the car, she'd never felt more alone.

"HI, EM." Gram smiled at her from the doorway. "Come in. Is everything okay?"

Emily knew the answer was written all over her face. After Diana left, she'd called Alex, needing her best friend to help talk her through it, but it was Frankie's birthday, and they were out to a fancy dinner together. So, she'd come to her grandmas' new house, desperate for some advice and a shoulder to cry on.

She gave Gram a weak smile as she stepped inside. "I'm not interrupting anything, am I?"

Gram placed a hand on her shoulder, guiding her toward the living room. "You see, that's the beauty of being retired. Your grandma and I were just ordering prints of our vacation photos and trying to decide what to have for dinner. We'd love to have some company."

Grandma stood from the couch. She'd come home from their cruise more deeply tanned than Emily had ever seen her. They both had a happy glow about them these days. Retirement looked good on them. "Em? What's wrong?"

Emily knew she was the farthest thing from glowing right now. She blinked as her eyes filled with tears. "Diana and I..."

"Oh no. Did you two have a fight?"

Emily nodded. "We didn't say the words, but I think we might have broken up, and I think...it's my fault."

"Well, let's not lay blame yet," Gram said. "Blaming yourself is never helpful in a breakup. We brought home some lemon chiffon tea from France that is absolutely divine. Why don't I put on a pot, and you can tell us everything?"

"Okay." She let Gram guide her to the kitchen. Ten minutes later, they were seated at the table with an ornate teapot between them...another European purchase. Grandma poured them each a cup of amber-colored liquid that smelled a bit like lemon meringue pie.

"So sweet you won't even need to add sugar," Grandma said.

"Now." Gram covered Emily's hand with her own. "Tell us what happened."

Emily sipped her tea—which tasted as good as it smelled—and sighed. "Diana had put in an offer to buy a hotel in Maryland, and it fell through. They sold to her father's company instead. She was upset about it, so she decided to head back to Boston a few days early."

"Her father's company undercut her deal?" Grandma grimaced. "That's awful. I'm even more glad we didn't sell to Devlin Hotels if that's how they treat people."

"Agreed," Gram said. "So how did you and Diana end up having a fight?"

"I got upset that she was leaving." Emily's bottom lip

trembled. "She said I could come with her if I wanted, and she'd come back for the summit hike next week, but then we started arguing about how things were going to work long distance. I said I'd never move to Boston, and she said she'd never move to Vermont, and then she made me admit that deep down, I'd been hoping she would. I wanted her to stay. And then she left."

"Okay." Grandma gave her a shrewd look. "Let's talk more about this realization that deep down, you wanted her to stay."

Emily stared morosely into her tea. "She's always made it clear that Boston is her home, so that part's on me, definitely. But we had so much fun together the last few weeks. She seemed to be really enjoying herself here, and my stupid romantic heart started hoping, you know? That Crescent Falls could be enough for her. That *I* could be enough. That she'd decide she wanted to stay... for me."

"Oh, Em." Gram wrapped an arm around her. "I love that you have such a big romantic heart, but surely you can't expect Diana to move to Vermont after you've dated for what, two weeks?"

"When you put it that way..." Emily's throat hurt when she swallowed, and tears stung her eyes. "She wanted to keep dating, to do the long-distance thing, and I...I fucked up."

"If you think long distance could work, then you might have," Grandma said gently. "But it's probably not unfixable, if you apologize. Look, you might not want to hear it, but I think part of what's happening here doesn't have anything to do with Diana. You have abandonment issues from the way your mom left, so Diana leaving probably brought up some insecurities for you."

Emily sipped her tea as her tears spilled over. "Don't forget Jenny. She left me to move to the city too."

"Right." Gram gave her a sympathetic look. "So, maybe you overreacted to Diana leaving, or maybe you just forced her to have a real conversation about the future now instead of putting it off. Maybe long distance was never going to work for you two. Your heart is in Crescent Falls, Em. You're content here, and that's okay."

Emily stared into the amber depths of her tea. Was she content here? She was comfortable, certainly. Crescent Falls was her home. She loved it, and she felt safe here. But there had always been that little part of her that yearned for more. She looked up. "What if...I'm not content?"

Grandma's eyebrows rose. "You're not?"

"When I was younger, I wanted to see the world...like what you guys just did. I wanted to paint faraway places, flowers I've never seen before. Mountains. Cities. Oceans."

"What's stopping you?"

"I don't know." She gulped from her tea, burning her mouth in the process.

"Is this because of your mom too, do you think?" Gram asked softly, hesitantly. "Do you feel like, if you leave Crescent Falls, you'll be like her in a way you don't want to be?"

"I don't know...maybe?" Emily's eyes stung, and her heart ached too.

"Sweetie, she abandoned her *child* to go see the world. She let you down, but honestly, she was little more than a child herself at the time. She'd been struggling for a while, and she got overwhelmed." Grandma reached out and took Emily's hand. "She was doing the best she could, the same as any of us, so please don't let her actions hold you back from whatever you want to do. You aren't letting anyone down if you leave. On the contrary, you're letting yourself down by staying, if it's not what you want. Go. Spread your wings. See the world."

"But first," Gram added, "you'd better get over to Diana's cabin and apologize before she leaves town."

EMILY KNEW AS SOON as she pulled into Diana's driveway that she was too late. The silver Lexus was gone. Only Carter's SUV remained. Emily's eyes, already sore from crying, welled with new tears. Her chest was heavy with regret. Still, she went to the door, just to be sure.

Carter opened it, his expression guarded. "She's gone back to Boston."

"Oh." She felt like she'd shrunk six inches, like her body was caving in on itself. Diana was gone. And Carter wasn't his usual friendly self, which meant he knew about their fight. Somehow it hurt even more to think of Diana venting to him about Emily before she left. "What...what did she say?"

His lips thinned, and for a moment, she thought he would close the door in her face rather than answer. "She didn't say anything, not really. It was how she *looked*. She almost cried, and I've never seen my aunt cry." He looked down at his feet. "Anyway, she's not here, so..."

"Right. I'll go. Thank you." She turned away as the door closed solidly behind her. A gust of wind stung the tears on her cheeks. She couldn't even imagine Diana crying. It was too much. *I did that to her. I hurt her.*

Emily drove home in a stupor, but when she pulled up to her cottage, she didn't get out of the car. She just sat there in the dark and let the tears fall, her mind drifting to what her grandmothers had said about abandonment issues. Emily hated that term, but if the shoe fit...

Impulsively, she picked up her phone and dialed a number she hadn't called in years.

"Em...Emily? Is that really you?" Her mother's voice sounded exactly the same, instantly evoking a million painful memories, like being thrust back in time to the worst day of her life.

"It's me," Emily managed, her voice little more than a whisper.

"It's been so long. Are you okay?"

"No," she admitted, balling a fist against her thigh. "I'm not okay. I screwed something up tonight, something big, and I just... Why did you leave, Mom? Why wasn't I enough?"

"Oh, Emily..." Violet sighed, and Emily had been wrong. She didn't sound the same at all. Her voice was deeper, *older*. Emily's mother would be fifty-one now, and the years had taken a toll. "I'm the one who wasn't enough. I was so young when I had you. I felt like I was losing myself. I can look back now and see that I was just an immature kid, but at the time...I felt like I was drowning, and I just kept screwing up with you. I knew Mary and Eva could give you so much more than I could, so I left."

"That's bullshit. You were my *mother*," Emily said, low and shaky. "I needed you, and you left. *That's* what screwed things up for me."

"Oh, I screwed up plenty before that too. You were just too young to see it," Violet said, something self-deprecating in her tone. "After you got hurt when we tried to hike to the top of the mountain together, your grandmothers were furious with me. They really let me have it for endangering you like that, and it wasn't the first time, but I decided it would be the last."

"You could have decided to become a better parent."

"I could have. I'm sorry I didn't." Violet's voice cracked. Emily had expected the usual light, flippant attitude she got from her mother. This was different. "All I can say is that, at the time, I was convinced you were better off without me. By the time I realized I'd made a mistake, it was too late."

"It would never have been too late!"

"It was, though." She could hear her mother crying now, and it made Emily's chest feel overinflated, like she was going to burst. "Whenever I came back to visit, you wanted nothing to do with me. You were happier with your grandmothers, and I get that. I do. They did an amazing job raising you, so much better than I could have. I still tag you on Facebook, so you know I'm thinking about you."

"Tagging me on Facebook is a cop-out!" Emily cried. "When you came to visit, you'd talk about your boyfriends and all the places you'd been, like your life was so much better without me in it. You never apologized for leaving. You never came *back*. Visiting for the weekend isn't the same thing. Of course I didn't know how to act when you showed up. It hurt to realize I didn't know you anymore!"

A sniff carried over the line. "If it's any consolation, I have so much regret for the choices I made. I think I've spent my whole life running, trying to escape my own guilt."

"And I've spent my whole life stuck here, right where you left me."

"Could I... If I came to visit now, would you see me?" her mom asked tentatively. "I could stay awhile, try to get to know you for real."

"I don't know." Emily was seething. She'd called to vent,

to tell her mom all the ways she'd screwed up. Maybe she'd wanted to cast blame, so she didn't have to feel as bad about what she'd done to Diana tonight. She hadn't expected apologies or remorse, and now she had no idea what to think or how to feel.

"What if I come for Thanksgiving? I'll rent one of those vacation cabins and cook a turkey. Darren and I, we've been together a few years now, and he's taught me how to cook."

"I don't know. Maybe."

"I'm going to book it when we get off the phone," Violet said, sounding more certain now. "I'll stay awhile this time. No more running."

Emily swiped angrily at her overflowing eyes. "I'll believe that when I see it."

"Fair enough," her mom said. "For once in my damn life, I'm going to try to make you proud and earn your forgiveness. I only hope I'm not already too late."

Emily thought of Diana on a dark mountain road somewhere, fleeing Vermont. Fleeing Emily. And she hoped she wasn't doomed to repeat her mother's mistakes.

DIANA REGRETTED her impulsive decision to drive to Boston tonight. She was too tired, and her emotions were too raw. Driving alone like this, she had no distraction from her pain, nothing to do but sit with her own chaotic thoughts. Her heart pounded. Her eyes stung. Her iron grip on the steering wheel made her hands ache.

Somewhere in New Hampshire, the tears began to fall. She blinked and sniffled, trying to get herself under control, but it was no use. Diana hardly ever cried, but on this absolutely shitty night, the dam broke, as if a decade's worth of tears had chosen this moment to come pouring out. Eventually, she pulled over at a gas station because it was dark, and these roads were already hard enough to navigate without tears blurring her vision.

She sat there in the parking lot, rubbing her calming strip until she'd cried herself out. Then she rested her forehead against the steering wheel, more exhausted than ever. She did feel calmer for having let it all out, though. Luckily, the gas station was still open and had a bathroom she could use to clean herself up. On her way out, she bought some snacks and a coffee for the road. Hopefully caffeine and sugar would see her the rest of the way to her town house.

She couldn't believe Carter had decided to stay in Vermont. Or maybe she could. She'd watched him blossom over the last few weeks. And he was going back to school. All of it made her happy, even if she'd gotten used to having him around. It would be hard to visit him in Crescent Falls without bumping into Emily.

Unless...

No. She was angry. She was upset. She was *hurt*. She wasn't even going to think about Emily tonight.

Except...

That little voice had been whispering in the back of her mind all evening. She'd started hearing it almost as soon as she learned Devlin Hotels bought the Cornflower Hotel. Her brain had immediately started working, pondering how she could do better next time, how she could set herself apart from Devlin Hotels, and the first step was obvious.

Aster only bought small, unique hotels. It embraced all the things that made those hotels special instead of making them conform to a corporate brand. Small towns and tight-knit communities were her bread and butter now.

So, if she set up Aster's headquarters in a small town

instead of Boston...well, that would further cement her brand. Not to mention, the office space would be exponentially cheaper. She'd struggled to find an affordable office in Boston, but if she opened an office in Crescent Falls...

It would be convenient for Carter. It would give her an excuse to visit Emily. And it would help her strengthen Aster's brand identity.

But right now, she didn't want anything to do with Crescent Falls, not after Emily had practically shoved her out the door after Diana said she needed to come home a few days early to regroup after her loss. Tears pricked her eyes again, and she huffed with annoyance.

When was the last time she'd cried over a woman?

Probably never. She and Emily needed to talk. She knew that. But first, she had to process. They probably both needed a few days to cool off. Diana forced thoughts of Emily from her mind as she reached Boston so she could focus on her driving. Luckily, entering the city at 10:00 p.m. on a Tuesday night meant there wasn't much traffic. Still, she exhaled with bone-deep relief as she finally pulled onto her street.

Even luckier still, she managed to find a parking space not too far from her town house. She rarely parked here at home, only on random nights like this one when she'd just gotten back from a work trip and hadn't returned her rental car yet.

She carried her suitcase and laptop bag down the street. She dropped them inside the front door and went back to the car for the plants she'd brought to Vermont. Everything else could wait until tomorrow. Inside, she was pleased to see that the plants she'd left here were faring much better this time since she'd visited only a few days ago. As much as she wanted to get right to work, it was late, and her brain was mush.

After washing up, she climbed into bed and was asleep almost immediately. She didn't stir until she was awakened by morning sunshine pouring in through her uncovered windows. In her exhaustion last night, she'd forgotten to close the curtains.

Today, she needed structure. She needed to stay busy to keep from moping. So, she went for a run, followed by a shower and breakfast on the back deck. And then, she went upstairs to her office and got to work. It was satisfying to be back in her space, at her own desk. The window let in plenty of sunlight, and several of her favorite plants were arranged below it.

Her spider plant had sprouted several new little spider babies while she was away. There were so many sprouts hanging off it now, she might have to clip some of them off soon.

No forest beckoned outside the window, only the familiar facades of the brownstones that lined the opposite side of the street. A steady stream of traffic passed by, and her next-door neighbor was playing the violin. The sights and sounds of home.

Diana's first order of business this morning was to reach out to the owners of the other two hotels she was interested in buying. She had a nice conversation with each of them and arranged times to visit both. Then she started looking at available office space in Boston. Whatever romantic notions she'd had in the heat of the moment last night about opening an office in Crescent Falls had been impractical.

Diana lived in Boston. Therefore her office needed to be here too.

She was deep in corporate real estate listings when she

heard a knock at the door. Frowning, she glanced at the clock on her laptop to see that it was just past eleven. Who in the world would be knocking on her door? She rarely had uninvited visitors, and no one even knew she was back from Vermont yet.

For the first time, she understood the value of those video doorbells. Since she didn't have one, she walked downstairs and pressed her eye against the peephole just as the person outside knocked again, nearly deafening her at such close range. She jumped backward, but not before she'd glimpsed the face on the other side of her door.

It was Emily.

TWENTY-SIX

Diana's heart was pounding, both from the knock against her ear and from seeing Emily. A confusing mix of emotions fizzed in her stomach, but one thing she was sure of: she wasn't mad anymore. Hurt? Oh, yes. Her heart was tender and wounded, but she wasn't angry.

Diana opened the door just as Emily raised her fist to knock a third time.

"Hi," they said at the same time, then gave each other stilted smiles.

Diana stepped back to invite her inside. "This is a surprise."

"I'm so sorry." Emily surged forward, flinging her arms around Diana. Her cheek was wet with tears where it pressed against Diana's, and Diana was powerless to push her away. They needed to talk. It had been killing her not knowing where they stood.

"Come in," Diana said when Emily released her.

"Thank you," Emily said breathlessly, her gaze roaming around the entranceway as she followed Diana inside.

Diana led her to the kitchen at the back of the house.

Coffee might go well with this conversation, and brewing a fresh pot would give Diana something to do while she corralled her rampaging emotions. They were both quiet while the coffee machine gurgled. Then Diana poured two mugs and handed one to Emily.

Emily gave her a hesitant smile as she took it. They both bypassed the kitchen table to stand near each other at the counter overlooking the backyard, which might have been awkward, but Diana needed the ability to move more freely right now. She was too anxious to sit. Maybe Emily was too.

"Thanks," Emily said after the silence had stretched a few moments too long. "Your town house is every bit as beautiful as I expected, and...I'm so sorry for being such an idiot yesterday. I overreacted and made a huge mess of things while you were trying to deal with what your dad did...which was really shitty, by the way."

"It was shitty, but I probably should have anticipated it. I tend to get tunnel vision when I'm focused on something, as you know. You're better at seeing the big picture."

"I want to be," Emily said quietly. "I want to expand my horizons. I want to go places and do things...with you, if you'll have me."

Diana's breath caught in her throat, her heart thudding against her ribs as hope bloomed there. She sipped her coffee to control her reaction. "Which places do you want to go?"

"Anywhere you're going. Diana...I'm so scared. I don't know why it's so hard for me to leave Crescent Falls. My grandmas think it's got something to do with how my mom left, that my stupid brain thinks if I leave too, I'll be like her. Speaking of my mom, I actually called her last night, and we had a surprisingly good conversation. She wants to come for

Thanksgiving, which is... I have no idea how to feel about that."

"Sounds like a big deal," Diana said.

"It is...if it happens. I guess...it seems like people are always leaving Crescent Falls, leaving *me*. First my mom, then Jenny, then my grandmas, and Jack, and *you*." She made a strange noise that turned into a sob. "In my heart yesterday, I wanted someone to pick me for once. I wanted *you* to pick me. But that was stupid and unfair, and honestly, it's not even a choice. You can have both. You can have Boston *and* me. Once I'm not working at the inn anymore, I can come stay here sometimes, and you can visit me in Crescent Falls, and...we'll work it out. I know we can. If you'll forgive me for yesterday." She finally paused for breath, tears streaming over her cheeks.

"Emily..." Diana put down her coffee and pulled Emily into her arms. "I knew all those facts separately, but I hadn't put them together, and I had no idea you felt that way. I didn't choose Boston over you. I wasn't leaving you at all. I just wanted to come home for a few days to work on my business plan. I was upset too, and neither of us was thinking very rationally."

"Can you forgive me?" Emily looked at her with flushed, tearstained cheeks.

"Of course." She held Emily close, marveling as the ache in her chest went away, her wounded heart healing itself now that Emily was back in her arms. It was that simple. She needed Emily. She *loved* Emily. Everything else would work itself out.

It had to, because Diana was going to put her full effort into making it so, and this time, she wasn't going to fail. This time, her eyes were wide open, and she was looking in every direction. She saw all the obstacles in her way, not blindly focused on the finish line.

She breathed in Emily's scent, calm and resolute in her decision. "I think I have the perfect solution to our logistical problem."

"You do?"

Diana nodded. "First of all, Carter told me last night that he's staying in Crescent Falls. He's starting college there after the new year."

"Oh, that's so great." Emily smiled through her tears.

"Office space is a lot cheaper in Crescent Falls than it is in Boston, and since Aster caters to small, unique hotels, it strengthens our brand—and helps differentiate us from Devlin Hotels—to have our headquarters in a small town, especially the town where our flagship hotel is located. Devlin is corporate America. Aster is small town America. Crescent Falls should be its home." She paused, meeting Emily's eyes as her skin flushed hot and her heart began to pound. "Plus, the woman I love lives there."

"Oh, shit. Oh my God," Emily spluttered, her face beet red. "You...the woman you love?"

"Yes. It hurt like hell leaving you last night. Right here." She pressed a hand over her heart, which was still beating out of control. She'd never told a woman she loved her before...or heard those words in return. "I realized something when I was with you in Vermont. In the past, I shied away from relationships because deep down, I feared career retribution. Devlin Hotels has some toxic ideas about family values. But at Aster, I can be the boss *and* have a love life. What do you think?"

"I think...I think...I love you too," Emily blurted. "And... does this mean you *are* moving to Vermont?"

Diana shook her head, her skin even hotter now because

Emily loves me too. Her eyes were wet, and her hands were shaking. "I didn't say that. I still love this town house as much as you love your cottage in Crescent Falls, but why can't we have both? I own this property, and you own that one, and we can split our time between them. It's not a long-distance relationship if we're both in the same place at the same time."

A luminous smile bloomed on Emily's face, as bright as the flowers she loved to paint. "I think it's perfect, and I love you, and..." Emily pressed her lips against Diana's for a kiss that soon had Diana panting, her body awakening the way it always did when Emily kissed her.

"So you want to travel with me?"

"Fuck fear," Emily gasped. "I've always wanted to see the world. I only wish it hadn't taken me so long to realize what was holding me back."

"It doesn't matter," Diana murmured against her lips. "We're all constrained by fear in one way or another. I hid my fears behind a mask of confidence. You're the first person to show me that I can let my guard down, I can be vulnerable, and you won't take advantage. You let me be myself and appreciate me for exactly who I am—flaws and all—and I...I didn't know how much I needed that until I found it."

Emily blinked at her through glossy eyes. "I...really?"

Diana nodded. "Want to start our travels in North Carolina next week? I just made arrangements to visit a hotel in the Blue Ridge Mountains."

"I want to bring lots of canvas and paint," Emily whispered.

"I can't wait to see what you create. As you know, I was taken with your art from the moment we met." She gestured to the painting in the hall, the purple aster Emily had been painting that fateful afternoon.

"You bought that?" Emily's jaw dropped. "I had no idea...oh wow." More tears spilled over her cheeks. "That's so romantic. Oh, Diana..."

"I named my new company after that painting. After *you*, really. I never stopped thinking about you when I came back to Boston."

"That's so beautiful. Oh my God, I love you so much." Emily wrapped her arms around Diana, grinning as she spun her.

"As much as I want to take you straight upstairs to celebrate in my bed, I also want to take you out to lunch and show you some of Boston." She wanted to show Emily the world—*right now*—but damn if she wasn't already aroused by their closeness.

"The theme of the day, Diana, is *both*." Emily beamed. "Let's do both, but maybe lunch first because I was too upset this morning to eat breakfast, and now I'm famished. And after that, who knows? We might not leave your bed for the rest of the day."

"We won't have to," Diana murmured against her lips. "You may not know this—having lived in Crescent Falls your whole life—but food delivery exists. Whatever cuisine you want, you can have it...in bed... with me."

"I love it. Two minutes in, and you're already broadening my horizons."

"Why don't we go out to lunch first and see a bit of the city," Diana suggested, "and then we can stay in this evening?"

"Perfect."

"Come on, then, darling. Let's go see Boston."

"YOU WERE RIGHT. That was so much fun," Emily said with a happy sigh as they reentered Diana's town house later that afternoon, having enjoyed sumptuous lobster rolls on the waterfront, followed by several hours of walking around some of Diana's favorite parts of the city.

Diana pressed Emily against the wall in the entrance way and kissed her soundly. "I love Boston, but I love it even more when you're with me."

"I feel so alive." Emily kissed her back, hands on Diana's waist as she nipped Diana's bottom lip before soothing the sting with her tongue.

Diana throbbed between her thighs. "Keep that up, and we'll wind up in bed sooner than later."

"The sooner the better," Emily murmured. "After all, we still need to have makeup sex."

"Mm, the only good thing about fighting with you." Diana pushed a thigh between Emily's, and if the windows beside her front door didn't overlook the sidewalk, she'd have taken Emily right here. The bedroom was only one flight of stairs away, though.

"I wish we hadn't fought." Emily's expression filled with regret. "I feel like I need to apologize again for my behavior yesterday...and to tell you how sorry I am about what your father did. Have you spoken to him yet?"

Diana felt herself tensing, but she resisted the urge to pull away. "No, I haven't, and I know I need to. I just...well, I was preoccupied with everything else going on, worrying I might have lost you. I didn't have the bandwidth for that conversation yet."

"I understand, and I feel terrible that I wasn't more supportive yesterday when you needed me." Emily's eyes shimmered with unshed tears. "That I hurt you when you were already down."

"You've already apologized for that, and I've accepted your apology." Diana ran a finger over Emily's sweater, soothed by its soft texture...and by Emily herself. "The truth is, I haven't spoken to my father since the day I handed in my resignation, and now, I have to wonder if that was a mistake. Maybe he wouldn't have done this if I'd made more of an effort to smooth things over between us."

"From what you've told me, he's the one who should have made that effort—not you—but at this point, I do think you should call him. If I've learned anything over the last twenty-four hours, it's that it can be worthwhile to suck it up and have a tough conversation instead of just making assumptions and letting hurt feelings brew."

Diana sighed, resting her forehead against Emily's. Emily's arms folded around her, wrapping Diana in the warmth and comfort of her embrace. "I know you're right, and I'm not usually one to put off a difficult conversation."

"So call him." Emily sounded more assertive now. "Just get it over with. If you do it right now, we can spend the rest of the day in your bed. You can even introduce me to food delivery."

"Among other things." Diana gave her another hungry kiss, but her focus had shifted. Emily was right. She needed to make this call. Reluctantly, she stepped out of Emily's embrace. "Okay, I'll call him."

Emily squeezed her hand. "I can go explore your backyard to give you some privacy?"

"No." Diana held tight to Emily's hand. "Stay."

"Okay," Emily whispered.

Diana walked to the couch and sat, still clinging to Emily with one hand as she used the other to bring up her father's name in her cell phone. He'd be at work right now, but she selected his cell, not his office phone. This was personal.

It only rang twice before the call connected. "Diana? This is a surprise."

"An overdue one, I'm afraid." She exhaled, grateful to her medication and Emily's presence for helping to keep her anxiety under control.

"I wasn't sure...well...what's this about?" He sounded brusque and businesslike, but there was something beneath it that she wasn't sure how to read. It might have been residual anger over how she'd left Devlin Hotels.

"We need to talk...about the Cornflower Hotel." The words came out haltingly, and she realized belatedly that she should have thought through what she was going to say before making the call.

"The what?"

"The hotel I tried to purchase for my new business that you outbid me for. I know you haven't forgotten, but Dad...I don't want to do this. I don't want to fight with you, and I don't want to compete with Devlin Hotels. In fact, I was specifically trying to buy smaller hotels you wouldn't be interested in. I want Aster to be its own unique brand." She paused for a breath, surprised to look down and see that she was rubbing Emily's hand as if it were a calming strip. "So let's talk. Surely there's a way we can agree to be civil with each other instead of you trying to put me out of business because you disapprove of my life decisions."

There was silence on the line. Total, devastating silence. Diana's pulse raced and her stomach cramped, but she kept her breathing under control. No need for him to know the effect he'd had.

"I wasn't aware we had bid on the same hotel," he said at length.

She huffed. "Oh, come on. I'm not naïve. This wasn't a hotel that would ordinarily have been on Devlin's radar. Don't try to tell me it was a coincidence."

"I never said it was a coincidence. I said I wasn't aware." He paused, and Diana held her breath, at a loss for what he meant or what to say in response. "Harrison did mention the acquisition of that hotel, but not that you'd been involved. I suppose he was trying to make a point about the way you'd treated the family, but I'll speak to him, because that's not how we do business around here."

"Oh." She exhaled roughly. Her brother had sabotaged her. Not her father. Was that better or worse?

Her father cleared his throat. "Your mother's been after me to call you, actually, to...clear the air. She's missed seeing you at family dinners. I, well...we both have. I still disagree with your decision to leave, but I'd like to think we can move past it."

"I'd like that too." Diana was reeling. That was a heart-felt apology as far as Edward Devlin was concerned. She inhaled, suddenly aware of how tense she'd been and the fact that she could breathe freely again now.

"Good. I'm on my way to a meeting with the board. Come to dinner on Friday?"

She gulped, meeting Emily's eyes. There was only one way to respond, and it terrified her more than making this call in the first place. "If I can bring my girlfriend with me, then yes, I'd love to come to dinner."

Another silence, and more throat clearing. "That's fine."

"Okay, then, Emily and I will see you on Friday."

"Until Friday."

With a click, the call disconnected.

Diana turned to Emily, drawing several deep breaths before she could speak. "How much of that did you catch?"

"Enough to get the basics." Emily squeezed Diana's hand, and when Diana looked down, she saw that hers was shaking. She didn't pull away, though, even though she knew Emily could feel her trembling.

"I should have asked you first," Diana said. "If you don't want to go to dinner, I can—"

"I do," Emily interrupted. "I want to share everything with you, remember? And this is a big deal, right? You told me before that you've never brought a woman home to meet your parents."

Diana nodded, swallowing roughly. "You'll be the first."

"That means a lot," Emily told her with quiet sincerity.

"*You* mean a lot." She met Emily's eyes. "It may be awkward, though. My family isn't the easiest."

"I'm not looking for easy, Diana. I'm here for the good, the bad, and the awkward."

"Me too. God, I love you so much." She tugged, and Emily slid into her lap, her hips pressing against Diana's. And just like that, the heat was back. It had been an emotional whirlwind of a day. Two emotionally chaotic days, actually, and all that turbulent energy seemed to ignite under the warm press of Emily's body, resulting in a sense of urgency that quickly overwhelmed Diana's senses.

She shifted against the couch, frustrated to have her thighs pinned together beneath Emily's weight. She anchored her hands in Emily's hair so she could kiss her, licking her way hungrily into Emily's mouth. Maybe it was the thought that she had almost lost this—lost *Emily*—that left her feeling so frenzied now.

"You mentioned makeup sex?" Diana tried for playful, but her voice came out rough and needy.

"I'm wholly in favor." Emily rocked her hips against Diana's, her eyes reflecting the same heat that was scorching Diana from the inside out. Without another word, Emily slid her hand down the front of Diana's pants. Her fingers wiggled against Diana's wet flesh, and she had to bite back a moan. "Miss me?" Emily asked with a wicked grin.

"So much." Diana pushed herself more firmly against Emily's hand.

And just like that, Emily withdrew. She stood, extending her hand to pull Diana to her feet. "Show me your bedroom?"

Diana nodded. Yes, a bed was a good idea. She'd mostly been joking earlier when she suggested they spend the rest of the day there, but it felt like a real possibility now. Keeping Emily's hand in hers, she climbed the stairs, closing the door to the master bedroom behind them. She wasn't expecting him, but Carter *did* have a key to the house.

"Nice." Emily swept her gaze around Diana's bedroom, taking in the gray walls and understated art Diana had chosen. "There's just one thing that doesn't match your décor." She pointed to the brown shipping box on Diana's bedside table, the box Diana had once been so desperate to get her hands on and then hadn't found time to open after her return from Vermont.

"Funny story about that box." She skimmed her hands up Emily's sides, bunching her shirt under her arms before she lifted it over Emily's head.

"I love a good story." Emily's hands were busy too, lowering the zipper on Diana's pants.

"I ordered it while I was in Vermont. I was...frustrated." She hissed as Emily's fingers slid over the front of her underwear. "I was so fucking attracted to you, but I couldn't have you, and I was so anxious, especially at night, all alone in that house."

Emily blinked at her out of wide eyes, her mouth forming a silent O.

"I was desperate for some relief, but sometimes it's hard for me on my own when I'm that anxious." Diana flicked her gaze to the box in question, surprised to realize how much easier it had already gotten to discuss her anxiety with Emily. "So I bought some toys for a little battery-powered assistance, but I forgot to update the shipping address, and they came here."

"You poor frustrated thing." Emily rubbed her over her underwear, and the ache between Diana's thighs intensified. "You mean to tell me, the whole time you were in Vermont, you were in this state?"

"Not one orgasm." Diana rocked her hips against the pressure of Emily's fingers. "I was feeling pretty desperate before we got together."

"I bet." Emily rubbed faster as she nodded toward the box. "Do they come charged?"

"Um." Diana was having trouble thinking through the haze of arousal that had overtaken her senses, but the idea of using her new vibrator with Emily sounded irresistibly hot. With some difficulty, she pulled away from Emily's touch. "I think they do."

She crossed the room and picked up the box, fumbling with the packing tape, her fingers clumsy with desire. Emily plucked it from her hands, easily peeling away the tape. She sat on the bed as she began to unpack the box.

"Nice," Emily murmured as she lifted the wand. She set aside the clitoral suction device Diana had been so excited to try. "If anyone's going to suck your clit today, Diana, it's going to be me."

Diana swallowed with a click, her throat gone dry in anticipation.

"Strip for me while I open this." Emily sounded as commanding as she had that first night, and just like she had then, Diana went absolutely *weak* for her. She shed her clothes and slid onto the bed as Emily went into the bathroom to wash the new vibrator.

Diana tried to calm her breathing as she waited for Emily's return, but she was a lost cause. Her core ached relentlessly, and she couldn't seem to be still, anticipation supercharging her system so that her legs slid restlessly against the comforter.

And then Emily was walking toward her, deliciously naked and holding the wand in her right hand. In all the nights Diana had wished for that wand, she hadn't thought to wish for *this*. She pressed her thighs together.

"Do you want this?" Emily asked as she crawled onto the bed to hover over Diana. Her fingers slid over Diana's wet flesh, discovering just how much Diana wanted it.

"Yes," she managed, her hips pushing against Emily's hand.

A faint buzzing sound reached her ears, and Diana felt herself grow even wetter. Her breath quickened, harsh and ragged.

"I love seeing you like this." Emily licked her lips as she hovered over Diana. The buzzing intensified, and Diana felt the sound in her clit, even though she still had no idea where the vibrator was. Emily grinned. "I love it when you're so worked up, you're about to lose control, and I haven't even touched you yet."

Diana moaned, her hips lifting in search of the elusive vibrator, Emily's fingers, *anything* to provide the stimulation she needed.

"It's hot," Emily murmured, her voice rough with her own arousal. *"You're* hot."

Without warning, the vibrator pressed firmly against Diana's clit, and she jolted in surprise before gasping with pleasure, because *yes*, God, it felt good. Its velvety, soft surface was already warm from Emily's fingers, and pleasure swept through Diana's system. She pulled Emily down on top of her, the vibrator rumbling between them.

"Yes," Diana gasped, hips rocking beneath Emily's, seeking... "More."

The vibrations grew stronger. Emily was breathing harder now, her hand wedged between their bodies to control the vibrator, rubbing it rhythmically against Diana, and she was...*oh*, she was already so close.

"I'm...Emily...oh..." Diana arched beneath her as sparks began to light in her core. The heat and pressure built, and then it burst as the orgasm rushed through her. She gasped and writhed, her hands gripping Emily's ass to press her impossibly closer as she rode out her release.

When it became too much, she slid the vibrator from Emily's grip and brought it between Emily's thighs, groaning when she felt how wet Emily was. She stroked her with the wand as Emily ground her hips down against it, and within minutes, she was coming too. Her whimper of pleasure awakened Diana's body all over again.

They were definitely not leaving this bed anytime soon.

"That was a first," Emily managed between gasping breaths as she reached between them to shut off the vibrator. Her sweat-dampened body relaxed, one thigh between Diana's as she rolled them to face each other.

"Using a vibrator with a partner?" Diana asked, pressing herself a bit more firmly against Emily's thigh.

Emily shook her head with a delighted smile. "You coming first."

"Oh." Diana exhaled, her skin flushing warm. "I guess I *really* missed you."

"You must have," Emily agreed as her fingers found Diana's clit, beginning to stroke. "And I loved every moment. I love *you* so much, Diana."

Diana smiled, biting back a groan as her arousal grew. "I love you just as much. We're going to share so many firsts together."

"A lifetime of firsts."

EPILOGUE

SIX MONTHS LATER

Diana's hiking boots had gotten a lot of use over the past year, but today, they were going to serve their original purpose and carry her to the summit of Crescent Peak. The forest around her was a kaleidoscope of green and brown, the trees all decked out in their brand-new spring leaves. The air smelled fresh and earthy, invigorating her with each breath.

In the end, she and Emily had been exploring the mountains of North Carolina when the Adventurers hiked to the summit last fall, and then the weather had quickly gotten too cold and drab to enjoy the hike, so they'd decided to wait until spring. Now, it was finally time. Today, she and Emily would enjoy the view from the top...together.

"Oh look, there's the rock you painted. I remember that from my first attempt." Diana pointed at the rock beside the trail, adorned with a colorful daisy. "We hadn't even met yet, and you were already encouraging me to stop and smell the roses, so to speak."

"Aww," Emily nudged her shoulder playfully. "The

forest service commissioned me to paint five of them along the trail system, but that's the only one we'll see today."

"I want to see them all this summer," Diana told her. "An Emily Janssen scavenger hunt."

Emily's smile was luminous. Since last fall, she'd quit her job at the inn and painted full time. She'd invested a lot of time and effort into growing her website—with Carter's help—and now she was living her dream, supporting herself with her art.

Her mom had indeed come to town for Thanksgiving, and they'd all spent the holiday together at Eva and Mary's new house. Emily and her mom would probably never have a traditional mother-daughter relationship, but they were talking more frequently now, mending old wounds while they got to know each other.

Diana was doing pretty damn well these days too. She'd successfully purchased two more hotels, bringing Aster's current portfolio to three properties. It was headquartered right here in Crescent Falls in an adorable little office on Main Street. Last month, she'd hired a full-time office manager, and Diana worked there whenever she was in town.

She tried to make sure she was here the second Monday of every month for the women-in-business meeting. Through that group, she'd met so many other female entrepreneurs in the area. Her people. Some of them had even become friends.

She and Emily were still splitting their time between Crescent Falls and Boston, sometimes spending a whole month in one location before returning to the other or setting out to scout new properties for Diana to purchase. Both of their homes were filled with Emily's paintings and Diana's plants, a cheerful combination that Diana loved.

Aster's new office space had come with a studio apartment upstairs, a space Diana initially hadn't known what to do with, but it had turned out to be a perfect first apartment for Carter while he finished his degree. He and Drew had gone from casual to serious, and it made Diana so happy to see him thriving like this.

She'd finally told Carter about her anxiety, and he confirmed what she'd suspected: he'd been struggling in that area too. He'd gotten it under control on his own now that he'd switched schools, but he promised he'd get help if he needed it. They were both making an effort to be more open with each other about things their parents had discouraged them from talking about.

Ironically, things were okay with Diana's family too. She and Emily had had dinner with her parents several times now, and they'd been cautiously accepting of their relationship. It was as much as she could hope for.

"Diana..."

When she looked over, Emily's brow was pinched. "Yes, darling?"

"What if we don't make it to the top?"

"Then we'll try again next week, but we're going to make it." Diana knew she sounded as confident as she felt. She was even more motivated to make it to the top today than Emily knew. "We're going to have a picnic at the summit, take one of those silly kissing selfies, and you're going to paint the tower."

"Okay," Emily said, but her face was the picture of self-doubt.

Diana gave her a reassuring smile, confident enough for them both. Her backpack contained their picnic lunch while Emily's was filled with painting supplies, an empty canvas strapped to the back. But Emily didn't know that

Diana had a surprise tucked into the side pocket of her pack.

"This is where I got lost last time," Diana commented when they reached the ridgeline. Today, she could easily see where she'd gone wrong. The trail diverged from the ridge-line early on, heading back into the trees. This time, she followed the markers. She had plenty of water. Her legs were stronger, toned from almost a year of Vermont's steep inclines. And she had Emily, who—despite her doubts—was more than capable of guiding them to the top.

About an hour and a half into their hike, they reached the infamous ravine. Diana stood at the edge, staring into the opening. The bottom, about ten feet below, was strewn with loose rocks and tree branches, plus a hat, sunglasses, and other items hikers had dropped. It was deeper and more ominous looking than she'd expected.

"Ready?" Emily asked.

Diana nodded, swallowing over her sudden fear. It was only a two-foot gap. She could almost step across. She wouldn't hesitate to make the same jump in another situa-tion where there wasn't so far to fall.

Her pulse spiked. This was her fatal flaw. She got tunnel vision when she focused on a successful outcome, to the point that she often failed to consider the possibility of failure. She underestimated the obstacles she'd have to over-come along the way.

What if she fell? What if Emily did?

"Diana?"

She resisted the urge to reach for the calming strip dangling from her backpack. Instead, she leaned over and gave Emily a kiss. "Here I go."

And then, she jumped.

"OH SHIT!" Emily screeched as she leaped after Diana. Her stomach swooped, her head spun, and then her feet slammed into the ground on the other side of the ravine. The weight of her backpack threw her off-balance, and she stumbled into Diana, both of them laughing as they staggered forward.

"We did it," Diana panted, relief visible in her blue eyes, and only then did Emily realize she'd been nervous about the jump.

"Nothing's going to stop us now," Emily decided, taking her hand as they hiked on. "The hardest part is behind us. We've conquered most of the elevation, and the ravine, but...oh no." She'd forgotten about the cliffside walk, which had just come into view ahead of them.

Here, the path had been carved into a particularly steep and rocky part of the mountain, where the ground rose almost vertically to their left and dropped off treacherously to the right. The path widened to accommodate the dangerous terrain, about three feet across, but still...

"Don't look down," Diana said. "Walk behind me and keep your left hand on the wall. You can use my backpack as a focal point if you need one. Got it?"

"Yes." Emily gulped as she put her left hand against the rock face, her gaze flitting briefly to the drop-off on her right. If one of them stumbled...

"Here we go. One minute and we'll be on the other side." Diana walked at a brisk pace, not giving Emily time to falter.

She kept her gaze on Diana's back, placing one foot in front of the other, and before she knew it the landscape had leveled out, tall trees rising on both sides of the path. Now, they really had made it past all the most difficult hurdles, but Emily didn't want to jinx herself again by saying it out loud.

The last stretch of the trail was steep and rocky. They were both struggling for breath by the time Emily glimpsed a distinct stone shape through the trees, the shape she'd dreamed of seeing in person her whole life.

"The tower," she gasped. "I see it!"

"So do I. We're almost there." Diana had started to lag slightly behind Emily over the last few minutes, but she picked up speed again, surging forward now that the end was in sight.

Wordlessly, they scrambled to the top of the incline and entered the grassy clearing where the tower stood. The ground around it was gently curved, a sloping hillside that marked the summit. To their right, the landscape opened up with sweeping views of the valley. The waterfall the town was named for poured over a rock face below, mist glistening in the sunshine.

From this vantage point, they could see the falls' distinct crescent shape. Hell, from this vantage point, they could see the whole world. The town lay sprinkled below them in the valley. Emily could even see the inn, although her cottage was shrouded by the surrounding forest.

Tears flooded her vision. "It's everything I hoped for."

Diana wrapped Emily in her arms, and for a few minutes, they just stood there, holding each other as they caught their breath and took in the awe-inspiring beauty of their surroundings. The tower indeed looked like it had come from a medieval English castle, gray stones reaching toward the sky. Emily could almost imagine Elizabeth

Abington in her long flowing dress standing in front of it after she'd had it built.

They posed for several kissing selfies, and then broke apart for a much-needed drink of water. Diana set her backpack down on a patch of grass with a perfect view of both the tower and the valley below. While she started spreading out their picnic blanket, Emily wandered over to the tower. Its doorway was just an arch-shaped opening in the stone. She stepped through it, pausing to look up at the circle of sky visible overhead.

"This is so cool," she murmured as she took a picture looking up. Then she moved to the window in front so she could peek out and catch Diana by surprise.

"Hey, look—" Emily's words got stuck in her throat as she stuck her head out the window and saw Diana kneeling in the grass in front of her.

On one knee.

With a ring box in her hand.

"Oh...oh my God..." Emily's voice wavered. Tears rose in her eyes.

"Emily Janssen, I had no idea when I met you last June on this very mountain how much you would change my life. Of course, you literally *saved* my life that day, so maybe that should have been a hint. I've always had big plans for myself, but they didn't always involve having a partner at my side. With you, I feel safer, happier, and more loved than I ever knew possible. I'm a better woman with you beside me. Will you do me the incredible honor of agreeing to be my wife?"

Emily was still head and shoulders through the window of the tower, tears wetting her cheeks, and now she wedged herself a little farther through the opening, trying to reach

Diana. "Yes. Oh God, yes. A hundred times, yes. Please get over here and put that ring on my finger because I think I might be stuck."

Diana smiled as she stood to slide the ring onto Emily's finger. The ring sparkled and shone as the diamond solitaire caught the sun overhead. It was set in a silver band engraved with delicate flowers. Simple. Beautiful. And *so* Emily.

"I love it," she whispered, dazzled. "I love *you*."

"It looks good on you."

Emily beamed at the ring before pulling Diana in for a kiss. "When I was a little girl, I dreamed about this moment, the romantic engagement and the fairy-tale wedding. I always knew I wanted to get married at the inn just like my grandmothers, but the rest was less certain. Prince? Princess? Someone else? I never could have imagined anyone more perfect for me than you, Diana. You complete me."

"We complete each other." Diana gave her a tender kiss, her own eyes suspiciously glossy. "And I'd love to marry you at the inn, if that's what you still want. I can't think of anything better."

"It'll be perfect." Emily clutched at her, hampered by the stone window.

Diana chuckled. "Come out of there before you get stuck for real, Rapunzel, and let's celebrate properly. I brought champagne."

"On my way." Emily yanked herself back through the window, chafing her sides against the stone in the process. She rushed out of the tower and into Diana's arms. In her excitement, she lifted Diana right off her feet and spun her in a circle.

Diana wriggled free, but she held tight to Emily's left

hand. She lifted it so they were both looking at Emily's diamond ring against the backdrop of the waterfall and valley below. A tear slipped over Diana's cheek. "I knew I wanted to see the view from the top, but this...this is a view I didn't know I was waiting for."

ACKNOWLEDGMENTS

It's been over four years since I launched a new indie series. So much has changed since then (I was just getting started as a sapphic author, still living in North Carolina and blissfully ignorant that I would launch that series – Midnight in Manhattan – just one month into the pandemic, when everything was so scary and uncertain.)

Now, here I am living in Vermont as an established sapphic romance author. The world is still scary and uncertain, but there's one thing I know for sure: I love this book SO much, and I'm so glad I get to introduce you to the fictional town of Crescent Falls, Vermont. Writing in my new home state of Vermont has been an absolute joy! I can't wait to return to Crescent Falls for future books.

As usual, I have so many people to thank, starting with my critique partner, Annie Rains, and my editor, Linda Ingmanson, who both offered invaluable insight to guide this book to its final form. A huge thank you also to my beta readers, Samantha Forster, Willow Hayward, and Declan Smith. I appreciate you all so much!

One of my favorite things about writing an indie book is the freedom to choose who I want to work with for every aspect of the process. I had been an admirer of Cath Grace Designs' gorgeous book covers for a while, and I just knew she would be the right person to illustrate the cover for *The View from the Top*. I couldn't be happier with how it turned out! Thank you, Cat.

And I get to work with the absolutely fabulous Quinn Riley for narration! As I write these acknowledgements, she hasn't recorded the book yet, but I know she's going to do an outstanding job. She's already blown me away with her narration on *Stars Collide* and *Cover Story*. Quinn, you are an absolute gem of a person, and I'm thrilled to partner with you again on *The View from the Top* - thank you for everything!

Thanks also to Nancy Holten and Dana Braeden who saw my pictures of Pinnacle Tower in Dorset, Vermont, and said, "You should set a scene in your Vermont book here!" Well, I created a fictional version of that tower for my fictional town, and it played a small but pivotal role in the book. I hope you enjoy it, and thank you for the idea!

This book is dedicated to my grandma, Mary Eva. She inspired the names for Emily's grandmas, Mary and Eva (though my grandma didn't answer to either of those names individually – you could only call her Mary Eva or Mae, at least, if you wanted her to answer you.) She was such an inspiration to me, both in the way she modeled unconditional love, taking in her gay nephew after his parents disowned him back in 1960s small town Georgia, and in her fearless optimism despite the many challenges she faced. I only wish I had known she was an author while she was still here to talk to me about it! (Finding her unpublished manuscript after she passed away was so bittersweet...)

To every reader, reviewer, and author friend who has been a part of my journey, I appreciate your support and your friendship more than you could possibly know. You mean the world to me!

Thank you all!

xoxo

Rachel

KEEP READING

Have you read my standalone, stranded sapphic romance, *Lost in Paradise*? Turn the page to read the first chapter...

LOST IN PARADISE

CHAPTER 1

Nicole Morella rested a hand on the doorway as the floor shifted beneath her feet. It had been eight hours since they set sail from Naples in southern Italy, and she hadn't found her sea legs yet. Was it called setting sail on a modern-day, engine-powered boat? Nicole steadied herself as she took in the lounge before her. Couples and groups lingered over drinks at the various tables and sofas filling the room. Laughter and conversation drifted on the air, undercut by gentle strains of jazz music.

Her gaze wandered to the bar, which was just as crowded. A man sat alone at the near end, watching her as he sipped from his drink. She looked away, determined not to lose her nerve and retreat to her cabin on her first night at sea. This trip was her post-divorce gift to herself, and she was going to make the most of it. Tonight, she was going to enjoy a drink at the bar—alone—and she was going to have fun doing it.

About halfway down the bar, a blonde in a red dress sat talking to the man beside her. The seat to her right was empty, and Nicole decided to take it. She crossed the room and slid onto the empty stool, setting her black clutch on the polished wood in front of her. Keeping her back angled slightly toward the man on her other side, who had already begun to eye her with curiosity, she held the bartender's gaze as he sidled over. "Do you have a house red?"

"Yes, ma'am. It's a cabernet blend from Veneto. Very smooth. Would you like to try it?"

"If you like red, you should try the Petit Verdot," a husky British voice said. "It's from Bordeaux, very full-bodied, with just a hint of berries."

Nicole turned to find the woman to her left watching her out of sky-blue eyes as she swirled the contents of her wineglass. "The Petit Verdot?"

"It's excellent." The blonde swiveled to face her, tucking an unruly strand of thick, wavy hair away from her face. She looked to be about Nicole's age—mid-thirties. Light freckles spattered her forehead and chest that, combined with her wild hair and direct stare, lent her a sort of unconventional beauty that Nicole found it difficult to look away from.

"I'll, um, I'll try a glass of that," Nicole told the bartender.

He nodded, moving down the bar to pour her drink.

"American, hm?" the blonde said, still watching her.

Nicole nodded, inexplicably flushed and tongue-twisted when she herself hadn't had even a sip of alcohol yet tonight. She'd booked herself a private Mediterranean cruise to find her footing after the divorce, and she had every intention of doing it alone. Yet, here she was, heart racing for a total stranger. It had been a long time since she'd felt this kind of attraction and even longer since she'd felt it for a woman. "I'm from New York. And you?"

The blonde swirled her wineglass again before taking a

sip. "I live just outside Nice, along the southern coast of France."

"Oh, I thought you were..." Nicole fumbled, grateful as the bartender interrupted to hand her a glass of wine identical to the one the woman beside her held.

"I'm an expat," the blonde said, tossing an amused glance over her shoulder at Nicole. "Born and raised in London."

"Right." Nicole lifted the glass and took a sip. The wine was rich, spicy but fruity. It tasted expensive. And exotic. A lot like the woman next to her. "It's good."

"Glad you think so," she said.

Nicole couldn't figure why the blonde was still talking to her, why she'd basically turned her back to her date when Nicole sat down. But then again, maybe he wasn't her date at all, because he was sitting there now, looking annoyed but also interested, his gaze flicking between the blonde and Nicole. Maybe he was just a random guy hitting on a single woman in a bar, and that woman was now giving him the cold shoulder.

Nicole found her spirits buoyed at the good fortune to have sat next to another single woman...for casual conversation purposes, anyway, not because she was ridiculously attracted to her. "I'm Nicole," she said.

"Fiona," the blonde replied. "Are you here alone, Nicole?"

She nodded. "You?"

"Unfortunately, yes." Fiona dropped her gaze to her wineglass, and Nicole couldn't help admiring the swell of her breasts beneath the formfitting bodice of her dress. Every inch of her was foreign and beautiful, dangerous for a woman committed to a week of solo soul-searching. "I was supposed to meet someone on the boat...a man."

"Oh." Nicole went for casual and hoped she succeeded. It was a good thing if Fiona was straight. It meant Nicole could sit and chat with her harmlessly. Safe.

"He stood me up," Fiona continued, a sharp bite to her tone. "The bastard."

"Aren't they all?" Nicole mumbled, reaching for her wine.

"Indeed," Fiona agreed. "I thought this one was an exception, at least good for a week of sex on the high seas."

The man on the other side of her choked on his drink, and Fiona cast a disapproving glance in his direction at his blatant eavesdropping. Nicole swallowed her laugh with another sip of the luxuriously rich wine Fiona had recommended. So much better than the house red she would have gotten otherwise.

"It's why I generally prefer women to men," Fiona said, a bit louder, and her would-be paramour's cheeks darkened before he turned away.

It was Nicole's turn to choke on her drink. She coughed and spluttered as wine burned its way down her esophagus while Fiona gave her a knowing look that said she'd read her interest and—God, was it possible she returned the feeling?

"So that's my sad story," Fiona said, still holding Nicole in her intense stare. "Why are you all alone on this lovely, romantic boat?"

"It's my post-divorce splurge for myself," Nicole said, clearing her throat and wishing she had a cup of water to cool the burning sensation from inhaling her wine. "I came here to rediscover my sense of adventure or find myself... something like that."

Fiona's eyes crinkled in a warm smile. "I must say I prefer your story to mine. Not the divorce, but making your own adventure. I like that."

"Thanks." Her cheeks were burning. They were probably as red as Fiona's dress. She really needed to get a grip. Her fingers tightened around the stem of her wineglass. "I'd always wanted to visit the Mediterranean—my family's from Italy originally—and I'd always wanted to take a cruise. So, here I am."

"Ballsy of you," Fiona said, her gaze sliding to the simple gray knit dress that Nicole wore.

She crossed her legs involuntarily. "Do you know this area pretty well, then?"

"I do. It's lovely," Fiona said, tossing her hair over her shoulder as she returned her attention to the wineglass in front of her, leaving Nicole feeling somewhat bereft after the intensity and heat of her gaze. "Although I prefer the French Riviera to Italy or Greece."

"Is that why you moved there?"

"Mm. My favorite place in the world."

"I was in Paris once, for business," Nicole said, remembering that she'd been somewhat lonely and off-balance on that trip too. That was two years ago, when she'd first begun to realize how unhappy she'd become in her marriage. If only she'd known then just how much worse things would get.

"Paris is charming, but if you really want to get the flavor of France, you've got to visit the countryside," Fiona said, swirling her wine.

"I'll have to visit sometime." Nicole felt a tingle in the pit of her stomach, as if she'd somehow accepted an invitation to visit her, when in reality, Fiona was just making idle conversation. Likely, the attraction was entirely one-sided. After all, it had been an eternity since Nicole had flirted with anyone, gone on a date, done anything but steel herself for another battle of the wills with Brandon. She wasn't sure she even remembered how to flirt at this point...

"And what is it that you do for work?" Fiona asked.

"I'm the senior marketing manager for an investment firm in Manhattan."

"Sounds very...corporate."

"It is." Nicole released a sigh that seemed to reach all the way to her soul. "I've been so caught up in work, I'm embarrassed to tell you how long it's been since I took a vacation."

"I'd say you needed this one, then," Fiona said.

"I did. I really did."

The man on the other side of Fiona was watching them again. She gave him an irritated look before her gaze darted back to Nicole. "Care to go for a walk?"

"Um, sure."

"I could use some air." Fiona stood, reaching for her wineglass and a small white purse that she slung over her shoulder.

Nicole followed, bringing her own wine and her black clutch. Alcohol hadn't improved her seaworthiness, though, and she stumbled as they reached the doorway.

"Careful," Fiona murmured, the "r" lost to the cadence of her accent as her free hand grasped Nicole's elbow. Her fingers were warm, her grip surprisingly strong, and Nicole was almost positive that Fiona lingered several moments longer than was strictly necessary.

FIONA BOONE LED the way onto the deck, dotted here and there with couples in search of fresh air and darkness to cover their actions. She'd thought this cruise was going to be dreadfully dull after Dimitris stood her up. That was before she met Nicole.

She led Nicole toward the rear of the boat to a quiet spot she'd discovered earlier. The curve of the deck hid them from view, but the protruding hulk of one of the lifeboats kept it from being a popular spot...unless one was looking for a place to hide from prying eyes, and right now, that was exactly what Fiona was going for. She leaned her elbows on the railing, taking in the glittering lights of the Italian coastline in the distance. "Beautiful, isn't it?"

"Yeah." Nicole's voice was softer now, as if hushed by the night.

The ship's engine hummed beneath them, accentuated by the splash of water against the hull. Rhythmic and soothing. Fiona had always loved the sea, although she preferred to enjoy it with her feet on dry land. She dangled the wineglass in her left hand, watching the play of white against black as water sprayed out of the darkness below. "I like places like this...out of the way, private. I'm not much for crowds."

"You seem like you could handle just about anything." Amusement laced Nicole's tone.

"I didn't say I couldn't handle them. I just prefer solitude, that's all."

"And here I had you pegged as a social butterfly."

Fiona turned her head, meeting Nicole's gaze in the near darkness. "Is that how you had me pegged?"

"Among other things." Nicole licked her lips, and they glistened in the moonlight, driving Fiona to distraction.

"Good, because I'm many things."

"Tell me a few of them. What do you do for work?"

"I'm an artist." Fiona watched the lights bobbing on the horizon, twinkling like fallen stars.

"Oh, really? What kind of art? Do you paint?"

"Digital mostly, but yes, I do paint." She slid her gaze to Nicole, who was watching her intently. They stood close enough that Fiona could inch her elbow to the right and bump Nicole's. Could have, but she didn't. Not yet, anyway. "Graphic design pays the bills. I paint mostly for myself, although I sell some locally."

"Landscapes or people?"

"Both." She let her gaze drop from Nicole's face to her body, endless curves highlighted by her formfitting dress. Brown hair, hazel eyes, olive-tinted skin. Earth tones. She'd look so much more vibrant in a mossy-green dress than this gray one. "I could paint you, but I'd use brighter colors."

"Like Jack draws Rose in *Titanic*?" Nicole's voice had dropped an octave or two, into the timbre of Fiona's lusty daydreams.

She scoffed. "Hardly. That's a rubbish movie. The ship sinks, and they all die, even poor Jack because Rose's too selfish to share her bit of wood with him."

"Why, Fiona, are you a romantic at heart?" Nicole asked, shifting subtly closer.

"I can be romantic." She lifted her right hand from the railing and brushed it against the curve of Nicole's waist, lingering for a moment there. An innocent enough gesture if Nicole didn't want this to happen, but Fiona had pretty good radar about these things, and she was confident she hadn't read her wrong. Nicole wanted her as badly as she wanted Nicole.

She sucked in a breath at the contact, her eyes finding Fiona's in the dark. Fiona was fairly sure Nicole's interest had more to do with avoiding memories of her ex-husband than Fiona herself, but she didn't mind. She was only looking for a distraction, someone to pass a lonely night or two with here on the ship. It had been months since she'd had sex, too many months, and she was ridiculously horny, an itch she'd been counting on Dimitris to scratch. But now, she found herself even more excited by the prospect of it being Nicole.

In the distance, another boat motored in their direction, engine rumbling in the night. Fiona reached out, sweeping the dark curtain of Nicole's hair over her shoulder. Her fingers brushed Nicole's neck, and she felt goose bumps rise beneath her touch. Fiona leaned in, her pulse going haywire the closer her lips got to Nicole's. They met in a rush of hot breath, noses bumping as their lips pressed together. Nicole let out a hum of pleasure, her eyes sliding shut as Fiona pressed a light kiss against her cheek before bringing their mouths back into alignment.

This time, Nicole opened to her, and Fiona slipped her tongue into her mouth, tasting the same wine she herself had been drinking. Somehow, it tasted sweeter in the hidden pleasure of Nicole's kiss, heady and lush as the Italian countryside they'd left behind that morning. Fiona slid her free hand to the hollow of Nicole's back, pressing her closer, kissing her deeper, drinking her in, suddenly certain this kiss was a hundred times better than anything she would have shared with Dimitris this week.

"Whoa," Nicole whispered as she lifted her head.

"Is that a good thing?" she asked, feathering a hand through Nicole's hair.

She nodded, her face bobbing in Fiona's vision as a shy smile played around her lips. "Better than good."

"I thought so too." Fiona brushed her fingers over the soft fabric of Nicole's dress, smoothing it over the dip of her waist. "In fact, I'm very glad to have been stood up."

"Is he your boyfriend?" There was something hesitant in Nicole's voice now.

Fiona was a lot of things, but she wasn't a cheat, and she wouldn't have Nicole feeling any guilt over Dimitris. "No. He's my... Even lover is too familiar a term. He's a businessman who travels almost exclusively. Occasionally, maybe once or twice a year, if he's in town and we're both currently unattached, we'll get together for a few nights. It's just sex, and in this case, he was called away on business last minute, so I wound up all alone on this lovely boat."

"That's..." Nicole's brow furrowed. "I was married for so long, I don't have any experience with an arrangement like that."

"It's the only kind of relationship I have experience with," Fiona said, a warning in case Nicole wasn't interested in a night of casual sex.

"Oh," she said quietly.

"Your divorce is recent?" Fiona asked.

"Three months. I'm supposed to be using this trip to figure things out by myself."

Fiona sipped her wine, feeling slightly desperate at the thought of having to let her go. She so rarely experienced such an instant connection with someone, let alone this kind of sizzling chemistry. "Would you like me to leave you to it, then?"

"No," Nicole answered quickly, stepping closer.

Fiona met her gaze. "Good."

The other boat had drawn closer, its engine obnoxiously loud. It seemed like their boat, the *Cyprus Star*, had picked up speed, perhaps trying to put more space between itself and its new neighbor. Fiona wished for a table so she could set down her wine. Nicole was stuck carrying wine in one hand and her clutch in the other, no free hands for touching, and maybe Fiona hadn't planned this little rendezvous as well as she'd thought.

"Do they seem too close to you?" Nicole asked, turning her attention to the approaching boat. It seemed to be heading straight for them.

"Mm," Fiona agreed, annoyed at the interruption.

"Maybe it's the Coast Guard?"

"Could be." But the other boat had drawn close enough now that its outline was visible in the night, and it didn't look like an official vessel. There were no identifying marks she could see, no maritime flag or police lights. Instinctively, she stepped into the shadows, drawing Nicole with her.

The approaching boat drew alongside the *Cyprus Star*, and with a horrible screech, their hulls bumped and rubbed, sending a shudder through the deck beneath her feet.

"Oh my God," Nicole whispered.

Almost immediately, men dressed in black tossed ropes to secure their vessel to the *Cyprus Star*. The engine roared belowdecks, an apparent attempt by the captain to shake free, but it was too late. The marauders threw a ladder that hooked onto the *Cyprus Star*'s railing and began scaling it one after another.

"Fuck," Fiona mumbled. She tossed her wineglass into the seething depths of the Mediterranean, then grabbed Nicole's and sent it after hers. She crouched, drawing Nicole down with her, and they pressed themselves into a darkened recess in the side of the ship.

"What's going on?" Nicole whispered. Her hand, still clutched in Fiona's, shook.

"Shh. I don't know, but I don't think it's anything good."

Men's voices shouted in Greek, too jumbled for Fiona to pick out more than the fact that they'd just been boarded by some kind of maritime pirates, and *fuck*, this was bad. She wrapped her arms around Nicole, who promptly buried her face against Fiona's chest, something she would have appreciated a lot more five minutes ago. Now, her heart was about to burst out of her chest, and she wasn't the least bit aroused.

"Everyone listen to me!" a man shouted, followed by the *pop pop pop* of gunfire, and Fiona recoiled. A shaft of moonlight passed overhead, illuminating her red dress like a beacon in the night.

ALSO BY RACHEL LACEY

Ms. Right Series

Read Between the Lines

No Rings Attached

Midnight in Manhattan Series

Don't Cry for Me

It's in Her Kiss

Come Away with Me

She'll Steal Your Heart

Crescent Falls Series

The View from the Top

Standalone Books

Cover Story

Stars Collide

Lost in Paradise

Hideaway

Short Stories

Off the Rails

Out of the Blue

ABOUT THE AUTHOR

 Rachel Lacey is an award-winning contemporary romance author and semi-reformed travel junkie. She's been climbed by a monkey on a mountain in Japan, gone scuba diving on the Great Barrier Reef, and camped out overnight in New York City for a chance to be an extra in a movie. These days, the majority of her adventures take place on the pages of the books she writes. She lives in the mountains of Vermont with her family and a variety of rescue pets.

facebook.com/RachelLaceyAuthor

x.com/rachelslacey

instagram.com/rachelslacey

amazon.com/author/rachellacey

bookbub.com/authors/rachel-lacey

Printed in the USA
CPSIA information can be obtained
at www.ICGtesting.com
LVHW021121011224
798049LV00007B/58